THE HAIGERLOCH PROJECT

THE HAIGERLOCH PROJECT

Ib Melchior

HARPER & ROW, PUBLISHERS
New York, Hagerstown, San Francisco, London

FIRST EDITION

Designed by C. Linda Dingler

Library of Congress Cataloging in Publication Data

Melchior, Ib.
  The Haigerloch project.
  Bibliography: p. 315
  I. Title.
PZ4.M51457Hi [PS3563.E435]   813'.5'4   76–26272
ISBN 0–06–012946–8

---

77 78 79 80 10 9 8 7 6 5 4 3 2 1

To Cleo
Alle gode gange tre . . .

CONTENTS

To the Ministry of War
Berlin   25.4.1939
   We take the liberty of calling to your attention the newest development in *atomic physics*
which in our opinion can produce an explosive
that is many orders of magnitude more effective than any conventional ones. . . . That country which first makes use of it has an unsurpassa-
ble advantage over all others.

—PROFESSOR PAUL HARTECK
Hamburg

AUTHOR'S NOTE

Although *The Haigerloch Project* is fiction, the existence of the project and many of the elements and incidents of the story are based on actual events and upon the author's personal experiences.

I. M.

**Der Reichsmarschall
des Großdeutschen Reiches**

**Präsident
des Reichsforschungsrates**

Der Bevollmächtigte
für kernphysikalische Forschung

Tgb.-Nr. Prof.G./W.

Berlin-Dahlem, den 26.2.45
Boltzmannstr. 20
Tel.: 763244/45

An den

Leiter der Kriegswirtschaftsstelle
im Reichsforschungsrat

Berlin-Steglitz
Grunewaldstr. 35

Geheime Reichssache

Vorgang: Schreiben vom 24.2.45, A. - Z,: Bb.Nr 1523/45 g

Betrifft: Notprogramm: Energiegewinnungsvorhaben.

I. Für die Endentwicklung des Vorhabens "Energiegewinnung aus Kernprozessen"
ist voller Schutz erforderlich. Die leitenden Arbeitsstellen sind:

Arbeitsgruppen KWI (für Physik und Chemie) (Berlin, Heidelberg, Hechingen
und Tailfingen).

   "   des Bevollmächtigen in Stadtilm, Haigerloch und München.

   "   Prof. Harteck (Inst. f. phys. Chemie, Hamburg, Celle und
Anschütz & Co.)

   "   Prof. Kirchner - Prof. Riezler (Phys. Inst. Köln, Zwst.
Garmish-Partenkirchen)

   "   Phys. Inst. Wien (Prof. Stetter)

   "   Strahlenschutz und Dosimetrie (PTR und KWI Berlin-Buch.

Vorhaben SH 200 (bes. I.G. und Bamag-Meguin)

   "   Spezialmetallfertigung (Auer, Degussa)

   "   Zyklotron (KWI Heidelberg, Siemens-Halske)
(Bemerkung: Materialbedarf gedeckt, nur noch Fertigmontage)

   "   Elektronenschleuder (gemeinsam mit uK geführt.

Diese Vorhaben sollen den vollen Energie-, Material- und Personalschutz des
Führernotprogramms entsprechend Führererlass von 31.1.45, 23 Uhr erhalten.

The Reich Marshal
of the Greater German Reich
President
of the Reich Research Council

———

The Authority
for Atomic Research

Berlin-Dahlem, the 26.2.45
Boltzmannstr. 20
Tel.: 763244/45

To the
Chief of the
War Management Office
of the
Reich Research Council

Berlin-Steglitz
Grünewaldstr. 35

Ref. No. Prof. G./W.   Secret State Matter

File: Letter of 24/2/45 A.-Z.: Bb. No. 1523/45 g

Regarding: Emergency Program, Power Yield Projects.

I. To accomplish the final development of "Power Yield from Atomic Action" full protection is imperative. The leading work sites are:

Work Group   KWI (for Physics and Chemistry) (Berlin, Heidelberg, Hechingen and Tailfingen)

"   the authorities on Stadtilm, Haigerloch and Munich

"   Prof. Harteck (Inst. for Physical Chemistry, Hamburg, Celle and Anschütz & Co.)

"   Prof. Kirchner—Prof. Riezler (Phys. Inst. Cologne, intermed. sta. Garmish-Partenkirchen)

"   Phys. Inst. Vienna (Prof. Stetter)

"   Radiation Protection and Dosimetry (PTR and KWI Berlin-Buch.)

Project   SH 200 (esp. I.G. and Bamag-Meguin)

"   Special Metal Processing (Auer, Degussa)

"   Cyclotron (KWI Heidelberg, Siemens-Halske) (Note: Material requirements covered, though only final assembly)

"   Electron Centrifuge (conducted in coaction)

These projects shall be afforded the full power, material and personnel protection of the Führer Emergency Program according to the Führer Order of 23 hours, 31/1/45.

/s/ Walther Gerlach

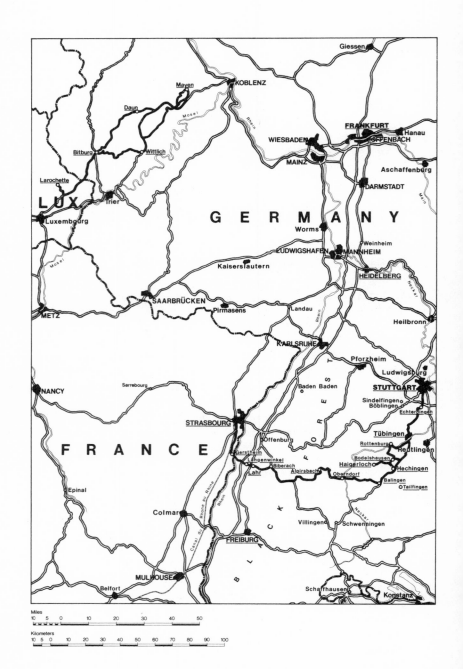

Miles
10 5 0   10   20   30   40   50

Kilometers
10 5 0   10   20   30   40   50   60   70   80   90   100

PROLOGUE

Fear clamped an icy vise on every nerve end in his body, threatening to numb his fingers as he tapped the worn Morse key—
QSP . . . QSP . . . QSP . . .

He listened. . . .

His earphones were filled only with static. There was no acknowledgment.

Urgently his fingers resumed QSP . . . QSP . . . QSP . . .

His eyes roamed the dark cellar room. His self-imposed prison.

His—crypt?

He knew he had been on the air too long. Any moment he would hear the motor of the monitor truck grind to a halt outside.

QSP . . . QSP . . . QSP . . .

Still no contact.

He clamped his jaws tight.

He could wait no longer. He had to take a chance. Perhaps they could read him—even though he could not read them. He'd send his message. Blind.

And hope . . .

Hurriedly he started his transmission. Call letters. Identification. Message in cipher. His fingers flew on the key. Groups of five letters . . .

IDUGS HBAFN RTJNV . . .

Finished. Almost finished . . .

Suddenly he stopped.

He tore the earphones from his head.

Too late.

He could hear the rifle butts battering the wooden door at the top of the stairs.

The dead-bolt would not hold for long. . . .

Automatically he finished the last letter group of his message. He signed off—

EULE.

Owl.

A cry for deliverance . . .

He struck a large wooden match and held his hurriedly scrawled message to the flame. His hands shook. He let the paper flare until it singed his fingers, then let it drop to the cement floor next to his stool.

He watched it writhe into a black curl before grinding it to ashes with his foot.

He heard the hobnailed boots pound down the stairs.

He stood up. Leadenly.

He turned.

He knew what he would see.

There were two of them. Hard-faced. Jet-black uniforms. On the left sleeves the blood-red armbands with the angular black swastikas in their white circles. On the black caps the gleaming death-head emblems of the SS . . .

But his eyes were inexorably drawn to the muzzles of the two Schmeisser submachine guns pointed directly at his gut.

He knew he was dead.

He only hoped death would come quickly.

He also knew it would not.

Unless—

Suddenly, with a cry of despair, he lunged at one of the SS men. . . .

He saw the all-devouring muzzle of the submachine gun jerk up, and—

PART I

The Month of
28 Feb 1945—28 Mar 1945

1

He had no doubt how it would turn out, and it annoyed the hell out of him. Still, he couldn't bring himself to capitulate without at least a show of rebellion. Any damned fish worth netting ought to do some struggling before being reeled in.

He glared at his commanding officer.

"Tell G-2 to shove it," he said angrily.

Major Wallace, Stanley H. Wallace—H for Homer after his paternal grandfather—CO of Counter Intelligence Corps Detachment 212, calmly studied the young officer standing stiffly at the grimy-paned window in his office. He knew him. Well. Knew he always bitched like hell before taking on an assignment not of his own choosing. But he always did take it on, and lit into it with imagination and guts. It would be no different now.

Major Wallace turned to a large area map on the wall behind him.

"It's thirty-two miles from Bitburg to Mayen," he said.

"And thirty of them held by the Krauts!" the young officer flared and turned away from the map deliberately to stare out the window into the gray, dismal morning.

Below lay the little town of Fels, virtually untouched by the war. The bustling military traffic flowing around the Corps HQ buildings seemed totally out of place—like close-order drill in a convent.

The Forward Echelon of XII Corps had moved to the county-seat town of Fels—or Larochette, depending on your ethnic preference—on February 23, a short week before, and set up shop in a drab three-story hotel, a textbook firetrap with narrow corridors and steep, winding stairs. All the rooms were small with depressingly low ceilings, the CIC office on the third floor most certainly no exception. The town was nestled in a heavily wooded and hilly section at the edge of the High Eifel in Luxembourg, hard on the German border, a resort area often called Little Switzerland.

For a brief moment Lieutenant Martin Kieffer, counter-intelligence agent, CIC Det. 212, stared at the scene before him. The forest-clad hills ringed the little town. From among the dark evergreens the twisted, naked branches of leafless trees reached upward toward the leaden sky—skeletons of winter waiting to be fleshed out with new spring growth.

It would be the last one, he thought—the last Corps CP before entering enemy territory.

He turned to Major Wallace.

"You know what they'll do to me if they nab me, don't you? I'm Jewish."

Wallace nodded. "Half Jewish. Your mother was Catholic."

"Dammit, Stan, I'm circumcised."

"Big deal. So am I. And I'm Presbyterian." The major rose. He walked up to Kieffer. "Look, Martin," he said quietly, "I know it's a helluva thing to ask. And nobody's ordering you to do it."

Kieffer felt a wave of frustrated anger surge through him. That was the worst part of it. It would be his choice. He couldn't hide behind an order. He himself would have to make the decision to get his ass shot off, to take on the goddamned stupid assignment.

"Shit!" he said. "Let me see that message again. The decipherment."

Wallace took a piece of paper from his desk and handed it across.

Frowning, Kieffer studied it.

IMPORTANT DEGUSSA SCIENTIST JOHANN
DECKER BELIEVED READY DEFECT STOP
PRESENT MAYEN OSTBAHNHOFSTR FROM 24
TO 28 FEB THEN TRANSFER INTERIOR
STOP EVACUATION VITAL STOP EULE

He looked up at Wallace.

"How was it sent?" he asked. "What's the cryp history?"

"Double transposition cipher," Wallace answered. Inwardly he smiled. Kieffer was hooked. "The standard OSS thing. Eule, the German underground operative in Frankfurt, sent it by short wave to a collection center in Switzerland. The monitoring agent there sent it on to London, and London shot it over to SHAEF—"

"—and it ends up in our eager little hands," Kieffer finished for him.

"With an order for immediate action." Wallace nodded. "And a lot of pressure from SHAEF."

Kieffer looked at the message in his hand. Absent-mindedly he turned it over.

"Someone's worried about something," he said pensively. He looked up at Wallace. "We know anything else?"

"Yeah. Degussa. It's a big Frankfurt outfit. Working on top-secret projects."

"Another goddamned secret weapon to win the war."

"Don't sell it short," Wallace said soberly. "V-1 and V-2 are no toys. Ask any poor bastard in London."

"CIC is not supposed to operate behind enemy lines, Stan, and you know it. It's an OSS job."

"No time for them to mount a mission."

"Sure. They waited to the last fucking day."

"Didn't get it before."

"Damned SHAEF snafu. Why us?"

Wallace shrugged.

"We're here."

"Why me? It's not my meat. I've never operated behind enemy lines before."

As he said it—he knew it wasn't true. But Wallace didn't know that. He'd never told his CO about the time he'd taken the wrong road and lost his way. It was shortly after the Siegfried Line had been smashed. He'd ended up in a small Kraut village on the Prüm River that hadn't been taken yet. Only he didn't know that. He'd strutted into the Bürgermeister's office, kicked the man out and replaced him with a non-Nazi farmer. He'd ordered the townspeople to dismantle a half-finished tank obstacle across the main drag on the double, and generally thrown his weight around. And he hadn't known that the cellar of damned near every house was filled with Waffen SS troops lying in ambush—any minute expecting the cock-sure *Ami* officer's support troops to roll in. He'd only learned that two days later when the town *was* occupied and he'd dropped in on the man he'd installed as mayor. He'd had one helluva time pretending that he'd known the situation all along.

But this time it was different. This time he knew.

"Your German is perfect," Wallace said.

"Who is this Decker guy?"

Major Wallace just shrugged.

"Don't know. All I know is, they want him. Badly." He glanced sideways at Kieffer, then looked back at the wall map. "You'll have to infiltrate to Mayen," he said briskly. "Find Decker on Ostbahnhofstrasse and transport him back here."

"That all?" Kieffer said bitingly. He threw the message on the CO's desk. "That damned message says *believed* ready to defect. What if the bastard doesn't want to go?"

"Persuade him."

"As in kidnap? You're out of your fucking mind!"

"Play it as it comes."

For a moment Kieffer stared silently at the map. Then he turned to Wallace.

"Okay," he said. "Okay. I'll go get him." He glared at his superior officer. "But I'll do it my way!"

"And what way is that?"

"First, I go in uniform. Infantry insignia. Dogtags. The works. I don't want to be stood up against the nearest wall if they catch me."

Wallace nodded. It made sense. Anyway, German troops had captured a lot of GI equipment and clothing during their abortive Ardennes offensive. They were putting it to practical use in the cold weather. A bastard American get-up would not attract attention.

"I'll go in by jeep," Kieffer continued. He was getting caught up in the challenge of the mission. His eyes flew across the wall map. "I'll scrape off the stars. Muddy the numbers." He turned to Wallace. "And I want a driver. Marshall. Jerry Marshall. That sergeant in the motor pool. He's crazy enough to go along."

"Marshall?" Wallace was startled. "He can't speak a word of German."

"But he can make a bathtub run like a Rolls. He's one damned good mechanic, and that's a helluva lot more important to me than language. I don't want to be stranded in a conked-out jeep in the middle of nowhere thirty miles into Kraut country. If we get into a situation we have to talk ourselves out of, we've had it anyway."

"It's okay with me—if Marshall agrees."

"He will. He's always bitching about not seeing any action."

"You'll have to get Decker out tonight. Tomorrow he'll be gone."

"Yeah. Do tell."

"You will be jumping off tonight," Wallace went on, briskly authoritative now the matter was settled. As he had known it would be. "From Bitburg. They're mopping up now. You will contact Major Baldon at Eleventh Infantry CP. He will have further instructions for you. He will get you through the American lines. From then on you're on your own. Any questions?"

"Yeah, one," Kieffer said dryly. "How do you get out of this chickenshit outfit?"

Wallace grinned.

"Section Eight . . . ?"

It was 1647 hours on February 28 when CIC agent Martin Kieffer and Sergeant Jerry Marshall drove into Bitburg.

The fields along the road on the outskirts had been blanketed by a paper blizzard. Surrender leaflets, dropped by the Air Force. And obviously ignored.

The town itself had been taken that same day by units of the 11th Infantry Regiment, 5th Division, who'd fought their way in from the south against heavy opposition. Air had plastered the important road junction, and Corps and Division artillery had slammed barrage after barrage of steel and high explosives into it. The place was one huge pile of muddy rubble.

Kieffer looked around with awed curiosity as Marshall threaded the mud-caked jeep through the half-cleared streets, following the signs to Regimental CP. He knew that the famous Long Tom 155 mm. gun of the 244th Field Artillery Battalion had been brought into action to soften up the burg before the infantry assault. To reach its target with the required accuracy, the gun had been hauled so far forward that it was placed up among the mortar crews firing infantry support for the advance. The mortar men had bitched like hell. They'd caught a lot of the incoming mail of the German counter-battery fire searching for Long Tom. Judging from what he saw—and smelled—the gun had done its job on the town of Bitburg.

Major Baldon eyed Kieffer and Marshall with obvious wariness. He'd been handed a hot potato by Corps—and didn't like the possibility of getting his fingers burned.

"If you ask me," he said, "you're nuts!"

Kieffer ignored him.

"Have you any idea where you want to cross?" the major asked testily.

"More than an idea," Kieffer answered. "I've picked the exact spot." He pulled a dirty, creased map from his pocket. It was a Wehrmacht area map he'd traded for a pack of Luckies with the IPW's who interrogated the prisoners. He'd carry it on the mission instead of a U.S. Army issue. Just in case. He spread it out on Baldon's desk. "I'll show you."

He found the spot on the wrinkled map and traced his route with his finger as he talked.

"Right—here. There's a timbering path running through a forest. The contour lines show it sloping down toward the Kyll River valley, joining a small country road—here."

"The Kyll bridges are all out," Baldon interrupted. He seemed smugly pleased with the intelligence.

"I know. We'll ford it."

"The river's pretty swollen." The major sounded doubtful.

Kieffer felt a surge of impatience. He didn't feel like wasting his time explaining to the contentious officer that he had just spent several hectic hours interrogating the half-dozen members of a Luxembourg hunting and fishing club he'd been able to round up. In better days these sportsmen had fished in every river and stream in the area—including the Kyll. They'd trudged along its banks, stood planted in the middle of the water and searched for the places richest in trout. Better than anyone, they knew the width and depth, the current and bottom conditions of every inch of the river—swollen or not. From their information he had picked his spot.

"We'll make it, Major," he said curtly.

He returned to the map.

"The road runs roughly parallel to the main highway to Mayen and joins it here—near Daun."

Baldon looked at the map, orienting himself in the jumble of unfamiliar symbols.

"You'll have to cross in Able Company's sector," he said. "Lieutenant Kinsey."

Kieffer nodded.

"The Krauts are reported regrouping in the entire area," he said. "The situation may be fluid enough to let us pull it off without a hitch. We've had reports of sporadic motorized activity. The sound of our jeep shouldn't cause any raised eyebrows."

He folded up the map, missing the original creases, and put it away.

"You brief Kinsey we're coming up now, Major. We'll make our final arrangements with him directly."

Baldon looked at him sourly.

"When do you want to take off?"

"After dark. At 2100 hours."

2

Sergeant Marshall was coaxing the jeep along the muddy, bumpy back road at what seemed to Kieffer a lazy snail's pace. They had put the top up. They usually didn't—and somehow the jeep looked less GI to them. To the Germans as well, he hoped. The road was dark, and the shadows from the trees lining it heightened the gloom. The blackout hoods over the headlights permitted only two thin slivers of light to probe the blackness ahead.

Kieffer felt keyed up. For the hundredth time he took stock. The jeep was unidentifiable as belonging to the US Army. It could easily be a captured vehicle pressed into service with the Wehrmacht as were countless others. Both he and Sergeant Marshall were clad in a conglomeration of nondescript uniform items. They'd checked each other out before taking off, like a pair of paratroopers before a jump. He wore a wool cap pulled down over his ears; a wool scarf which effectively hid his collar tabs with his US insignia; a dirty, loose US mackinaw coat; and mud-caked paratrooper boots. His dogtags around his neck were stuck together with chewing gum to prevent their rattling. His underwear was fresh. If he got into trouble and was hit, the clean fabric forced into the wound would be less likely to cause infection and perhaps gangrene than dirty cloth. In his mind he repeated the passwords he and Kinsey had picked: *Homecoming—Highball.* It had been decided they'd cross back at the same place they left, at 0430—with or without Decker.

So far the mission *had* gone off without a hitch. Too easy. It made him uncomfortable. Something was bound to happen. He wished it would. He needed to cope with—something. . . .

He and Marshall had located the forest path quickly. For a couple of hundred yards it sloped gently down toward the Kyll valley. They'd coasted slowly and silently until the jeep finally had come to a halt. There had been no challenge.

They'd started up, and had soon joined the back road that crossed the river.

As the Luxembourg fishermen had described, the river widened there and formed a natural ford, reinforced with bottom rocks and logs just below the surface of the rushing water.

The current had been strong. The jeep had labored on its buffeted course across the slippery rocks, but they'd made it without getting more than tolerably wet.

They had seen no activity at all. Only heard what sounded like light armor moving in the distance. . . .

In a couple of miles they would join the highway to Mayen.

The trees were thinning out, the gloom was becoming less intense.

Suddenly Marshall pointed.

"Holy shit!" he whispered. "Look!"

Ahead of them was the road junction. And on the highway, directly across from the back road they were on, sat the massive hulk of a heavy transport truck hooked up to an artillery piece, a 15 cm Schwere Infantrie Geschütz. Around a fire were half a dozen of the crew; the others were working on a damaged driving track on the truck in the beam of a battery work light.

It was their first sight of the enemy.

It was expected, and yet Kieffer felt a quick surge of panic. He suppressed it angrily.

Automatically Marshall slowed down.

"Keep going," Kieffer snapped. "And keep your trap shut!"

He resisted the instant impulse to grab his gun.

The jeep edged onto the highway.

The Germans stirred at the sight of the American vehicle. Guns in hand, a couple of them, one a Feldwebel, warily started across the highway toward the jeep.

Kieffer leaned out.

"Hallo! Am Kraftwagen!" he called. "Hey! At the truck!— *Wie weit noch bis Mayen?*—How far to Mayen?"

"Fufzehn Kilometer," the Feldwebel answered in typical Berliner dialect.

Kieffer beat his arms around him elaborately.

"Kreuz-Donnerwetter-Papenheim-Herrgott-Sakrament-Zum-Teufel-Nocha'mal!" he swore. "It's cold in this damned *Ami Klamotte!"* He prayed his thick Bavarian oath would allay any budding suspicions the Berliner might have about his accent. He knew his German was good, though it wasn't good enough for him to be taken for a nextdoor neighbor. But for someone from a different part of Germany. He hoped.

Irrelevantly he had a flash vision of his mother's scandalized face as he'd pronounced that oath the first time. He'd been twelve. Blasphemous, she'd cried, white-faced with shock. It *was* a little strong—especially to Catholic ears. *Crucifix-Thunder-Home of Popes-Lord God-Sacrament, to the Devil, Twice Said!* For days she refused to speak to her brother, who was visiting the States from Bavaria and who'd taught the boy the curse.

He turned to Marshall.

"Los, Fritz," he said. He pulled his wool cap even farther down over his ears. "Before I freeze my balls off!"

The Berliner grinned.

"Mensch!" he said. "You are warming the wrong end!"

They started down the highway.

No one stopped them.

It was 2237 hours when Kieffer and Marshall brought their oddball jeep to a halt at the Mayen railroad yards in back of the main station. The sprawling yards were utterly deserted and dark, yet not dark enough to hide the sweeping devastation. Mayen, a town of some 16,000, was an important junction on the Andernach-Gerolstein Railroad, vital to the rail traffic in the Rhineland-Palatinate, and as such the town had been the target of heavy Allied bombing raids. The railroad marshaling yards were a mass of corkscrew iron rails, shrapnel-shattered rolling stock and jagged mounds of masonry rubble.

Though it had been late when the two Americans drove into town, there was still considerable traffic abroad, both military and civilian. The streets were only dimly lit, a fact they welcomed; electricity obviously was scarce, but even in the dimness the old town, which had begun as a Roman settlement, clearly showed what the bombers had done.

Driving through the center of town, Kieffer and Marshall had passed only one large building which miraculously showed no damage except for a few boarded-up windows—the huge, castlelike hospital, shored up with massive concrete buttresses. They had steered clear of the area. The hospital was obviously in the process of being evacuated, and there was too much activity for comfort. The Germans, anticipating the impending occupation of the town, were transporting their wounded soldiers to the rear—so they might be patched up to fight another day.

They had found a spot next to a mangled tie-tamper between two badly shot-up boxcars and stashed their jeep in the black shadows. Kieffer had decided to track down Decker on foot. It would eliminate the risk of having to park the jeep on the street. Marshall threw a couple of loose boards against the vehicle as camouflage. He opened the hood and removed a small object. He threw it to Kieffer.

"Hold on to that," he said, closing the hood. "It's our ticket back home."

"The rotor?" Kieffer asked, pocketing the little object.

"Right." Marshall patted the jeep. "Nobody's going to start this baby without it." He looked at the jeep. "You know," he said, "I never really thought we'd pull it off. But I'll be damned if the Krauts didn't act as if they saw a US Army jeep driving through their burg every day. . . ."

"That's just fine with me," Kieffer said. "Let's keep it that way."

He turned toward the town.

"Okay. We've gotta start someplace," he said, keeping his voice low. He was annoyed to note that he couldn't keep his tension from showing. "We have to find Ostbahnhofstrasse first. Then Decker's house number."

He looked toward the looming hulk of the main railroad station.

"Probably not too far from here," he said. "Bahnhofstrasse means Railroad Station Street." He nodded toward the building. "That's where we'll start. The railroad station. There'll probably be a street map of the town somewhere."

He turned to Marshall.

"You stay glued to me," he said. "And don't open your mouth. If there's any trouble, let me do the talking. You pretend to be a—a foreign worker. A Pole. French. Anything but US."

Marshall nodded vigorously.

"Got you. Mum's the word."

The station complex itself had sustained heavy damage. The place was only sparsely lighted. But through the shattered glass high above, a feeble moon stabbed at the gloom below and made the twisted iron framework look like an enormous, sooty spiderweb suspended over the passenger rotunda and track platforms. Under this giant web a mass of people seemed to be imprisoned. The railroad station was the only hope of escape for the many who feared the imminent onslaught of the enemy, and the dimness was filled with the whispered voices and shuffling feet of refugees waiting for a place on one of the few trains still able to run.

Kieffer and Marshall made their way through the milling crowd as unobtrusively as possible, looking for a street map. The walls still standing and the makeshift partitions hastily thrown up around bomb-damaged areas were covered with proclamations, bills, slogans and posters.

Nearly all the cheerful advertising and travel posters that adorn every railroad station were gone. In their places were Nazi political placards and old recruiting posters—all torn and soiled. . . .

A stirring scene of gallant battleships steaming forward against a background of a huge Navy flag: "EINSATZ *der Deutsche Kriegsmarine*—CONTRIBUTION of the Germany Navy," it proclaimed. . . . The noble Aryan profile of an airman superimposed on a Luftwaffe emblem: "*Unsere* LUFTWAFFE—Our AIR FORCE." . . . Grim, attacking soldiers: "INFANTRIE *Königin Aller Waffen*—INFANTRY, Queen of All Arms." . . . Even "HER ZU UNS," a proud Hitler Youth holding a swastika banner: "*Hinein in die Hitler-Jugend*—Into the Hitler Youth." . . . And, of course, a picture of a stern, imposing Adolf Hitler and the drumbeat slogan "EIN VOLK, EIN REICH, EIN FÜHRER—One People, One Country, One Leader." . . .

Finally, next to the ominous admonition "FEIND HÖRT MIT! —The Enemy Listens," they found a town map.

Ostbahnhofstrasse began close to the station. It was not a long street. One building on it was marked with a red circle. Jäger-hof. Apparently a notable tourist hotel in happier times.

Kieffer was suddenly aware of a commotion nearby that was coming closer. A small group of tired-looking Waffen SS soldiers headed by an Unterscharführer came marching toward him. The people scrambled out of their way. Kieffer found himself pressed up against the wall. He turned his face to it, earnestly studying the street map.

The palms of his hands were suddenly clammy. Were they headed for him? Had he and Marshall been noticed? Had someone turned in the alarm?

The measured footsteps came closer.

Any second he expected to hear the sergeant bark the command to halt—and to feel the enemy's hand on his shoulder. The skin on his back crawled.

He stood rigid. And the footsteps passed. The crush of people at once let up.

He could feel himself shaking slightly, as after great exertion.

He turned to Marshall.

He was gone.

He looked around wildly before he caught himself.

Easy—

His mind raced.

What had happened? Had Marshall been pushed aside in the crush? Swept away—without being able to call out to him?

Where the hell was he?

Suddenly he heard loud, angry voices not far away. He turned —and froze.

Not twenty yards away stood Marshall, ashen-faced, fright-ened, surrounded by a group of Germans angrily shouting at him, brandishing their fists in outrage. Marshall was shaking his head desperately, gesticulating with his hands and frantically looking around for his comrade.

At once Kieffer was icily calm.

He started toward the knot of angry people.

And stopped short.

Interfering now would only make matters worse. *Two* men in outlandish uniforms would certainly arouse suspicion. They would both be lost.

Quickly he looked around.

A man ahead of him was just going through a door marked HERREN—*Men.*

At once he ducked in after the man.

The stranger was entering one of the small stalls.

Kieffer hurled himself against its door, sending the man sprawling over the yellowed porcelain bowl. In the same motion his right hand found and grabbed the gun in his shoulder holster. He whipped it out and dealt the man a crushing blow on the temple. Without a sound he collapsed.

Kieffer at once slipped into the stall with him and pulled the door shut.

He listened.

Someone came in and began to use the urinal.

Kieffer tore at his clothes. He ripped off his wool cap; he pulled his scarf from around his neck and wriggled out of his grubby mackinaw jacket.

He began to take off his paratrooper boots. It was incredibly cramped. He started to sweat. There was so little time. . . .

He turned to the unconscious man. He wrestled the large raincoat from the limp body. Was he still alive? He pulled off the man's shoes and jammed his feet into them. They were too small—but he gave it no thought.

He struggled into the raincoat and grabbed the man's hat from the moist floor where it had fallen. He clamped it on his head.

Again he listened.

The man at the urinal was washing his hands. Someone else entered and made his way toward the stalls.

Kieffer waited until he heard the door to another compartment open, then he stepped out, closing the door to his stall behind him.

He moved quickly to the exit.

The man at the washstand paid him no heed.

Outside the WC his eyes went at once to Marshall. He was still there—obviously panic-stricken. Even as Kieffer watched, one of the angry Germans gave him a rough shove.

God, Kieffer prayed, as he hurriedly walked toward the group, *don't fight back, Jerry! Don't!*

As he strode toward the disturbance, he buttoned up his coat close to his chin and pulled the hat down on his head. He buried his hands in his pockets.

The thought struck him like lightning.

He was no longer in US uniform. He was in disguise—a spy.

And he reached the group.

Pushing the agitated Germans aside, he stepped up to Marshall. His hand shot out—and he grabbed his friend's arm, twisted it around to his back and yanked it upward with all his might.

Startled, Marshall cried out in pain. Tears welled in his eyes. His face twisted.

Kieffer glared at the suddenly silent Germans.

"Gestapo," he growled. "What goes on here?"

With his hands busy holding the armlock on Marshall, he hoped no one would ask for any identification. . . .

No one did.

A babble of irate explanations beat against him—anger mingled with wariness.

He listened for a moment, glowering at them. He let go of Marshall's arm with one hand, keeping his painful hold with the other.

He held up his free hand imperiously.

"Schon gut!" he said curtly. "Enough. We know what to do with him."

Without waiting for any reaction, he began to march Marshall away.

The crowd parted for him.

No one followed.

Pedestrian traffic in the streets of Mayen was growing lighter. It was late. There were still little groups of grim people around a cart or bicycle being pushed down the street and heaped with household goods and bedding.

Marshall had only partly regained his composure.

"Jesus Christ," he muttered. "Jesus Christ . . ."

He swallowed hard.

"I sure as hell thought I'd had it." He looked pleadingly at Kieffer. "I didn't do nothing. What the hell did I do?"

"Why did you walk away from me?" Kieffer countered.

"I didn't. I swear I didn't. The damned fools pushed me away

—trying to make room for those marching Heinies. I was on my way back to you. I stopped to look for you. But I didn't *do* nothing!"

"You did." Kieffer grinned. "You stepped into a line waiting at a priority transportation center. They thought you'd bucked the line."

"Je-sus Kee-rist," Marshall whispered.

"At least you kept your head," Kieffer said. "And kept your mouth shut. They thought you were a foreign laborer trying to beat them out of a chance to get away from the front." He looked at Marshall. "They were ready to tear you apart."

Marshall shook his head. "You sure took some chance— marching me off like that."

"Hell, no," Kieffer said. "If I'd thought there'd have been any risk, I'd have let you stew in your own juice. I just didn't think any of those noble travelers would want to lose their place in line, following us!"

"Thanks a heap, fella." Marshall rubbed his shoulder. "You nearly pulled my damned arm out of its socket."

"Had to, old buddy," Kieffer said brightly. "It had to look good." He glanced at Marshall. "And I didn't know how good an actor you were."

He looked up at a metal sign on the side of a shrapnel-scarred house.

"Ostbahnhofstrasse," he read. "Let's start looking."

They started down the street.

Kieffer walked rapidly toward the nearest building entrance. He was acutely aware of one chilling fact. He no longer had the protection of his US uniform.

Capture now would mean death.

A most unpleasant one . . .

It was well past midnight when they finally gave up.

With typical Germanic orderliness, almost every residential building on Ostbahnhofstrasse had name plates listing the occupants in the entrance hall. But no Decker. Kieffer was getting worried. In just four hours they were committed to cross back into friendly territory.

Pedestrian traffic on the street had virtually disappeared. Only occasionally would someone hurriedly pass by. Kieffer felt increasingly conspicuous. It made him uneasy. Impatient.

He had a sudden crazy urge to get out in the middle of the street and shout at the top of his lungs: Hey, Decker! Where the hell are you? In times of stress he often let his mind flit to some such outrageous action. Never acted upon, these fantasies somehow helped put things in their proper perspective. He wondered if others had nutty reactions like that.

Okay, so shouting for Decker was hardly the thing to do. But —how the hell *was* he going to find the man?

A little distance away loomed a large building. He could barely make out a sign on the front.

JÄGERHOF.

The hotel.

It was a chance he had to take. . . .

The night porter rose from a chair behind the reception desk when he saw the two men enter the empty hotel vestibule. He began to button the green collar on his threadbare dark-blue tunic, but stopped when he got a better look at the two late visitors. They were hardly potential guests. He eyed them suspiciously.

"Guten Abend," Kieffer said pleasantly.

"Was wollen Sie?" the porter said sourly. "What do you want?"

He scowled at them with mean little eyes; he had bushy brows and an equally luxuriant mustache—a real *Schnurrbart.*

"I wonder if you could be of help to us," Kieffer said politely. "We are trying to locate a gentleman named Decker. Johann Decker. He is an important man. With important friends. He is to leave town tomorrow morning early, and we are supposed to fetch some boxes from his house. For storage."

He glanced at the porter. The man looked bored. Unfriendly. He went on.

"Unfortunately, we have forgotten the number of his house. It is, however, on Ostbahnhofstrasse. Perhaps you know this man? Perhaps you could tell us where he lives?"

The porter shook his head impatiently.

"I know no such man," he said coldly.

Kieffer sighed.

"That is too bad." He carefully pulled out a half-full pack of

Lucky Strike cigarettes and placed them on the counter. The porter's beady eyes grew round. He stared at the treasure.

"Herr Decker is a generous man," Kieffer said. "He gave us a whole pack of real American cigarettes. On account. He had them from the colonel who took them from a war prisoner." He laughed. "They are lucky, *die Kerle*—those fellows who get to the *Ami* prisoners first—not so . . . ?"

The porter nodded—mesmerized by the crumpled pack of cigarettes.

"Ah, well," Kieffer sighed again. "It is pity you cannot help us."

He picked up the cigarettes and started away.

"Moment mal!" The porter's voice was hoarse with greed. "Just a moment!"

Kieffer turned back. He held the pack of cigarettes in plain view.

"Yes?"

The porter scratched his mustache.

"Decker," he mused aloud, "Decker . . ."

He looked pointedly at Kieffer.

Kieffer placed the cigarettes on the counter once again.

"Die Witwe Decker—the Widow Decker," the German said eagerly. "In number one thirty-two. Perhaps—"

"Vielen Dank," Kieffer interrupted. "Many thanks. We shall try there."

He turned and left with Marshall.

He did not have to see the cigarettes disappear into the porter's blue tunic.

Ostbahnhofstrasse No. 132 was a modest three-story apartment building. There were name plates in the entry hall on the street level. But no Decker.

Kieffer pressed the little wall button marked LICHT, which would provide a dim light on the stairs for a measured time only. They started up the steps.

A yellowed porcelain plate on a door on the second floor read: S. DECKER.

There was a white bell button next to the entrance.

Kieffer motioned Marshall to one side of the door. He reached for the bell button.

The light went out.

Kieffer swore under his breath.

He groped his way in the dark to the landing wall, found the LICHT button and pressed it. They would have another two minutes of light.

He returned to the door.

He pressed the bell button.

Inside, a rasping sound could be heard.

And silence.

Again he pressed the button. Again the rasping sound.

He waited.

He glanced at the dim light bulb overhead on the landing. How much time left? Come on, he thought. Answer the damned bell!

Suddenly a man's voice called from behind the door.

"Wer ist da?—Who is there?"

Kieffer tensed. Automatically he glanced down at the wrinkled civilian raincoat he was wearing.

"Kieffer," he answered. "Martin Kieffer, Herr Decker." He took a deep breath. "I am an American Intelligence Officer. I should like to speak with you!"

There was a pause.

Not a sound was heard.

Tensely Kieffer waited.

Suddenly the door opened.

Silhouetted against a dim light in the hallway beyond stood a man.

He wore the long, wide-lapeled, leather greatcoat of a Wehrmacht officer. In his hand he held a gun—aimed directly at Kieffer's belly.

And the light on the landing went out.

3

Kieffer stared at the German.

There was a thin, enigmatic smile on the man's lips. Softly he said:

"I suggest you stand perfectly still."

Kieffer's mind whirled. Who was this German officer? Why was he there? . . . Marshall! He almost turned to look for his companion still standing out of sight on the landing. What would he do? Please, no heroics, he prayed. Or I'm dead. . . .

The German slowly backed toward a small side table in the hallway. On it stood a telephone.

Kieffer's thoughts churned.

He watched the German move toward the telephone. The action seemed to be played out in slow motion, a sinister somnambulistic ballet.

He frowned in concentration.

There was something—something he had sensed but not yet consciously recognized. Something out of context.

Suddenly he knew. The hallway floor was bare wood. But there was no sound of the German officer's boots as he moved. Only a soft shuffling.

He looked down.

Below the leather greatcoat he could make out the bottoms of thin, striped pants. And felt slippers on bare feet.

The German reached for the telephone.

"Wait!" Kieffer said, his voice urgent, strained.

The German hesitated.

"You are Professor Decker?" Kieffer asked quickly. "Professor Johann Decker?"

The German nodded curtly.

"I am," he said.

He picked up the telephone receiver and placed it on the table. His gun never wavered from Kieffer. He gave the handle a short crank, picked up the phone and listened.

He gazed steadily at Kieffer; his enigmatic smile returned.

"Give me the Gestapo!" he said into the phone.

Kieffer acted.

In two strides he was at the table. He pressed down on the phone jack, at once cutting off the German. He reached out and took the receiver from the unresisting man's hand. He replaced it.

The German backed away a step.

Kieffer stared at him. He was suddenly aware that Marshall was crouched in the open doorway behind him, covering the German.

The officer looked back at Kieffer.

"Did you really find this necessary, *meine Herren?*" he asked bitingly. "Did I pass your little test?"

He placed his gun on the table.

"Have I proven my loyalty to your satisfaction?" He sounded bitter.

"Herr Professor," Kieffer said quietly, "I *am* an American."

Without turning around, he continued.

"Jerry. Close the door. Keep him covered."

He heard the soft click as the front door to the apartment was closed.

The German stared at him, white-faced, his little smile gone.

"I—I do not believe you," he said, obviously shaken. "*You* are the Gestapo! Trying to trick me into betraying pro-American sentiments which I do not possess. You are *not*—Americans! . . . It is impossible!"

Kieffer opened his raincoat. Even in the faint hallway light the US emblems on his collar could be seen. He pulled his CIC credentials from his pocket and held them out to Decker.

"I am," he said.

Wordlessly Decker took the credentials. For a moment he stared at them. Slowly he shook his head.

"The Gestapo makes the finest document forgeries in the world," he said, his voice dull.

Kieffer unbuttoned his shirt. He pulled out his dogtags.

"And these," he said, "they are *American* identity tags."

Decker stared at them. He said nothing.

Kieffer gave a hard yank on the tags, breaking the chain around his neck. He held the tags out to Decker.

"Kieffer, Martin," he said, "ASN 0346249. Blood Type O."

Decker took the tags. Slowly he turned them over and over in his fingers. He tried to pry them apart. The gum stretched stickily between them. His eyes gray with uncertainty, he looked up at Kieffer.

"Chewing . . . gum?" he asked tonelessly.

Kieffer nodded.

"To keep them from rattling," he said.

Decker sank down on a chair.

"I—I could have killed you," he whispered. "Or . . ." He glanced at the phone. He looked up at Kieffer, his eyes haunted. "I—could have shot you. . . ."

"No," Kieffer said.

"How could you know?"

"I knew you were Johann Decker," Kieffer said. "Not someone else. Not an officer waiting here to trap me. He would not have worn pajamas and slippers under his coat. Only you. And you would not have shot me—whether you thought I was American or Gestapo."

He took his dogtags back and put them in his pants pocket.

Decker nodded.

"Everything is packed away," he said. "My robe. For tomorrow." He looked up at Kieffer. "I am a scientist," he said. "I am also a major in the Wehrmacht. That is how I shall travel." He sighed. "Even in that, rank has its privileges."

"Professor Decker," Kieffer said urgently. "You know why we are here?"

Decker nodded fearfully. "I—I can guess."

"We have very little time, Professor Decker. Will you return with us? To the American lines? Now?"

Decker put his face in his hands. He shivered slightly. Perhaps it was because of the cold in the apartment. Kieffer said nothing. Finally the scientist looked up at him. His eyes were harrowed.

"I—I do not know . . . ," he whispered.

"Your family?" Kieffer asked gently.

Decker shook his head. "There is only my mother. She left for Munich this morning. She will be safe."

"Your—loyalties?"

Decker looked away.

"Loyalties?" he whispered. "To what? Inhumanity? Deceit? Fear? That is not my Fatherland. Not my people . . ."

He raised his tormented eyes to Kieffer.

"It is very simple," he said quietly. "I am not a brave man. My imagination is too vivid to allow me to be brave. . . ."

He looked down at the floor.

"If—if we were caught . . ." He shook his head. "No. I—I cannot do it."

"There is a way," Kieffer said quickly.

Decker looked up.

"We can take you by force. We can make it appear that we are abducting you against your will."

"How?"

"We will—bruise you on your head. Lightly. To make it appear that you have been knocked out. We will tie you up. We will keep you in the back of our jeep."

Decker looked troubled.

"If we are stopped," Kieffer hurriedly went on, "you can denounce us. You can say you were taken by force. You can show them your bruise. Your bound hands. No one can blame you. You will be safe."

Decker stood up. He suddenly looked excited.

"Will you come?" Kieffer pressed. "There is no time to waste!"

Slowly Decker nodded.

"Yes," he said. "If you do this, I will go with you."

"Good!" Kieffer felt relieved. It would have been damned awkward if he'd really had to knock the guy out. "Get dressed," he said. "Our jeep is not far from here."

"No!" Decker sounded alarmed. "I cannot go with you to your jeep. You must get it yourselves. I will wait for you. Here. Alone. I can be seen with you only when I am—tied up. You must both go. . . ."

Kieffer knew it was no use arguing. The man was too afraid.

"All right," he said. "Wait for us downstairs. In the hallway."

He shrugged out of his raincoat.

"Wear this," he said, "and the hat. Give *me* your officer's coat. Do you have a cap?"

Decker nodded. He opened a closet and took down an officer's peaked cap from a shelf.

"Here."

Kieffer put it on. It was too big. He looked around. On the table lay a magazine. *Berliner Illustrierte Zeitung.* He tore a strip of paper from it. Irrelevantly he noticed it was an article headed ALLIED TERROR BOMBERS RAID DRESDEN CULTURE CENTER. He wadded it up and placed it inside the headband. The cap fitted.

He shrugged into the leather greatcoat.

"We will not be too long," he said. "Wait for us."

Decker nodded. "I will be there."

Kieffer looked at his watch. 0047 hours. There was not much time.

Marshall was at the door. Cautiously he opened it. The darkened stairway was empty. Kieffer joined him. He turned to look back at Decker.

The German scientist stood watching them. He looked oddly forlorn in his striped pajamas and felt slippers, cradling a rumpled raincoat and a battered hat in his arms.

He will be waiting for us, Kieffer thought grimly. He—or the Gestapo. . . .

He left quickly.

The borrowed leather greatcoat softly slapped Kieffer's calves and shins as he and Marshall hurriedly made their way through the gloomy, bomb-pocked railroad yards to the spot where they'd hidden their jeep.

It was still there, undisturbed.

They exchanged silent glances of relief. Marshall at once removed the camouflaging debris. He opened the hood and turned to Kieffer, holding out his hand.

"Okay," he said. "Give!"

Automatically Kieffer put his hand in his overcoat pocket and froze.

Marshall bent over the engine.

"Come on," he urged. "The rotor. Our ticket to Home-Sweet-Homesville!"

The rotor . . .

With the futile urgency born of desperation, Kieffer felt around in the alien pockets of the Wehrmacht officer's greatcoat, knowing that the vital little part would not be there.

The rotor . . .

He knew with bleak certainty where the damned thing was. In the pocket of a grubby mackinaw coat flung across the slimy toilet bowl in a stinking stall of the men's room at the railroad station!

Impatiently Marshall looked up from the engine. His eyes met Kieffer's. The truth rushed upon him. He paled.

"Jesus," he whispered hoarsely. "Jee-sus . . ."

For a brief moment the two stood staring at one another. In his mind each blamed himself. . . .

Had I not gotten into trouble . . .

Had I only remembered the damned rotor . . .

Marshall shook his head.

"No way," he said tonelessly. "No way the damned jeep will run without the rotor."

"There's gotta be a way," Kieffer said vehemently. "Damn it to hell, we've gotta get out of here. And Decker is expecting us to come for him any moment. . . ."

"Shut up!" Marshall said sharply. "Let me think. . . ."

Frowning in concentration, he looked around the yard, his head moving in quick, jerky motions, his eyes searching the misshapen shadows.

They came to rest on the wrecked tie-tamper nearby.

"What's that thing?" he asked, walking rapidly toward the mangled rig.

Kieffer followed.

"No idea," he said. "Railroad maintenance equipment of some sort." He frowned. "Why? It's smashed all to hell."

"Yeah," Marshall mumbled. He seemed deeply preoccupied. "Yeah . . ."

He climbed up on the battered tamping machine. "How's the damned thing powered . . . ?"

He peered into the mass of twisted metal, broken wheel disks and tangled tubing.

"Looks like an internal-combustion engine all shot to hell," he muttered. He tore at some cracked and buckled metal sheathing. He looked up, his eyes excited. "It is! Give me a hand."

Working feverishly, the two men tore at the jagged metal, oblivious to the cuts and gashes they inflicted upon their bare hands.

"There it is," Marshall said tautly. "The distributor."

His hands worked deftly on the device. "Cross your fingers, Marty," he breathed. "Cross everything you can—that it's still there."

Carefully he reached.

He turned to Kieffer. He grinned.

"Got it!"

He held the small object up to his eyes for inspection.

"A Kraut rotor," he said. "I'll be damned!"

"Will it fit?" Kieffer asked anxiously.

"Don't know." Marshall frowned. "Looks about right."

He jumped from the damaged tamper. Together they hurried to the jeep. Marshall at once bent over the engine.

Kieffer looked at his watch. He was acutely aware of time quickly draining away. How long would Decker wait? Would he think he'd been tricked after all? Would he play it safe and call the Gestapo?

Marshall straightened up.

"Shit!" he said with black disgust. "The fucking thing's too big."

He examined the rotor closely. "Maybe . . ." He turned to Kieffer. "Give me that knife of yours."

Kieffer at once reached under his greatcoat. He always carried a paratrooper knife in his belt. In the small of his back. It was a trick he'd seen in an old gangster movie. It had impressed him. He gave the knife to Marshall.

Carefully the sergeant began to whittle away at the German rotor. He ducked under the hood.

Kieffer waited tensely. Time seemed to rush by with breakneck speed. What was Decker doing now . . .?

Finally Marshall called softly.

"Try it. Try to start her up."

Kieffer at once jumped into the jeep. He turned the ignition switch.

The engine caught, sputtered—and died.

"Hold it!" Marshall called.

Kieffer could hear him hacking and scraping at the hard little distributor part.

"Try it again!"

The engine caught—and kept running. Roughly. Faltering. But it ran.

Marshall pushed in behind the wheel. He nursed the uneven engine along.

"I don't know how long she'll last," he said. "I wouldn't want to run no Indianapolis Five Hundred with that gizmo. But at least—she runs."

"Let's get out of here," Kieffer said. He glanced at his companion. "I thought you were supposed to be a top mechanic," he said more calmly. "Sure took you one hell of a time just getting a jeep to start!"

Marshall eased into gear. Slowly, with an occasional cough and jerk, the jeep started off.

"Just you hope," he said dryly. "Just you hope it'll take a lot longer before she stops. . . ."

Kieffer motioned for Marshall to stop a couple of houses before Ostbahnhofstrasse No. 132.

"You wait here," he whispered urgently. "I'll go take a look."

He reached in the back of the jeep and brought out a small roll of webbing.

"If I get in trouble, you barrel the hell out of here, got that?"

"Got it." Marshall sounded reluctant.

"If everything's okay, I'll wave you on," Kieffer said. He looked closely at his friend. "Keep the engine running—and wait!"

"Okay, okay . . ."

Kieffer dismounted and walked rapidly toward Decker's house.

For a brief moment he had a strangely vivid sense of standing aside, detached, watching himself. Or rather—both sides of himself. One was deeply, desperately afraid; the other lucidly calculating. He knew he wasn't free to choose his course of action. And yet at the same time he realized coldly that the slightest miscalculation could cost him his life.

As he neared the front entrance to the Decker apartment building, he slowed down, every sense alert.

He stopped.

There was no sound.

He looked back at the jeep. Still there.

Did he need reassurance that badly?

He looked at the front door to No. 132. The faintest glow of light could be seen through the frosted-glass panes. He knew what it was. The feeble bulb showing night visitors the way to the LICHT button for the stairs.

He walked up to the door, opened it and walked through.

The thought lanced his mind: If they're laying for me, now's the time they'll take me.

The place was quiet, empty.

He glanced quickly around the darkened entrance hall.

Decker was not to be seen.

He went to the LICHT button and pressed it.

There was a soft sound behind him.

Pressed into the shadows of a corner, half hidden by the stairway, stood the figure of a man.

Decker.

White-faced, he stared at Kieffer.

"Gott sei dank!" he whispered. "Thank God! It is you." He stepped forward. He was shaking badly. "I thought—I thought you would not come. I—"

"We are here," Kieffer interrupted sharply. It was obvious—but he had to break in. The man was losing control. "Let's get on with it, Herr Professor."

Critically he inspected the man standing before him. The rumpled raincoat was short in the sleeves, the hat not quite big enough.

"What do you have in your pockets?" he asked.

Decker looked startled.

"Pockets?"

"Yes. What are you carrying with you?"

Decker began to fumble through his pockets.

"My—identification—"

"Keep it."

"—a little money . . . Keys . . . A—a handkerchief . . ." Decker stammered through the list. "Nothing—nothing else. Only—only this . . ."

He brought out a small leather-covered notebook.

"Let me see it."

Kieffer took the notebook. He opened it. It was a folder holding two photographs. An elderly man and an elderly woman smiling gently from opposite sides.

"My—parents," Decker said. He sounded apologetic. He held out his hand for the photo folder.

"You'll have to get rid of it," Kieffer said gruffly, angry at the man's stupidity. "It cannot be found on you if we are stopped and you are searched. A man being abducted hardly has time to pick up a family photo album."

"No," said Decker. His outstretched hand began to shake.

"It's for your own protection, dammit!"

"No. I shall keep it."

Kieffer glanced at the German. He recognized the look of near-panic in the man's eyes. Perhaps the photos were *his* assurance, he thought. His link to sanity. He could not take the chance of having the man lose control. Not now.

"All right," he said shortly. "But *I* shall keep it—until we are safely across the lines." He put the little folder in his pocket. "That's it," he said firmly.

Decker looked down.

"Anything else?"

Decker shook his head.

Kieffer unrolled the webbing.

"Put your hands behind you," he ordered.

Wordlessly the German obeyed.

Quickly Kieffer made an eight-loop with the webbing, slipped it over Decker's hands and pulled it tight. He wound it around the man's waist and tied it securely in the back.

He stepped in front of the trussed-up scientist.

"Your choice," he said quietly. "You still want that knock on your head?"

Decker looked petrified. Two terrors fought in his mind. The fear of getting hurt—and the greater fear of falling into Gestapo hands without every possible proof of innocence.

He nodded.

Kieffer took the soiled hat from the man's head. He brought out his gun from its shoulder holster.

Decker shivered. He screwed his eyes tightly shut.

Kieffer quickly struck him a glancing blow on the temple, hard enough to break the skin.

Decker sagged, but caught himself.

He opened his eyes. He looked surprised.

Kieffer grinned at him.

"It's a beaut!" he said. "No one can doubt you've been hit over the head." He replaced the hat.

Decker smiled weakly. A trickle of blood seeped from under the hat rim and oozed down his cheek. Kieffer did nothing to stem it. He took Decker's arm.

"Let's go."

They walked to the entrance. Cautiously Kieffer looked outside. The street was empty. He stepped from the doorway and waved to the waiting jeep. At once Marshall drove up to the door.

Quickly Kieffer bundled the trussed-up Decker into the back seat and jumped in beside Marshall.

The jeep motor sputtered, missed, caught under Marshall's educated manipulation, faltered for a beat and started down the deserted Ostbahnhofstrasse.

4

Kieffer looked at his watch. 0212 hours. If all went without a hitch, they'd have no trouble making the crossover rendezvous on time.

Mayen had been left behind. According to Kieffer's map, the road on which they were traveling should join the highway to Wittlich-Bitburg in less than a mile. It was a different route from the one they'd taken coming in. Kieffer had decided not to pass through the hospital area and the evacuation activity there but to get out of town the quickest way possible. It was a slightly longer route, passing through Kaisersesch instead of Daun, but there was time enough.

Decker had uttered not a word since getting into the jeep. He was huddled in a corner, his head lowered to his chest. Kieffer could almost feel the tension emanating from him. The jeep engine with the makeshift German rotor had developed a wheezing, clicking sound and missed quite often. It obviously worried Marshall, who sat rigidly hunched over the wheel. Kieffer tried not to think what would happen if the damned thing gave up altogether.

He peered into the night darkness ahead.

In the distance he could make out a row of trees marching across the countryside, diagonally to the road. That would be the highway.

They drove on.

Kieffer strained to see. He thought he could make out some darker shapes at the road junction.

They were almost there.

Suddenly the scene stood out clearly. A chill of alarm hit him. Roadblock!

Two-wooden barriers strung with barbed wire had been placed across the road. Two motorcycles with sidecars were pulled off the road nearby, and four soldiers stood at the barriers, Schmeissers at the ready. German MP's.

One of the MP's stepped forward. He raised high his *Verkehrsanzeiger*—his traffic baton—an imperative order to halt. The red illuminated dot in the disk on the end of the baton glowed malevolently.

Marshall drew in his breath.

Kieffer turned to him.

"Jerry!" His voice was urgent, taut. "Stop the jeep fifty feet before the roadblock. Keep the motor running." He gave a short nod toward the man in the back of the jeep. "Keep him quiet," he growled, "any way you have to!" He buttoned up his greatcoat and pulled the officer's cap firmly down on his head. "If anything goes wrong—you run that damned roadblock! Get Decker back!"

Marshall started to protest.

"Do it, dammit!" Kieffer snarled vehemently. "And keep your mouth shut!"

The jeep came to a halt. The MP walked purposefully toward them.

Kieffer jumped from the jeep. Quickly, impatiently, he strode toward the approaching MP. He met him halfway. He scowled at him. In his hand he held the Wehrmacht map. For show.

A glance etched the man on his mind. Single silver cord and orange piping on his shoulder strap: Unteroffizier—Sergeant—Military Police. Half-moon chest plate with its two prominent dots, Nazi eagle and the word FELDGENDARMERIE—Field Police—daubed with luminous paint.

The MP non-com saluted smartly.

"Heil Hitler!"

With a show of irritation, Kieffer returned the salute.

"What the devil is the meaning of this, Sergeant?" he barked. "Get that damned roadblock the hell out of the way!"

"I am sorry, Herr Major," the MP said stiffly. "It is not possible. I am under orders to let no traffic onto the highway. It is to be kept clear for a top-priority convoy, Herr Major. It is due any minute."

Kieffer glared at the man. His mind whirled. He knew they could not turn around and take the other route. There was no time. And he could not wait for the convoy to pass. It would take too long. . . .

"You hear me well, Sergeant," he snarled, emphasizing each separate word. His voice was dangerous, rising in anger until he was shouting. "I am Major Ritter. I am escorting Standartenführer Adolf Himmler to the front! The front, dammit! It is of the utmost importance that we get there as quickly as possible. You understand me?"

Pointedly he narrowed his eyes, glaring at the MP.

"I am sure you know Colonel Himmler's *uncle,* Sergeant!"

The MP looked apprehensive.

"Jawohl, Herr Major," he said. "May I—"

"You may not! Delay is out of the question!" Kieffer shouted. "Have I not made myself clear? *Verdammt nochmal!* How dare you defy a superior officer?"

The MP non-com was visibly shaken.

"I have—orders—" he started.

"Orders!" Kieffer screamed. "To the devil with your orders!" He suddenly drew himself up, shaking with rage. "Very well, Sergeant. I shall inform Colonel Himmler right now that you refuse to let him pass!"

He turned on his heel, stopped short and whirled on the terrified MP. He whipped Decker's photo folder from his pocket. Imperiously he held out his hand toward the MP.

"Your pen!" he demanded curtly. "I shall want your name. Your service number. For the record." He smiled maliciously. "The Reichsleiter will wish to know exactly *who* delayed a mission in which he is vitally interested!"

The MP was chalk-faced with fear.

Suddenly the low, dull roar of many motor vehicles intruded on their attention. Automatically they both looked toward the highway. Driving with blackout lights only, the convoy was bearing down on the road junction—a giant, growling shadow snake with a thousand slit-orbed eyes.

The sergeant wet his bloodless lips.

"Herr Major," he said, "the convoy is going to the front. Perhaps—if the colonel would join—"

"Good!" Kieffer interrupted him curtly. "See to it! At once!"

He turned on his heel and stalked back to the jeep.

"Come on, Jerry," he said. "We—" His voice broke. He was suddenly aware of his heart pounding in his throat. He swallowed hard. "We're joining that Kraut convoy," he finished. "Get going!"

"Jesus!" Marshall whispered. He eased the jeep into gear. There was a rough, grating sound, a dull backfire; the engine sputtered, coughed—and died.

At the roadblock the MP's were pushing the barriers aside. The non-com stepped out onto the highway—raising his traffic baton. . . .

Kieffer whirled on Marshall. He was about to shout at him, shake him. . . . He stopped. It would do no good.

Marshall was intent on the jeep. He played the ignition, the throttle, the choke, the clutch like an organ virtuoso.

The MP non-com turned toward them and waved them on.

Oh, God! Kieffer prayed. Let it start. . . . Let it start. . . .

The engine turned over; it coughed . . . missed . . . sputtered and the jeep moved.

They drove through the roadblock. The MP non-com stood on the highway, holding up his baton, stopping the convoy so the jeep could join it.

He peered into the back of the vehicle as it passed. He was curious. He could just make out the figure huddled there. Imagine. Heinrich Himmler's goddamned nephew! He considered himself lucky. He'd come out of a run-in with a real *Bonze*—a real big-shot—without getting his balls crushed. . . .

He gave Kieffer a stiff-armed salute.

It was returned with an impatient wave of the hand.

Staring at the truck ahead of him, Kieffer was suddenly aware of the fact that he was shivering with cold. The sweat that drenched him was drying on his skin.

He looked back at Decker. He wondered what the man thought. Had he known how close it had been?

"Colonel Adolf Himmler"—in a wrinkled raincoat and a grimy hat, petrified with fear . . .

He wondered if Himmler actually did have a nephew. Possible. He did have an older brother.

Anyway—Standartenführer Adolf Himmler had done a *prima* job!

Kieffer followed the progress of the convoy on his map. The Wehrmacht map was thoroughly detailed and he'd been able to keep himself oriented on it every foot of the way. They had passed through the town of Wittlich and turned onto the Bitburg highway, and he'd located a small country road which connected with the one leading to the rendezvous point.

But he had not been able to shake the tension which knotted his shoulders and chilled his limbs. Every time the jeep coughed or sputtered, alarm shot through him.

They were making excellent time. The convoy had slowed down as it made its way through Wittlich, a town only a little smaller than Mayen, but they were in no trouble as far as time was concerned.

He turned to Marshall.

"Jerry," he said, his voice strained, "about a half-mile to go before we hit the side road."

He studied the map intently.

"It's a wooded area," he said. "A hill on the left; almost level on the right. There's a bend to the left. That's where the side road is—coming out of the bend."

He looked up and peered ahead. The jeep was keeping the correct convoy distance from the two red dots on the rear of the truck in front of them. He turned to look back at the vehicle behind them. It, too, was observing the proper distance.

"Okay, Jerry," he said. "Here we go! . . . Pull up as close to the truck as you can. We should hit the turnoff in less than a minute. Just before you make the turn—douse the lights."

"Got you."

"Once you're on the damned road—don't stop for anything."

They were only a jeep length from the truck in front.

Kieffer pointed.

"There it is!" he whispered.

At once Jerry turned off the jeep lights. He swung onto the dirt road and careened away through the trees into the gloom of the forest.

No one followed.

The jeep, lights out, was creeping along the narrow forest path. Ahead, the darkness grew less intense where a small clearing straddled the path.

Kieffer felt exhilarated. They'd pulled it off! They had it made . . . almost. Across the clearing was their starting point, the outpost of Able Company.

The ride back through the forest had come off without incident. Even the jeep had behaved. Either it was getting used to the Kraut rotor or Jerry was learning to handle it better.

They came to the edge of the clearing.

"Hold it!," Kieffer whispered.

Marshall stopped the jeep. He kept the motor running. He patted the dashboard affectionately.

"Good girl!" he said softly.

Kieffer listened.

Only the normal night noises of the forest could be heard.

He looked at his watch.

0337 hours. They were almost an hour ahead of time. He grinned. Who could have figured on a convoy escort to speed them on their way? Should he wait? Rendezvous at the exact time agreed on?

He looked back at Decker. Once away from the convoy, they had untied his hands to make him more comfortable. Kieffer hoped he was worth all the sweat. The scientist sat bolt upright, staring silently ahead. His drawn, pale face was a patch of white in the darkness.

Hell, no, Kieffer thought. Better get him back as quickly as possible. Before he starts to fall apart. Anyway, if we kill the damned motor we may never get it started again. He turned to Marshall.

"Okay, Jerry," he said, "let's go. Home . . ."

Slowly Marshall started the jeep across the clearing toward the American outpost.

Any split moment Kieffer expected to hear the challenge— *Homecoming!* He had his countersign ready on his tongue— *Highball!* His eyes were riveted on the spot where he knew the outpost was dug in.

Closer . . .

Suddenly he saw a burst of flash points spit from the forest edge. In almost the same instant the deafening chatter of machine-gun fire slammed against his ears. The windshield shattered, showering him with glass shards. He looked over at Marshall just as the young sergeant's face disintegrated in a crimson blur and he slumped over the wheel. Kieffer threw himself from the jeep. He felt something punch him on his left shoulder, spinning him around. He hit the ground. He screamed into the night.

"Highball! You bastards! . . . *Highball!*"

At the same time he heard a voice in the distance bellow: "Knock it off, you idiot! It's *our* guys!"

The firing stopped.

Kieffer knew he was to blame. They should have waited. Because they were too early, some trigger-nervous Repple-Depple GI had fired before asking questions. . . .

He crawled to the bullet-riddled jeep—only mildly surprised that his left arm hung useless at his side. He was dimly aware of figures running toward him across the clearing.

He pulled Marshall from the steering wheel—avoiding the sight that seared his eyes.

He turned to Decker.

The German was slumped in the back seat. His eyes were closed in agony, his hands clasped tightly against his chest. Bright red blood seeped between his rigid fingers.

With his one good hand, Kieffer took the scientist by the shoulder. The man opened his eyes and stared into Kieffer's face—uncomprehendingly, accusingly. . . .

"Decker," Kieffer whispered, his voice hoarse. "You must talk. Now!"

Decker's lips moved.

No sound came out.

Kieffer bent down over him.

"Try," he urged. *"Try!"*

"They—they have finished—setting up." Decker's voice was barely audible. "Find—Himmelmann. In—Haigerloch—near Hechingen. . . . They are—close. . . ."

He stopped.

"Who?" Kieffer asked desperately. "What were you working on in Frankfurt? . . . What are *they* working on?"

Decker's eyes—pits of anguish—locked onto his.

"Kernphysik," he breathed.

He coughed; he shuddered. His hands relaxed—and fell away.

Kieffer pressed his hand against the open wound in Decker's chest, trying to stem the flow of blood. Help would come. . . .

He stared into Decker's face. The man's warm red life was spilling out over his hand.

He looked at Decker's bloodless lips, slightly parted as if in a sardonic grin. Their last words had made his own blood freeze.

Kernphysik . . .

Hitler's ultimate weapon?

Kernphysik—atomic research . . . !

5

Major General James Edward McKinley stared frowning at the Intelligence Summary dated 3 Mar 45 that was lying on the desk before him. His fingers curled and uncurled one corner of the paper. Two items in it raised his hackles and he couldn't shake the feeling of foreboding they evoked.

Item . . . A German scientist supposedly working on atomic research claiming near-success before being killed by friendly fire during an attempt to defect . . .

Item . . . The German-ordered evacuation of several small settlements in the barren region around Norway's northernmost seaport of Hammerfest, sealing off the area . . .

Unrelated bits of intelligence—and yet . . .

If the Nazis *were* close to perfecting an atomic bomb, they would need a place to test it.

Was *that* what they were preparing on the remote Norwegian ice fields?

Until about a month before, the Intelligence Summaries had contained regular reports on the progress of German atomic research. They had given no cause for alarm. It had been generally assumed that the Nazis were far behind what had been achieved by the Manhattan Project. But since then such reports had virtually ceased coming through.

Intensified security because of an expected breakthrough?

McKinley was acutely aware of the super-strict security imposed on the US effort to perfect an atomic weapon. Ever since the project had been code-named the Manhattan Engineering District and General Groves had been placed in command,

McKinley had kept his boss, the Secretary of War, fully informed on its progress.

The sprawling plant at Oak Ridge in Tennessee was finally turning out significant quantities of U-235, the fully enriched uranium necessary for the construction of an atomic bomb, and shipments of U-235, the fruits of three long years, were ready for delivery to Project Y, the bomb design and development phase at Los Alamos in New Mexico.

He had visited the place. He had found it ideal for its purpose.

Atop a lonely mesa along the Los Alamos Canyon at 7200 feet above sea level a small town of green-painted buildings had sprung up, surrounded by a double row of heavy barbed-wire fencing. Cradled in an arc of hump-backed green hills to the west, the mesa overlooked a vast desert wasteland of sand and cacti to the east, stretching away below as far as the eye could see, marked only by a thin, verdant strip of fertile ground along the winding path of the Rio Grande. It was a town that was not indicated on any map. The Hill, they called it. To the rest of the world it did not exist. It had been the site of a boys' boarding school before being taken over by MED, but the studies being pursued at Los Alamos today were very different. Different—and deadly. How deadly would be learned at Alamogordo, 190 miles to the south as the crow flies, the site selected for Trinity —the test explosion of the first atomic bomb Los Alamos would produce. Preparations for Trinity were going into high gear. They expected the blast to be equivalent to five thousand tons of TNT, but they could be wrong. Either way . . .

Was that barren Norway site the Nazi Alamogordo?

He stood up, walked to the window and stood for a moment staring into space. His Pentagon office windows opened on the landscaped, five-acre, pentagonal court in the center of the mammoth building. It was restful and pleasant. Yet he could never escape the feeling of being imprisoned.

McKinley had a photographic memory. Anything he'd *seen,* he remembered. He still recalled the poop sheet they'd handed him two years ago when the Pentagon had been completed. Trivia on an incredible scale. The world's largest office building . . . 4200 clocks . . . 685 drinking fountains . . . 280 restrooms —he wondered briefly if an architectural study had been made on the correlation of drinking fountains to toilets—and corridors, seventeen and one half miles of corridors. He must have walked every goddamned mile of them.

They could all disappear in the flash of absolute annihilation an atomic bomb might unleash.

An American bomb. Or a German . . .

He returned to his desk, stared at the Intelligence Summary. Should he alert Groves? As soon as the thought occurred to him, he knew he would not.

Groves had stopped a top OSS agent, that baseball player . . . Bates. Burns. Berg—that was it—Moe Berg . . . from going into Germany to check on the Nazi atomic project. Into the same damned area—Hechingen—mentioned in the report.

McKinley sighed.

Groves felt—and he had been right—that if Berg was captured, the Nazis might sweat more information out of him about *our* project than he could have learned about *theirs.*

McKinley flipped the switch on his intercom.

"Barnes," he said, "the MED offices are still in the War Department Building?"

"Yes, sir," his aide's answer came over the speaker.

"Get hold of their head of security. Colonel—eh—"

"Reed, sir. John Reed."

"—Reed. I want him here in my office in two hours."

"Yes, sir."

"Also that major from Donovan's outfit—"

"Major Rosenfeld, sir. David Rosenfeld."

"Right. The one we've dealt with on OSS matters."

"Yes, sir. Anyone else?"

"That's all."

"Yes, sir. Colonel Reed and Major Rosenfeld. Your office at 1330 hours, sir."

There was a click from the intercom.

McKinley sat back in his chair. He knew both Reed and Rosenfeld. He respected them. They were men like himself who believed in getting a necessary job done—even if it meant not going through channels but taking direct action.

And action *had* to be taken.

He'd damned well better get some hard facts about the Nazi bomb.

A few months before, Groves had been wise in choosing to

stop direct penetration of the suspected project area.

This time there was *no* choice. They had to go in. . . .

He stared at the Intelligence Summary. Slowly he reread the first item:

1 Mar 45. Sector of 11th Inf vic Bitburg, Germany (Q 822 877). German scientist, Johann Decker, believed active with Degussa, Frankfurt, killed during exfiltration attempt. Decker states that individual named Himmelmann in Haigerloch ten miles west of the town of Hechingen (P 654 667) may have information re: German progress in atomic research. States further that German physicists are close to success. . . .

McKinley sighed again. Decker. Johann Decker . . .

Who the hell was Johann Decker?

6

The slim file folder on the desk before Standartenführer Werner Harbicht bore the legend printed in black block letters:

GEHEIME STAATSPOLIZEI
Amt IV E-1   Stuttgart, Wkr V

A handwritten case number, 3-72P, had been entered in the appropriate box in the upper right corner—and beneath it a name in bold lettering: **DECKER, JOHANN.**

Colonel Harbicht, Chief of Amt IV E-1—Counterespionage—Regional Gestapo Headquarters, Stuttgart, contemplated the file. He knew every word it contained. It had been lying on his desk in a stack of new cases to be brought to his attention when he had returned to his office early that afternoon. It was now close to 1800 hours and Harbicht had just made up his mind. He knew exactly what he had to do.

He felt the familiar exhilaration course through him and welcomed it, a well-trained hunting dog sniffing a fresh spoor.

Seeing the name on the case file folder, he had recognized it at once—even though years had gone by since he had last been involved with Johann Decker. In 1934, as a young officer in the then year-old Gestapo organization in Berlin, he had investigated Decker, who had suddenly been publicly spotlighted because of getting the Nobel Prize. There had been rumors that Decker was hostile to the rising National Socialist movement, and Harbicht had investigated the man. He had found no concrete evidence to support the allegations, and no action had been taken.

Now—more than ten years later—the name of Johann Decker had reappeared.

Decker should have reported in Haigerloch on March 1. It was now March 3—and the man had not arrived. He had, in fact, disappeared.

Harbicht was acutely aware of the security measures that surrounded the entire project at Hechingen and Haigerloch. He knew how vitally important the undertaking was to the Reich—and to ultimate military success. Although Decker had last been seen in a town outside Harbicht's jurisdiction, the man's destination had been Haigerloch. And Haigerloch *was* in his territory. He had at once requested a full report on the Gestapo investigation in Mayen, Decker's last known whereabouts.

For several years Decker had worked at the Degussa uranium-refining plant in Frankfurt. After the massive RAF raid in mid-September of '44, which gutted large parts of the facilities, the plant machinery and remaining raw materials and supplies had gradually been evacuated to Rheinsberg near Berlin and the plant personnel reassigned. Decker was one of the last to leave.

In his mind Harbicht reviewed the meager—and puzzling— facts. . . .

Decker had been staying for a few days in the apartment of his mother, who had left for Munich the day before Decker himself was supposed to leave for Haigerloch. His luggage was still in the house. He was known to be traveling in the uniform of a Wehrmacht major. This uniform was gone, including greatcoat and cap but not the boots. Harbicht frowned. It irritated him that he could not determine the significance of this single little fact. The apartment showed no signs of any struggle. Only one item was out of the ordinary. Part of a page had been torn out of a magazine lying on a side table in the hall. The *Berliner Illustrierte Zeitung.* The scrap of paper was not found in the apartment. The torn page had been reconstructed. On one side of the missing piece was a portion of an ad for Electrola Musikplatten; on the other, part of a report about a bombing raid on Dresden. It made no sense. The gramophone-records ad had listed several selections with ordering code numbers. EJ443 . . . EH607 . . . EG861 . . . and so on. Could easily be a more sinister code as well, he reasoned. The standard five-letter or five-digit group of a Morse code transmission? Was that why the ad had been torn out? He made a mental note to follow it up.

The local Gestapo had turned up only one additional piece of information. The hotel porter in the Jägerhof Hotel. This man informed the investigating agents that during the night of February 28–March 1 two men had inquired about Decker. The men, who said they were movers, were strangers to him. Although he did know where the Decker family lived, he denied giving the strangers any information, and his description of them was vague. He thought they had worn some kind of field uniform, but he had been unable to make any identification.

Harbicht smiled a thin smile. He wondered idly how efficient the interrogation of the porter had been. He had no doubt the man was lying. It was logical. It was also unimportant. Decker *had* disappeared—with or without the unintentional help of the night porter.

It was not much to go on. But Werner Harbicht had a sharply analytical mind—as orderly and crisp as his SS uniform. He was convinced the Decker case was of paramount importance, and he was determined to find out exactly what that importance was. He felt wholly alert. His powers of analysis extended to himself, and he was thoroughly aware that he welcomed challenges; thrived on trouble. The more difficult the problems, the more cunning his opponents—the greater his satisfaction in defeating them.

His superiors at Gestapo Headquarters in Berlin had recognized this characteristic in the young officer. That was the principal reason for transferring him out of the Prinz Albrecht Strasse offices and promoting him, at the age of thirty-seven, to Standartenführer, placing him in charge of the Stuttgart Regional Gestapo Headquarters in the highly sensitive Wehrkreis V, which included the vital Hechingen-Haigerloch Project. The other reason had been a vague feeling on the part of his immediate superior of a predatory threat in the intensely ambitious young officer—a danger which the older man preferred to keep at a distance. . . .

Harbicht pressed a button on his desk.

At once an SS Scharführer appeared at the door.

"Zu Befehl, Herr Standartenführer!" The sergeant clicked his heels. "At your orders, Colonel!"

"I shall be leaving for Hechingen in one hour. I want the local office informed. See to it," he snapped.

"Jawohl, Herr Standartenführer!"

"I shall be gone indefinitely. Sturmbannführer Meister will take over here. Have him report to me at once."

"Jawohl, Herr Standartenführer, sofort—at once!"

The man's hand shot out in a stiff-armed Nazi salute.

"Heil Hitler!"

He left.

Harbicht sat back in his chair. He would not be unhappy to be leaving Stuttgart. With the presence there of the Daimler-Benz aircraft-engine, truck and tank factories, the Bosh electric plant and the important railheads, the city had become a prime target for Allied air raids.

But that was not the reason he had decided to go to Hechingen and take charge of the Decker case himself. It was the only logical decision he could make.

Why had Decker not shown up in Haigerloch?

What had happened to him?

He was eager to come to grips with this new challenge, and even swollen with the influx of workers and technical personnel on the project, Hechingen was a small town. Fifteen, twenty thousand people. He would be able to hold it in an iron fist.

He had never yet emerged a loser.

7

It was precisely 1330 hours when Captain Barnes ushered Colonel Reed and Major Rosenfeld into General McKinley's office. The general looked at his aide.

"No interruptions," he said quietly.

"Yes, sir."

Barnes left.

McKinley gave each of the officers a copy of the Intelligence Summary.

"Read the two marked items," he said.

He studied the two men as they read. Rosenfeld, the OSS officer, was in his late thirties, a linguist-sociologist, European languages. He had expert knowledge of six or seven and spoke every one of them with an atrocious Midwestern accent. Reed, the MED security chief, was a few years older, with an extensive background in law enforcement and as a special agent in the FBI.

The two men finished reading at almost the same time. They looked up at the general. Their faces were grim.

McKinley turned to the senior officer.

"Reed?" he asked quietly.

"What's the reliability rating of the Norwegian source?" the colonel asked.

"High," McKinley answered. "A member of Milorg—the Norwegian Resistance Organization."

Reed nodded thoughtfully.

"It's a new ballgame, sir," he said slowly. "Taken in context with other intelligence, it sure looks as if the Germans are

up to something. Getting ready for some action. Possibly—
atomic . . ."

McKinley glanced at the summary.

"Do you know who this Johann Decker is?" he asked.

"The name is not familiar."

McKinley flipped the intercom switch.

"Barnes," he said, "is that biographical information on Johann
Decker—reference, Intelligence Summary, third March, page
two—ready?"

"Just transcribing it, sir."

"Also find out who was interested in exfiltrating him. And—
why."

"Yes, sir."

"Bring it in when you have it."

He flipped off the switch and turned back to Reed.

"Degussa?"

"A Frankfurt corporation, sir. They have an outstanding reputation in the field of metal refinement. Pre-war, they used
small amounts of uranium for the manufacture of ceramic coloring. We have had unconfirmed intelligence that indicates considerable quantities of uranium products recently shipped to
their plant." He thought for a moment. "But we have no reli-
able information on any current project. Degussa security has
been extremely strict. We assume it to be a uranium-reduction
project."

McKinley nodded.

"And—Himmelmann?"

"Probably Gustav Himmelmann. An Austrian physicist involved in atomic research. One of the scientists whose whereabouts Alsos has been trying to pinpoint." He frowned. "Apparently he is in Haigerloch." He paused. "Only—ten miles from
Hechingen . . ."

"Yes. Hechingen," McKinley said. "Again . . ."

His mind raced back to the fall of the year before. It had been
their biggest scare. Aerial photographs taken on a series of
sorties had revealed a construction program of considerable
magnitude mushrooming with extraordinary speed in the Hechingen area. Railroad spurs, power lines and storage tanks had
sprung up; what appeared to be a number of medium-sized
industrial plants and factory buildings with tall chimneys had

been erected and a grid of pipes laid out on the ground, and storage depots with mountains of material dotted the region. The project had obviously been given the highest priority; three large forced-labor camps had been built literally overnight. Since a flock of German atomic scientists had already been sent to Hechingen and surrounding villages, everyone from Groves on had felt the project might well be a Nazi version of Oak Ridge and Los Alamos rolled into one. The complex was finally determined to be a new form of shale-oil-cracking plant, and that explanation had been accepted then. Indeed, there were deposits of low-grade oil shale in the region. Now he felt suddenly uneasy. Extracting oil from shale was inefficient. Was the operation actually a cover for the construction of an atomic bomb?

He turned to the OSS major.

"Rosenfeld?"

"They are obviously going full steam on some top-secret project—atomic or not," the officer said. "We will have to find out exactly what."

"You recommend an OSS mission?"

Rosenfeld nodded. "I do."

McKinley turned to Reed. "What about Alsos?" he asked.

He already knew the answer. . . .

Alsos was MED's own scientific-intelligence unit, formed in the fall of 1943. Its primary mission was to collect intelligence of atomic developments in Italy and Germany. Alsos agents advanced with and operated closely behind US military forces —but never in enemy territory. The highly knowledgeable Alsos scientists and specialists were far too vulnerable to risk capture and interrogation. Alsos' German operation had begun only a week before near Aachen, too recently for any significant results.

"It's not an operation for Alsos," Reed said.

"The only agency with operatives working in the 'black' inside Germany proper, sir, is our Secret Intelligence section— OSS-SI," Rosenfeld added.

"Any of them qualified to handle this?"

Rosenfeld shook his head.

"I am certain not," he said. "We only have a handful of agents inside."

There was a knock on the door. Captain Barnes entered, handed a sheet of paper to McKinley and left.

The general read the information aloud:

"Decker, Johann—physicist. Born Düsseldorf, 1901. Professor theoretic physics, Heidelberg. Investigated disintegration products of radium, thorium and actinium, and the behavior of beta rays. Investigations in the field of quantum theory and atomic structure and behavior. Worked on development of quantum mechanics, 1931. Nobel Prize in physics, 1934. Professor in Berlin; member of Kaiser Wilhelm Institute of Physics, 1937. Joined Degussa, Frankfurt, 1944—position and activities unknown. Considered one of Germany's leading scientists in the field of atomic research. G-2 states exfiltration request originated with Manhattan Project."

McKinley looked at Colonel Reed.

"Seems your people wanted this Decker fellow," he said. "And I can understand why."

Reed was turning deep red.

"Yes, sir," he said with obvious difficulty. Then he could no longer contain himself. "Damn that Need-to-Know nonsense!" he exploded. "How in hell can I function when my right hand doesn't communicate with my left—even in sign language?"

McKinley smiled.

"Don't let it get you down, Reed," he said. "I've got the same problem right here."

He turned to Rosenfeld. He grew sober.

"It's your baby, Major," he said. "How do you want to handle it?"

Rosenfeld frowned lightly in concentration.

"Probably as a one-man infiltration—rather than a team effort," he said. "The man would have to penetrate a strict security project in the heart of enemy country."

"He'd have to be one hell of an agent," Reed commented.

"He would." Rosenfeld looked at General McKinley. "I can profile him."

"Go," McKinley said.

"He'd have to speak German like a native, know his way around the country. He must be thoroughly trained and have experience in the field. He must be a scientist with enough knowledge in the atomic field to know what he is looking for—

and to recognize it if he finds it—but not enough knowledge of our own progress to be a real danger if captured." He thought for a moment. "He must be in good enough physical condition to be able to handle himself in any tight situation, and he would have to have a good cover with a valid excuse for not being in the German armed forces, if he is to be able to move around."

"Pretty tall order—even for your OSS," Reed commented dryly.

"Can you lay your hands on a man to fit that bill?" General McKinley asked. "Fast?"

"How fast?"

"Forty-eight hours."

Rosenfeld looked startled. "We can try."

"Get on it," McKinley said. "Keep me fully informed."

"Yes, sir."

McKinley stood up. He walked over to the window. The sky was as blue as he had ever seen it. He weighed his options. . . . Johann Decker's statement was unconfirmed, but he felt in his gut it was valid. Attempts could be made to verify it. Were significant amounts of uranium actually going to Haigerloch? That was a key question. What were the realistic risks in sending into Germany an agent who knew about the Manhattan Project, however sketchily? He suddenly appreciated Groves' stand on that baseball-player incident; saw the dilemma clearer than ever. If the man was caught, he would be made to talk. Eventually. McKinley had no illusions about that. Would the risks be outweighed by the possible benefits? If the Nazi undertaking at Haigerloch definitely *was* an atomic-bomb project— was there any choice at all?

He turned to Rosenfeld.

"Major," he said, "I want a penetration mission prepared as quickly as possible, ready to jump off at a moment's notice."

"Yes, sir."

"I will tell you *if*—and *when.* Understood?"

"Yes, sir."

McKinley walked back to his desk. He turned to Reed. He looked deeply troubled. He hesitated. Then—

"Reed," he said soberly, "has the Manhattan Project been penetrated?"

Reed slowly shook his head.

"Half an hour ago I would have said no," he answered slowly. "Absolutely not . . ."

He looked grimly at the general.

"I—don't know."

8

He squinted through the grimy window at the crisp morning light. From the shadows of his dingy room he cautiously looked up and down the alley below. Only two days before, he had almost been caught. . . .

He'd barely walked out of the fleabag on Lee Street near the B&O Railroad when a carload of eager-beaver FBI men had barreled up. It had taken all his sang-froid to join the small, curious crowd that quickly gathered to watch as two of the agents rushed in the front while others raced to cover the rear. He had to hand it to them. He'd been on the air less than fifteen minutes. . . .

He glanced at his watch. It was almost time.

He took a deep breath. A sharp pain knifed through his chest. That damn wound. About time it stopped bothering him.

He took stock. Again.

He realized that was a weakness. Checking and rechecking. And checking again. Not because of caution, but because of nerves. Something to do. Something to replace sweaty, apprehensive waiting. Like his habit of yawning when he was on edge.

Maybe it wasn't such a bad thing after all. Better than wetting his pants.

He breathed a little more cautiously.

It had been ridiculously easy.

The people of Hagerstown, Maryland, had been cooperative to a fault. Information had been freely—sometimes even proudly—given. He'd had no trouble getting access to town records and plans. He had been able to construct a complete picture. He knew every target point in detail: power stations, sewer system, water supply, industry, transportation, communication and defense—the works. He knew exactly how to paralyze this entire city of over thirty-thousand people quickly and effectively. And for a period long enough to destroy completely the entire complex of Fairchild Aircraft Corporation factories straddling the railroad junction at the northern outskirts of the town. The drop could be made at their test field. The entire operation would take less than twenty-four hours.

He took off his watch and laid it on the table next to his set. Contact time in less than eight minutes.

He looked at the thin wire running from the set. The hotel was in the old part of town. His room was on the top floor. He had planned on putting up his antenna on the roof—but a tight-faced spinster in a room across the hall was using it to dry her underwear. He didn't want to take the chance. Instead he was using the bed. The springs made an effective antenna. He had good contact. And he'd grounded the set with the central heating pipes. It worked.

He pulled his lined pad to him.

He yawned.

He wanted to make his message as short and sweet as possible. He wanted to be on the air as brief a time as possible. He knew the minute he began transmitting, the FBI monitors would pick him up—and he already knew how damned fast they could react.

He printed his message on the paper in block letters. He always waited till the last possible moment before putting anything down. It was a good precaution.

ALL TARGET POINTS LOCATED STOP, he wrote. TAKEOVER CAN BE EFFECTED WITH ONE PARACOMPANY STOP. That ought to do it. ACTIONREADY VAN G8, he finished.

He at once began to encipher the clear text. He used the standard double transposition cipher, which required nothing but pencil and paper and the memorizing of two key words. It eliminated the necessity for an agent in the field to carry incriminating encoding paraphernalia. His key words were OPERATIONAL and SUPERSENSITIVE.

Quickly he printed key word number one and made the

number conversion, using one for the first letter of the alphabet that appeared in the word and so on along the line.

```
O   P   E   R    A   T    I   O   N   A   L
7   9   3   10   1   11   4   8   6   2   5
```

He counted the numbers of letters in the clear. Eighty-five. Seventeen groups—right on the button. He did not need to add any nulls. He grinned. He was getting too damned good at this message-writing crap.

He quickly lined out his grid under the converted key word —his cross lines making uneven, careless squares—and wrote his clear below it.

```
O   P   E   R    A   T    I   O   N   A   L
7   9   3   10   1   11   4   8   6   2   5
A   L   L   T    A   R    G   E   T   P   O
I   N   T   S    L   O    C   A   T   E   D
S   T   O   P    T   A    K   E   O   V   E
R   C   A   N    B   E    E   F   F   E   C
T   E   D   W    I   T    H   O   N   E   P
A   R   A   C    O   M    P   A   N   Y   S
T   O   P   A    C   T    I   O   N   R   E
A   D   Y   V    A   N    G   8
```

He scribbled his second key word, number-converted it and penciled in his message horizontally below it, starting with the vertical line numbered *one* and reading down. . . .

```
S   U    P   E   R   S    E   N   S   I    T   I    V    E
9   13   7   1   8   10   2   6   11  4    12  5    14   3
A   L    T   B   I   O    C   A   P   E    V   E    E    Y
R   L    T   O   A   D    A   P   Y   G    C   K    E    H
P   I    G   O   D   E    C   P   S   E    T   T    O    F
N   N    N   A   I   S    R   T   A   T    A   E    A    E
F   O    A   O   8   L    N   T   C   E    R   O    D    T
S   P    N   W   C   A    V   R   O   A    E   T    M    T
N
```

He glanced at his watch. Two minutes, twenty seconds. Quickly he copied out his enciphered five-letter groups, again starting with the key-word line numbered *one* and reading down. . . .

BOOAO WCACR NVYHF ETTEG ETEAE KTEOT APPTT
RTTGN ANIAD I8CAR PNFSN ODESL APYSA COVCT
ARELL INOPE EOADM

He was pleased. With only seventeen groups, he should be on
and out in a few minutes.

He turned on his set.

It was time.

He began sending his call letters.

In less than forty seconds he'd made contact. He was just
about to start his transmission when the letters QSP, QSP, QSP
crackled in his earphones.

The code letters for ACCEPT MY PRIORITY MESSAGE.

Shit, he thought. There goes the fucking ballgame. By the
time those bastards transmit their damn priority message, whatever the hell it is, and I get it deciphered and answered and get
my own message sent—the FBI'll be able to locate Judge Crater!

Angrily he snapped off QRV, QRV—I AM READY. He hoped
his fist showed his annoyance.

He poised his pencil and listened. He held it frozen in astonishment as the transmission began: SENDING CLEAR—

The words came crisply over his earphones. He began to
write:

GIVE YOUR LOCATION STOP WAIT FOR PHYSICAL CONTACT STOP AC-
KNOWLEDGE PAUL

His mind raced. What the hell were they doing back at B-2?
Was it a trick?

Paul *was* his contact's name. Was it *his* fist? He could not be
sure. Had the FBI cracked his frequency? Did the transmission
actually come from the home OSS camp—or the FBI?

He had a sudden icy vision of Ramon, his Filipino classmate.
The guy looked just like a Jap. He'd been picked up by the
police in some little Midwestern town where he'd been sent on
his field problem. It was a good idea—the field problem. It was
as close to the real thing as a novice agent could get—without
laying his life on the line. He'd be up against the FBI and local
law-enforcement agencies who didn't know him from the real
article. It wasn't always a picnic. The local gendarmes who'd
picked up Ramon thought they'd captured themselves a real,

hot-off-the-griddle spy. They'd beaten the shit out of him. Broken his nose, half his teeth, seeing themselves making the Midwest safe for democracy. They didn't know, of course, that Ramon was one of the good guys, and they took their own sweet time calling the Washington executive number he'd finally given them.

The FBI knew just as little about him, he realized. They didn't know he was on an OSS field problem. He had no identification. It was a kind of getting-back-in-shape exercise after his abortive mission. His chest and elbow suddenly hurt. He swore under his breath. Shit! They'd play it for real, too. . . .

He adjusted his head-set. It felt sweaty. Did his ears sweat, for crissake?

He had to make sure. If it was an FBI intercept—he'd better beat it the hell out of there. Fast!

His fingers flew over the keys.

IF PAUL WHAT IS MANNY'S RETREAT?

He waited.

Almost at once the answer came.

SHITHOUSE.

He sighed.

WILCO, he sent. HOTEL ADAMS FRANKLIN NEAR POTOMAC OUT.

He sat back. He was conscious of his body relaxing. He had not been aware of his tenseness.

It had to be Paul. Only *he* could know that the camp latrine was nicknamed Manny's Retreat because Mannering, the mess sergeant, spent all his leisure time there reading girlie magazines.

He ripped up his enciphered message. He packed up his X-35 set that looked for all the world like an ordinary portable typewriter. An Underwood.

He contemplated the antenna rig.

The hell with it.

Dirk Vandermeer, OSS agent Van G-8, stretched out on the bed to wait.

9

Major Rosenfeld felt like a salesman—with a second-rate product to sell. The worst of it was that he *had* to make the sale. He had nothing better to offer. And General McKinley was no easy mark.

He glanced at Colonel Reed. Your turn is coming up, Buddy, he thought without satisfaction.

He cleared his throat and continued his presentation. His sales pitch.

"Vandermeer possesses the following qualifications necessary for the job, sir," he said persuasively. "He was born in Rotterdam in 1919 and came to the States as a pre-teenager. His father, still living, is a cheese importer in Brooklyn. The boy spent his high-school vacations in Holland and practically crisscrossed Germany as a *Wandervogel*—"

McKinley raised an inquisitive eyebrow.

"A term for young hikers, sir, making their way on foot through the country," Rosenfeld explained. "He learned to speak German fluently on those trips," he continued. "Not a difficult thing to do for someone brought up speaking Dutch."

He referred to some notes.

"He joined the OSS immediately after Pearl Harbor," he went on, "and finished all training courses in the top ten percent." He frowned slightly. "He—he did not like being addressed by his OSS code name, Van G-8, and chose to be called by his own name, Dirk, contrary to instructions." He glanced at the general. "He is—eh—somewhat of an individualist, sir, but most effective. He has already proven himself courageous, imaginative and resourceful. He—"

Hold it, he thought. Don't oversell. He cleared his throat.

"He has had field experience on two OSS missions in Holland. The first an unqualified success. The second terminating in quite serious injuries. He—"

"How serious?" McKinley interrupted.

"One rib on his left side was partly sheared away, sir. His left elbow was shattered. He has regained only partial use of the arm. About eighty percent. He can, however, function perfectly all right and has recuperated remarkably well. But those wounds will provide him with a bona-fide excuse for not being in uniform in Germany."

"He hasn't come up—eh—gun-shy in any way, has he?"

"No, sir. There have been no indications that he has."

McKinley nodded. "I see." He paused.

Here it comes, Rosenfeld thought bleakly.

"What are his scientific qualifications, Major?" the general asked.

Rosenfeld looked him straight in the eyes.

"None, sir," he said. "None whatsoever."

McKinley frowned. He sat back in his chair.

Okay, Reed, Rosenfeld thought, take it, dammit, take it!

"Sir." It was Colonel Reed. "We do have another possible subject."

"Let's have it." McKinley sounded cool.

"His name is Brandt, sir. Sigmund Brandt."

"Another OSS agent?"

Reed looked uncomfortable.

"Yes, sir," he said, "and—no. . . ."

"Which is it?" the general asked icily.

"*Yes*, sir. Since this morning."

"What training has he had?"

"None."

"You can't send in an untrained man, Colonel," McKinley said. He was capable of making his voice sub-arctic. "You might as well shoot him here."

"OSS has no available trained agent with all the necessary qualifications including scientific knowledge, sir," Rosenfeld came to the rescue.

"When I briefed General Groves on the immediate problem," Reed took up the relay staff, "he remembered Sigmund Brandt. He suggested I contact him. The general has been very much impressed by him."

"In what way?"

"Brandt runs a manufacturing company in New Jersey that he took over from his father when he retired, sir. An electro-chemical plant. It's a prime contractor on the Manhattan Project." He paused, searching for the right words. "When the project hit a—a snag which none of the major corporations could solve, General Groves approached the senior Brandt. Brandt turned the problem over to his son, who told General Groves *'Can do'*—and he did. In fact, he invented a whole new electrochemical process. The general was very impressed with his imaginative approach."

"Why is he a subject for the Hechingen mission?" McKinley asked.

"He has the scientific knowledge, sir. Just enough—without being too great a danger if captured. He had to be briefed on the rudimentary aspects of the project in order to solve the problem handed him." Reed was warming to his subject. "He also has other qualifications necessary to the mission," he continued. He is a naturalized US citizen, born in Zürich in 1914, and he speaks German, French and English fluently—as well as Switzerdeutsch, the Swiss dialect. With proper papers as a Swiss-national technician, he should be able to sustain a safe cover in Germany."

He looked at McKinley.

"He—he has agreed to join the OSS, General," he said. "But —he has no prior intelligence training. In fact—no military training at all. Major Rosenfeld and I—"

"I agree," McKinley interrupted him.

"Sir?" Reed looked puzzled.

McKinley smiled imperceptibly.

"I assume you are about to suggest that Vandermeer and Brandt be teamed to go on the mission to Hechingen," he said matter-of-factly. "You were going to point out to me that *together* the two of them would make one hell of an agent. I agree."

Rosenfeld and Reed exchanged glances. A wave of relief washed over Rosenfeld. The sale had been made.

"The mission will by mounted by OSS-SI," he said. "From London. We will monitor it from there."

"What is your next step?" McKinley asked.

"Both men are now at B-2, the OSS camp at Catoctin Manor in the Blue Ridge," Rosenfeld answered briskly. "Brandt will undergo a two weeks' crash training course with Vandermeer before going on to London."

"Make it ten days," McKinley said. "Four days saved now may be worth forty later."

10

Sigmund Brandt cursed the day he'd first laid eyes on that Rosenfeld from the Office of Strategic Services. He had been summoned to the major's office in Temporary Building Q in Washington, D.C.: urgent and vital. He'd naturally assumed it had something to do with his contractual work for the Manhattan Project. He'd been wrong.

He should have known from the start that he was getting himself involved with a screwball outfit. The OSS. That file cabinet behind Rosenfeld's desk in his office should have tipped him off. Three drawers. On the top one a sign in big black letters —TOP SECRET. The next one down was marked MIDDLE SECRET —and the lowest, BOTTOM SECRET. Really!

He'd been snowed. But good! Rosenfeld had told him that the mission for which he was being asked to "volunteer" was of the utmost importance to the security of the Manhattan Project, of which he, Sigmund Brandt, was such a vital part. In fact, the job was vital to the safety of the entire United States of America, his chosen country. He hadn't been able to muster the guts to say no. There *was* a certain hazardous element involved, Rosenfelt had hinted; it would be behind enemy lines, but he had not been at liberty to tell Sig *exactly* what the mission was.

They still had not told him. He wondered wryly if they ever would—or if he would have to sally forth to fight windmills blindly. But Rosenfeld had assured him he'd be okay. He would be given a thorough training course which would prepare him for—anything. A crash course, he'd called it. Crash was right. He felt as if he had indeed crashed—from somewhere on the top floor of Temporary Building Q.

He shifted his position cautiously. The ground was damp and cold. Every muscle in his body seemed to ache.

He glanced at his companion lying quietly, fully alert beside him. The man reminded him of a coiled spring. Dirk. Or Van G-8, as the OSS characters insisted on calling him. Just as he, Sig, was Sig S-2. For ten days the two of them had trained together. Studied, eaten and rested together. Used the latrine together. And yet—he did not feel any real companionship with Dirk. They were two men going through the same motions, separate and independent of one another, giving each other a hand, of necessity. Except, dammit, Dirk was far and away the superior physical specimen of the two—despite the handicap of his injuries.

Sig sighed—much put upon.

Anyway. The immediate problem was that damned obstacle course. The culmination of ten days of grueling instruction and training. They'd been given a crude map with the layout of the course so they could familiarize themselves with it, and they'd walked it the day before with their instructor. It was laid out in the wooded hills, crossing back and forth over a little stream. It was also well marked. He felt confident that part of it would present no difficulties. He always liked to anticipate any eventualities that might arise and have some possible counter-action in mind. He liked to know where the back door was. Always. He thought he knew, this time. He'd studied the obstacles they would be encountering. It remained to be seen if he could master them. He had inspected them all—except one. The barn. The last part of the obstacle course. Station #13. A large, forbidding, wooden building without windows. The barn. The only unknown factor. No one would tell him what to expect in there. It made him uneasy. He wondered if his companion knew. He retraced the course in his mind. It seemed impossible that anyone could actually complete the damn thing—let alone in the twenty-one minutes forty-two seconds that was the camp record. If he, Sig, could do it at all, it would take him more like twenty-one hours. . . .

He shifted again. The course was being readied for them. They were waiting for the signal to start.

He looked at the barbed-wire fence in front of him. Ten feet

high. That was the first obstacle. Station #1. The fence had to
be scaled—without inflicting too many cuts on hands and arms
and legs. Once on the other side, they would tackle Station #2.
At a little distance stood a sentry. He had to be disarmed. He
had his back to the fence. He knew, of course, that they would
be coming for him, but he was instructed not to turn around
unless he actually *heard* them. If he caught them—it was back
to the damned fence again. If they could sneak up on him and
punch him on the back, simulating a kill, they had it made. They
could then take the vehicle the sentry had been guarding and
use it . . . if they could get it started. There would be one small
thing wrong with it. Some little mechanical disorder. Anything.
They had to find it. Correct it. And the vehicle could be anything from a jeep to a German staff car. Station #3. Once they
got it going, they could drive the half-mile to Station #4, where
the rest of the course began—drive at breakneck speed to save
time. If they failed, they had to run a winding trail through the
woods, two miles long, which led them to the same spot.

From there it would become really difficult.

He shifted once more. He realized he was getting impatient.
Eager to get started. He was surprised how keyed up he felt.

He was suddenly transported back to his high-school days in
Montclair, New Jersey. He'd been on the school track team. A
sprinter. He'd felt exactly the same excitement as he crouched
on the line in the start position for the hundred-yard dash. Once
when he'd been the anchor man on a relay team, he'd become
so excited waiting for his teammates to sprint around the track
and reach him that a spurt of blood had suddenly burst from his
nose. He'd run his lap with blood streaking out behind him like
crimson streamers. But he'd won. He had a twinge of regret
that he'd not kept himself in top physical condition. Weekend
tennis didn't really do it. His aching muscles attested to that.

He glanced up as two men approached them. One was their
instructor, who for obvious reasons was called Slim. The other,
Major Rosenfeld.

Come up from the big city for the festivities, no doubt, Sig
thought sourly.

Slim was carrying an obviously heavy backpack in his hands.
He plunked it down with a thud next to Dirk.

"For you," he said amiably. "A little something extra."

"What the hell is that supposed to mean?" Dirk asked suspiciously.

Rosenfeld answered.

"It's an—afterthought, Van, my boy." He seemed to be enjoying himself. "Getting through the course just by yourselves is not really enough, is it? In the field you'd have your gear to worry about. Well—that's it. Forty pounds of selected Maryland rocks! Where you go, it goes!"

"Oh, shit!" Dirk said. He stood up, eyeing the pack with distaste.

"I was going to give a pack to each one of you," Rosenfeld added magnanimously. "But I thought I'd make it easy on you. You can share—if you can agree on how to do it. . . ."

Dirk gave the pack a kick with his boot. Rosenfeld shook his head reprovingly.

"Temper," he admonished. "I'd treat the thing with some respect. Don't be too rough on it. You see, there is one more thing in there. A glass Mason jar. Resting nicely among the rocks." He paused significantly. "I want to see that jar *whole* at the end of the run." He smiled. "You can think of it as the precious little tubes in your X-35!"

Dirk gave him a dirty look. He glanced at Sig, who had looked on in silence. Resignedly he bent down, lifted the heavy pack and slung it on his back, shrugging his arms through the shoulder straps. He hefted it, testing its ride.

"Let's get on with it," he grumbled. He took up his waiting position on the ground.

Slim brought out a stopwatch.

"Okay, this is it," he said with great originality. "I won't raise my voice." He nodded toward the sentry standing in the distance, his back to them. "Wouldn't want to alert Station Two, would we?" He held up his hand—

Sig was aware of his heart racing, pumping adrenalin through his system. He stared at the ten-foot fence in front of him. He'd never get over it. . . .

The instructor's hand came down.

"Go!"

Dirk was on his feet at once. Without a word, he whirled on Sig. He held up his hand, stopping him from rushing at the fence. Quickly he pointed to himself—then to Sig. Not waiting to find out if he had been understood, he ran to the nearest wooden pole holding up the barbed wire. Alternately placing a foot close to the pole on one side or the other of the wire fastened to it, he used it as a spike-studded ladder, quickly reaching the top. He switched over precariously—the heavy pack threatening to throw him off balance—and swarmed down the other side.

Sig had started up right behind him. He was excited and awed at Dirk's instant leap to action. Would he himself have thought of using the pole? He was shocked to realize he had given no thought to *how* to scale the fence. Wincing as one of the sharp barbed-wire spikes cut the fleshy part of his left hand, he was over the top and starting down the other side.

Dirk had discarded the pack. It was lying on the ground. He was already cat-running toward the tensely listening sentry. He stopped within twenty feet. Sig stood stock still, watching him, hardly daring to breathe. Slowly, stealthily Dirk crept up on the sentry. Ten feet.

The sentry switched his weight from one foot to the other. Dirk froze. Sig felt his heart skip a beat—then pound the next one. Silently Dirk moved again. Five feet. Suddenly he leaped forward, striking the man a blow on his neck with his out-stretched hand. The man fell to the ground.

Sig sprang into action. Grabbing the pack—My God! Did forty pounds weigh that much?—he ran toward Dirk, already at the vehicle. The grinning guard was sitting on the ground.

The vehicle was a German BMW R750 motorcycle combination. Ten days ago he'd never heard of one, let alone seen it. Now he and Dirk had to fix it—and drive it.

The cycle was battered and the sand-colored paint chipped. Must have picked the damned thing up in North Africa, Sig thought, as he carefully placed the pack on the ground. The spoked spare wheel was missing from the back deck of the side car, but the two Wehrmacht plates were still on—the long, curved one along the front-wheel fender and the one in the rear under the taillight. WH727694. The bike had been stripped of its armament—the MG34 unbolted from its seat.

Dirk was already astride the bike. He tried to start it up. The engine turned over—but did not catch. He stared at the motor. He made an adjustment. He tried again. No go.

Sig stepped closer.

Dirk was poring over the bike engine. He was frowning.

"The hot wire," Sig said suddenly. "From the coil to the distributor. Check it. It could be loose."

"Got you."

Dirk peered at the engine. The damned hot wire was difficult to see. Figured. There—

"That's it," he said.

He worked quickly.

"Grab the damned pack and hop in!" he snapped. He gunned the bike. It roared to life.

Spurting gravel, they took off down the dirt road—half a mile to Station #4. . . .

Station #4 was at the stream. The flow had been widened to a width of about twelve feet. They were instructed to leap across it—preferably without getting their feet wet. When Sig had inspected it earlier, it had not seemed too difficult. What was the world-record broad jump? Better than twenty-six feet? Hell, this was less than half. But as Dirk brought the bike to a sliding halt at the stream's edge, it looked to Sig twice as wide as before—and his combat boots suddenly weighed a ton. Each.

"Throw me the pack," Dirk called. He took a running start and leaped across the stream.

Sig swung the heavy pack a couple of times and hurled it out over the water. He was aware of the station instructor watching them. Dirk caught it.

Sig was already taking his running start for the jump. He pushed off with his right foot and sailed out over the water.

I'll make it, flashed through his mind.

At one thought-synapse he exulted—at the next the world exploded beneath him.

An ear-shattering blast slammed into him and a geyser of water shot up from the stream to engulf him and catapult him to the far bank of the stream, where he landed in a heap. Instantly he tried to get up. His legs were like oatmeal mush.

He was aware of Dirk bending over him.

"One of their little surprises," he said, grinning. "There'll be others." He spoke quickly. "Don't worry. It was only a small TNT charge detonated under water. You'll be okay in a minute. I'll get the damned pack up the slope. Get going as quickly as you can."

He took off.

Sig was still trying to orient himself. He glanced toward the embankment. Station #5. A twenty-foot rise so steep it was almost perpendicular.

How the hell was he ever going to cimb it—without legs?

He tried to stand up. To his surprise, he was able to get to his feet. He started toward the slope. He was wobbly—but he moved. He looked up. Dirk was just crawling over the top, hauling the pack after him.

Sig started up the rise—and stopped in dismay. The cascading water from the explosion had drenched the earth. The dirt had turned into mud. The slope was as slippery as a greased pole.

He scrambled up, digging his fingers and boot toes into the wet ground. Halfway there—and he slid back.

He swore. He was getting angry. They were not playing fair, dammit! Nobody'd said anything about TNT or mud when he'd walked the course before. He resented it. But in the back of his mind a thought intruded upon his anger. The unexpected was happening. Certainly. But would that not also happen in the field? Could one *ever* plan for all eventualities?

He clamped his jaws shut stubbornly—and tackled the muddy slope again. He plastered his entire body against the rise and worked his arms and legs like a swimmer. Slowly—inch by inch—he oozed upward. Almost . . . He felt himself beginning to slip. . . .

Suddenly a hand grabbed his fatigue jacket at the shoulder. He felt himself being hoisted up, sliding along the mud bank to the top.

Dirk was lying on the ground, breathing heavily. He'd anchored his feet around the heavy pack for added leverage. He was rubbing his left elbow.

"Come on," he said, jumping to his feet and grabbing the pack. "Let's go!"

Ahead rose the grassy slope of a hill, and at the crest stood Station #6.

It was a solid fence eight feet high made of wooden planks. It had to be scaled.

Dirk was the first to arrive at the obstacle. At once he knelt down close to the fence and clasped his hands firmly in front of him, fingers entwined.

"Right foot!" he called as Sig came running up.

Sig was winded. He had regained the use of his legs, but they tingled as if they'd been asleep. He placed his right foot squarely in Dirk's hands and felt himself being propelled toward the top of the fence. He barely managed to catch hold of the edge, breaking his momentum as he tumbled over and down on the far side, landing on his hands and knees with a tooth-rattling jar.

"Catch!" Dirk shouted from the other side of the fence.

Sig looked up just in time to see the heavy pack come sailing over the top. He reached out and grabbed at it, cushioning its fall. It hit him on the chest, sending him sprawling and knocking the wind out of him. His ribs suddenly hurt. Hell, he thought cynically, what's a couple of cracked ribs as long as that damned Mason jar doesn't break!

Dirk jumped down to the ground next to him. He at once yanked the pack off Sig.

"Come on!" he called, loping down the hillside toward the little stream.

Sig followed.

Halfway down the staked-out path was Station #7, a large box placed on a spread-out half of a pup tent.

It was filled with hand guns. US Army .45 automatics; German Walthers, 7.65; 9 mm. Lugers '08 and P-38s. All of them field-stripped—their disassembled parts mixed together along with the different kinds of ammunition needed for each weapon.

Object: Assemble two guns, one each, and load them with a full magazine.

Dirk upended the box, unceremoniously spilling the jumble of gun parts and ammo out onto the green canvas.

"Go for the forty-fives," he said. "You pick out the parts and throw them in the box. Also the ammo." As he was talking, he was already grabbing a slide and a barrel. "I'll assemble and load."

"Okay." Sig at once got to work. He was impressed with Dirk's division of labor. Efficient. And the .45 parts were the easiest to distinguish. He pawed through the jumble, rejecting and selecting. . . .

A jeep came careening up to them. Slim was at the wheel, Rosenfeld beside him.

"Hey! Come on!" Rosenfeld called to them. "That's not a picnic basket, for crissake! Get the lead out!"

"Don't let the bastard get your goat," Dirk snapped. He did not bother to look up. "He's trying to rattle you. Part of the act. Keep the damned parts coming!"

"You're taking one hell of a time," Rosenfeld taunted. "We were looking for you at Station Nine!"

Sig suppressed his irritation. Dammit, he was working as fast as he could. He could do without the gratuitous harassment from that clown Rosenfeld. Or—could he? What kind of pressures would he have to work under in the field? His respect for the obstacle course and its surprises slowly grew. . . .

Dirk snapped the magazine into place on the second .45, pulled back the slide and let it go. He flipped the safety on and handed the gun to Sig.

"Loaded," he said. "Cocked and locked."

He started down the path toward the stream—and Station #8. . . .

At the bottom of the hill the stream had gouged out a small ravine some thirty feet across. The steep sides were overgrown with dense shrubbery. A log had been placed across the crevasse from the hillside to a tree trunk surrounded by brush on the opposite bank. The little creek flowed placidly twenty feet below.

Station #8.

Gun in hand, Dirk turned to Sig.

"You go first," he said. "Keep your eyes on the trunk on the other side. Don't look down. I'll cover you."

Sig glanced at the log. It looked no wider than a strand of spaghetti.

"Trick is, *run* across!" Dirk said quickly. "It's easier. No time to lose your balance. Go!"

Sig ran out onto the log. He kept going. He suddenly felt completely confident. It's like riding a bicycle, he thought—the faster you go, the easier it is to keep your balance. It's only when you go slow you flounder.

Halfway across, two shots rang out behind him. He started, but he did not lose his stride. In the same instant a target in the shape of a German soldier jumped up in the shrubbery on the bank before him. He pumped two rounds at it. He had no idea if he hit or missed.

Another target jumped up and again he fired. He was aware of Dirk racing across the log behind him, firing his gun. . . .

And he reached the tree trunk. It was a drop of six feet to the ground. He jumped down.

Almost at once Dirk joined him.

Together they ran through the underbrush.

A target flew up. And another . . .

They emptied their guns.

They did not stop to check for hits. . . .

And Station #9 came into view.

Two tall trees stood opposite each other on either side of the stream—fifty feet apart. Each had a small wooden platform built twenty feet in the air—and between them a steel wire was stretched taut. A second thinner wire was fixed five feet above the first, running parallel to it across the creek. A heavy rope led up to the tree platform on the near bank. . . .

Climb the rope. Cross the wire to the other tree—and climb down.

Simple.

There were two ways of trying it. *One* that worked.

You could hang beneath the heavier bottom wire on hands and knees and push across. At least, you could try. But half-way there you'd find that the wire cut into your hands and made them slippery with blood. You'd have to let go—and fall to the stream below. No one had ever made it that way.

With a forty-pound pack strapped to your back, it was an utter impossibility.

The other way was to walk the bottom wire—holding on to the top one, trying to balance yourself and keeping the two wires exactly in line, one atop the other. If you did *not* and they spread apart, you found yourself hanging with your hands on one wire and your feet on the other, parallel to the ground twenty feet below. . . .

But it was the only possible way—*if* you could keep your balance with forty pounds of rocks and a Mason jar on your back.

Dirk shinnied up the rope with the pack on his back—although it was obvious that his arm bothered him. Sig, too, made it to the platform, but his hands hurt.

He looked across to the second tree.

Jesus! Had to be in another county—if not another state. . . .

Slim and Rosenfeld drove up to the tree on the far side. Rosenfeld got out and leaned against the jeep, making himself comfortable. He lit a cigarette.

Dirk took his first tentative step out onto the wire.

"Come on, Wallenda!" Rosenfeld shouted across the stream. "Do your stuff. Your audience is waiting!"

Dirk ignored him. Slowly he pushed away from the platform, grasping the top wire firmly with both hands.

"I brought a set of dry underwear," Rosenfeld called.

Sig watched his teammate. He hardly heard Rosenfeld's taunts. A minor irritation. It quickly became obvious that Dirk had trouble balancing himself on the wire with the heavy pack strapped to his back. He started to sway. The weight of the pack made him overcompensate. He was losing his grip. . . .

Sig reached out as far as he could. He grabbed Dirk's belt— and pulled him to safety on the platform.

"Shit and double shit!" Dirk said. "That fucking pack's screwing up everything." He stepped onto the wire once more. "I'll try again. I've got—"

"Wait," Sig interrupted. "Take the pack off."

Dirk looked at him in exasperation.

"Why? If *I* can't—"

"Don't argue!" Sig snapped with sudden authority. "You're wasting time. Take it off!"

Dirk stared at his companion in astonishment. Quickly he shrugged the heavy pack off his shoulders. Without a word, he handed it to Sig.

Sig at once unsnapped both the shoulder-strap hooks from the pack rings.

"Get on the wire," he ordered.

Dirk obeyed.

Sig snapped one of the strap hooks onto the bottom wire and let the pack hang below it. The other hook he linked to Dirk's combat-boot strap.

"Slide it across," he said. "Go!"

At once Dirk began to cross the wire. The heavy pack acted as a stabilizing weight on the lower wire and he quickly and easily pulled it along as he moved his foot along the wire. He was across in a few seconds. Sig followed as Dirk hoisted the pack back up and reconnected the shoulder straps.

Sig was within a few feet of the far platform when his foot slipped. He caught himself—but he was thrown off balance. The wires started to spread. Desperately he struggled to check their swaying. Bleakly he knew it was a losing battle.

He heard Dirk call to him.

"Grab my hand!"

In a glance he saw his partner holding on to a tree branch with one hand and leaning toward him with the other arm stretched out. Only a foot from reaching him. Twelve lousy inches . . .

The wires were swinging, the momentum increasing as they kept spreading farther apart. Any second he would lose his footing and be left hanging by his fingers on the thin top wire. He knew with absolute certainty he would not be able to hold on.

Dirk's voice seemed to reach him from an enormous distance.

"Let go the wire, Sig! *Grab my hand!*"

Let go?

He glanced down at the ground—miles below. . . .

He let go.

He thrust both his arms toward Dirk's outstretched hand. He felt his feet shoot off the wire. He felt himself fall. . . .

And his hand found his partner's reaching arm. With desperation he grabbed hold. As he swung down, one knee hooked over the bottom wire and checked his plunge. Straining, Dirk hauled him to safety.

Sig's legs were trembling. His hands were sore. He ignored them.

He'd made it!

Dirk turned to him.

"You're okay, Siggy baby!" he said with a huge grin. He began to climb down the tree. "Onward and downward!" he called. "Station Ten waits without!"

Slim and Rosenfeld were nowhere to be seen as they arrived at Station #10 at a trot.

Sig was breathing heavily. The pace was beginning to tell. His legs were leaden. His chest ached as he gulped air.

How long?

It seemed hours. . . .

At Station #10 a small spring trickled down the hill toward the creek, running parallel to it for a short distance before joining it. Erosion had carved out a narrow stream bed, providing a hundred feet or so of defiladed area. A shallow ditch. On the side away from the creek the hill rose again.

Ducking down in an awkward, crouching run, it was possible to move through the muddy stream bed of the little tributary, protected from enemy observation—and fire.

Sig was running in the lead. His back hurt. The muscles in his calves and thighs knotted and pulled from the cramped, crouched gait. He suddenly dreaded getting a charley horse. Not now, please God, not now . . . !

Suddenly the staccato coughs of machine-gun fire shattered the silence. Sig jumped with shock. Then he remembered. Blanks. They were shooting blanks—to give realism to the problem.

Blanks?

They were *not* blanks! He was all at once vividly aware of the plops and sprays of dirt that erupted as the rounds slammed into the hillside beyond.

They were shooting live ammunition, dammit! Another of their goddamned surprises.

"Hit the dirt!" Dirk shouted.

Sig threw himself into the muddy water at the bottom of the ditch.

"And keep your butt down—unless you want a second crease in your ass!" Dirk finished.

Sig crawled on as fast as he could. He had been badly startled, even though reason assured him the bullets were whizzing well above him. He did not raise his head to find out. . . .

After the shooting-gallery crawl, Stations #11 and #12 were almost like amusement-park rides—easy, had he not been exhausted to the point of pain:

Climbing the tree at #11, leaping into space to grab hold of a rope six feet out and sliding down . . . Making like a GI Tarzan at #12, swinging on a chain across the stream at a widened stretch . . .

Every muscle in Sig's body protested at the abuse, and fatigue dulled his brain.

Dirk's old injuries were obviously giving him trouble; he was favoring his left arm.

But they both plodded on. Running, stumbling—making headway.

Finally they stood before Station #13.

The barn.

A vehicle was parked at the corner of the massive, windowless building. An Army ambulance. Two attendants were sitting on the ground, leaning against the barn. They eyed Dirk and Sig curiously as they made for the single door leading into it.

Sig had a twinge of apprehension. Ambulance? What the hell for? . . .

And Dirk threw open the door.

The room immediately inside was unexpectedly small, its walls of unfinished lumber. It was lit by two strong naked bulbs hanging from the ceiling. Behind a plain table in the middle of the floor sat Major Rosenfeld. Gone were his taunts, his levity. He looked sober. Grim. He pointed to two piles of ammunition lying on the table before him.

"Six rounds each," he said. "Load your guns."

Dirk and Sig at once began to load their magazines. Rosenfeld watched them solemnly.

"This is the last station," he said quietly. He glanced back over his shoulder. "You will go through the door behind me." He placed a stopwatch on the table before him. "You will have exactly seven minutes. If you do not reach the exit at the other end of the barn within that time, you will have failed the entire course."

He looked searchingly at them. "Ready?"

They nodded.

Sig's hands were suddenly clammy. What the hell—it was only a test. What could happen to him?

Rosenfeld stood up. He picked up the stopwatch.

"Stand by the door," he said.

Dirk and Sig took up positions facing the door, guns ready.

"Remember what you have been taught," Rosenfeld said softly, his voice concerned. "If—if anything should happen, we'll be standing by." He looked from one to the other. "Be— be careful!"

He held up the watch.

"Go!" he said.

They entered.

The door closed behind them with the emphasis of finality. They peered ahead. . . .

Sig could not shake the feeling of apprehension. Why the hell was Rosenfeld so damned gloomy? What *did* lie ahead of them?

The wide, bare corridor in front of them was lit only by dim bulbs set far apart in the ceiling.

For a moment they stood stock still. Gradually their eyes adjusted to the faint light.

Dirk gestured to Sig: *Take the right side.* He himself moved toward the left. Slowly, cautiously they started down the corridor.

And the lights went out.

The place was suddenly shrouded in total darkness.

Sig started.

He clutched his gun before him, locked firmly against his abdomen as he had been taught.

Where was Dirk?

He strained every nerve to distinguish any sight or sound. He heard Dirk whisper.

"Move to the center, Sig. We've got to stay together."

"Right." Sig's whisper came out hoarse and strained. Slowly he moved toward the middle of the corridor, feeling his way with his feet.

Where was Dirk?

He must be almost to the left wall by now. *Where the hell was Dirk?*

The soft whisper came only inches from his ear.

"Okay. Let's move on. You cover the right. I'll take the left. No use shooting the balls off each other."

Suddenly the rough floorboards under Sig gave way, sagging down several inches, creaking loudly.

Involuntarily his finger tightened on the trigger—but in the last instant he caught himself and eased off.

They went on.

The gloom was impenetrable. Sig felt strangely disembodied. The absolute darkness seemed to permeate his whole being. He felt gripped by a tension greater than any he had ever experienced.

He almost screamed when something brushed softly across his face. He stopped dead. He had a flash impulse to turn and run back. The specter of panic bloated and trembled in his mind. Then he was aware of Dirk standing next to him.

"Burlap," Dirk whispered. "Strips of fucking burlap!"

Sig reached up. He felt around in the blackness, somehow surprised that it wasn't solid. Several pieces of shredded burlap were hanging across the corridor at face height.

They kept going.

Suddenly a door in the right corridor wall creaked open, spilling a faint yellow light onto the floor.

Both men whirled on the door. They froze.

Sig threw a quick glance at his partner. The dim light from the open door was barely enough to be able to make him out.

Dirk motioned to him. *On the floor. Cover me. I'll move in!* He understood at once.

Noiselessly they moved toward the open door.

Not a sound was to be heard.

Nothing moved.

They stopped.

Dirk nodded to Sig.

At once Sig hurled himself to the floor in the doorway—his gun held out in front of him—

In the same split instant Dirk crashed through the open door—

The small room beyond was completely empty.

They resumed their slow progress down the corridor. A few feet farther on, it turned sharply to the left. A dim light seeped around the corner.

Sig felt his body harden with tension. Something *had* to happen. What? When?

They negotiated the corner. The corridor made a sharp U-turn and continued. Once again a string of dim bulbs cast a faint light from above. Several stacks of crates and boxes lined the walls.

They moved steadily on.

How much time had gone by?

Suddenly, from behind a stack of crates on the lefthand side a target, a German-soldier cut-out, jumped into view. Even as Dirk's gun barked twice, another target shot out on Sig's side. Instantly he shifted to face it squarely—and fired. Two rounds.

He felt an enormous excitement course through him.

A shooting gallery . . . The barn was one huge house-of-horrors shooting gallery!

In a flash he was back at Coney Island. When he first came to the States, he had often taken his girl there. He'd loved the rides, the bizarre attractions and the shooting galleries. Especially the shooting galleries. Shooting at the bear going back and forth through the little painted metal forest, making him turn and turn and turn. The row of paint-chipped ducks keeling over one by one. The shooting galleries had been great. But nothing like the barn!

Dirk grinned at him.

"Let's go get 'em!" he said.

Sig enjoyed himself immensely. He'd been enormously gratified to find that he'd hit the first unexpected target squarely. Right through the chest . . .

The corridor had made another U-turn, this time to the right. There had been two more targets for each of them—and finally they stood before a closed door at the end of the corridor.

The exit.

Had to be.

They exchanged quick glances. They had it made.

Quickly they burst through the door.

And stopped dead.

Before them was a large, well-lit enclosure. A deep, wide trench had been dug wall to wall in the dirt floor, cutting the area in half. From the ceiling a large, heavy net was suspended, a transparent curtain dipping down into the middle of the trench. A single, narrow, twelve-foot plank had been placed across the trench, running through a vertical slit in the coarse netting. In the far wall was a door.

It was marked: EXIT.

Off to one side an instructor sat at a small table. Stony-faced, he made a notation in a logbook as Dirk and Sig entered.

Dirk looked around quickly.

"Oh, shit!" he swore. "A fucking Noodle Test!"

Sig looked at his teammate with a questioning frown.

"To test your smarts," Dirk said. "Some goddamned stupid problem to solve."

"How much time have we left?" Sig wanted to know.

"Beats me."

Sig glanced toward the silently observing instructor.

"Can we ask him?"

Dirk did not bother to look. "That SOB wouldn't tell you the time if you loaned him your watch," he said. He walked up to the gangplank. A sign next to it read: MAXIMUM LOAD CAPACITY 200 POUNDS.

"Figures," Dirk said. "I'll just be able to squeeze across." He shrugged off the pack. He glanced at Sig.

"A hundred eighty-five," Sig said. "How do we get that damned forty-pound pack across?"

"That, my boy," said Dirk, "is the Noodle Test!"

Sig's mind raced. There had to be a way.

"Okay," he said crisply. "Let's look at what we can *not* do." He frowned. "Neither you nor I can carry the pack across. Too great a combined weight. We can't go around. We can't toss it across the trench because of the net. . . ."

"We can break out the pack and haul a few rocks at a time. Make several trips," Dirk suggested.

Sig shook his head.

"Take too much time. No go . . ."

Dirk glared at the pack.

"Too bad the damn thing can't walk across by itself," he said bitterly.

Sig looked up quickly.

"Why not?" he said.

Dirk glanced at him sharply. He said nothing.

"Go on across," Sig said hurriedly. "Wait on the other side."

Without hesitation, Dirk started across the narrow plank. He slipped through the slit in the net and hurried to the far side. He turned toward Sig.

Sig had the pack on the ground next to the plank. As soon as Dirk stepped off, he lifted the plank end up—and slipped it through the shoulder straps of the pack.

"Hold on to your end!" he called to Dirk. "Keep it on the ground."

He took hold of his end of the plank and lifted it. Higher.

Higher—until it was above his head. Slowly the pack began to slide down the slanting plank. It gathered momentum, slid through the opening in the net and came to rest at Dirk's feet!

At once Sig replaced the plank on the ground and sped across to Dirk. . . .

Seconds later the teammates burst from the barn into the bright sunlight.

Rosenfeld and Slim were waiting for them.

Rosenfeld clicked his stopwatch. He glanced at it.

"Six minutes, forty-seven seconds," he said. "Cutting it close."

Slim consulted his stopwatch.

"Twenty-nine minutes, thirty-eight seconds total," he announced. "Just under average."

Despite himself, he sounded impressed.

Sig sank down on the grass. It seemed ages ago he'd been lying on the ground before the barbed-wire fence at Station #1. A lifetime of happenings ago.

Rosenfeld's briefing suddenly rang in his mind. The obstacle course is a test, he'd said. A test designed to measure your physical fitness at the end of your training period, your agility and coordination. To make you rely less on gadgets—more on ingenuity. To test your courage, your alertness and your ability to follow instructions. Your initiative, imagination and power of analysis. Your endurance. And—your teamwork. . . . He had been mildly amused. It had seemed to him nothing but a string of self-important words and phrases.

He had changed his mind. He had learned a lot about himself —in just half an hour. And about Dirk.

Not a bad guy to have on your side.

Somehow all his self-doubt and misgivings about their mission had evaporated.

If they could beat that damn obstacle course, they could do anything!

Dirk was shrugging out of the heavy pack. He stretched luxuriously.

He, too, felt good. He'd actually enjoyed running the damn course.

Sig stood up. He rubbed his ribs. They were still tender. He turned to Rosenfeld.

"Is the jar okay?" he asked.

Rosenfeld looked blank.

"What jar?"

"The jar. In the pack. With the rocks."

Rosenfeld laughed.

"Hell—there's no jar! Just thought we'd worry you a little. . . ."

Sig felt the blood rise to the tip of his ears. He looked at Dirk, deeply affronted.

"Scheissdreck, nochmal!" he swore. "Shit and double shit!"

The corners of Dirk's mouth twitched. He began to laugh. Sig stared at him; then suddenly he, too, was laughing.

Rosenfeld regarded them soberly.

"Okay," he said. "Come on. Back to camp. There is a lot to be done. You leave tomorrow for London."

Sig looked at the OSS officer. To do *what?* he thought. It's about time we found out. He opened his mouth to speak. Dirk beat him to it.

"Isn't it about time you told us what the hell this is all about?" he asked tersely.

Rosenfeld nodded solemnly.

"It is."

He told them.

11

Dirk was bored.

He considered Captain Cornelius Everett, Jr., USA, a colossal pain in the ass.

He and Sig had arrived five days before at the secluded OSS training-and-staging center at Milton Hall, a grand old manor house a hundred miles from London—and ever since they'd had to listen to Everett run off at the mouth. He talked and talked and talked with the stilted verbosity of a dull book. Too damned bad, Dirk thought wryly, that he couldn't be shut up the same way.

He knew the captain from his last mission, which had also been mounted from London.

Everett had shown up at Milton Hall directly from the States in early February of '44—about the time the first "Jeds" began to arrive at the Hall. The special Jedburgh teams were formed there, made up of three agents from each of three countries, England, France and the States, in any combination. They were to be dropped into France to help prepare the Maquis for their role in Operation Overlord—the invasion of Europe.

Except for Scandinavia, which the British considered their special domain, there had been, and still was, close cooperation between the OSS and the SOE—the British Special Operations Executive—on actions in Europe, and Everett had soaked up the British methods like a sun-dried sponge. He'd adopted every ploy and every trick he could ferret out. And he'd used them all. Still did.

Dirk had been incredulous when Everett pulled the routine

"old buddy" test on him and Sig when he'd picked them up in London to escort them by train to the Hall. The coaches on the British trains are divided into compartments, and as Everett had been helping stow Dirk's and Sig's gear in the overhead racks, he'd spotted a British officer, obviously an old buddy of long standing, less obviously an MTO—a Military Testing Officer—assigned to the test. There'd been a lot of back-slapping, small-talking and old-boying—all of which clearly established that Everett and his buddy were intimate friends. Once the train was under way, Everett had excused himself on some pretext or other and left "old buddy" alone with the two pigeons. That was supposedly the moment of truth. Or rather— of withholding the truth!

To be capable of surviving within a totally hostile environment, an agent must above all be discreet—in fact, have a veritable passion for anonymity. How careful would Sig be in talking about himself to this "old buddy," so obviously "one of the gang," under gentle, friendly probing? Would he be tempted to brag a little about his important job? Quite a few candidates had wondered why their one-way journey to Milton Hall had turned into a return trip.

But not only had Sig clammed up and not burned himself or the mission—he'd barely been civilized to the "old buddy"!

Dirk forced himself to return his attention to Corny's lecture —something about eating habits.

"It is nearly always the little things that betray the agent," Everett was saying, "—give him away as a foreigner. Such as the eating habits we've discussed. Remember—never put down your knife and pick up your fork in your right hand to eat. You might as well wear an American flag sticking out your ear!"

He paused dramatically to let his witty wisdom sink in.

Doesn't the dope realize that both Sig and I were born in Europe? Dirk wondered.

"Then, of course, there is the language factor," Everett continued. "Multilingual or bilingual people instinctively lapse into their native language when they pray or swear. When they count—or screw!" He smiled thinly.

"And finally—be aware of involuntary muscle habits that may give you away. You must be so saturated in your cover story that even unconscious expressions or gestures inconsistent with it become inconceivable—in any situation that may arise. For example, a Catholic priest would hardly reach for a gun in a shoulder holster at an unexpected loud noise behind him. An agent would. You must be thoroughly familiar with your adopted cover."

Familiar? Dirk thought. Hell—they'd gone over and over and over their cover stories so often in the past few days that he wasn't sure anymore which was his cover name and which his real one. . . .

"Never for a moment forget," Everett intoned, "that you will be operating in the black in the heart of enemy country. You must constantly think of yourselves as hunted men. A spook who forgets *that* is not apt to live very long!"

Everett looked at his watch.

"2145 hours," he said. "We'll call it quits for tonight. At 0700 tomorrow we will start a thorough briefing on your contact in the anti-Nazi resistance group in Hechingen. The man's name is Storp. *Otto Storp.*" He paused significantly. "You will appreciate the not inconsequential feat of locating this man within the severe time limitation imposed on us. Of course, there *are* several small illegal groups of active anti-Nazis in Germany. They are, in the main, unrelated to one another and without any central direction. Fortunately, we knew of Storp through an underground agent in Frankfurt, who—eh—is no longer active. The German underground must be highly secretive to survive. The Gestapo is a formidable adversary, make no mistake about that!"

He looked at the two young men lounging comfortably in easy chairs in the small, beautifully appointed room annexed by Everett for his briefing talks.

"In the afternoon," he continued, "you will be taken to London. The Moles have your ID and outfits ready for you." He stood up. "That's all for today."

He marched smartly from the room.

Sig looked after him.

"Seems to know what he's talking about," he said.

Dirk raised an eyebrow.

"Corny?" he said. "He's an alchemist's nightmare."

It was Sig's turn to do the raised-eyebrow routine.

"You pour golden information into him and it comes out

leaden platitudes!" Dirk said with a grin and settled into his chair, draping himself over the arm like a Dali watch. He looked forward to their visit with the London Moles. They were fantastic. It was their responsibility to equip the spooks in the field with all the physical gear necessary: identity cards, clothing, every little personal item, and their stuff was indistinguishable from the real thing—mainly because it *was* the real thing. The Moles scrounged their enormous inventory of clothing and all the rest from pawnshops and secondhand stores in New York and London that were frequented by refugees from Nazi-occupied countries. They collected European suits and coats and underwear, fountain pens, calendar notebooks, shoes, watches, suitcases, spectacles and anything else an OSS agent might need to sustain his cover.

They also operated an efficient little printing press, turning out false documents and identification papers of all kinds, complete with seals and signatures that would defy the most minute examination. Often the Moles themselves would wear the clothing and carry the false documents around in their pockets for a while to give the proper aged look to them. They could turn a New York university professor into a French farmer or a Chicago lawyer into an Italian priest at the drop of a secondhand hat. It was damned important work. And top secret. The Moles got to know a lot of agents—and their covers. But they hadn't lost their perspective—nor their sense of humor. Dirk recalled the sign on the desk of one man who was busily sewing a false pocket into a jacket: DON'T GET THE IMPRESSION I'M INEFFICIENT, it read. THE NATURE OF MY WORK IS SO SECRET IT DOES NOT ALLOW ME TO KNOW WHAT I AM DOING!

He wondered idly if they were called Moles because they made it possible for the spooks to go underground.

He rubbed his elbow. It was becoming a habit. One of Corny's muscle habits? Couldn't hurt. He *did* have a bum elbow—and it *was* part of his cover.

Sig watched him.

"Bother you?"

"It's okay."

"How did it happen?"

How? Dirk thought. . . . It had been in Holland. He'd been on a mission against the V-2 launching sites on the Dutch coast north of Amsterdam near Bergen aan Zee. The RAF had blasted most of them, but they couldn't get to the rest without specific information. Someone had to get it. London was being clobbered. He and his Dutch underground contact, Jan, had entered a bombed-out assembly plant, destroyed in a prior raid. Cautiously, ever wary of booby traps, they had entered an office in their search for a vantage point from which to observe a launching pad nearby. . . . He could see the scene. He would always be able to see it. The cracked walls and ceiling and the shattered windows; the debris-strewn floor, the broken furniture and the big desk—all covered with the fine white dust of crumbled plaster which coated every surface. And the single sheet of paper that looked like a folded blueprint lying on top of the desk with the word GEHEIM—Secret—showing through the dust! They had stopped. They had looked around carefully. . . . He saw the tiny patch of fresh yellow sawdust under the desk —in the same instant Jan reached for the document. He screamed his warning—which was drowned out by the blinding roar of the explosion. Jan had literally disintegrated. His own left side had been peppered with shrapnel and splinters from the massive desk. Had he not instinctively turned away, he would have been blinded. As it was, he was unable to hear and could barely see. The blood was running into his eyes. But he'd managed to crawl from the building and hide. He'd been found by a Dutch girl with a round red face, a huge bosom—and the gentlest hands in the world. She had nursed him back to a semblance of health—and the underground had managed to evacuate him to England in the bilge of a fishing boat. . . . It had been a booby trap. The most ingenious he'd ever run across. And so simple. A small hole bored through the desk top and lined with a metal ring; a wire taped to the underside of the document lying over the hole, running down through the middle of the ring—without touching; the batteries of the electrical firing device hidden in the drawer below and wired to a couple of grenades. When the document was moved—and contact was made—*boom!*

The damned mission had been a bust. He'd brought nothing back—except a piece of shrapnel in his ass. . . .

He looked at Sig.

"How did it happen?" He shrugged. "I goofed."

"Was Captain Everett—eh—Corny your control officer before?"

"No," Dirk said. "He's supposed to be tops—however hard *that* is to believe. . . ."

His mind was suddenly filled with thoughts of the mission ahead of them. Foreboding chilled him.

The Nazi atomic bomb . . .

Three things, they'd told him and Sig, three elements were absolutely necessary in order to make this bomb. The basic fuel —probably uranium or plutonium; the laboratory and industrial set-up to develop and build a prototype; the know-how in the persons of a sufficient number of top scientists and technicians to mastermind it . . .

The Germans had all three.

The big question was—How far had they progressed? How close were they??

The answer to *that* was the mission.

He glanced at Sig. He wondered if his teammate realized how inextricably close their relationship would have to be. How completely they would have to depend on one another.

Their mission had been given a code name:

Operation Gemini.

We make a hell of a pair of twins, he thought caustically. A battered spook and a professional civilian!

He yawned and glanced at his watch. 2200 hours.

"Almost ten," he said. "Come on, Siggy, let's haul our asses out of here. Time to grab some bunk fatigue. . . ."

12

General McKinley could feel the pressure he was under as a dull ache building up behind his eyes, hard thumbs of pain pushing into his temples.

He was already deep in one crisis with no immediate solution in sight. And now another had been dumped in his lap.

He deliberately tensed every muscle to the point of trembling—then consciously relaxed. He felt better.

He looked at the clock on his desk, the one Helene had given him on their twenty-fifth anniversary. 1917 they had been married. War was ripping the world apart then. He sighed. The world had done a lot of running just to stay in the same damn spot. . . . The clock showed close to 1600 hours. He flipped the switch on the intercom.

"Barnes," he said, "it's about 2200 hours in London."

"Yes, sir."

"Get me that OSS captain—the control officer on Gemini—eh—"

"Captain Everett, sir."

"Yes, Everett. Priority communication. He'll probably be at Milton Hall."

"Yes, sir."

McKinley sat back in his chair. He'd have to deal with this new crisis immediately. Push the other out of his mind.

And how the hell did you do *that?*

Congressional trouble was always a sizable pain in the balls. When it threatened to involve the security of the Manhattan Project, it was a monumental one.

The Trinity test at Los Alamos was obviously a project of topmost priority. Now it had become figuratively as well as literally explosive. The congressional bloodhounds had nosed a quarry. Pointed questions about the "squandering" of millions of taxpayer dollars were already rumbling from certain factions on the Hill. They might have to go through the same damned rigmarole they'd already suffered once, when questions in Congress had gotten the Special Senate Committee to Investigate the National Defense Program into the act. Thank God Truman, then chairman, had realized the risk in an investigation of the Manhattan Project and had promptly agreed to postpone action until after the war.

The most vociferous Congressman then had been Representative Engel of Michigan. And now Engel was making noises again. He had to be placated again. It would require supremely delicate handling at the highest level. Groves? Stimson? Marshall?

He pushed that problem aside and fingered the cabled report brought to him a short while before. Top secret. From London.

He began to read it once more, although he knew it by heart. He saw only one word.

OHIO.

The current code word meaning *uranium.*

A German encoded message had been intercepted and deciphered. It was an order to ship at once all available uranium mined at the Joachimthal mines in Czechoslovakia and processed at the Auer-Gesellschaft near Berlin to Haigerloch at Hechingen.

There it was. The first time *Haigerloch* and *uranium*—the core element of an atomic bomb—had been definitely linked!

He had no doubts about the authenticity of the intercepted message. He had come to rely implicitly on reports such as this one. It had originated with Ultra.

Ultra messages awed him. He knew he was one of a handful of senior US officers and officials who were privy to the awesome secret of this vitally important British operation. It was an appalling responsibility. Were the Germans to learn or even suspect that the British had cracked their supposedly unbreakable coding-machine system, the Enigma, and were literally reading every top-secret High Command document and order it encoded, they would immediately discontinue using it, and thus deprive the Allies of an invaluable intelligence source. The British called their decoding set-up the Ultra Operation. And it was. The vitally essential intelligence gathered by Ultra had to be jealously safeguarded—and backed up with conventional intelligence to allay any possible enemy suspicions.

With a cold lump in the pit of his stomach, he recalled a high-level rumor early in Ultra's existence.

Ultra had picked up the bombing orders for the Nazi Luftwaffe to blitz the cathedral city of Coventry supposedly well before the scheduled attack occurred. Evacuation might have been achieved—but such a move would certainly have alerted the enemy to the existence of Ultra. McKinley felt cold. The decision to do nothing and doom an entire town in order to safeguard Ultra must have been agonizing.

He took a deep breath. Now—another Enigma signal with the potential of an immensely greater disaster had been intercepted. Coventry would be a Bible-class outing in comparison. And the report was on *his* desk. If the Coventry story was true, he fervently hoped that the decision he'd just made would help justify in some small measure the earlier decision. . . .

Should he consult Stimson? Notify him?

No. He'd act on his own. Hell, he'd had his ass in a sling before. . . .

He had a fleeting moment of doubt. *Was* it a wild-goose chase? Would he be jeopardizing the Manhattan Project needlessly? Was the Haigerloch Project just another of Hitler's screwball secret weapons? There'd been detailed reports of literally hundreds of them. True, a few *had* turned out to be highly effective. The V-1 buzz bombs. The V-2 rockets. Jets. But most had never reached the production stage. Just as well. Some that were actually tested and employed in strictly limited situations might have become real headaches. The *Krummlauf Gewehr,* for example, a rifle that could shoot around corners. Actually worked. A curved barrel with a Zeiss optical sight mounted on an MP 44. . . . A whole slew of Buck Rogersish aircraft. His favorite had been the Dornier DO-335. Someone had obtained complete blueprints of the damn thing. It was a fighter plane of extreme maneuverability. It had a propeller mounted at each end of the fuselage—a regular aeronautical *pushmi-pullyu* dreamed up by some Nazi Dr. Doolittle. He'd had fantasies of building a model of it for his grandson. . . . Or the *Bombersäge*—the Bomber Saw. That's what it was. A plane designed to saw a bomber in half, for crissake! It had a row of bazooka-like rocket weapons mounted vertically on the fuselage. All the fighter had to do was to fly *under* the bomber's vulnerable belly and push a button. Couldn't miss. . . . Hell, they'd even worked on making their damned planes invisible to radar. They'd developed a paint. Called it *Schornsteinsfeger* —Chimney Sweep. When smeared on the planes, it would trap incoming radar signals—and the presence of the planes would not show up on the radar screen. So far they'd perfected it for only one radar wavelength, however. God only knew when they'd be able to go all the way. . . . Even their subs had their secret devices. How about the *Pillenwerfer*—the Pill Thrower, an anti-detection device for U-boats? Turned the whole damned ocean into a giant Bromo-Seltzer. The device shot out perforated cans with a special chemical that immediately effervesced in the water and formed millions of bubbles that enveloped the sub and completely hid it from sonar detection. Every damned U-boat that had actually used it had escaped. . . .

Was the project going on at Hechingen and Haigerloch in this category of never-rans? Or would it be the one that would give the Nazis their final triumph?

The intercom buzz interrupted his thoughts.

"Sir. Captain Cornelius Everett, Jr., Control Officer of Operation Gemini, is on the line."

"Good."

McKinley picked up the receiver. Without preliminaries, he demanded:

"Everett. What is your time frame for making Gemini operative?"

"Five days, sir."

McKinley looked at the report on the desk before him.

"You will have to speed it up," he said grimly. "I want Operation Gemini launched within twenty-four hours!"

13

Sig leaned against the dirty, cracked plaster wall in the farm-house. It was cold and rough. His rucksack was lying beside him on the plain wooden bench. He felt keyed up. His mind still whirled with the hectic activities of the last twenty-four hours. One moment he and Dirk had been anticipating another five days of training and mission instruction—the next, after a crash-and-cram briefing session and a continuing flood of frantic preparation, they'd found themselves on a USAF plane bound for who-the-hell-knew-where. It had been Thursday when the floodgates broke. Thursday the twenty-second of March. It was now Friday. He glanced at his watch. A little before eight in the evening. Or—2000 hours according to GI lingo. Better get used to that, he thought.

He shifted on the hard bench. He fingered the coarse material of the jacket he was wearing. He was surprised how comfortable he felt in the clothes the London Moles had given him. It was the first time in his life he'd worn some-one else's secondhand clothing. It wasn't the only *first* he was about to tackle.

In two hours he'd be well into Germany. Enemy country.

The plane had taken them to Strasbourg. He knew now that the little village they'd been rushed to immediately after land-ing was called Gerstheim. They had shown it to him on the map and told him it was totally evacuated. It was situated twenty-five miles south of Strasbourg between the Canal du Rhône au Rhin and the Rhine itself; a stone's throw from the river—and the enemy—in the sector of General de Lattre de Tassigny's French First Army.

He suddenly felt a wave of cold fear surge through him. *What in the name of hell was he doing here?*

When Corny had first told him of the decision to infiltrate them by land rather than by parachute, he'd felt greatly relieved. He couldn't see himself leaping out of an airplane in the dead of some dark night. Corny's reasoning had been utterly logical. He and Dirk would have had to jump blind into enemy territory without a reception committee. The drop plane over the sensitive area might well have alerted the enemy—and there had been too little time to train him, Sig, thoroughly in proper jumping procedure, making an accident upon landing a high-risk proposition. And finally—it would be quite impossible for Dirk to jump with his scarcely healed chest injury anyway. He snorted cynically to himself. That last reason would have been enough all by itself for anyone—except perhaps for Corny. . . .

He glanced at Dirk sitting close by, his eyes closed. He seemed utterly relaxed, calm. Almost too calm. Is that *his* way of being nervous? Sig wondered.

He looked around at the other men crowded into the farmhouse. Twenty-two of them. He'd counted them. Several times. Twenty-two. Including the sergeant, a forbidding, six-feet-four giant of a man with the magnificent name of Abu Kamir Hassan, who hadn't said two words to them since they had joined the patrol.

In a little while his life—and his partner's—would be in their hands. . . .

He studied them with an odd, morbid fascination. How many of them would come back? How many would die? Would—*he?*

They were a strange group. Swarthy-skinned, with piercing dark eyes, rugged faces and close-cropped black hair; a special combat patrol mounted by the Premier Groupement de Tabors Marocains—the First Group of Moroccan Tabors. They looked fierce, hard, totally deadly as they checked their equipment and weapons with the quick, meticulous care of professional killers. In addition to their guns, every one of them carried a long, razor-sharp knife and several grenades hanging from his belt. The French officer who'd briefed Dirk and Sig on the line-crossing operation had referred to the Moroccans as *goumiers,* men specially trained for infiltration operations in rugged terrain. He had sounded awed.

A thought flashed into Sig's mind. World War II. It really was a world operation. Here he sat, a Swiss in a US Intelligence outfit, in a French farmhouse, surrounded by a band of Moroccans, with a Dutch partner and with clothing and equipment supplied by English Moles!

He looked at Dirk.

"I don't like it," he said darkly.

Dirk kept his eyes closed.

"What's not to like?" he commented airily. "Just because you might get your ass shot off paddling across the river and crawling through the Siegfried Line?" He shrugged. "You'll get used to it."

Sig glared at his partner in irritation. If the SOB was nervous, why the hell didn't he show it? Why so goddamned smug and calm?

"Sure. I forgot," he said sarcastically. "You're the expert. *I* think we're being committed too damned fast!"

Dirk opened his eyes. He looked at Sig.

"Relax, Siggy baby," he said quietly. "I'm scared too. Only damned fools don't get scared."

"I hadn't figured on ending up in the French Army," Sig said. He felt an overwhelming need to say something—however inane.

Dirk shrugged.

"It's their sector," he said. "Closest point on the front to Hechingen."

"I *know* that, dammit!" Sig snapped. He was aware that he was being unreasonable, but he could not help himself. "I know this spot was chosen because the Westwall is supposed to be weak here. I just hope to God that's true. The damned Black Forest is supposed to be enough of an obstacle itself. Sure." He glanced at the grim Moroccans. "I also know these bastards can hardly wait to get into a fight."

Dirk looked up at him.

"How do you know that?"

"I do speak French," Sig snapped. "Or had you forgotten?"

Dirk held up his hands. He knew his partner's irritation was an outlet for his pent-up apprehension. He felt it himself, but he'd had time to learn to cope.

"The First French has been holding a passive front along the

Upper Rhine for too damned long, according to these guys," Sig continued. "Ever since their outfit hit the Siegfried Line north of Strasbourg this morning, they've been hopping mad because they were kept out of it to go on a nursemaid expedition!" He scowled at the Moroccans. "They'll probably go looking for trouble."

Sergeant Abu Kamir Hassan stood up.

"Partons!" he said sharply.

Dirk climbed to his feet.

"I guess that means 'get your ass in gear!' " he said. "Come on, Siggy, up and at 'em!"

The sky was overcast. The night was dark. Dirk slid over the bloated rim and huddled on the bottom of the rubber boat as he had been instructed. He cradled his rucksack protectively between his legs. It contained his lifeline—his radio. The other five men assigned to his boat were already in place. Four of them would paddle.

Dirk was impressed. He had not thought it possible for twenty-two men to move down the riverbank and launch four boats in the water without making any sound at all. But if he'd closed his eyes, he would have thought himself utterly alone with only the sounds of the gently lapping river waves and softly rustling leaves.

He could barely make out the boat on his right. Sig would be in that one, with the big Moroccan sergeant, Hassan. The Moroccan had curtly ordered them to split up when they'd headed for the same boat. He grinned to himself. Sensible not to put all his agents in one basket . . .

He was not aware of any command having been given, but suddenly the rubber boat was gliding silently across the black water into the darkness toward the ebony horizon—and Germany. . . .

Sig was crouched in the middle of his boat behind the hulking Moroccan sergeant. He was aware of the fact that his heart was pounding. It was loud in his ears. He could hear nothing else except the silken sound of the paddles softly dipping into the inky water. He touched his breast pocket, where his new ID papers were safely tucked away. They'd made it easy for him. The Moles had prepared all his papers in his real name, his real nationality, background and occupation. He had nothing to memorize and only one thing to forget—the fact that he had ever been in the United States. Dirk's cover was not so simple, but he seemed to have mastered it without difficulty. Sig peered into the darkness, trying to see Dirk's boat, thought he could make out a darker shape sliding noiselessly over the water close by, could not be sure. What if they got lost? He had a flash of panic, but he shook it off. The broad back of the Moroccan non-com kneeling before him was surprisingly reassuring.

The Schwarzwald—the Black Forest.

He knew the area, although he'd never been there. It was the birthplace of the mighty Danube. He still remembered the pictures in his schoolbook in Zürich. He frowned. What the hell was a memory like that doing in his mind now? But irrepressibly he recalled what he'd known then and coupled it with his recent mission briefing. They would be landing in the region called Mittlere Schwarzwald—the Middle Black Forest, a region of forest-clad, rolling hills where the mountains were lower and the forest less dense and forbidding than in the Nordschwarzwald to the north or the Hochschwarzwald—the High Black Forest—to the south. They would be able to link up quickly with the Kinzig Valley, which crossed almost the entire area. He had to admit that Corny had chosen the best possible spot.

He was suddenly aware that the gentle motion of the rubber boat had stopped.

The Moroccan sergeant turned to him. He motioned him to follow. Noiselessly he climbed from the boat. Sig followed.

The riverbank was gravelly and made a small grating sound as he stepped on it. He froze. Dammit! They must have heard it in Berlin. The sergeant motioned him on. The bank rose gently toward cultivated land. A vineyard, he thought. He crept up the slope after the Moroccan. His rucksack seemed heavy on his back. At the edge of the vineyard he stopped. Out of the darkness two figures approached. Dirk and one of the *goumiers.* Dirk grinned at him, gave him a thumbs-up sign and lay down beside him.

In silence they watched their escort patrol secure their beachhead.

The Moroccans moved swiftly, noiselessly, knowingly. The

four boats were carried a short distance up the bank and laid down close together. Two men melted into the ground beside them. The rest quickly fanned out along the vineyard and disappeared in the darkness.

The sergeant came up to the tensely waiting agents.

"You," he whispered hoarsely. "Both. Stay tight behind me."

"Sergeant," Sig breathed, "how—"

"I am called Abu," the Moroccan interrupted.

"Abu. How far up is the fortified line?"

"Not far. You see."

He turned to his right. He held up his hand. He turned to his left and repeated the gesture. At once he started into the vineyard, moving through the rows of staked vines in a low crouch.

Dirk and Sig followed.

Dirk's every sense was strained to full capacity. He could hear faint rustles on his right and left as the *goumiers* made their way through the vineyard. He could hear Sig breathing close behind him. The vineyard seemed to go on forever.

Suddenly Abu stopped.

Before them stretched an open space, a pasture dotted with an occasional tree. Beyond rose the wooded hills of the Black Forest.

Dirk crept up to the Moroccan.

Wordlessly the man pointed to his right and to his left. Dirk strained to see.

At the far edges of the clearing he could make out two dark, squat shapes—like massive building blocks.

"Blockhäuser," Abu whispered in heavy-accented German, "bunkers. The Westwall fortifications."

He pointed straight ahead.

"Between them—clear." He nodded at the open space before them. "That is their field of fire," he whispered. "We must cross."

He beckoned for Sig to join them.

"You—" he pointed to them both—"stay five steps behind me," he breathed. "Do as I do. I take you through."

He stood up. Slightly crouched—his gun held at port arms— he began to walk out across the open field.

Dirk counted his steps. . . . Three . . . Four . . . Five . . . He started out after the Moroccan, closely followed by Sig.

Slowly, steadily they moved up the slope toward the forest edge. Dirk was aware of shadowy forms advancing on his right and left. Any second he expected a burst of enemy fire to erupt from one of the bunkers and sweep across them—although he knew they were all but invisible in the darkness. . . .

They were halfway across. More . . .

Suddenly he heard it.

For the span of a single thought frame he was back in a bombed-out V-2 assembly plant. *Damn Jan!* . . .

The sound knifed through his mind. The muffled click of the detonator mechanism on an anti-personnel mine being set off!

Abu.

He'd stepped on a Bouncing Betty!

He heard the Moroccan swear. One low word.

"Merde!"

"Mine! Hit the dirt!" Dirk hissed at Sig as he threw himself to the ground. He knew that in three seconds the mine would be catapulted eight feet into the air from its shallow tomb in the earth and explode a lethal hail of steel balls and metal fragments in all directions. They were certain to be hit!

Sig was standing frozen. Dirk grabbed at his partner and yanked him down.

The second Abu hit the dirt the mine would shoot from the ground. . . .

But Abu did not move. He stood rooted to the spot.

Dirk felt himself go cold. He knew with sudden lucidity what the Moroccan was doing.

The man stood erect, his foot firmly planted on the deadly device. The mine would *not* shoot up. It *would* explode in the ground! It would—

Dirk was on the ground, his face close to the earth. He threw his arms up to protect his face—in the exact instant the mine went off and the raw blast of the explosion slammed across his ears.

Abu's booted foot disintegrated in a crimson splatter. His uniform ripped open as the steel balls tore from the ground up through his mangled leg and through his jacket. Two long red gashes appeared on Abu's face, gone gray with shock, as fragments from the mine gouged the flesh away and sheared off an ear.

Almost at once Dirk heard the machine-gun fire from the forest ahead of them.

He hugged the ground, pressing himself into the soft dirt to get away from the probing bullets. . . .

He took his arms from his face.

Sig was lying next to him—his face ashen, his haunted eyes fixed in horror on Abu.

The Moroccan was huddled on the ground. One of his men was already slashing the tattered, bloodied pants leg from his raw stump, using the long knife. White-knuckled, Abu's strong hands held his leg tightly encircled above the knee, stemming the flow of blood as best he could until his comrade could apply a tourniquet. He seemed oblivious to his injuries as he turned to Dirk and Sig.

Off to the left, the Moroccan patrol was returning the fire from the German MG position. The black night was rent with streaks of fire and reverberated with the sounds of death.

"You go," Abu said, his voice surprisingly strong. "Get through alone. When you hear grenades explode, you go quick." He winced as his comrade tore at the blood-soaked cloth stuck to his stump. "You go right." He nodded. "That way. Stay low. Move fast." He pointed. "The forest will hide you."

Sig crawled closer.

"We can't leave you here like this," he said hoarsely, his voice indignant. "We'll get you back!" He turned to Dirk. "We'll—"

"No!" Abu spat out the word with startling vehemence. "No! They said to me it was important you get through. And you will!"

"But—"

"Do not argue!" Abu snarled his order in a fury. "Men will die on this foul earth. Here. This night. So that *you* may get through," he growled. *"My* men. I—perhaps . . . " His dark eyes bore into Sig's. "There will be no prisoners. No one to betray you. Have no fear!" His voice was bitter. "It shall *not* have been for nothing! Go *on*—damn you!"

Suddenly, at a distance, two explosions in quick succession blasted the night air—followed by yet another. The German MG fire died abruptly, to be replaced almost at once by fire from the bunkers. Heavy MG's, searching for this new source of danger . . .

"You go! Now!" Abu raged. *"Now!"*

For a brief moment Dirk and Sig stared at the Moroccan; then they jumped to their feet, making for the edge of the forest in a broken-field run. Behind them the fire from the bunker guns raked the clearing. Within seconds the din was punctuated by the carunching blasts of exploding mortar shells.

Where there was one mine there would be others. Racing through the pasture, Sig close behind him, at every step—every time his pounding feet hit the ground—Dirk expected the explosion. He had to fight down his impulse to stop and stand—just wait. . . .

Thirty more feet . . . The firefight raged with renewed fury behind them.

Abu . . .

The Moroccan *goumiers* . . . How many would return?

Dirk felt his eyes smart. Damn—trying to see in the fucking dark . . .

And the underbrush closed in around them.

They kept running. The forest thinned. Ahead of them stretched a patchwork of fields. Close to the edge of the woods stood a barn.

They ran to it, entered it cautiously.

It was deserted.

They sank down on a pile of hay inside the door.

For a moment they sat in silence—each with his own thoughts.

Sig's face was pale, his eyes bleak. He looked out through the open barn door—out over the night-darkened land before him.

Germany.

Their passage into enemy country had been dearly bought.

Dirk stood up, walked over to the wall.

"Look," he said. "Look what I found!"

He hauled out a rusty man's bicycle, wheeled it into the faint light from the doorway, examined it.

"Two flat tires," he said. "Otherwise as good as new." He turned to Sig. "How are you on riding the bar?" he asked.

It was rough going on the flat tires. Sig was perched uncomfortably on the bar of the frame. It cut into his buttocks. His rucksack was fixed to the handlebars. Dirk was pumping along the country road. They were a couple of miles from the deserted barn. A broken signpost had read: LANGENWINKEL, 2 KM.

The rolling hills on either side were cultivated. Fields and pastures lined the roadway. Ahead they could make out the darker shapes of farmhouses and barns. That would be the village of Langenwinkel.

They were coming up on a little roadside shrine. There would be the painted figure of a Madonna under the peaked roof, Sig thought.

Suddenly two figures stepped out from behind the shrine. They planted themselves firmly in the middle of the road, effectively blocking it. One of them, a burly, powerfully built man, raised a gun, aiming it directly at the two riders.

"Halt!" he commanded.

Dirk stopped at once. He almost lost his balance, but managed to steady himself. He was staring down the two black holes of a double-barreled shotgun.

"Get off!" the man ordered. "And raise your hands. *High!*"

14

Standartenführer Werner Harbicht was tired. Tired and irritated. He glanced at the sallow-faced, middle-aged man sitting stiffly perched on the straight-backed chair across from him. Beads of perspiration stood out on the man's bald pate and glistened on his upper lip. Distasteful.

It was getting late. Past 2300 hours. He had spent hours questioning the frightened little milksop. And had learned nothing. The man had come prepared with reams of records and sheaves of invoices documenting the fact that the gramophone-records company Electrola Musikplatten had used its ordering-number code system for years. With charts and graphs the man had explained their marketing methods ad nauseam. Harbicht had a sinking feeling that he was getting nowhere. But why the devil had that page been torn out? There had been no new developments in the Decker case; the man had vanished without a trace, and now his hunch concerning the Electrola code seemed to be thoroughly refuted.

But his mind still itched. . . .

He contemplated the record-company executive resentfully. He did not like failure. In others—or in himself. He knew he could, of course, get the man to admit to anything. He wouldn't shy away from a little—persuasion, if it would give him information he wanted, but it would be of no value, and he resented the sweating little man for that. He was also offended by the stink of fear that enveloped him.

There was a knock at the door. Harbicht looked toward it with annoyance.

"Herein!" he called sharply. "Come in!" *Verflucht nochmal!*
—Dammit!—Rauner knew better than to interrupt him during
an interrogation.

The door opened. His aide, Obersturmführer Franz Rauner,
entered and clicked his heels.

"I beg your pardon, *Herr Standartenführer,"* he said gravely.
"But I thought you would wish to see this at once."

He walked over to Harbicht and handed him a note.

Harbicht glanced at it, frowning, then stiffened. He turned to
the apprehensive little man watching him.

"That will be all, Herr Staudinger. For tonight," he said
curtly.

The little man looked pathetically relieved. He bobbed his
bald head.

"Jawohl, Herr Standartenführer," he said. "Of course. Thank
you, *Herr Standartenführer!"*

He was feverishly stuffing his papers, his charts and graphs
into his voluminous black briefcase.

"I suggest, Herr Staudinger," Harbicht continued, his voice
like poisoned honey, "I suggest that you give our little talk some
serious thought." He smiled—but with his lips only. "You are a
pleasant gentleman, Herr Staudinger. Cooperative. Loyal to
the Führer and your Fatherland, I am certain. . . ." He frowned
ruefully. "I should very much regret if our—ah—relationship
should—how shall I put it?—deteriorate. . . ."

Staudinger stared at the colonel, fear darkening his eyes. He
licked his bloodless lips.

"Of course, *Herr Standartenführer.* Of course."

"I want you here at eight o'clock tomorrow morning. Precisely! Understood?" Harbicht's voice was suddenly sharp and
authoritative. He had, of course, no intention of wasting more
time on the miserable little wretch, but it never hurt to let them
sweat—literally and figuratively.

Staudinger bobbed his head.

"Gewiss, Herr Standartenführer—certainly."

"You know what we shall be—ah—discussing." Harbicht
waved a hand in dismissal. "You may go."

"Thank you, *Herr Standartenführer. Heil Hitler!"*

He was gone.

Harbicht turned to Lieutenant Rauner.

"Get me the commanding officer of Sector 47-R," he snapped. "At once!"

"*Jawohl, Herr Standartenführer!*"

Rauner hurried from the room.

Harbicht felt uneasy while he waited for his call to come through. He drummed his fingers on the desk top. Something he could not pin down was gnawing at the edges of his mind. Was the action just reported to him designed to test the strength of the Westwall in that particular sector—several units having been pulled north just that morning to oppose the French assault on the Siegfried Line? Possible. Or did the operation have a different purpose?

His thoughts were interrupted by the single shrill ring of his telephone. He grabbed the receiver.

"Harbicht!" he barked.

The voice on the phone sounded distant. Guarded and formal.

"*Hier Major Alpers*—Major Alpers here."

"Alpers—what the devil is going on in your sector?" Harbicht demanded.

There was a slight pause.

"I am addressing Standartenführer Werner Harbicht? Gestapo?"

"*Ja!*" The word exploded into the phone.

"*Herr Standartenführer,* I am not familiar with—"

Harbicht interrupted the officer.

"Major Alpers," he said, his voice dangerously low. "I shall say this only once. I suggest you listen—and listen carefully. I have personally taken charge of security in the Haigerloch-Hechingen area seventy-five kilometers east of your sector. Is that understood?"

"*Selbstverständlich*—naturally, *Herr   Standartenführer,* but—"

"*Wir sitzen auf einem Pulverfass!*" Harbicht broke in. "We are sitting on a powder keg! I want to know about everything that occurs in a hundred-kilometer radius from here. I want to know of every pin that drops. Is that clear? I have the authority to demand your full cooperation. Or do you wish to contradict me?"

"No, *Herr Standartenführer.* Certainly not, *Herr Standarten-*

führer." A note of alarm had crept into the officer's voice. "I—I, too, am concerned about security, of course. That is why I—I merely wanted to—"

"I am waiting for an answer to my question, Major!" Harbicht's voice was cold.

"A combat patrol, *Herr Standartenführer,*" Alpers said quickly. "Strength, twenty to thirty men. Not an effort in force. They have been repulsed—with heavy losses—retreating across the river."

"Any prisoners?"

"No, *Herr Standartenführer.*"

"Major. Could it have been a cover for a penetration attempt? Could the patrol have been an infiltration escort?"

"Infiltration, *Herr Standartenführer?*" Alpers sounded surprised. "I do not believe so. No one was observed."

"I see. I want you to send out patrols, Major. Cover an area up to twenty kilometers behind the lines."

"Herr Standartenführer, we are—not up to strength. We—"

"I don't care *how* you do it, Major!" Harbicht exploded. "Use your clerks. Your cooks if you have to. But I want those patrols out! At once!"

He slammed the receiver down.

15

Sig stared at the two men looming before him. Both seemed middle-aged, dressed in coarse clothing with dirty, scuffed boots. Obviously farmers. The man with the shotgun wore a stained leather cap.

Sig clenched and unclenched his fingers. He was surprised how fast his arms, held high above his head, were becoming numb. Defeat soured his mouth. They had barely begun their mission—and they were already caught. . . .

The burly man with the shotgun never took his eyes from his captives as he spoke to his companion, his voice grim.

"Get Karl and Anton," he said. "Bring them here. *Los!*"

Without a word, the man turned on his heel and hurried toward the dark shapes that were the houses of Langenwinkel.

The man with the shotgun glowered at his two prisoners.

"If you have ever seen a roebuck with its belly blasted open by a shotgun, you won't move an inch," he drawled. "I do not know who you are, but I will blow you wide open if you try anything, the both of you!"

He looked from one to the other.

Sig's mind was in turmoil.

If the man searched them—opened Dirk's rucksack and found the OSS radio—it would be all over before it had begun. Back in London they had been assured that they would *not* be searched in Germany. It wasn't like an occupied country. It was the Fatherland. Not unless suspicion had been aroused for some other reason.

The farmer would have to be killed. Whatever happened . . .

He could not be left alive to make a report on them. Any half-baked intelligence officer who learned of two strangers showing up immediately after a combat-patrol assault on the front could put two and two together. And the man holding the gun on them could supply an accurate description.

But killing him would also create a problem. Set off a search. And what about the other man?

Whatever they decided to do would be wrong. . . .

He'd been instructed by Corny to let Dirk take the initiative in any situation that called for violent action, and he was more than willing to follow instructions. He had no doubt that Dirk would pull it off. Somehow. But they would have to act soon— before the reinforcements arrived.

Neither of them carried any weapons. It would have been too risky. But he knew that Dirk had been trained to kill—without them. And *he* would help.

He looked at the farmer with a sudden hollow feeling in the pit of his stomach. He had never killed a man before. What would it be like . . . ?

The incongruity of his thoughts suddenly struck him. Here he and Dirk stood, both unarmed and defenseless, held at bay by a determined man armed with a shotgun the size of a cannon —and he was wondering how *they* would kill *him!* He marveled at what a few weeks of OSS training had done to his powers of reason. . . .

"Who are you?" the farmer asked. "Where do you come from?" He looked closely at them. "I myself am Ortsbauern-führer Eichler," he said. "Village leader of Langenwinkel. I know every man around here. That is my responsibility. I do not know you." He gave a brief nod toward the forest from which they'd come. "There has been much shooting in the restricted zone tonight," he continued, weighing his words significantly. "That is why we are guarding our village. We are so close." He peered at the two men before him. "Who are you?"

They did not answer.

Sig's nerves were taut to the breaking point.

Any moment Dirk would fly into action. Sig had to be ready. . . .

"You will say nothing, will you?" the man said. "No matter.

We will turn you over to the garrison commander. Major Alpers will know how to deal with you."

He shifted the weight of his bulk from one leg to the other. For a split second he was off balance.

Now!

Suddenly Dirk spoke.

"Please, *Herr Ortsbauernführer!*" he whined, his voice shrill with alarm. "Please don't turn us over to the military police! Please! Don't hurt us! I'll—I'll tell you anything you want to know!"

His voice broke. He trembled with fear.

Sig went cold with shock.

Dirk?

The farmer seemed taken aback. He obviously had not anticipated the pitiful outburst.

"Tell me?" he questioned. "Tell me—what?"

"You have already guessed it, *Herr Ortsbauernführer,*" Dirk said. "I am certain of it." He paused indecisively. He licked his lips nervously. His eyes flitted quickly toward his partner.

"We are—" he began. "We are—"

"No!" The cry of protest escaped unwittingly from Sig.

"Shut up, Sig!" Dirk spat at his friend. "Don't be stupid. Don't you see? It is no use. . . ."

Sig stood frozen as Dirk turned back to the farmer, the picture of servility. He was literally cringing before the man.

"We are—black-marketeers, *Herr Ortsbauernführer!*" The words poured from him. "Twice every week we have been foraging for food. Eggs. Chicken. Butter. We pay good prices, *Herr Ortsbauernführer.* We harm no one. . . ."

"Where are you from?" The man sounded dubious.

"Lahr, *Herr Ortsbauernführer.* We come from Lahr."

The farmer frowned.

"Lahr is not big enough to have a black market," he said suspiciously.

"Of course not, *Herr Ortsbauernführer,*" Dirk said at once. "Of course not! That is where we live, *Herr Ortsbauernführer.* Now. We supply a ring. They operate in the city of Freiburg."

The farmer stared at him. He said nothing.

Sig felt sheepish. How could he have doubted Dirk? They had told him always to try to bluff his way out of a tight situation.

Nine out of ten times it would work. He realized he'd been so flustered and tense that he'd been unable to remember what he'd been taught. He vowed to himself it would be the last time that happened.

Dirk was going on.

"We have a—a contact in another village near here, *Herr Ortsbauernführer,*" he explained. "But we did not get there tonight. There was much firing and shooting, and we turned back. We took a different road—and that is why we are here, *Herr Ortsbauernführer.* We fell in a hole in the dark and my friend's bicycle was broken. Both wheels bent. We had to leave it. And my tires were ripped open. We have had much bad luck. Please do not turn us in," he pleaded. *"Bitte. Bitte."*

The farmer looked at him pensively.

"That other village," he said slowly, "that would be Allmannsweier?"

Dirk's mouth fell open in astonishment.

"Yes, *Herr Ortsbauernführer,* exactly!" He turned to Sig. "There you have it, Sig," he said reproachfully, "the *Herr Ortsbauernführer* knows. It would have been foolish to try to keep the truth from him."

Sig nodded, hanging his head in shame.

"Your contact," the farmer said, "who would that be?"

Dirk looked stricken.

"Please, *Herr Ortsbauernführer.* Please do not make me tell. He would be most angry. I would lose him."

"It would not be the *Grossbauer*—the big farmer Alois Degener, would it?" the farmer suggested shrewdly.

Again Dirk's mouth fell open. He stared at the man with wide-eyed wonder.

"The *Herr Ortsbauernführer* knows already?" he asked with awe.

The man spat on the ground.

"I know that thieving *Schweinehund,* I do!" he snarled maliciously. "He is nothing but a fart from my asshole!"

"We have given him much money," Dirk said. "We pay well for what we get. . . . Only—tonight—we got nothing."

The farmer looked crafty. He glanced at Dirk. He had let his gun sag, holding it casually in the crook of his arm. Both his prisoners had taken their arms down. He didn't seem to notice.

"You will still be looking for something to buy, then," he said, his voice calculating. "Eggs? Sausage? Good homemade sausage?" He glanced in the direction of the village Allmann- sweier. "I can give you food as good as that *gauner*—that crook Degener. Better!" He turned back to Dirk. "How much do you pay?" he asked.

"We pay three times the store prices for everything," Dirk said quickly.

"Well now . . . " The man licked his lips. "And—you have the money?"

"Yes, *Herr Ortsbauernführer*. We do."

Dirk slapped his breast pocket, with a kind thought toward the London Moles. . . .

"That is good." The farmer nodded. "Then—perhaps I can help you. You do not have to go all the way to Allmannsweier. Not again." Once more he spat on the ground. "I am certain that *verdammte* Degener has been cheating you as he has cheated me. But I will not do this."

"We would be very grateful, *Herr Ortsbauernführer!* Most grateful! It is well!" Dirk turned to Sig, full of enthusiasm. "You see!" he said. "I told you this was going to be our lucky night! After the rotten eggs Degener fished out of his water-glass barrel for us the last time!"

Three men came running from the village. They hurried up to Eichler.

"Schon gut," the farmer grumbled. "It is all right. These two are from Lahr. I know of them." He turned toward the village. "They will come with me to my house. For a schnapps." He turned back to the men. "You stay here. One does not know what a night like this will bring."

He beckoned to Dirk and Sig.

"Come with me," he said.

The large black cooking stove in the spacious *Bauernstube,* the combined kitchen-dining-living area of the Eichler farm, kept the big room warm and cozy. The strong schnapps did the same for the three men.

Eichler had awakened his wife and daughter. The woman, drab and heavy-set, was heating a kettle of water on the stove for the ersatz coffee. The girl, a nubile, blond seventeen-year-old, had been sent out to scrounge up any eggs that might have been laid since the last gathering. Already a couple of large, fragrant sausages, a big package of freshly churned butter and two loaves of *Landbrot*—homemade country bread—were stacked on the big wooden table around which the men were sitting.

The woman poured the steaming black brew into heavy mugs and placed one of them before each man.

Dirk observed her out of the corner of his eye. She was definitely not the friendly type. Perhaps it was just the customary wariness of strangers; perhaps she resented being dragged out of bed in the middle of the night. He hoped it was not more than that.

The girl came back. She had a basket over her arm.

Eichler looked up.

"How many, Erika?"

"Sixteen, *Vati*," the girl replied. She glared at Dirk. There was a sullen animosity in her eyes. "I suppose he gets them all?" she said.

"We can make it an even twenty," Eichler said. "With what we have in the house." He turned to Dirk. "Will that be enough?"

"Prima!" Dirk replied. "It is very generous. Please add it all up, *Herr Ortsbauernführer,* and I shall pay you right away."

With a little gesture of anger, Erika plunked the basket of eggs down on the table. Tossing her blond hair, she turned and joined her mother at the stove.

Dirk watched her. He was concerned. He did not want to leave behind any kind of antagonism—which might be expressed to the wrong person at the wrong time. Or the right time, depending on your point of view. . . . When he and Sig left, he wanted only two feelings to linger. Goodwill—and greed. He would have no trouble with the second, but the girl presented a dilemma in regard to the first one. How in hell could he overcome her hostility?

Eichler was frowning in concentration over a scrap of paper, writing on it with a stubby, blunt pencil which he periodically wet on the tip of his tongue. Arithmetic obviously was not one of his strong points.

Dirk turned to the woman.

"We must thank you for your hospitality, Frau Eichler. You and your daughter have been most gracious." He looked at his watch. "But we must soon be on our way. I want to be in Lahr first thing in the morning. And with only my broken bicycle for the two of us, it will take a good deal of time."

Eichler looked up from his labors.

"We can fix your bicycle for you," he said.

"You can?" Dirk asked eagerly. "You have extra tires? Tubes?"

"We do." Eichler licked his lips. "They are of first quality. But they will not cost you too much," he added quickly.

"That would be great," Dirk said. "Say—perhaps you even have an extra bike? We would purchase it. We need it badly— and we would be willing to pay well for it."

Eichler thought. He nodded slowly.

"Yes," he said. "I have such a bicycle."

Erika whirled on her father.

"No, Vati!" she cried. "It is Konrad's!"

Eichler refused to look at her.

"He will not need it," he stated flatly. He glowered at the table top. "He was killed," he explained quietly. "My son. Only last September. In Holland." He looked up at his daughter defiantly. "Better his bicycle should help his family than turn to rust in the barn!"

Erika turned away, bitterness in her face.

Dirk had a sudden idea. It was worth a try. It had been the only big action in Holland at that time.

"Herr Ortsbauernführer," he said solemnly, "you said your son fell in Holland? In September?"

"Yes."

"Was it—was it at Arnhem, by any chance?"

Eichler looked at him in surprise.

"Yes. It was. Arnhem."

Dirk shook his head in wonder.

"Unglaublich," he said. "Incredible . . . " He looked at Eichler. "I was there!" He pointed to his arm. "That is where I got mine!"

Eichler stared at him.

"Konrad was a *Panzergrenadier*—in the Armored Infantry," he said slowly. "With the Tenth SS Panzer Division."

"Oberführer Heinz Harmel's Frundsberg Division!" Dirk exclaimed. "Of course. Their home station is Stuttgart. Wehrkreis V!"

A sudden bond had sprung up between Eichler and Dirk. The two women were listening with evident interest.

"You were in the same division?" Eichler asked.

"No," Dirk answered regretfully. "I was in the Ninth SS Panzer Division. Same corps, though. The Hohenstauffen Division. Under Standartenführer Walter Harzer. We were on Frundsberg's right flank on the river." He shook his head. "Those boys from the Tenth—they fought like demons."

The two women had drawn near, listening to Dirk.

He rolled up his left sleeve. The long, deep scar running across his elbow looked red and shiny fresh.

"I nearly left an arm and a lung there," he said, patting his side.

The Eichler woman stared, wide-eyed. She crossed herself. "Josef-Maria," she mumbled. The daughter took her mother's arm. She looked at the scar in fascination.

"It would have been a small loss against the one you suffered," Dirk said gravely. He rolled down his sleeve. "Imagine," he said. "Your son and I. Both in the Second SS Panzer Corps!"

He looked earnestly at the woman.

"I am sorry your son had to give his life for the Fatherland, Frau Eichler. But you can be proud of what he did."

The woman sniffed loudly. Once. She turned to her daughter. "Perhaps Konrad's *Feldkamerad* would like some more hot coffee," she said.

"Ja, Mutti." Erika lifted the pot from the stove. She filled Dirk's cup.

"Dankeschön," he said. "Thank you very much." He smiled at her. For a moment their eyes met.

The animosity was gone from her face.

"Bitte," she said.

Dirk looked away. He did not want the girl to see the relief that would certainly show in his eyes. . . . Hell—in another few minutes he could have her in the sack! He sighed to himself. It would be some time before that sort of pleasure became a priority matter again.

Eichler turned to his daughter.

"Erika. Go to the barn and get the bicycle," he said. "And the set of fine new tires and tubes."

"Ja, Vati."

The girl hurried from the room.

"I have made the total count," Eichler said ponderously. "Including the bicycle. Perhaps you had best look it over." He handed the paper to Dirk.

Dirk took it. He placed it on the table for Sig to see. Together they made a show of going over it, item by item. Dirk didn't give a damn how badly the old bastard was gouging them. The man had not the slightest idea of his real contribution. . . .

Suddenly he stiffened.

From outside came the unmistakable sound of a motor vehicle approaching on the road.

For a moment everyone in the room remained frozen.

It seemed that the vehicle would pass—when it suddenly stopped.

The four people in the *Bauernstube* hardly breathed.

Suddenly the motor started up again. The sound seemed abnormally loud as they heard it turn into the farmyard.

"Quick," Dirk whispered. "Hide the food!" With surprisingly fast reaction Frau Eichler scooped up the sausages, the bread and butter and swept them into a deep drawer in the table. She grabbed the basket of eggs and made for a cupboard gaily painted with flowers.

Dirk turned to Eichler.

"It might be best, *Herr Ortsbauernführer,* for us all," he said gravely, "if we were not found here with you at this hour." He looked soberly at the farmer. "Explanations—however reasonable—are always difficult."

Eichler nodded.

"This way," he said.

Dirk and Sig grabbed their rucksacks. Eichler hurried them toward a door. He flung it open.

"In there," he breathed. "In the storeroom."

Quickly Dirk and Sig entered the cramped and cluttered storeroom. Eichler was closing the door behind them when there was a sudden, loud banging on the front door.

"Aufmachen! Feldgendarmerie!" a deep voice shouted. "Open up! Military Police!"

Dirk had a last glimpse of Frau Eichler quickly removing the extra mugs and schnapps glasses from the table. Good woman, he thought as the door snapped shut, snuffing out the last slit of light. He thought of Erika. Where was she? This hastily chosen hiding place would become a trap—if the girl had given them away. . . .

He heard the front door being opened. He strained to listen. The storeroom was totally dark; the door thick. He was aware of Sig close behind him, standing utterly still and stiff. Muffled voices came through the heavy wooden door.

"Guten Morgen—Good morning. *Heil Hitler!"* A strange voice.

Eichler answering. *"Heil Hitler!"* I am Ortsbauernführer Gerhard Eichler. What do you want?"

"Beg your pardon, *Herr Ortsbauernführer.* We have orders to search for enemy soldiers."

"Enemy soldiers? Here?"

"There has been an attack. Across the river. They were driven back."

"Yes. We heard the shooting. What—" Eichler's voice became inaudible. Dirk strained to hear. The other voice said a few words. He could not make them out. He could feel the sweat trickle down his sides from his armpits. Speak up, dammit!

"—of the enemy soldiers may have escaped. There are patrols out. Looking for them. We saw your lights on, *Herr Ortsbauern-führer.* We thought—"

"The shooting woke us up." It was Eichler interrupting. He sounded impatient. "I am Ortsbauernführer here. I felt it my duty to be ready to—"

The scrape of a stool on the floor drowned out the last few words.

"Of course, *Herr Ortsbauernführer.* May we—"

"Would you and your men like a cup of hot coffee, *Herr Obergefreiter?* Ersatz, of course." It was the woman.

"Bitte, gnädige Frau—yes, thank you, Lady."

Cup noises. Kettle noises . . .

Where the hell was the girl?

"You have not noticed anything out of the usual, have you, *Herr Ortsbauernführer?"* It was the corporal.

"Unusual?"

There was a pause.

What the hell is he waiting for? Tell him *no,* for crissake!

"No," Eichler drawled. "Nothing—unusual . . ."

"Gerhard." It was Frau Eichler. "Perhaps you should tell the corporal. About the two men."

Dirk froze. He more sensed than heard Sig draw in his breath sharply.

"*Ach, ja!*" It was Eichler. "Of course. We stopped two men. Down by the road shrine. Where my men are watching even now. We checked them out. They were from Lahr—and they have gone on."

"Thank you, *Herr Ortsbauernführer.* We talked to your men. That is what they told us."

The sudden noise of a door opening.

Shit! Erika walking in with bicycle tires and tubes! Even Eichler couldn't get out of that one—however much he wanted to hang on to his newfound suckers. . . .

"No one on the grounds." A new voice.

"Good."

"Where do you go now, *Herr Obergefreiter?* If you do not know the area well, perhaps I—as an official—can be of help?" It was Eichler.

Sounds of rustling papers.

"Hugsweier."

"*Ach, ja,* Hugsweier. You turn left. Just outside the village. There is a sign. Three kilometers. You cannot miss it."

"Thank you, *Herr Ortsbauernführer.* And thank you for the coffee, *gnädige Frau. Heil Hitler!*"

"*Heil Hitler!*"

The front door opening and closing . . . The faint sounds of a motor vehicle starting up—and driving away.

The door to the storeroom opened. Eichler stood in the doorway.

"You must leave here," he said. "It will be safe. No one will come here again for a time."

Dirk, blinking against the light in the *Bauernstube,* stepped from the storeroom with Sig. He saw that Frau Eichler had already brought the food out of hiding and was piling it on the table. Dull she may seem, Dirk thought, but she's sure on the ball—or whatever the saying is with a Frau. . . . He noticed she'd added a bottle of local huckleberry brandy to the loot.

He and Sig began to stuff the food into their knapsacks. Dirk chose one of the large bread loaves to rest on top of his radio. He pushed a sausage down beside it. And the brandy. From now on, he thought, communication with Corny will make my mouth water. He was about to share his joke with Sig when he stopped himself. After all, the Eichlers weren't co-conspirators.

The front door opened and Erika came hurrying in.

"I saw them, *Vati!*" she cried excitedly. "I saw them arrive. In their Wehrmacht Volkswagen. I was getting Konrad's bicycle from the harness room when they stopped on the road. I hid!"

Eichler nodded.

"Did you bring the bicycle? And the tires?"

"Yes, *Vati.* I—I replaced the old ones already." She threw a quick glance at Dirk.

"Good."

Everything had been stuffed into the two rucksacks—except the eggs. Sig held the basket in his hand—undecided. Eichler watched him.

"You may keep the basket," he said. "Bring it back next time you come. Agreed?"

"Agreed, *Herr Ortsbauernführer,*" Sig answered. "Thank you."

"When will that be?" Eichler wanted to know, licking his lips.

"We shall return in two days," Dirk said. "That is our usual schedule. Will that be convenient, *Herr Ortsbauernführer?*"

Eichler nodded.

"It would be well to leave a small deposit on the basket," he said. "Ten marks?"

"Of course, *Herr Ortsbauernführer.* Very proper." Dirk dug into his pocket. *"Bis Übermorgen*—until the day after tomorrow," he said.

Eichler nodded.

"You will—come *here,* then?" He lowered his voice. He licked his lips. "We are agreed?" he said. "No longer will you go to that *gauner* Degener in Allmannsweier?"

"We are agreed." Dirk, too, spoke confidentially—man to man. He winked at Eichler. "A choosy dog barks up a forest full of trees before he finds one to piss on!"

Eichler nodded solemnly.

"That is true," he said. He offered Dirk a work-hardened hand. *"Auf Wiedersehen,"* he said.

Dirk turned to his wife.

"Thank you again, Frau Eichler."

The woman looked at him. Her eyes were suddenly bright with unshed tears. It is her Konrad she is saying goodbye to, Dirk thought. The woman's eyes flitted to his arm. Suddenly she gave him a brief hug.

"Sei vorsichtig!" she whispered. "Take care. . . . "

Dirk returned her hug.

He turned to Erika.

She was watching him.

On impulse he put his arms around her and hugged her. What the hell—the precedent had been set. He felt her stiffen—then almost at once she was straining against him. Oh, Christ, he thought. Out there is a barn full of hay. . . .

Sig was at the door. Dirk joined him. He looked back at the Eichlers. Damned if he didn't like them—even greedy old Gerhard. . . .

"Grüss Gott!" he said. "God be with you!"

It was Eichler who answered him.

"Heil Hitler!"

They were pedaling down the country road toward Lahr. It would soon be dawn. The bulging rucksacks were strapped to the handlebars of their bikes, the egg basket secured to the package rack behind Dirk.

Sig looked back at the Eichler farm.

He had just left ten years back there. In a cluttered, pitch-black storeroom.

He glanced at Dirk.

"I don't mind telling you," he said, "you had me going there awhile back. When you went into that black-marketeer bit."

"You may nominate me for an Academy Award." Dirk grinned. He felt good. Things had turned out fine. They were on their way.

"I'll say this for you—you make one helluva subservient bastard."

"Some first-class cringing was expected, Siggy baby," Dirk quipped. "Remember the old French proverb? *When the Hun is out and down, he's the humblest man in town. But when he mounts and holds the rod, he has no love for man or God!*" He grinned broadly. "Seemed to me that as a good Kraut I'd better be damned humble. I sure wasn't holding the rod!"

Sig shook his head.

"I didn't know you were at Arnhem either," he said.

"Arnhem?" Dirk grinned. "Never heard of it! Hell—in September last year I was flat on my ass at Walter Reed back in D.C.!" He sent a fleeting thought of appreciation to his talkative roommate at the hospital where he'd been recuperating from the fiasco with Jan. The guy had been a captain in G-2. From the 82nd Airborne. Been in the thick of the mess at Arnhem, and he'd never stopped yakking about it. At the time it had annoyed the hell out of Dirk. You never know. . . .

An hour later dawn was lightening the sky. Dirk and Sig were nearing the town of Lahr.

Lahr was crucial. A town of some twenty-thousand souls, situated on the little Chutter River like a tight cork in a narrow bottleneck, it guarded the only access through the mountains to the vital Kinzig Valley. The town could not be bypassed. They had to get to the valley. They would have to brazen their way through. . . .

They turned a bend in the road—and braked.

In the gray morning light the roadblock across the highway into town could be clearly seen. A wooden barrier painted with broad black and white stripes. It looked more forbidding than the black mountains surrounding them. A Wehrmacht non-com stood up from his perch in the open door of a Volkswagen parked on the road shoulder and walked purposefully to the front of the barricade as he saw the bicyclists approaching. Two men flanked him—machine pistols at the ready.

Imperiously he held up his hand.

16

Dirk and Sig brought their bikes to a halt before the barricade.
The Wehrmacht non-com—a sergeant, according to the piping
on his uniform shoulder strap—walked up to them.

"Papiere herzeigen!" he ordered curtly. "Show your papers!"

Sig fumbled his identification papers from his pocket. His
work permit. He felt excited. It would be the first test of the
effectiveness of the work of the London Moles. Dirk handed the
sergeant his dog-eared *Soldbuch*—his army paybook. The sergeant glanced through it.

"Wounded," he commented.

"Yes," Dirk said pleasantly. "Unfortunately, they got me bad
enough to make me no longer *kriegsfähig*—fit for field duty,
the devil take it!"

The non-com gave him a sour look. He examined Sig's work
papers.

"Swiss," he said.

"Technical specialist, *Herr Unteroffizier,*" Sig said politely.
He wondered briefly if he should cringe. He decided it wasn't
called for.

"You come from Hechingen," the sergeant said, frowning.
"What are you doing in this area?"

Dirk answered.

"We earned some time off," he said cheerfully. "At long last.
We decided a change of scenery would do us good. We visited
a friend of mine. In Langenwinkel. He is the Ortsbauernführer
there. I served in the Panzer Corps with his son, Konrad—God
rest his soul." He looked at the barricade and the armed sentries

with mild curiosity. "Say—we went to Langenwinkel only a couple of days ago and we took a different route. But we didn't see any barricades. What's up?"

"Who the devil knows?" the sergeant grumbled. "It's the damned brain-child of some *Bonze*—some big-shot in Hechingen with nothing better to do than piss in the punchbowl. Took over only a few days ago. Real ballbuster. Roadblocks on every damned road. *Blödsinn ist das!* Idiocy! We have spent hours just sitting around stretching our assholes."

"Say," Dirk said brightly, "I bet you could do with a little something to fill your stomachs. My friend Eichler gave us some food. Some sausage. And real *Landbrot*. Fresh. Frau Eichler baked it herself." He started to open his rucksack. He stopped and looked inquiringly at the sergeant. "It is permitted to open the rucksack, *Herr Unteroffizier?* To make a present of a little sausage and bread?"

The sergeant nodded.

"It is permitted," he said.

Dirk hauled a sausage from his knapsack. He held it out to the sergeant.

"Bitte," he said. "Please."

The sergeant handed the identification papers to Sig and took the sausage. He looked pleased.

"It is a fine sausage," he said, sniffing it.

Dirk brought out a loaf of bread.

"Give me your bayonet," he said ingenuously to the sergeant. "And I'll cut half of this *Landbrot* for you."

For a moment the non-com looked startled; then he drew his bayonet from its scabbard and handed it to Dirk.

Dirk cradled the big loaf in his left arm and, slicing toward him, cut the bread cleanly in half. He handed the bayonet and the half-loaf to the sergeant.

"Eat it in good health!" he said.

He replaced the other half of the bread in his rucksack and closed it.

"Push your bikes around the barrier," the sergeant said. "We do not want to have to move the *verfluchte* thing more than we have to!"

"Thank you, *Herr Unteroffizier,"* Dirk said, as he and Sig wheeled their bicycles around the end of the barrier.

"When you come to the Kinzig," the non-com called to them, "take the road just south of Biberach. Or you will run into another roadblock."

Dirk waved his thanks as he and Sig mounted their bikes and pedaled off toward the town of Lahr. . . .

Lahr was in the fitful process of waking up. The tree-lined streets were beginning to come alive with pedestrians and bicyclists hurrying to work. Dirk and Sig blended in perfectly.

Sig looked around curiously. He felt a vague, comforting kinship with the old, picturesque, half-timbered houses with gaily painted window shutters and steep, shingled roofs. The town showed none of the usual intrusive signs of industrialization. The occasional Nazi slogans painted on walls and the propaganda posters tacked on fences seemed out of place. Even the admonitory query "WAS HAST DU HEUTE FÜR DEUTSCHLAND GETAN?—*What Have* YOU *Done for Germany Today*"— seemed irrelevant.

On the eastern outskirts of town where the road entered the forest, cutting through the wooded hills, a road sign read: BIBE-RACH 12 KM.

It was still early. They were making good time.

Dirk was whistling a German marching song as he and Sig pumped along the road. It had been hard riding on the hilly stretches, and they had been forced to dismount and push their bikes up especially long and steep slopes. They had entered the Kinzig Valley, bypassing Biberach to the south, as the roadblock non-com had advised, and were already more than eight miles south of town. It was close to 0930 hours.

The valley road was quiet and pleasant, snaking through well-cultivated farmland. They had run into very little traffic except for farm wagons and other bicycle riders. Only rarely had they been passed by a motor vehicle—except for a small military convoy on the way toward the Rhine positions. They had dismounted and waited in the ditch for it to pass.

Suddenly there was a rubbery pop and a sharp hiss.

Dirk at once slowed down, wobbling to a halt.

He stared at the flat tire on his front wheel.

"Shit and double shit!" he swore. "So much for that fart

Eichler's tubes of first quality!"

He kicked the limp tire.

"That damned rubber wouldn't have held up through a good fuck!"

Sig was secretly pleased. Getting off his bike for a while felt good. His thigh muscles were beginning to pull. His shoulders ached. And the hard seat was chafing his crotch. He needed to stretch a bit.

They had been trudging along the road, pushing their bikes, less than a quarter of an hour when they heard it building behind them—the labored growl of a truck engine approaching in the distance. They looked at one another.

"Why not?" said Dirk. "Germany is, after all, the cradle of hitchhikers."

They placed their bikes on the right shoulder at a ninety-degree angle to the road and waited.

Presently the vehicle lumbered into view. It was a large, battered farm truck, its paint job scratched and chipped, leaving a splattering of rust spots.

Dirk waved his arms, flagging down the vehicle.

The driver slowed and came to a stop. He leaned toward the open window of the cab.

"Holla!" he called. *"Was ist los?—*What's up?"

"How about a ride?" Dirk asked. "We had a flat—and we lost our repair kit. Just to the next village?"

The driver, a stocky, middle-aged man, contemplated them. He scratched the side of his nose with a blunt thumb. His small, close-set eyes in his weather-worn, stubble-coarsened face shifted back and forth between the two men.

"Where are you going?" he asked.

"Hechingen," Dirk answered.

The man nodded. "Hechingen," he said. "What have you been doing out here?" His mouth suddenly split in an oily leer, exposing bad, tobacco-stained teeth. "Screwing the farmers' daughters? Or—just scrounging?"

Dirk grinned.

"A little of both. Too little—more's the pity!"

The driver opened the cab door.

"I am going half the way to Hechingen myself," he said.

"Oberndorf. I will take you that far."

"*Prima!*" Dirk exclaimed with pleasure.

"Put your bikes and your gear in back," the man said. "There is plenty of room."

Dirk and Sig pushed their bikes to the rear of the truck. Dirk jumped up. The truck bed, crusted with dried manure, was empty except for a large, dented gasoline can lashed to the rear of the cab under the grime-streaked rearview window. Sig handed the bikes up to Dirk and joined him on the truck.

Dirk glanced toward the cab.

"Shifty bastard!" he said in a low voice. "Looks like he'd give you change for a six-dollar bill!"

Sig grinned. "Yeah. Two threes!"

"I don't trust him much," Dirk said. "But the ride'll come in handy. Watch him."

Sig nodded.

They jumped from the truck and walked toward the cab. Dirk carried his rucksack. Sig had left his with the bikes and the basket of eggs. They climbed into the cab.

Sig sat next to the driver. The man stank. Sig tried to identify the offensive odor. . . . Manure, certainly. The pungent-sour smell of old sweat. And—motor oil.

The driver glanced at Dirk's rucksack.

"Why did you not leave that thing back there?" he grumbled. "It is going to be crowded enough with the three of us up here."

"Do not worry, friend," Dirk said. "I shall keep it on my lap."

The driver gave him a flat stare. He started up. He glanced out of the corner of his eyes at his two passengers. He scratched his nose with his stubby thumb.

"You live in Hechingen?" he finally asked.

"At present," Dirk answered. "We work there."

"Hummph," the man snorted.

For a while they drove in silence.

The man scowled sideways at Dirk.

"You could have left that damned rucksack in back," he grumbled sullenly.

"Well—I tell you," Dirk said cheerfully, "I have a bottle of huckleberry brandy in there. I thought, with your permission, it might come in handy after a while."

The driver suddenly looked cheered.

"*Ach, so!*" he said. "You have good reason!" He began to whistle. Off key.

"I am going to Oberndorf," he volunteered after a while, "to pick up a tractor. For my farm near Biberach."

"A tractor?" Sig asked.

"Yes. A tractor! The Widow Schrader is selling it to me. Her husband died and she will go to live with her sister in Nürnberg. She is giving up the farm."

"She a friend of yours?" Dirk asked idly.

"Frau Schrader? I have not met her." He grinned at them shrewdly. "But she will sell me her tractor. For little money. She needs money. She does not know the true value of such a tractor!" He looked enormously pleased with himself. "There are not many tractors in the Schwarzwald. Only on the biggest farms. I, Ludwig Brause, will have such a tractor now."

"Sounds like a good deal," Dirk commented. He was beginning to dislike the man intensely. He leaned back and closed his eyes. It was one way to discourage conversation. . . .

He'd actually dozed off.

He jerked awake so abruptly that monstrous shadows from a nightmare—Jan; a gouging of flesh; a crimson splatter in a field —were trapped briefly in his conscious mind.

He sat bolt upright, instantly aware.

The truck had come to a stop.

"We are about five kilometers from Oberndorf," Sig said. "Let me out, will you? I've got to take a crap. This monster rides on square wheels. I think everything's been shaken loose inside and collected at the bottom!"

Dirk climbed from the cab. He looked around. The truck was halted on a narrow road winding through steep mountains. They had obviously left the main road and were cutting across the forest to the Neckar River valley and Oberndorf. He must have been dead to the world for a couple of hours. Good enough. That was one thing you learned quickly in the field. Get your sleep where and when you can.

Sig made for the woods. "Be back in a few minutes," he called. "Probably several pounds lighter!"

Dirk stretched. He started back up into the cab.

"*Moment mal,*" the German said, eyeing him. "Just a moment. While you are there, take a look at your bikes. They have been rattling around. You would not want to injure them."

Dirk stopped. A warning bell went off in his mind.

He glanced at the rucksack lying on the seat. Dammit, he couldn't leave it there! His muscles tensed to grab it, but with a conscious effort he relaxed. No. It would most certainly be suspicious if he carted the damned rucksack around with him like the family jewels. He could not afford to kindle any suspicions in the farmer's mind. He would have to take a chance.

"I will look," he said.

He walked to the back of the truck and jumped up. He examined the bikes. They seemed okay. On impulse, he quickly walked to the cab and peered in through the grimy rearview window.

A chill shot through him.

The German was bent over the open rucksack. He straightened up. In one hand he held the bottle of huckleberry brandy. In the other—the earphones from the OSS radio!

The bottle fell from the farmer's hand. He stared at the radio head-set. . . .

Dirk leaped from the truck. He lost his footing and fell to one knee. At once he got up and raced for the cab door—as the truck suddenly leaped forward and started down the steep road, spewing dirt from its spinning wheels.

Sig came running from the trees.

"What happened?" he called. "What the hell's going on?"

"The bastard found the radio!" Dirk snapped. He looked after the truck careening down the road. Ahead of it was a sharp hairpin curve to the right. Dirk ran to the edge of the road. He peered down through the trees. A couple of hundred feet below he could make out the road—switchbacking through the steep hills. At once he started to race down the slope.

"Come on!" he called.

Sig ran after him.

The sound of the laboring truck changed in pitch as it precariously negotiated the hairpin curve, gears grating metallically.

Dirk bounded headlong through the trees down the steep slope. He riveted his full attention on the ribbon of road visible below, letting his pounding feet find their own path as he pitched down. The rough branches of the underbrush wrenched and tore at his clothing, a continuous flail of stinging slaps on his face and his hands, held protectively before him. He was oblivious to the gashes. He was aware only of Sig crashing after him—and the strip of narrow road below. . . .

Almost there. He threw a quick glance toward the sound of the roaring truck. The speeding vehicle was just lurching out of the curve. . . .

The trees thinned just before reaching the road. On the far side of the roadway the mountain fell away sharply. Quickly Dirk looked around. A few cords of cut wood were stacked at the roadside. He dismissed them at once. Too damned heavy to move quickly. A large pile of half-withered branches lay nearby. He headed for the heap. He tore at the thick, entangled branches. As Sig came dashing up, he shouted to him, his voice winded.

"Grab them! Heave them out on the road!"

He flung a bough onto the narrow roadbed and at once tugged at another, ignoring the sudden stab of pain in his arm.

Sig followed suit. He looked toward the on-roaring truck only a few hundred feet away. . . .

"It won't stop him!" he shouted. "He'll ride right over them!"

"Get 'em out there!" Dirk screamed at him.

A couple more leafy branches were hurled onto the road—and the truck came racing down on them. Without slowing, it plowed into the flimsy barrier. For a moment, sheer momentum carried it on, dragging some of the branches with it as it slewed down the road. Suddenly the driver stomped on the brakes. He was losing control. Some of the branches were caught and wedged in the steering lever under the truck. The front wheels had locked. . . .

With screeching brakes the truck skidded along the dirt road, raising a cloud of brown-gray dust. It hit the shoulder, leaped across it and hurtled down the steep slope, caroming from rock to rock like a pellet in the tilt of a nightmare pinball machine. . . .

Dirk and Sig raced across the road.

The truck was plummeting down the hillside.

Dirk stood rigid at the edge of the ravine. He watched the precipitate plunge of the bucking truck as if everything was being played in slow motion. . . .

One of the bikes, flung from the truck, hurtled through space to smash into a tree, buckling instantly and wrapping its steel frame grotesquely around the trunk. Sig's?

The truck-bed gate wrenched off as the body glanced off a massive rock outcropping, shooting sparks like a giant flintlock struck by its steel hammer. . . .

Bits of metal and splintered wood spewed from the body in a flurry of debris. . . .

He saw the final impact as the front end of the truck slammed into a huge boulder covered with green moss and jolted to a stop, wedged tightly between the rock and a squat, weathered tree stump. He saw the windshield shatter and cascade in a glittering shower. A split second later he heard the crash. . . .

For a moment there was utter silence—as if the entire forest was in shock. Then, as if with one voice, a host of startled birds set up a cry of outrage.

In the same moment, as if he'd been waiting for this raucous signal, Dirk—who had stood rooted to the spot at the edge of the road—jumped down and raced toward the wreck. . . .

The truck was lying on its side, wheels slowly spinning. There was a dull whoosh—and flames shot out beneath the engine and the cab, licking upward. Dirk strained to quicken his scrambling rush. He caught his foot in a gnarled root, tumbled to the ground and rolled sprawling down the embankment. He caught himself and leaped to his feet. He glanced toward the burning truck. . . .

He saw the German farmer slowly rise up through the empty cab window—like a lazy jack-in-the-box. Writhing, pushing, wedged in the opening, he struggled desperately to free himself. His horror-stricken face was streaked with rivulets of blood from a deep gash in his scalp. He looked around him wildly. He spied Dirk.

"Get me out!" he screamed. "For God's sake—*get me out!*"

He twisted violently in the grip of the tortured metal. "My legs!" he shrieked. "Oh, God! My legs! They—are—burning!" His mouth opened in a cry of agony. . . .

Dirk was at the wreck. He gave a fleeting thought to the big can of gasoline lashed to the back of the cab. In only a matter of seconds it would explode. . . .

He leaped up on the wreck—and he saw it.

Wedged in the broken windshield, held by a jagged glass splinter, was his rucksack. It was burning.

He closed his ears to the screams of the farmer. He ignored the pain in his bleeding hands. He reached. The hair on the back of his hands was instantly singed away. He yanked and tore at the pack. It came free. He leaped from the truck, stumbled a few feet with the blazing rucksack and threw it to the ground. At once he shoveled dirt and sand upon it with his hands, smothering the flames.

He turned to run back to the truck. Sig, too, was running toward it. . . .

There was a deafening explosion as the gasoline can blew up, showering the man wedged in the cab window with blazing gasoline. At once he flared up—a writhing torch. He tried to scream, but no sound came from his scorched vocal cords, seared instantly by the flames he inhaled. His hair flared up in a brief gust of flame; his eyes burst from the heat. . . .

Sig had hit the ground. He stared with incredulous horror at the blackened apparition still twisting in its deadly vise. Was the man still alive? No . . . No. It was the burning and the charring of his fire-bloated body that was causing the macabre dance of death. Had to be. . . .

He turned away, unable to bear the sight.

Dirk came up to Sig. Spent, he sank down beside him, the smoldering rucksack at his side. For a moment they sat in silence—not looking at one another.

Gradually the fire died out. The searing heat was replaced by a sickening stench. Sig swallowed. Hard. The stench flooded his nostrils with sweet nausea. It seeped into him through every pore. He turned to look at Dirk. His eyes were sandy.

His partner had opened the rucksack. He had the OSS radio in his hands and was staring at the head-set. One of the earphones had melted into a shapeless mass.

"It . . . it'll be okay," he said tonelessly. He ran his fingers probingly over the set. "I *had* to save it," he said. "Without it the mission would be a bust. We'd be dead. . . ."

Sig swallowed. Again.

"But—that man . . ." It was a whisper of horror.

Dirk shook his head dully. "It would have been no use," he said, his voice flat. "We could not have freed him in time."

"We—could have tried. . . ."

Dirk looked at his friend. He spoke quietly.

"Sig. Never again say *'We could have . . .'* " He turned to stare at the smoking wreck. "That poor bastard was dead when I left him alone with my damned rucksack," he said bitterly.

Sig glanced at him quickly.

"Dirk. I—I didn't mean . . ."

Dirk whirled on him savagely.

"Shut up!" he cried with sudden vehemence. "Just—*shut up!*"

Sig stared at him, ashen-faced. He understood.

He shut up.

They continued to sit there, each with his own grim thoughts.

Dirk looked bleakly at the charred rucksack. "This thing's no damned good," he said. "Raise too many Kraut eyebrows lugging that around." He frowned. "We'll have to find some other way to carry the radio and the rest of the stuff."

"*My* rucksack," Sig said. "It was thrown clear of the truck." He looked up the slope. "I saw it on the way down." He stook up. "I'll get it."

"Great." Dirk started to get to his feet. "We've got to get the hell out of here." He took a step—and stumbled in pain. He looked down at his right foot.

"Shit!" he said with utter disgust. He tested the foot. It hurt like hell to put his weight on it. "I've sprained the goddamned foot!"

He sat down. He touched his ankle. It felt puffy. He remembered: the race down the steep slope; the wrench as he caught his foot in the root; tumbling head over heels . . .

He considered his swollen ankle.

They were only halfway to Hechingen. . . .

17

Below them, in the verdant Neckar Valley, peacefully nestled on the river, lay the picturesque little village of Oberndorf.

Dirk was sitting on the grassy bank of the shallow ditch running along the road shoulder. He looked drawn and sweaty.

Sig watched him with concern. It wasn't just the sun and exertion that made his teammate sweat, he thought; his ankle must hurt like the devil. If only one of the damned bikes had been usable . . .

He rubbed his shoulders. The straps of the heavy rucksack had been biting into his skin. His thoughts briefly went back to Major Rosenfeld and his damned obstacle course. It was for real now. This time the make-believe Mason jar was a real-life radio transmitter.

Dirk rubbed his ankle gently. He'd bound it up tightly with strips of cloth torn from the tail of his shirt. At least that support had made it possible to get this far. Dammit! Of all the fucking luck! And there'd been no traffic on the road; no chance to bum a ride again. It was only a light sprain, he realized, but he needed to rest the damned foot. With rest, the swelling and pain would probably subside, but not if he kept trudging all over the goddamned Kraut countryside. But they didn't have the time to rest. . . .

He glanced at his watch, and looked at Sig.

"Two hours," he said bitterly. "Six lousy miles in two hours!" He swore under his breath. "We've still got thirty or thirty-five miles to cover. We'll never make it this way." He looked at Sig. "You know what we'll have to do?"

Sig nodded. "It's a risk." He looked soberly at Dirk. "Will it work?"

"It had better."

The Schrader farm lay east of Oberndorf on the far side of the river. The villagers had been most helpful with directions.

Sig and Dirk entered the farmyard. At a hand pump in front of the house, a young man was filling a wooden bucket. He glanced up at them—but continued his task. They walked over to him.

"*Grüss Gott,*" Sig said pleasantly. "The Widow Schrader. Is she here?"

The young man hefted the filled bucket from the pump. "*Frau im Haus,*" he said, his German betraying his foreign origin. "Woman in house." Carrying the bucket, he walked off toward a hen coop.

Sig and Dirk turned to the farmhouse. As they started for the door, it opened. An elderly woman, gray hair gathered in a tight bun at the back of her head, stood in the doorway. She held her work-scarred hands in front of her, folded across a soiled apron. She watched them approach.

"Frau Schrader?" Sig asked politely.

She eyed him. Then Dirk.

"*Ja,*" she said guardedly.

Sig shrugged out of the rucksack and placed it on the ground at his feet. "*Gott sei dank!*" he said fervently. "Thank God! It has been hard walking to get here, Frau Schrader."

The woman's noncommittal mien did not change.

"And why *are* you here?" she asked.

"Ah—that is another story," Sig said. He took a deep breath and launched into his explanation. "We come from the farmer Ludwig Brause, Frau Schrader. From Biberach. And a pretty distance that is. Ludwig would have come himself, but some important matters came up and prevented his leaving the farm. And so, he sent us." He took a breath and went on. "We had a —a little mishap with our truck." He pointed to Dirk's foot. "My friend hurt his foot. And we had to leave the truck to be repaired in Alpirsbach. We walked from there. We have come for the tractor."

"*Ach, ja,*" the woman exclaimed. "The tractor." She looked

at Dirk's foot. "You should not walk on this foot," she admonished. "It will make it worse."

"It is good now," Dirk said. "We can ride the tractor back to the truck. It will be no trouble."

The woman looked dubious.

"Perhaps so," she allowed. "If the tractor will run. And if there is gasoline for it . . ."

Sig and Dirk exchanged glances.

"When was it last used?" Sig asked quickly.

The woman shrugged. "Not for some weeks now. My husband—God rest his soul!—was ill. And Adam, the Polish boy, he is a good boy, but he does not know how to drive the tractor."

"We will look at this tractor," Sig said. "Where is it kept?"

"No, no, no," the woman said emphatically. "I cannot let you do that." She looked down at Dirk's foot. "When I have done what can be done for this bad foot, then I will show you the tractor."

"Thank you, Frau Schrader," Dirk said quickly, "that is not necessary."

"It *is* necessary," the woman said sternly. "I have had a husband. A good man. I have raised two sons. I know what is necessary." She turned and started into the *Bauernstube*.

Dirk glanced at Sig. He shrugged. They followed the woman into the house.

Frau Schrader pointed to a bench. "You sit there," she instructed Dirk. "Take off your boot and your sock and roll up your trouser leg." There was no doubt who was in charge. "And be sure you sit in comfort. You will sit there for one hour."

Obediently Dirk began to carry out the woman's orders.

She brought over a large tub and placed it at his feet.

"Put your bad foot in it," she said. She looked at the swollen ankle marked with puffy rings from the makeshift bandages. She touched it gently. "It is bad," she said. "But I have seen them worse. It will be better. You wait now."

For a moment she left the room. When she returned she carried a large pail. From it she poured a heavy white liquid over Dirk's foot.

"Buttermilk," she said. "Cold buttermilk. It will draw out the swelling. It will take away the hurt. My mother and her mother before her did this thing for their men." She looked at Dirk.

"You sit. Quietly," she said firmly. "And I will get the tractor papers for Herr Brause and give them to your friend." She looked from one to the other. "You did bring the thousand marks, did you not?"

"We did, Frau Schrader," Sig said. "All is in order."

One hour later Dirk lifted his foot from the tub of buttermilk. He stared at it. The skin was wrinkled, but the puffy rings were gone. The swelling had almost disappeared. Gingerly he placed the wet foot on the floor and put his weight on it. It was tender —but the pain was gone. He looked at Frau Schrader, who was observing him critically.

"It is fine," he said. "It is really *prima!*"

"Naturally," the woman said.

Dirk wriggled his foot. "It feels much better," he said. He couldn't quite keep his surprise from his voice. "I am grateful." He glanced at the buttermilk in the tub. "But it is a shame about all the good buttermilk," he added.

"It will not be wasted," the woman said matter-of-factly. "The Polish boy likes buttermilk."

Sig looked at her, startled. "But—"

Frau Schrader turned to him. "What is not known to him will not hurt him," she said firmly. "And it is too good for the pigs."

The social order of the Third Reich, Sig thought wryly. On top the Germans, on the bottom the pigs—and somewhere in between the rest of the world . . .

Frau Schrader turned back to Dirk. "We will put a nice bandage around your ankle—and you will not walk much on it for a day, is that understood?" she asked sternly.

"Yes, Frau Schrader."

"Very well. As soon as you are ready, we will go and look at the tractor. . . ."

The tractor was kept in the barn. Adam, the Polish farm worker, threw open the big double doors to let in as much light as possible. The machine had obviously not been used for a while. It was rusty and ill-kempt, and clumps of wind-borne straw had collected in hollow places on it, some obviously having served as nests for roosting hens.

They examined it.

It was a Fordson. A grimy plate on it read: HENRY FORD & SON, LTD. CORK, IRELAND. MODEL N. It had two large cast-iron wheels with solid rubber rims in the back and two smaller ones in front. It had a belt pulley and a broad, rigid drawbar. It had probably been built some fifteen years before—although it looked older.

Sig inspected the engine. A side-valve four-cylinder unit that would probably run on either gasoline or kerosene.

"Let's try to start her up," Dirk said. "I'll work the crank."

Sure, Sig thought cynically. And if we do get the damned thing to run—how about operating it? They taught us to drive anything on wheels from Italian two-ton trucks to Russian baby-buggies—but nobody thought of a Fordson tractor!

They bent to the task of getting the battered tractor started. Miraculously, they succeeded.

Rasping, wheezing, knocking and sputtering—it ran.

But not for long.

With a spastic cough—it quit.

Sig inspected the gasoline tank.

It was empty.

He looked at Dirk. He shook his head. Dirk turned to Frau Schrader.

"Have you any gasoline?" he asked. "Or kerosene?"

The woman frowned. "I know nothing of this tractor," she said. "Emil took care of it. I have no knowledge if there is any gasoline."

"Could we get some? In the village? Buy it?"

"I think not. There is little gasoline for us these days. No one will give up what he has. You must come with your truck and take the tractor away." She looked at him defiantly. "It is yours now."

Sig and Dirk glanced at one another. That was that.

Suddenly Adam spoke.

"Machine no run," he said solemnly. "No petrol."

Thanks a lot, Dirk thought, we just about managed to figure that out for ourselves.

"Man take out," Adam continued.

Dirk looked at him quickly. "Herr Schrader took the gas out of the tractor?" he asked. "Siphoned it out?"

Adam looked puzzled. He shook his head. "Man take out," he repeated.

"Okay, okay," Dirk said impatiently. "What did he do with it? Where is it? Where?"

"He hide. No one will take."

"Where?"

Adam didn't answer. Instead he walked over to a row of battered milk cans standing against the barn wall. One of them had a piece of old burlap wedged in the opening by the dented lid. He pointed at it. "Petrol there," he said.

Dirk was at the can in two strides. He wrested the lid off. He sniffed the opening.

"Gas!" he said.

With his knuckles he rapped down the side of the can until the hollow, booming sound suddenly became a solid thud.

"Ten, twelve liters," he said to Sig.

"It will be enough, this gasoline?" Frau Schrader asked. "Enough to get you to your truck?"

Dirk nodded.

"Thank you, Frau Schrader," he said. "It will be enough."

The sign said simply:

HECHINGEN
Kreis Stuttgart

Sig and Dirk looked at it. Hechingen. It was more than an ordinary road sign to them. More than a milestone on their path. It was a good omen. They'd made it. *Hechingen* . . .

Dirk's foot gave him no serious trouble. Frau Schrader's home remedy and the rest he'd enjoyed riding on the tractor had done the job. They had covered over thirty miles from Oberndorf to the road junction with the Hechingen-Tübingen-Stuttgart highway. They had sold the tractor to a farmer near Balingen before going onto the main road, where it would have been out of place. At first they had thought of simply abandoning it—but that would have led to some sort of investigation when it was found, leading back to Frau Schrader. They could not risk that. But the farmer who bought it had gotten himself a good deal and was unlikely to go around shooting off his mouth. Twelve hundred marks, he'd paid. They had actually made two hundred marks on the transaction! "Just wait till old Corny hears that one," Dirk had said triumphantly.

Once on the highway, they had quickly thumbed a ride. A truck converted to wood-burning had picked them up. The driver had turned off less than a mile before the town limits of Hechingen, and they had walked the rest of the way, Sig carrying the rucksack so Dirk could go easy on his foot.

Dirk was looking at the signpost marking the town limits. A line . . . An imaginary line. But—to him—vitally important . . .

He was eleven years old. His parents had taken him to visit friends from the Old Country who'd settled in a small town on the Ohio-Indiana state line. In fact, the state line ran right through town, right smack through the house where their friends lived. His father had said that every day the lady cooked dinner for her family in Ohio and served it in Indiana! He had been awed, and he had been thrilled each time he walked across the invisible line. He had stood with one foot in each state. It has been magic. . . .

Now once again there was an invisible line to be crossed. But this time there was no magic of innocence. Only the promise of danger—perhaps death.

They walked on; two ordinary townspeople to be lost among the thousands of workers crowding the town. No one would pay them special attention. . . .

It was dusk. 1817 hours, Saturday, March 24, 1945, when Dirk and Sig entered Hechingen.

In his office at Gestapo Headquarters, Standartenführer Werner Harbicht sat staring angrily at a report brought to him earlier. He tapped his pencil on his desk in exasperation.

He was dealing with imbeciles!

18

The descriptions were of no earthly use.

Harbicht slapped the papers on his desk an angry, back-handed blow. *Zum Teufel damit!*—the devil take it! The investigating officer in the field must have been a first-class *Erdkloss,* he thought in disgust—one of those country clods, so dumb he couldn't find a turd in a cow pasture. The information the man had managed to obtain from his interrogation of the suspect was utterly inadequate: An Unteroffizier was under arrest, accused of stealing food from the local farmers while on duty. Routine. He had been discovered at his post on a roadblock near the town of Lahr eating a large, homemade sausage. The matter had been referred to the Hechingen Gestapo at once simply because the orders to establish the roadblocks had come from that headquarters. Harbicht scowled at the report. His first impulse had been to pick up the phone and thoroughly ream the ass of the unit CO responsible for bothering the Gestapo with such stupid trivia. But he had read on. The Unteroffizier had insisted that he had been given the sausage by two men passing through the roadblock. Two bicyclists carrying rucksacks. Time—Saturday, March 24, about 0600. *About!* Harbicht could taste his irritation. The inexactness was not to be tolerated. Their papers had been in order, according to the sergeant. *Soldbuch.* Work permit. The men were from Hechingen. *Hechingen?* But the descriptions of them given by the non-com were utterly useless. One of them was a discharged soldier. Wounded. But it was not known what kind of wound. The other was a foreign worker. Austrian? Czech? Italian? The Unteroffizier could not remember. The men were medium height. Medium build. Medium-color hair. Medium age. *Medium*—damn and double damn! The observations of an idiot—most certainly *below* medium intelligence!

Nevertheless, one statement in the report had caught Harbicht's interest. The men had mentioned to the Unteroffizier that they had been visiting in a village called Langenwinkel. With the family of the local Ortsbauernführer. And Langenwinkel was hard on the restricted zone, only a few kilometers from the front-line sector hit by the enemy combat-patrol assault that night. . . .

Who *were* the two anonymous bicyclists? *What* were they? Holiday travelers? Black-marketeers? Or—infiltrating saboteurs? If—*if*, in fact, they did exist at all except in the self-defensive imagination of the Unteroffizier . . .

He frowned. He would have that Ortsbauernführer brought to Hechingen. But it would have to wait. He was due at the Haigerloch plant in less than an hour. Berlin had requested that he attend an urgent, high-level conference. It was the kind of request not to be ignored.

He would get to the Langenwinkel matter as soon as he returned.

In addition to himself there were seven men seated around the conference table. Nearly all of them were smoking, Harbicht noted. The denseness of the smoke and the tension in the air were about equal, he thought. He knew all the men by name —and, of course, dossier—but he had met only one of them personally. Professor Reichardt. Dieter Reichardt, chief of the Haigerloch Project. The other men were top project scientists and an SS Obergruppenführer—SS General—from Berlin. A special representative of the Führer himself, flown down only hours before.

Harbicht looked at each of the sober men in turn. "The Uranium Club," they called themselves in private. He frowned at the frivolous breach of security—however "private" it might be. The code name for the group was actually the Speleological Research Unit. Aptly chosen, he thought. From the rear window in the Swan Inn, where the conference was taking place, he could see the heavily guarded entrance to the complex of caves that had been carved and blasted into the granite bowels of the mountain itself. Those caves housed the most sensitive phase of the Haigerloch Project. The atomic pile . . .

The SS general stood up, ramrod stiff, waiting until he had the full attention of all.

"Meine Herren," he said crisply, "I shall make this brief. I am flying back to Berlin within the hour. . . . I bring you the Führer's personal congratulations on your successful achievement here earlier today!" He looked around the room. "As soon as word reached Berlin that the Haigerloch pile had worked and your theories and methods had been proven correct, the Führer himself was informed. He at once called an urgent meeting with Reichsleiter Bormann, Reichsführer Himmler, Reichsmarschall Goering and Dr. Goebbels. I attended that meeting. I am here to make a personal inspection of your progress and to get definite answers to specific questions." He paused. *"Meine Herren,"* he said solemnly, "the Führer is assigning top priority to the Haigerloch Project. To the creation of an atomic bomb!"

Harbicht was wholly engrossed. He carefully considered the full ramifications of the general's statements. He was not surprised that Bormann, Himmler and Goering had at once thrown their support to the project. In the past they had all championed the cause of scientific research on behalf of the Reich. Their decrees had saved many a scientist from going to the front. *Der Dicke*—the Fat One—had been one of the first, setting up the War Research Pool in '44 when the scientists were in danger of being drafted into the armed forces. Bormann had followed in September with his decree shielding scientists from any kind of duty except in their own fields. But —the Führer? Atomic research had never interested him. *Judenphysik*—Jew physics—he had called it. As had Helwig, whose *Die Deutsche Physik* maintained that such inquiries were the work of alien, Jewish minds, which the pure German *Volk* must shun as racially incompatible. . . . The importance of that morning's achievement at Haigerloch must be—enormous. . . .

He felt a sudden chill of alarm. Why his presence now? Security, of course. But was there more? Had the Decker disappearance case come to the attention of Berlin? He still had no answers. And he vowed silently to double his efforts and to strengthen security still further in the Hechingen-Haigerloch area. But if nobody else brought the Decker case up now, he certainly would not.

He returned his attention to the general. The man's voice was getting on his nerves. It was thin and high-pitched, totally out of keeping with the importance of his rank.

The general brought out a small black notebook. He opened it.

"These are the questions I shall want answered," he said crisply. "First. When do you plan to conduct the final test of the uranium machine? Cause the pile to go critical?"

Reichardt cleared his throat.

"Yes?" the general asked sharply.

"We—we did not reach infinite neutron increase today," Reichardt explained, "because the size of our present pile is insufficient." Again he cleared his throat. "Increasing the size by fifty percent and using exactly the same geometry, a self-sustaining chain reaction will definitely occur. . . ."

"How will you accomplish this?"

"We must obtain an additional seven hundred and fifty kilograms of heavy water and a similar weight of uranium."

"Are these supplies available?"

"Yes. At Stadtilm and elsewhere. It is a matter of logistics."

"It will be arranged. At once. It is in accordance with the Führer Order of January Thirty-first." He looked straight at Reichardt. "With these supplies brought here—when can you conduct your final test?"

Reichardt glanced around at his colleagues. They remained silent. He sighed.

"The nineteenth," he said, "April the nineteenth."

One of the other scientists spoke up.

"Herr Obergruppenführer," he said quietly, "you do realize that even if we *are* successful, it will be many months after the pile has gone critical—before a bomb can be constructed?"

It was Himmelmann. Harbicht mentally reviewed what he knew about the man: Himmelmann, Gustav, physicist. Like Decker? Born in Austria. Not a party member. Believed apolitical—totally involved in his scientific work. . . .

The general waved a hand in dismissal.

"The Führer is aware of that. He has made plans for such contingencies. These plans will be revealed to you at the proper time." He consulted his notebook. "Secondly. What is the power of a completed atomic bomb?"

Reichardt cleared his throat. "Exact calculations cannot be made at this time, General. We—we estimate one bomb will have the power of several thousand tons of high explosive."

"So." The general was obviously impressed, trying not to show it. "It would level an entire city?"

"It would."

The general nodded with satisfaction. He made a note in his little book.

"There is, of course, also the possibility that once a chain reaction occurs—it cannot be controlled," Himmelmann said, his voice soft.

The general looked startled. "Meaning?"

Himmelmann shrugged. *"Total* annihilation."

The general turned to Reichardt. "Professor?"

Reichardt coughed nervously. "It—it *is* possible, of course," he said. "Although we—we have full confidence that we *can* control any such—ah—occurrence . . ." He cleared his throat apologetically.

"I see." The general paused. *"Meine Herren,* it is the Führer's wish that you proceed with all possible dispatch in an effort to bring the Haigerloch Project to a successful conclusion at the earliest possible moment. . . ." He frowned. "I must impress on you the utmost importance of your task—and the essential secrecy with which it must be carried out." He looked at Harbicht.

"Area security is under your jurisdiction?" he asked.

"It is, *Herr Obergruppenführer,*" Harbicht answered smartly. "Tight security is in force. All precautions have been taken. My command is on a constant alert status."

"Good."

Harbicht heaved a mental sigh of relief as the SS general turned back to the scientists.

"Meine Herren," the general said solemnly, "I have been authorized to impart to you the following top-secret information." He paused dramatically. "Two targets have been chosen for annihilation by atomic bombing. One of them—or both—

will be struck. Target number one requires particularly careful planning and precise execution. It will be mounted as a variant of the earlier combination relay plan for extreme long-range bomber operations which was discarded only because of the limitation on bomb-load capacity. A consideration which will now be eliminated! Target number two requires considerably less effort. Both Reichsmarschall Goering and Grossadmiral Doenitz have assured the Führer that all-out emergency measures would make both operations possible. The entire Luftwaffe and the Navy will, of course, cooperate to the fullest extent. Delivery of the bombs *is* feasible! . . . *Meine Herren"*— he looked gravely around the room—"gentlemen. The two targets chosen by our Führer, Adolf Hitler, are Washington and London. . . ."

Corny's instructions had been explicit. Sig and Dirk had had no trouble finding the address where they were to contact Otto Storp. Corny had assured them that by the time they got there Storp would be expecting them and be familiar with the passwords: *Gemini—Prussian Blue.* . . .

Hechingen had been the capital of the principality of Hohenzollern-Hechingen until 1850, when Prussia had "acquired" it. A few miles south of town the ancient Hohenzollern Castle imperiously crowned a mountaintop. They had seen it from the highway on their way to town.

The Storp house was a modest one-story building on a side street, much like the other houses on the street. Across from it was a tiny park—more like an afterthought for an empty lot. Two benches stood close together at one end.

Dirk and Sig sat on one of the benches, sharing the rest of the *Landbrot* baked by Frau Eichler—and unobtrusively observing the Storp house. They were eager to meet Otto Storp—and apprehensive. They knew how dependent they would be on him and how important to their success he would be. But they did not know *him.* Even though Corny had shown the highest respect for him and his resourcefulness, they still wondered what he'd turn out to be like. In a few minutes he would hold their lives in his hands. . . .

They had been sitting on the bench for over twenty minutes watching the house, munching the bread. During that time they had observed three persons entering the house—and leaving. One man, middle twenties, and one elderly couple. They had stayed inside only a few minutes before reappearing and walking rapidly away.

Dirk was uneasy. What was going on? It could have nothing to do with Storp's underground work, he felt; the man's cell would be extremely small with highly limited activity. What, then? Trouble?

It was getting dark. They would have to make their move. They could not afford to be caught in town with no place to spend the night.

Dirk looked at Sig. "Well," he said, "shall we?"

Sig nodded. "Let's do it."

They walked across the street. They rang the bell at the front door. After a short wait, the door was opened. A pretty girl in her twenties stood in the doorway. She looked at the two men questioningly.

"Bitte?" she asked. "Yes, please?"

"Excuse me, *Fräulein,"* Dirk said. "Is this the house of Otto Storp?"

The girl nodded solemnly. "You are friends?" she asked.

"Yes," Dirk said. "May we see him?"

Again the girl nodded. She stood aside to let them enter. "This way, please," she said. She started down the corridor. Dirk and Sig followed.

The girl stopped at a door. She opened it. *"Bitte,"* she said.

Dirk and Sig entered the room. Heavy drapes were drawn across the windows. The first thing they saw were the two large candles burning. The next was the open coffin cradling the body of a pale young man. Heavily applied makeup could not hide the ugly purplish bruise across his forehead and temple. . . .

They had found Otto Storp.

19

Sig stared at the waxen corpse in the coffin. He felt the blood drain from his own face. He turned to the girl.

"Is that—Otto Storp?" He blurted out the question.

The girl spun toward him. She glared at him—sudden, cold suspicion hardening her pretty face.

"You said you were my brother's friends!" she exclaimed. Her voice was coldly accusing.

"We *are*, Fräulein Storp," Dirk broke in quickly. "We are. But in a special way. We never met him."

"Who are you?" the girl demanded. "What do you want here?"

Dirk thought quickly. This was no time for sparring.

"*Gemini,*" he said quietly.

The girl drew in her breath sharply. Her eyes were wide and dark. But she said not a word.

Suddenly a deep voice broke the silence. "Hang the wreath on the door, Gisela. Lock it. We will have no more visitors tonight."

Dirk and Sig whirled on the voice before the first word was out. In the doorway stood a huge man. At least six feet two. He appeared to be in his early forties, but his rugged face made it difficult to tell with certainty. His ham-sized fist held a Luger pointed steadily at the two men before him.

"Do not move," he said calmly. "I will not hesitate to kill you both."

Dirk's mind raced. He realized they could do nothing. There were a thousand possible reasons for the predicament in which they found themselves—but only one possible reaction to it. He did not move a muscle.

"Put your hands on top of your head," the man ordered. "Lace your fingers. Tightly. I want to see white flesh."

Dirk obeyed. He glanced at Sig—relieved to see that he, too, was carrying out the command. He clasped his hands together till they hurt.

"Now," the man said unhurriedly. "What do you want here?" He studied them. "Who are you?"

"My papers are in my pocket," Dirk said.

The man shook his head. "Papers mean nothing," he stated flatly.

The girl was watching the two strangers, her face strained and bleak. Suddenly she spoke.

"Turn them in, Onkel Oskar," she pleaded, her voice hoarsely urgent. "Please! Do not get involved!"

The big man nodded slowly. "Gisela may be right," he said thoughtfully. "Can you give me one reason why I should not hand you over to the police?"

Sig had been following the exchange with rising, bitter anger. All their careful plans, all their damned trials and tribulations, the lives lost—all down the drain because of the one goddamned development no one could possibly have foreseen . . . The death of Otto Storp.

He glared at the girl, at the big man. Dammit, what the hell did they know? Or care? The frustration of the situation overwhelmed him.

The big man slowly looked from one to the other. "I have little choice, have I not?" he said. "Perhaps I—"

Sig could contain himself no longer.

"Save it!" he spat. "I know too damn well what you're going to say! You will *have* to turn us in. As good, patriotic Germans, you will have to hand us over. Whoever we are! If we are enemies, you will have to. Of course. If we are Gestapo trying to infiltrate your crummy organization, you will have to, to prove yourselves!" He glared resentfully at the girl. "You knew what Otto was," he growled. "You recognized the password." He snapped his head back to look at the big man. "You *know* who we are. Why we are here. Well, dammit, make up your minds. Turn us in, and save your own lousy skins—or give us a chance to talk!"

He stopped. He was literally out of breath. His hands, still clasped achingly on top of his head, trembled. For a moment there was silence. All eyes were on Sig. Then the big man turned to Dirk.

"Your friend is very hot under his collar," he said calmly. He grinned. "But—we must make sure." He gestured with his gun. "Show me your arm," he ordered. "The left one."

Dirk slowly took his hands from his head. He rolled up his sleeve and held his bare arm out for inspection. The long, deep scar seemed angrily inflamed.

The big man nodded.

"Prussian Blue," he said. "I am Oskar Weber." He put the gun in his belt. He turned to Sig. He grinned. "Welcome to Hechingen," he said.

Sig took his hands down. He scowled at the man. "Why the hell didn't you give us the password in the first place?" he growled.

Weber shrugged. "And if you had been Gestapo informers who somehow had learned of the arrival of two enemy agents *and* the passwords, where would we be now?"

The girl walked over to her uncle. She placed her hand on his arm. "Please, Onkel Oskar," she begged, "tell them to go. To leave us alone. Please! Do not get involved!"

The big man gently placed one of his huge hands over the girl's. "Gisela, my child," he said with surprising softness, "is that what Otto would have done, do you think? Is that what he would have wanted us to do now?"

Two tears gleamed in the girl's dark eyes. They caught the flickering light from the candle flames. She turned away. "I will make hot coffee," she said, her voice low. Quickly she left the room. The three men looked after her.

"Gisela can be trusted," Weber said, answering the unspoken question in the air. "When you know more about her, you will understand. Her parents—her mother was my sister—they were killed. Only a year ago. In Stuttgart. It was an air raid." He sighed. "It is difficult for her." He looked toward the open coffin.

"Last night," he said heavily. "Only last night the accident happened. It was at the railroad yards. We both work there—"

He suddenly stopped. *"I*—work there," he continued. "Otto slipped and fell between two cars being coupled." He turned away. "Together, Otto and I—we did what little we could down there to stop the war machine that is destroying our Fatherland." He looked earnestly at Dirk. "But only when we were a hundred and ten percent certain that we would not be caught. You understand, my friend, *we* must be more careful than anyone else. . . ."

Dirk nodded. "We understand," he said. "You are part of Storp's cell?"

"Cell?" Weber asked in surprise. "What cell? There were the two of us. And Gisela . . ."

Dirk and Sig glanced at one another. They had the same bleak thought. The forces they could count on in carrying out their mission consisted of one man, one reluctant girl—and one corpse. . . .

Dirk looked speculatively at Weber. "How much do you know?" he asked.

For a moment the big man fixed his pale blue eyes on Dirk, then he shrugged. "Only what Otto told me," he said. "What he thought I should know. . . . We were expecting you. Otto knows—Otto knew a man in Stuttgart. He operates a *Schwarzsender* —an illegal radio. We have no radio here. The man in Stuttgart told Otto about you."

"This man," Dirk asked, "who is he?"

Weber shook his head. "I do not know," he said. "I do not know how to find him. Otto thought it best."

Dirk nodded. He dismissed it. It was not of paramount importance. "Go on," he said.

"I know that you are here to learn about the scientific project at Haigerloch. The one Otto said is atomic research."

"Is it?"

Weber shrugged. "Otto said yes. To make a terrible bomb. He knew a man who works there."

"Himmelmann?" Sig asked.

"Yes. Gustav Himmelmann."

"Who is he?"

"A scientist. From Austria. Otto said he is a very good scientist. But he has become disillusioned. With the Nazis. He cannot bear to see his work in science being used for destruction. So

—he will do what he can to help stop this bomb project. Once such a bomb is made—he knows how it will be used." The big man looked solemnly at the two Americans. "Understand," he said in a low voice, "we are none of us traitors to our Fatherland. We love our country. We are not your allies to help destroy her —but to help her survive. Adolf Hitler and his gang have laid waste our Germany. They have pushed her to the brink of total ruin. We would try to save her. Stop this final cataclysm—if we can." He was silent for a moment. "We will help you, Gisela and I. But at all times our Fatherland and our people come first. You understand this?"

"It is understood," Dirk said.

Weber nodded solemnly. "It is good. Now, my friends, what would you have us do?"

"First—we need a place to stay."

"Here. There is a room in the basement which will be safe. And I will give you Otto's work papers. From the railroad yards. They may be helpful."

"Good. Secondly. How soon can we talk to Himmelmann?"

"I will get to him as quickly as I can."

"Okay," Dirk acknowledged. "That's our next step."

There was a small noise behind him. He turned. Gisela was standing half-hidden in the open doorway. When she saw him turn toward her, she stepped into full view. She was carrying a small tray with three steaming cups.

"Kaffee," she said tonelessly. "Ersatz, of course . . ." She gave the open coffin a quick look. "I will serve it in the parlor." She looked at Dirk and Sig—a look full of resentment and bitterness. She turned on her heel and walked away.

Dirk looked soberly after her. It was not her brother, Otto, who held their lives in his hands.

It was Gisela.

It was late when Standartenführer Harbicht returned from Haigerloch, but he went directly to his office. There was work to be done.

Despite a strenuous day and the late hour, he felt exhilarated. The Haigerloch Project might well be the key to final victory. With half-guilty wonder, he realized that in the hidden recesses of his mind he had actually begun to doubt the ability of the

Reich and the Führer to conclude the war victoriously. No more. The Haigerloch Project would ensure the ultimate triumph of the Third Reich.

Nothing must be permitted to interfere.

He pulled a large sheet of paper in front of him and began to write on it. Quickly, purposefully. Dividing the paper into two columns, he wrote:

FALL DECKER	*FALL LAHR*
The Decker Case	The Lahr Case
Time: 28 Feb.	Time: 23/24 Mar.
Place: Mayen.	Place: Route bt. Rhine front and Hechingen.
Decker, top atom. scientist, ordered to Haigerloch—disappears.	Top-secret Haigerloch Project at crucial stage.
2 men make inquiries about Decker.	2 men pass Lahr roadblock.
Descriptions of men sketchy. No descript. = no memorable features.	Descript. of men: 1 wounded ex-soldier (not verified). 1 *Ausländer*—foreigner—nationality unknown. No descript. = no memorable features.
Eyewitness: Hotel porter.	Eyewitness: Roadblock Unteroffizier. Stated: Ortsbauernführer from village of Langenwinkel.
Item: Electrola marketing code ad torn fr. mag.—missing.	Item: Combat patrol activity E of Langenwinkel.
Item: Decker luggage left in house. Uniform gone—except boots.	Item: 2 men placed in: Langenwinkel—Lahr; starting on way to Hechingen.

For a long while he sat studying the outline, analyzing each meager bit of information he possessed. He could not shake the feeling that the two cases were related. In fact, his conviction grew stronger. The pieces all belonged to one giant jigsaw puzzle. He could not fit some of them into it at all—such as the boots —but he knew with the certainty born of experience coupled with imagination that when he ultimately did find a way to fit them in, it would be well worth his while. . . . Some pieces were obviously unimportant—others, such as the Electrola ad, seemingly dead ends. But a strong, definitive picture did emerge. Enough to alert his sense of danger.

There were four possible explanations for Decker's disappearance, stated in broad terms: He could have had an accident. He could have elected to go underground for his own personal reasons. He could have defected voluntarily. Or he could have been kidnapped.

The first was unlikely. There would have been reports. The second presented no real problem: the man would ultimately be ferreted out. It was the last two possibilities that interested him. They were identical in their implications of danger; there was only one difference. Decker would talk quickly and freely if he had gone voluntarily. Slower and reluctantly if he had been taken by force. But talk he would. Eventually. Harbicht smiled a thin smile. They all did. . . .

The probability that Decker was in enemy hands was strong. Two strangers had been looking for him in Mayen on the eve of his scheduled departure for Haigerloch. He must have left his mother's flat in a hurry; his luggage had been left behind. All of it. And his uniform boots. Damn those boots! They were beginning to get on his nerves. He could see absolutely no reason for leaving them behind. . . .

What important information could Decker have given the enemy? His own involvement in uranium research, of course, and whatever he knew of the nature of the Haigerloch Project. Did he have enough information to be dangerous? Harbicht decided that he did. . . .

The assumption then had to be that the enemy had obtained enough information from Decker about the Project to be forced to acquire more. An espionage mission? Possibly. There would have been ample time to mount a mission between the Decker disappearance and the appearance of the two men at the Lahr checkpoint. . . .

Ah! The same two men who had been observed in Mayen? Perhaps. Possible. But not important. Important was the place and time of appearance. Two strangers showing up close to the restricted zone immediately following a combat-patrol assault which *could* have been the cover for a penetration. Two men, headed for Hechingen—first observed in the village of Langenwinkel.

He flipped the button on his intercom. Rauner's sleepy voice answered, *"Jawohl, Herr Standartenführer!"*

"Find out the name of the Ortsbauernführer in Langenwinkel," Harbicht ordered. "I want him here tomorrow!"

He flipped the button off without waiting for confirmation. It did not occur to him that his order would not be carried out.

He reviewed the facts again. He was convinced. Somewhere in the Hechingen/Haigerloch area were two men. Two enemy agents—on a mission to discover the secrets of the Haigerloch Project. No other logical conclusion could be reached.

He took a deep breath. He felt vibrantly alive. It was a challenge he would meet—and overcome.

Swollen as it was with the influx of workers and technicians involved in the Project or working in the expanded railroad facilities, the area held only fifteen, perhaps twenty thousand people. Even with his sketchy information about the two intruders, he could narrow the number of suspects down considerably. He would find them. It was only a matter of time.

The only question was—had he time enough?

20

The *Bierstube Zum Güterzug*—"At the Freight Train"—was jammed into the lower floor of an old building on a narrow side street near the railroad yards. Its patrons were almost exclusively railroad workers and train personnel. A pall of coal soot covered it inside and out, coating everything with a grimy film —including the dull, dirty-blond hair of the harassed waitress juggling her way through the crowd with four steins of beer in each hand and spilling not a drop.

The *Bierstube* was packed with men, all talking too loudly and laughing too boisterously. It sounded as if, for a brief span of time, they were trying to drown out the dismal voices of war. Every table was occupied and only a few scattered chairs were empty, one of them at the table Dirk, Sig and Oskar had taken. They had come early, before the shift break at the railroad yards had jammed the place. They had chosen a small table against the wall near the kitchen door, waiting until it had become available and barely beating two burly stokers to it. Dirk had selected it. The wall protected their backs and the door would provide a quick exit if necessary. It also afforded a good view of the front entrance and the side door to the rest room, the only other means of entering or leaving the main *Gastzimmer*. It was as safe as possible.

Weber had taken them to the *Bierstube*. He and Otto had met Himmelmann there before. It was always filled with customers intent only on their beer and temporary escape; a place where nobody paid anyone else the slightest attention. Himmelmann, who stayed in Hechingen, had a room nearby, and it was not unusual for him to stop in at *Zum Güterzug* for a short beer.

The three men had already emptied a couple of large steins of *Löwenbrau hell*—and Dirk's kidneys were quickly afloat. He had visited the cramped, pungent rest room—three urinals and two stalls. There was one small window with a sooty, cracked pane, easily opened, leading out to a narrow alley with an exit at each end. Good enough.

He watched the front door. Halfway up the two large windows that flanked it, heavy, streak-faded curtains hung from massive brass rings on sturdy wooden rods, making it impossible to see in—or out.

Oskar touched his arm.

The man who entered the *Gastzimmer* through the front door looked to be in his sixties. Unruly gray hair set him apart from the close-cropped *Bierstube* habitués. He was tall, six or six-one, Dirk estimated, with a slight stoop.

He looked around the crammed room and his eyes did not pause as they passed over the three men at the wall table near the kitchen door. For a moment he stood at the door acclimatizing himself to the din.

Oskar turned to his two companions.

"You may find the *Herr Professor* perhaps—strange to you," he said slowly, as if searching for words that eluded him. "You must understand," he said. "He is betraying his friends. His work. Himself." Oskar spoke with quiet earnestness. "He must hate himself for it—even though he knows he *must* do what he does."

Himmelmann began to make his way toward the table at the rear wall. Neither Oskar nor his two companions paid him any attention. Oskar took a healthy draft of his beer. He wiped his mouth with the back of his hand.

"But he is a man of vision, the *Herr Professor*," he said softly. "He has the power to see the oak tree where only an acorn lies."

Himmelmann came up to the table. He placed his hand on the back of the single empty chair.

"Ist dieser Platz frei?" he inquired.

Oskar glanced up. "Yes," he said. "It is free. Sit down if you wish."

"Danke."

The man sat down. Expressionless eyes flitted across the faces of Dirk and Sig. Then the newcomer turned to catch the eye of the waitress plowing her way through the throng. He held up one finger. Then he turned to Oskar.

"Where is Otto?" he demanded abruptly.

"He is dead," Oskar said quietly. Himmelmann started. Alarm showed briefly in his eyes. Oskar went on quickly. "It was an accident, Herr Professor. At the yard. No one suspects."

Himmelmann's tension eased. *"Tut mir leid,"* he mumbled awkwardly. "I am sorry. . . ." He turned to look at Dirk and Sig, his eyes hostile.

"You are Otto's—friends." It was a statement rather than a question.

Dirk nodded. "We are."

Sig looked at the German with distaste. How offhand the man had been in dismissing Otto's death. Was that what living in the midst of war did to you? Or living under the Nazis? Or—being involved in subversive work? He gave a quick glance at Dirk.

The plump waitress appeared at the table. She plunked down a stein of beer without disturbing the head and plunged back into the crowd. Himmelmann picked up the stein. Silently he contemplated the sparkling bubbles. Dirk spoke to him.

"You are Gustav Himmelmann?"

The scientist nodded. He regarded Dirk and Sig with hooded eyes.

"I am Van," Dirk said. "My friend's name is Sig."

Himmelmann nodded curtly.

"You will agree, *Herr Professor*, that we do not want to be seen talking too long or too seriously together—here."

Himmelmann nodded, his face cloudy.

"With your permission, then, I will ask a few questions."

Again the scientist nodded. He began to sip his beer.

"Very good," Dirk said. "First, the jackpot question." He took a deep breath. "Is the work at Haigerloch an atomic project?"

Himmelmann looked up. His cold eyes met Dirk's.

"Yes," he said evenly.

Sig had been watching and listening closely. Involuntarily he let out a deep sigh. It startled him. He had expected Himmelmann's confirmation. But it was quite another matter to hear it spoken so bluntly.

"Who heads the Project?" Dirk asked.

"Professor Reichardt. Dieter Reichardt."

Dirk frowned. "The name is not familiar. What kind of a man is he?"

"As a scientist he is brilliant. Politically he is naïve," Himmelmann said. "His standard for measuring intelligence in his colleagues is the degree of *their* acceptance of *his* ideas." He smiled a strange, cynical smile, the corners of his mouth pulling down instead of up. "Brilliance in blinkers."

"How long have *you* been involved with the Haigerloch Project?" Dirk asked.

"I have been working in atomic research directly for many years," Himmelmann answered, his voice flat. He regarded Dirk steadily. "The Project here and now is the culmination of years of extensive research and experimentation at several locations elsewhere in Germany." He took a deep breath and continued in a monotone. "Early this year the crucial heavy-water atomic pile, the B-VIII, at the Kaiser Wilhelm Institute in Berlin, was dismantled and moved by truck convoy to Haigerloch. I came with the convoy. At the end of February, reconstruction of the pile was begun."

He paused.

"What's the status of the pile now?" Dirk asked. "How—how close are you to being successful?"

Himmelmann's mouth drew downward in his disturbing smile. "Successful?" he asked, bitterness making his voice harsh. "The efficiency of the B-VIII pile has already far surpassed all previous results." His bleak eyes bored into Dirk's. "A couple of days ago—in the early morning of March twenty-fourth, to be exact—the pile almost went critical. We now have all the answers. Next time—in a matter of weeks, perhaps days—we *will* be successful." He looked away. "There is still time to build the Führer's atomic bomb. . . . Our work has been intensified. Speeded up. On his orders . . ."

"Have you any—"

Suddenly Oskar banged his stein down on the table, sending droplets of amber liquid splashing over the rim.

"I don't care what you say," he stated in a loud, emphatic voice. "The switch on number two works one hell of a lot better since they fixed it."

Dirk looked at him. He took a deliberate pull on his beer and wiped the foam from his mouth with the back of his hand, as he had seen Oskar do.

"That's *your* opinion, Oskar," he drawled. *"I* say it is still an ass-buster."

Oskar looked after a pleasantly open-faced young man with a grease smudge on his forehead who had just passed by the table. "Gestapo informer," he said quietly. "Works in the yard. He thinks he is undercover. Otto made him weeks ago."

Dirk turned back to Himmelmann.

"What about security?" he asked. "How thorough is it?"

The German frowned. "It is strict," he said. "Strict and all-encompassing. Since Colonel Harbicht took over—even more rigid."

"Harbicht?"

"Gestapo. Head of the regional *Abteilung* in Stuttgart. He has only recently taken personal charge of security in the Hechingen-Haigerloch area."

Dirk and Sig exchanged glances.

"What's *he* like?" Dirk asked.

"Cunning. Hard. Totally ruthless. He has the no doubt well-earned reputation for missing nothing. Visual or verbal." Again the man's mouth contorted into his disquieting, downward smile. "Harbicht is that epitome of efficiency—a morally lobotomized professional Gestapo officer."

"Where exactly is the pile itself located?"

"In the bowels of the mountain. Blasted into a cliff. An old complex of wine caves long ago hewn out of the rock has been enlarged and adapted to hold the pile."

"Accessibility?"

Himmelmann looked straight at Dirk. "Accessibility? For you?" The corners of his mouth drew down. "Non-existent!"

Dirk returned the German's intense gaze. *"Herr Professor,"* he said. "One final question. Why are you helping us?"

For a moment Himmelmann stared at him. Then he lowered his head.

"Because—I am a coward," he said, bitterness grating in his voice. "I abhor the use to which my work is destined. I detest the life I lead. Yet—I am reluctant to give it up. I have not the courage to take action myself." He looked straight at Dirk. "I *know* the evil of Adolf Hitler and his National Socialists. They *cannot* be permitted to control this ultimate source of power and destruction. . . . You? You are—unknown. So, I will help you destroy the known. You can be no worse."

Dirk turned to Sig.

"Sig?"

Sig was scowling at his beer. He looked up.

"Herr Professor," he said, "you say that the Haigerloch Project is indeed concerned with atomic research. With an atomic bomb. . . . How can *we* be sure? How can you prove to us that this is so?"

Himmelmann glared at him. Then the crooked smile appeared.

"You are a scientist, I perceive, not merely a—saboteur." He filled the word with abysmal contempt. "You must be shown before you believe." He shrugged. "Very well. We will show you—Oskar and I."

Oskar glanced at the German physicist, his eyes suddenly dark with shock. He opened his mouth—but Himmelmann stopped him.

"You brought them here, Oskar," he said chillingly. "Surely you can have no objection to their seeing for themselves!"

The streets of Hechingen were dimly lit, obviously in an effort to save energy, but although not bustling with people, they were far from deserted.

Dirk was uneasy as they walked along the narrow sidewalk. He felt exposed. Any second he expected the imperious "Halt!" of an enemy patrol. He realized it was a reaction left over from earlier missions to occupied territories with their rigid restrictions, curfews and ever-present military patrols. But he was *not* in an occupied country now. He was a German in Germany among other Germans. At least that's what his papers said. He regretted having allowed Corny to talk him into carrying no arms. He'd have felt a lot more secure with the solid heft of a .38 under his left arm.

Oskar stopped at a house with a store on the ground floor. The naked metal skeleton of an awning was folded above the display window like the waiting arms of a praying mantis.

The small, half-timbered building with its steep roof and

wooden shutters did not distinguish itself from the other houses on the narrow, cobblestoned street. Like many of them, it too had a stack of firewood piled on the sidewalk against one wall. A couple of houses away, on one corner of a street junction, stood a pump topped with the figure of a girl in the national dress of the Schwäbische Alb. A massive stone horse trough squatted before it. Empty.

Oskar stepped up to the door. Heavy curtains were drawn across the store window next to it, but there was obviously light behind them. A cardboard sign taped to the inside of the glass read: ANNA WEBER, NÄHERIN.

Oskar knocked loudly, opened the door and entered, followed by the others.

As the sign had indicated, it was a seamstress shop. Several racks held dresses, skirts and coats in various stages of repair. Other clothing lay piled on chairs and a wooden bench.

Directly under the single, naked bulb hanging from the ceiling and providing the only light in the place stood a large, ancient sewing machine, treadle-operated, with a multi-drawer, drop-head cabinet. An elderly woman sat hunched over the machine, her right foot working the treadle with a steady rocking motion, sending the flywheel spinning as she carefully guided a piece of cloth under the bobbing needle. The clacking whirring of the machine filled the room.

Sig felt a sudden pang of nostalgia. His grandmother had had just such a sewing machine. Back in Zürich. She had been so proud of it. He still remembered the name on it. In gold. BURDICK. He wondered if this machine was also a Burdick. He remembered the soothing effect on him of the cozy whirring of his grandmother's sewing machine.

The woman looked up as the men entered, but did not interrupt her work. Oskar walked up to her.

"Anna," he said, "I have brought—friends."

The woman nodded.

"It is necessary that we go into the back room."

The woman looked up at them. Dark eyes set deep in her wrinkled face were old and joyless with too much knowledge. Slowly she nodded—before immersing herself in her work again.

Oskar turned to Dirk and Sig. "Anna is my sister, Gisela's

aunt," he said. "She is a seamstress. A good one." He looked around the cluttered room, his face grim. "In these days she is busy. Old clothing must be made to last a long time."

He walked to a rack loaded with clothing at the back of the room and moved it aside. Behind it was a closed door. As he reached for it, it suddenly opened.

In the doorway stood Gisela.

Her hair was tousled. In her hand she held a basin with soiled water and a sponge. She stopped short as she saw the four men, looking at them with a shocked expression on her face.

"Gisela!" Oskar exclaimed. "I did not know you would be here tonight."

"Tante Anna has much to do," Gisela said, her voice strongly defensive. "I must do what I can to help." She put the basin down on a stool and ran her hands through her hair in a vain effort to smooth it. Her eyes met Dirk's. She looked away.

"What do you want here?" she asked tonelessly. It was obvious she already knew the answer.

"It is—Wanda, Gisela," Oskar said softly. "The Herr Professor wishes to—to discuss her with our—with Otto's friends."

Gisela looked resentful.

"You should not have brought them here," she said. "In a few days—it will be all over." She glared at Dirk and Sig. "Now—when they are caught—they will give us all away!"

Oskar looked at the defiant young girl. "Gisela—" he said.

She tossed her head. "I cannot stop you," she said. She stood aside.

Oskar turned to the men, his set face grim and pale. He nodded curtly—and entered the room. Dirk and Sig and Himmelmann followed close behind.

The room was small and they saw the bed at once—and the figure hunched upon it. They stopped dead.

It was a girl. Eighteen? Or a woman. Forty-eight? It was impossible to tell. . . .

She was wearing a flimsy robe. When she saw the strangers enter, she shrank into the corner of her bed against the wall, drawing her legs up, her hollow, dark eyes fixed on them with maniacal dread. Every inch of visible flesh was inflamed, festering with weeping sores. An infected eruption on one cheek was oozing pus. The hair on her scalp had come out in great tufts;

her eyebrows and lashes were reduced to a few strands. She drew her cracked lips back in a snarl of terror, exposing bleeding, ulcerous gums. Then she moaned: a soft, mewing sound of abject fear.

Dirk and Sig stood transfixed.

"My—God!" Sig whispered. His flesh crawled. "Oh—my dear God . . . "

"Do you recognize it, Herr Scientist?" Himmelmann asked. "Does it look familiar to you? The effects of atomic radiation?"

Sig wrenched his eyes from the cowering girl. He stared at Himmelmann.

"She—*she* was at—Haigerloch?" he asked in a stunned whisper. "There was—an accident?"

The corners of Himmelmann's mouth drew down. "Accident?" he said bitterly. "Not exactly. What you see is the work of our Nazi science. The result of a laboratory experiment. One dosage of gamma rays. Fourteen hundred Roentgen. With a dosage of beta rays thrown in for good measure."

"Dear—God!"

Sig turned back to the trembling girl on the bed. He was once again aware of the others in the room. And the smell. The pungent-sweet odor of decaying flesh. It burned his nostrils.

He heard Oskar's voice from far away.

"Her name is Wanda. She is a Polish Jew." His voice was dead. "She—she was part of a medical experiment carried out under the Applied War Research program. An experimental program spawned by the Section R experiments at Dachau Concentration Camp. The chief, Dr. Sigmund Rascher, used the camp inmates for his—purposes. Wanda is—"

Suddenly Gisela interrupted.

"No, Onkel Oskar! If they must know—let *me* tell them. Let them know the full story." She stepped close to the cowering girl on the bed, reached out and touched her reassuringly. Then she faced the men, her eyes boring into Dirk's and Sig's. "You will wish to know, will you not," she said bitterly, "so you may judge? Very well. You *shall* know. Everything Otto learned and told to me." There was a sudden catch in her voice. She glared at the two, her eyes unnaturally bright. For a brief moment she clamped her teeth together tightly.

"Dr. Rascher—and Nini, his wife. So pretty. I have seen pictures of her. In the *Illustrierte."* She spoke rapidly, defiantly. *"They* may be no longer. But their spirit—and their work at Dachau—goes on. . . . The low-pressure chambers that were meant to test how much an unprotected human being could stand flying at high altitudes. They may no longer be used for experimentation—but as execution chambers. But *then* the human guinea pigs were subjected to an ever-increasing vacuum until they screamed and tore their hair out to relieve the excruciating pressure in their heads; until they beat the walls, lacerated and ripped their own flesh with their nails; shrieked until their lungs burst. Now such experiments are no longer needed. Only executions. Exterminations. In a manner to amuse and distract the SS guards . . ."

She stopped. She gave a small sob. Tears glistened in her eyes.

"For Wanda—for Wanda all that might have been a blessing," she whispered.

"Gisela. *Liebchen,"* Oskar said gently, with deep concern. "You do not have to—"

"Yes, Onkel Oskar," the girl flared at him. "Yes! I do! They must know *why* Otto and you are willing to—to—" She glanced at Wanda. "Are willing to betray your own . . ."

Oskar sighed. He looked down. Gisela glared at Dirk and Sig, her face flushed.

"I will tell you about Wanda," she said. "I will tell you how she came to be—like this. . . . She is seventeen. And she will die now. Today. The day after—"

Sig started. He glanced at the girl still crouched in terror on the bed. He scowled at Gisela. She met his gaze.

"She will not understand us," she said, her voice flat. "She speaks Polish. Even if she spoke German—she would not understand. They made certain of that. They were experimenting at Dachau with the effects of cold. Of freezing. It had to do with air crews downed in Arctic waters. Wanda had just arrived at the camp with her family—her father, her mother and her younger brother—when such an experiment began. Her father was chosen. He and others were kept in icy water until they lost consciousness. And then followed the experiments to revive them. If they could be revived at all. With Wanda's father, they tried body contact. They tried to revive his poor, frozen body and mind by placing a warm, naked woman beside him. A prisoner from the camp. First one woman. Then two. Or three. And they wanted to discover if sexual stirrings would speed up the process. Or their absence slow it. So, wherever possible, they used members of the family. Wanda was chosen. Seventeen-year-old Wanda. She watched her father being frozen nearly to death. She heard his screams of agony. She was placed naked next to his icy body. She. And a stranger. And her mother. And she was ordered to try to stimulate her father sexually. . . . It was while they were watching *her* reactions that someone had the ingenious idea of using her in an experiment to determine the stages in the disintegration of a human mind. How much could it take? How long? . . .

"Her father was still alive—although nothing but a mass of pain. They used him to demonstrate to Wanda the expediency of the crematorium procedures. She watched while they killed him with their efficient *Genickschuss*—the neck shot which brought instant death. They made him kneel. They put a gun to the nape of his neck. With one shot they severed his spinal cord. They trussed his feet together and hung him upside down from a meat hook. They slit open his jugular vein and drained him of blood. Oh, it was very efficient. That way the empty body would burn a lot faster. In fact, two bodies could be crammed into the same oven at one time. They took their huge iron tongs and placed a prong in each of her father's ears—and clamped them tight. And she watched and walked with them while they dragged his thin body to the ovens. She was there as they tore out his gold-filled teeth—and as they stuffed the mutilated remains into the oven, using their blunt wooden poles to cram another corpse in beside him. And she heard the flames roar up. Saw the sooty, oily smoke spew from the chimney. . . .

"And they watched her as her mind began to crumble. . . . But—there was a long way to go. Still. It was only the beginning. . . .

"They forced her . . . it can only be imagined by what tortures . . . to perform, herself, all the horrors she had witnessed. First —on her own little brother. . . . Killed him . . . drained him . . . burned him . . . Then—on her mother. And they observed clinically the collapse of her mind. And made notes for articles in their scientific journals. . . ."

She stopped, brushed the tears from her eyes. Sig was staring at her incredulously.

"She is telling you the truth," Himmelmann said suddenly. "I have seen those journals. Those reports. Copies of them accompanied the girl when she was sent to the Project for the radiation test." He spoke in a low, dead voice.

"Oh, they were not through with Wanda yet," Gisela said. "They had killed her mind. Her tears had stopped coming. Her sobs had died away. She saw—without seeing. Heard—without hearing. Lived—without living. She'd entered into her own peculiar madness that made it possible for her to stay alive. But her body was still physically strong and healthy. They had seen to that. The breaking of her mind had to be accomplished by mental torture alone. Malnutrition or any other irrelevant weakness could not be allowed to interfere with the experiment. That would not have been—*scientific.*" Gisela spat out the word. "Oh, yes. They kept her well fed throughout her ordeal. . . .

"So, when they needed a healthy specimen for their radiation test, Wanda was the perfect subject. There had already been complaints that the majority of the concentration-camp inmates sent for medical experiments were useless. Their health could not be compared to that of the German people—to *ours* —for whose benefit the experiments were being conducted. But Wanda was a fine specimen. And—they subjected her to their radiation test. . . ."

Gisela's tears could no longer be contained, and she let them flow freely down her cheeks. She looked at the girl drawn up unto herself, cowering uncomprehending on the bed.

"And they—they observed her. And made their notes." She turned back to Sig and Dirk. She bit her lip and gulped a deep breath.

"And when they had observed enough, when her body too had been burned out, they discarded her. They packed her into an old *Sonderkraftwagen*—an S-truck—with a load of others, and sent her on her way to Dachau to join her family in the ovens. . . ."

Dirk felt his own sanity slipping as he listened. He knew he had to get a grip on something real or be lost. Something that was comprehensible to his horror-scourged mind.

"S-trucks?" he said. Was that his voice? He turned to Oskar. He could not bear to look at Gisela. "I don't know what S-trucks are."

"They are special trucks," Oskar said, his voice heavy. "Death trucks. They were built on direct orders of Himmler, already back in 1942. They are rigged so that the exhaust gas from the truck is funneled into the sealed cargo space. Fifteen, twenty prisoners can be crammed in. The carbon monoxide—" He stopped. He took a deep breath. "The ten or fifteen minutes' ride to the crematorium would be enough to—to kill the prisoners. The trucks were used mostly for women and children. There are still some of them in use. . . ."

"But how?" Dirk asked. "How did she—escape?"

It was Gisela who answered.

"Wanda was one of the last to be pushed into the truck," she said tonelessly. "Next to her was a large woman—panic-stricken. When the guards slammed the doors shut, this woman tried to stop their closing with her bare hands. One hand was caught and horribly mangled. But, as a result, the doors didn't close completely; a narrow crack remained. The woman screamed when her hand was crushed. A scream of agony—which changed to terror when the gas began to seep in. Wanda knew about screams. How they changed as the stimuli tearing them forth changed. The instinct to keep alive still existed in her mutilated mind. She cupped her hands over the narrow crack held open by the woman's mangled hand. And she breathed. The poisoned air made her sick. But she remained conscious, her face covered with a foul mixture of her own vomit and a dying stranger's blood. . . .

"Instead of taking the bodies to the overworked crematorium at Dachau, they took them to a lime pit in the forest. When they dumped them from the truck, Wanda was half-conscious. But she was alive. She did not move. She lay motionless among the corpses. When darkness came, some of the bodies were still unburied in the mass grave—and she crawled away into the wood—into the night. . . ."

"Otto found her," Oskar said quietly. "He speaks—he spoke a little Polish. He pieced together her story. He brought her here."

"We—we could not let her die alone," Gisela said. "We had

to try to help her through her last few days." She fell silent. Spent.

Dirk looked at Gisela. Otto's sister. The girl who had called on her uncle to turn him and Sig over to the police. The girl who cried in outrage and pity at the fate of a stranger and risked her own safety to minister to that stranger. The girl whose irresolute hands held the future of their mission—and their own—

And with sudden lucidity he knew what he had to do.

His face grew hard. "I hear you, Gisela," he said quietly. "I see your tears. But are they not the tears of a crocodile?"

Gisela stared at him in shocked incomprehension.

"Your tears, Gisela, on your cheeks even now. Like the tears a crocodile cries over its prey."

The girl's face flushed. Her lips trembled in an effort to speak.

"Take another good look at the abomination on that bed," Dirk said coldly. "Are you any better than the swine who did this to her?"

Gisela started to tremble. Her eyes were riveted on Dirk. The others in the room stood motionless, in shocked silence.

"You see their work!" He pointed at the girl on the bed. "There! *And you want it to go on. . . .*"

"No! . . . I . . . I—do—not. . . ." Gisela forced out the words. *"I—do—not!"*

"Yet you would deliver *us* into their hands," Dirk said vehemently.

"I—"

"You would stop us from destroying this evil. From ridding your country of this Nazi cancer you profess to abhor!"

"No! I—I—"

"You have a choice to make, Gisela. Now!" Again his finger aimed straight at Wanda. *"This*—or *us!"*

"Oh, God . . ." Gisela sobbed.

"Make up your mind. Your brother did. He gave his life. Your uncle is with *us.* What about *you?* Do you still want him to hand us over to *them?"*

"NO!"

"Then you will help? Help as Otto helped? Like your uncle?"

"I—"

She stopped. With an enormous effort, she regained control of herself. Her dark, terrible eyes bored into Dirk's.

"Yes . . . May God damn you! *Yes!*"

She gave a sudden sob—and threw herself into her uncle's arms.

Sig stared at Dirk. He understood fully what his partner had done. It was imperative to secure the girl's cooperation. They must be certain of her—even if something happened to her uncle. But could he, Sig, have done what Dirk just had?

He felt chilled to the marrow of his bones. The glimpse of hell they had been shown had made one thing monstrously clear.

The Haigerloch Project was in fact atomic.

21

"Herein!"

Standartenführer Werner Harbicht barked the order. He sat ramrod stiff behind his massive desk, glowering at the door. It was promptly opened and his aide, Obersturmführer Rauner, pushed a man into the room.

He was a civilian. A farmer. He stumbled—caught himself and stood uncertainly in the middle of the room, nervously clutching his grimy cap in big, callused hands, close-set eyes in a waxen face watching Harbicht with apprehension. Rauner closed the door behind him with a thud of finality and silently took up position beside it.

Harbicht glanced at the clock on his desk. It was precisely 0800 hours. Monday, March 26. He smiled inwardly. Rauner was learning to be punctual.

Deliberately he moved a file folder in front of him. He opened it. He began to study it, frowning. He was gratifyingly aware of the effect he was creating in the man standing in front of him. The man had been brought to Hechingen the night before. On orders from Harbicht, he had been treated coldly, roughly—and given no reason for his arrest and detention. His belongings, his suspenders, his shoelaces had been taken from him. He had undergone a humiliating search, and he had been kept in a bare, brightly lit cell overnight with nothing to eat. It was standard procedure to soften up a suspect before interrogation.

Harbicht took his time. The longer he could keep the man uncertain, giving his imagination ample opportunity to conjure up countless dark fears, the easier it would be to make him talk.

Finally Harbicht looked up, his face stern.

"You are Ortsbauernführer Gerhard Eichler from Langen-winkel?" he asked curtly.

Eichler started. He bobbed his head eagerly. *"Zu Befehl, Herr Standartenführer!"* he croaked subserviently. "At your orders! I—"

"Just answer when you are spoken to."

Eichler cringed. Harbicht consulted the file.

"During the night of the twenty-third/twenty-fourth you issued special rations to two men in your home." He looked up, fixing Eichler with a penetrating, hostile gaze. "Two enemies of the Reich!"

Eichler started convulsively. The last shade of color drained from his pasty face, leaving it a sickly gray. His legs began to tremble.

"No, *Herr Standartenführer!*" he cried, terror in his voice. "No, I—"

"Did you or did you not give food to two men?" Harbicht shouted at him.

"Yes, but the—"

"Silence!"

Eichler froze in mid-word. Horrified, he stared at Harbicht. The officer contemplated him coldly.

"You do not deny that you gave supplies to the two enemy saboteurs?" he asked. The tone of his voice was distant, yet murderous.

"I—I did not—I ha-had no . . . I—" Eichler stammered in terrified confusion.

"The men *were* there?"

"Yes, but—"

"You heard the firefight with the enemy patrol that brought them across the river?"

"I—I did. I went—"

"You *knew* who the two men were!"

"No!" Eichler was shaking uncontrollably. "No—I—"

"You were expecting them!"

"No! Please, *Herr Standartenführer. Please!* It was nothing like that!" He was wringing his cap in sweaty hands. *"Please . . ."*

Harbicht sat back in his chair. "Perhaps you had better tell me the whole story, Eichler," he said. "Every detail of it. Then we shall be able to determine if you are going to—eh, survive this little interrogation—a matter that is still not absolutely certain. . . ."

Eichler gaped at him, speechless.

"*Now,* Eichler!" Harbicht snapped impatiently. "I am waiting."

And Gerhard Eichler, Ortsbauernführer of Langenwinkel, talked. Talked as if his life depended on it. He was certain it did. . . .

Standartenführer Werner Harbicht felt cheated. The farmer Eichler had been no contest at all. Harbicht enjoyed the process of breaking a man's will. He liked the feeling of power it gave him. But Eichler had offered no such pleasure. He had talked. At once. He had poured out every detail of his sordid little escapade into the black market. The man was nothing but a stupid, avaricious hog. Beneath contempt.

Harbicht had had to cut through the feverish flow of words to get the few facts of any value. Eichler had been so intent on playing up his own alertness and patriotism that his account of his exploits that fateful night overflowed the borders of fact.

His description of the two men had been familiar. Useless. The men were—average. Looked just like native-born Germans. Harbicht felt a twinge of annoyance. Ridiculous. What does a native-born German look like? He could be anything from pure Aryan to Jewish. But the idiot *had* been able to corroborate some information he already possessed. The strangers spoke German. Fluently. They traveled on bicycles—and now he had a detailed description of one of those. And he *had* learned one important new fact. One of the men had a scar. A large, recent scar running across his left elbow. That was something. He felt excited as he put together the information from Eichler with what he'd learned from the non-com at the Lahr roadblock. He was beginning to form a real picture of his adversaries, and he was convinced they were enemy infiltrators. Two young men, well built, Nordic features. One a foreign worker, the other with a deep scar on his left arm; their papers in good order. Riding bicycles, carrying rucksacks—and headed for Hechingen!

He felt closer to his quarry as he pictured them. He thought of them almost with affection. He would make it impossible for them to do any damage to the Project—and they would provide him with an exciting chase. . . .

Eichler . . .

Harbicht frowned. His first impulse had been to have the man taken through the streets of the town. Eichler might have spotted the suspects. But that worked both ways. *They* might just as easily spot Eichler—and realize the Gestapo was on their trail. They would take precautions. And Harbicht would lose the valuable advantage of surprise: the fact that the enemy agents had no idea how much he already knew about them. How close he was . . .

Meanwhile he would keep Eichler in detention. He would come in handy for positive identification at a later time.

Harbicht had no doubt that time would come soon.

22

Looking at the paper on the scarred wooden workbench before him, Dirk estimated he'd have to be on the air between ten and twelve minutes. It was too damned long. Especially since he'd have to stick around for another few minutes to receive instructions for a contact schedule from Corny.

He felt relatively secure. Oskar had been extremely helpful when it came down to picking a place from which to transmit in reasonable safety. The Storp house was out, of course. Had to remain their safe house. And so was Anna's shop. He needed a place with a power source, a place where he could rig an antenna that wouldn't stick out like Gable's ears—and one he could get in and out of before being tracked down by the monitoring trucks that were sure to get on to him.

The shack on the fringe area of the railroad hump switching yard seemed made for the job. A lot of rubble and damaged equipment lay strewn about, and his rig would not stand out. Moreover, the shack had power—having once been used as a minor-repair shed.

Oskar had given him Otto Storp's yard pass and his bike, and he'd had no trouble at all entering the work area. The transmitter was hidden in a burlap sack wrapped up in a heavy work jacket, sharing the space with a battered lunchbox, the whole load strapped to his bike. No one had paid it the slightest attention.

They had decided that Dirk should go alone. He'd followed Oskar to the yard and through the checkpoint—and then taken off for the shack by himself. Sig had stayed with

Gisela. No reason to put all your aces on the line—however slight the risk.

The shack had turned out to be ideal. Isolated. Oskar had said that the only yardmen likely to come around would be foreign workers. All he had to do was shout at them in German to get the hell away and they'd obey. He had placed his bicycle on the ground among the rubble. It would be less noticeable from a distance that way. No reason to invite visitors.

It really had been a milk-run mission. They had obtained the information Corny wanted. In spades. And they had managed to get it without even raising an eyebrow of suspicion. He felt pleased with himself.

But—even so—he'd like to make his report as concise and brief as he could and be on the air as short a time as possible. No reason to tempt fate—however smiling a face she might present.

He reread the clear message. And again. It was the first transmission he would be sending to Corny and he had a hell of a lot to say. But there had to be something he could cut.

ARRIVED STOP OTTO DEAD STOP WORKING
WITH SUB STOP HIMMELMANN CONTACTED
STOP

Already cut to the damn bone. Nothing there. He studied the block letters he'd scribbled. There was the information from Himmelmann about the B-VIII pile being moved from Berlin during February and set up in Haigerloch; the uranium and heavy-water shipments from Stadtilm and other sites; the near-success in making the pile self-sustaining, with final success a virtual certainty. . . . There were the decrees by the top Nazis protecting atomic scientists, lending paramount importance to the Project; the discovery of Wanda—and Sig's scientific mumbo-jumbo proving atomic radiation. . . .

He frowned at the next passage:

REACTOR LOCATION IN DEEP MOUNTAIN
CAVES VIRTUALLY IMPENETRABLE STOP
SINGLE REPEAT SINGLE HEAVILY GUARDED
ENTRANCE—

He crossed out REPEAT SINGLE.

> —COMPLEX HOUSES THREE THOUSAND
> TECHNICIANS AND WORKERS STOP MANY
> GUARDS STOP—

He crossed out TECHNICIANS AND.

> —PROJECT DEFINITELY ATOMIC STOP
> SUCCESS IMMINENT STOP END MESSAGE
> VAN G-8

He contemplated the last sentences. Not strictly necessary. But sure as hell dramatic. Make Corny jump for that scrambler phone to Washington. What the hell. He'd leave it in.

It was time.

He opened one of the cracked, grimy windows. It faced a water tower on the far side of a service road running across the tracks and a semaphore signal on the shack side. He'd already decided to string his antenna wire from the window to the signal post. It would blend in with the other wires. As soon as that was done he'd encipher his message, send the damn thing —and get the hell out.

He dropped the antenna wire through the window and walked out of the shack. . . .

Helmut Zander put the old binoculars to his eyes. Yes, the *Scheisskerl*—the shitbum—was finally coming out of the shack again. He saw him look around and then walk to the far side and disappear around the corner. Helmut took the binoculars down in annoyance and resentment. He hated those damned foreign workers. A shiftless, untrustworthy mob they were. That one down there by the shack near Semaphore Signal #17 was typical. Shirking work. *Verdammter Faulenzer!*—damned slacker!

He'd seen the man arrive some time before—and had watched him through his binoculars. It was a slow time at his post up in the tower of Switching Station IV. It was always slow late in the afternoon—before shift break. The men had completed most of the switching lists by then. The yardman down there—without doubt a damned foreigner—had come pushing a bicycle with a sack strapped to the handlebars. Tools? He'd watched him unstrap the sack and lay his bicycle down among the debris at the shack. Typical. A German would have leaned it against the wall. The orderly way of doing it. And he'd watched the man go into the shack.

That was quite a while ago. What the devil was he doing in there? As if he didn't know. The damned, no-good *Ausländer*. Loafing, of course! Instead of doing an honest day's work for his keep. Rabble. That's what they were. Malingering rabble . . .

He glanced at his binoculars. They gave him something to do during the dull periods on station. They had been his father's. An old pair. French Army Issue. His father had brought them back after World War I. He sighed. The bitter lines around his mouth deepened. At least his father had brought back *something*. He himself had been less fortunate. He had left a leg.

He felt trapped sitting up in the switching station tower. It was so damned difficult to climb the steep ladder with his crutches that, once up there, he stayed until relieved. He hated to be a cripple.

He raised the binoculars and surveyed the shack. He had a clear view of it—beyond the salvage storage shed below him on the right, flanking the terminal sidings on the left, where the damaged rolling stock had been collected. The man was out of sight, but his bike was still lying there in the rubble. A thought suddenly struck him. The bastard probably hid the bike that way so it would be less noticeable; so a German foreman wouldn't spot it—while *he* took it easy. Flagrant loafing. Damned foreigner . . . Foreigners and cripples, that's who. That's who ran the *verschissene* railroad yard these days.

That worthless stiff down there. He should not be allowed to get away with it, dammit! Zander smiled a vindictive little smile. He'd cook his damned foreign-ass goose!

He picked up the direct line to the Central Control Tower and cranked the handle vigorously. He would bring the matter up with Günther. It was *his* responsibility, that foreign rabble. A nice cushy office job, Günther had. They called him by a nickname. *Raupe*—the caterpillar—because he'd gotten where he was by crawling.

"Günther," he said into the mouthpiece, his voice oily. *"Hier Helmut."* He paused conspiratorially. *"Hör mal*—listen. I just thought I'd let you know. Whatever is wrong with Semaphore Seventeen down by the watering tower—don't look for it to be finished for a long time."

He listened.

"What am I talking about? *Mensch*—I'm talking about that foreign bum you sent down to fix it. The lazy stiff is laying down on the job. He has even tried to cover his criminal idling. Hidden his damned bicycle in the rubbish. Didn't count on me and my binoculars, though!"

He listened again. He frowned.

"Do as you damned well please, Günther," he said acridly. "I could not care less. If you say there is no one there—then there is no one there. That must be the bastard I am watching!"

He slammed the receiver down.

He looked through the binoculars. The man was still behind the shack. Or he had gone back in. To snooze, no doubt . . .

Angrily he banged the binoculars down on his desk.

Günther, the *Raupe*, bit his lip. What was all *that* about a foreign worker loafing on the job? At Semaphore 17? He remembered no trouble with that signal. Or the watering tower. He'd sent nobody to fix anything. He frowned. He pulled a sheaf of work orders from a rusty nail and leafed through them. Nothing.

Could the General Yardmaster himself have dispatched someone? Not likely. Still—*if* he had, it might not be a bad idea to show him that he, Günther, was alert to the fact. Make him look good. . . .

Yardmaster Schindler was irritated. That little ass-kisser Günther had come sniveling to him with some cock-and-bull story about a foreign worker loafing on the job. Good God! Didn't they all? He'd sent the idiot packing, of course. He had more important things to worry about. That Gestapo officer who'd just showed up in Hechingen had insisted that security throughout the yard be doubled. Impossible. He could not play police and run the yard at the same time. He deeply resented the Gestapo meddling in yard affairs. He glanced at an official order lying on his desk, arrived only that morning. "Immediate reports are to be made of anything unusual," it read. Over the signature "Harbicht."

He suddenly smiled.

So the Herr Standartenführer Harbicht wanted strict security. Immediate notification of anything out of the ordinary.

Schon gut!—Very well! Perhaps *he* would like to take care of the mysterious, malingering foreign worker and his hidden bicycle at Semaphore 17!

He turned to his assistant.

"Get me the Gestapo," he said.

Harbicht slammed the receiver down.

"Rauner!" he bellowed as he hurriedly shrugged into his uniform jacket. *"Rauner!"*

The door burst open and the startled Obersturmführer came rushing in. Harbicht at once barked at him.

"I want two trucks. Personnel carriers. Twenty men. With *Schmeissers! Sofort!*—At once!" He strapped on his belt, began to check his Walther automatic. "You take one of them. I'll take the other. And get that—peasant Eichler. Bring him along."

"Jawohl, Herr Standartenführer. Where—"

"The railroad yard," Harbicht snapped. "The hump switching yard. I'll brief you. Get that detail together! *Los!"*

"Jawohl!"

Rauner left at a run.

By God! A foreigner acting furtively! A hidden bicycle! By God! His case could be breaking even sooner than he thought.

Harbicht hurried from the office. . . .

There he was. Going back into the shack. What the hell was he up to? Goddamned foreign bastard. Likely as not a Frenchman. Ought to be strung up for slowing up important work for the Reich. Zander could taste the gall of frustration in the back of his mouth. There was nothing he could do about it. . . .

He was just about to put his binoculars down when he stiffened in surprise.

Careening down the service road came a military truck. It skidded to a gravel-spurting stop at the watering tower, and a bunch of SS troops armed with Schmeisser machine pistols leaped to the ground, quickly fanning out to cover the tower and the signal.

Hardly had he recovered from his astonishment when he heard a second truck screeching to a halt on the service road below, directly in front of his tower station. He leaned out to look down. He could hear the shouted orders as armed SS troops tumbled from the truck and cautiously started to approach the old storage sheds.

He was thunderstruck.

Günther?

All *that* to capture a malingering foreign worker?

He glued the binoculars to his eyes. This he did not want to miss. . . .

He trained his sight on the shack—just in time to see the loafer duck out of the door and sprint for the cluster of damaged rolling stock on the sidings. He was carrying his burlap sack.

He leaned out the window.

"Hello!" he shouted. "Hello!" But the SS soldiers were already too far away. Only one man stood at the truck below. Looked to be a civilian. "Hello!" he called. "At the truck! He's over there! At the cars! *Over there! . . .*"

Eichler was apprehensive. All right—frightened. They'd hauled him out of his cell, pushed him into a truck and taken him on a wild ride to a railroad yard. The Obersturmführer had ordered him to stay put at the truck and not move until they came for him. What was it all about? And now some excited fool was shouting at him from a tower on metal stilts: *He's over there!*

Who? Over where?

Eichler turned to look toward the damaged railroad cars. He was able to see down the aisles between them. And suddenly he saw him. In the distance.

Recognition knifed through him.

It was one of the black-marketeers! The one who had said he served with Konrad. Who said he had been Konrad's friend! Lies! Lies he had told them. Lies about Konrad. Black rage roared in his ears. It was all *his* fault, damn him to hell! All this trouble he, Eichler, was in . . . *Get him!*

He looked around for the Obersturmführer and his men. They were already over by the sheds.

He ran toward the group of railroad cars. He ran around them, hoping to alert the soldiers from the other truck.

"Hierher!" he shouted hoarsely. "Over here!"

Harbicht's SS men were just approaching a broken-down shack.

Suddenly a man screaming something unintelligible came running around a railroad car in the distance, flailing his arms.

Even as Harbicht shouted "Don't shoot!" the soldiers opened fire.

The slugs from their machine pistols tore into Eichler, spinning him around, cutting him nearly in half.

He was dead before he hit the ground. . . .

Helmut Zander was shocked to the core. He stared in uncomprehending horror at the body sprawled grotesquely below.

He looked toward the round-up of rolling stock on the running-repair sidings. He could see nothing.

He picked up his binoculars. He searched among the cars. There!

Climbing into a gutted boxcar, hauling his sack with him, was the *Ausländer!*

He started to shout. He stopped. There was no one near enough to hear him.

He glanced at his stump. He cursed. He would never be able to get down in time.

He looked around.

Somehow. Somehow he had to let them know what he had seen. . . .

Dirk gulped air in short, painful breaths. His chest ached like hell. He was stunned. What had gone wrong? Had the others been caught? Oskar? Given the show away? Gisela? . . . He rejected it. Anyway—it was not important now. Only one thing. That he get away.

He glanced around the burned-out boxcar. There were gaping holes in both sides. Obviously he could not stay. It would be only a matter of minutes. . . .

His thoughts were interrupted by a rumbling sound. A train.

Cautiously he peeked out. The boxcar was standing on a siding next to a working track. A train approaching from the terminal was heading out of the yard. Flatcars loaded with damaged armor on the way to be repaired. Probably in Stuttgart. It would pass right by his boxcar.

He estimated the distance between the siding and the track; the speed of the oncoming train. A fleeting thought went back to Rosenfeld and his damned obstacle course. Bless him! It was possible. Just barely.

He had no choice.

The locomotive passed him, hissing and laboring to gather steam and speed.

The first few cars lumbered by.

He took a good grip on his sack with his right hand.

Now!

He jumped.

He landed heavily on the rear end of a flatcar. The jar rattled his teeth. Desperately he grabbed hold with his free left hand. And felt himself slipping. Pain seared his injured arm. He grabbed hold with the other hand just in time to keep himself from falling between the cars to the tracks below. As he did, the heavy sack hit the edge of the car and was bounced from his grip, plummeting down. In despair he saw it hit the rail. Saw the wheel of the following car roll over it, crushing the transmitter inside, mashing it into junk. . . .

He hauled himself up onto the flatcar.

He hid under a chained-down tank that was badly scorched and had both tracks missing. . . .

Helmut Zander desperately cranked the handle on his telephone. "Hello!" he shouted into the mouthpiece. "Hello! *Verdammt nochmal!*—Dammit! Answer! Answer!" But the phone remained dead. Where the hell was Günther? Where the hell was everybody? Taking in the show?

He'd seen the lousy foreigner jump onto the moving transport. He'd seen him clear as day through his binoculars. He'd seen him drop his sack. He had to tell somebody!

He turned the handle vehemently. Goddamn it! Answer!

He could reach no one.

He hobbled to the ladder and looked down. He had to get to someone. He cursed his missing leg. But it was the only way. He'd have to get down the damn ladder as quickly as possible.

He grabbed his crutches and threw them out the door to the ground below. He hopped to the ladder, turned his back to it and made an awkward, one-legged hop down the first rung. He clung to the handrail. Precariously, as quickly as he could, he hopped down, one rung at a time. . . .

Halfway. He looked down. The sweat was dripping from his forehead into his eyes. His hands were getting slippery. His foot ached.

Two more rungs . . .

Hurry.

Suddenly—in his haste—his foot slipped. He tried to hold himself upright with his sweaty hands, but he could not get a firm grip. His leg slid in between two rungs of the iron ladder. He felt himself falling backward. The leg bone—the tibia— snapped with an audible crack—and he fell heavily to the ground at the foot of the ladder.

He blacked out.

Harbicht was cold with fury. He'd had his prey within his grasp—and the man had slipped through his fingers. He found it difficult to excuse himself. In his mind he cast about for reasons. Why? Where had he made the mistake that cost him his quarry? Deliberately he suppressed those thoughts. For now.

He fingered the crushed and shattered pieces that once had been a sophisticated radio transmitter. American make. It was now utterly useless for anything except corroboration that the man in the railroad yard had indeed been an enemy saboteur. Undoubtedly one of the two agents who, he was now certain, had infiltrated near Langenwinkel. His men had found a yard-man, a switching operator, lying unconscious at the bottom of a ladder to a tower station, his one leg broken.

This man had given them a description of the fugitive that tallied with the one given by the farmer Eichler, the god-damned fool. . . . The yardman had also told them how the saboteur had left the area, and had steered them to the spot where the radio had been dropped.

Darkly he contemplated a bit of twisted and flattened metal from the *Schwarzsender*—the illegal radio. It was so completely smashed there was no way even to guess what it had once looked like.

He had a sudden twinge of uneasiness. He did not like the feeling at all. It was totally unfamiliar. The two enemy agents should not have been able to get this far. Certainly they should have been apprehended by now. Had he—underestimated them? It could not be allowed. Were they—his betters? It was unthinkable. . . .

Nonetheless, he would double his efforts to catch them.

Dirk watched the Storp house from the little park across the street. He was deeply shaken. His arm hurt. As soon as he had cleared the railroad switching-yard area, he had dropped off the train and made his way back to town.

There had been no activity at all at the house. No light showed through the blackout curtains. There was no way of telling if everything was okay—or if the place was crawling with Gestapo men. . . .

What had gone wrong?

They had come for *him.* Obviously. They had known *where* he was. *What* he was doing.

How?

The enormity of the whole thing struck him.

A couple of hours before, he had been supremely confident that their presence in the town was known to absolutely no one except Oskar and Gisela—and Himmelmann.

Now . . .

Was it Himmelmann?

Had they been betrayed?

He closed his eyes. Tightly. He had agonized over the same bleak puzzle again and again. There was no ready answer.

The answer lay waiting in the little one-story house across the street.

He would have to seek it there.

23

Dirk reached for the ornate brass handle on the door.

He hesitated.

If his friends were there, the door would be unlocked. It always was.

He pressed down the handle. The door opened.

The hallway beyond was pitch dark. For a moment he listened. He could hear nothing.

He stepped into the hall.

Suddenly two strong arms grabbed him from behind, pinning his arms to his side, making him gasp. He heard the door slam shut behind him.

Instantly, as he had been taught, he bent his knees and threw himself forward in an attempt to dislodge his assailant and send him flying over his head. But the man behind him crouched down with him, giving him no leverage. The iron bear-hug held.

Suddenly the light in the hallway blazed on—and Dirk found himself staring into the black-holed muzzle of a gun.

Almost at once the crushing grip around his chest relaxed. In a glance Dirk took in the scene.

Before him stood Sig, Oskar's Luger trained at his gut. At the light switch stood Gisela, eyes wide with alarm. Behind him stood Oskar, astonishment on his face. For a moment there was stunned silence. Then Dirk said dryly:

"Some welcome!" He looked at Sig. "You can put the gun away, Siggy baby. We're on the same side."

Sig lowered the gun. He stared at Dirk.

"Jesus Christ," he said fervently, "am I glad to see you! We —we thought—" He looked at Oskar. "We were told they killed a man at the railroad yard. We thought—"

"Eichler," Dirk said, his face grim. "The poor bastard got himself shot."

"Holy Jesus," Sig whispered.

Dirk took a deep breath. It felt good. He could feel the muscles in his shoulders and legs begin to tremble as the tension that had gripped them ebbed. He walked to a settee and sank down on it.

"To be honest with you, Sig," he said quietly, "I wasn't sure what—or whom—I'd be running into here. I—I thought they'd nabbed you." He looked at them, one at a time. "I sure am glad I was wrong."

He suddenly frowned.

"Shit!" he said heavily. "The radio. I—"

"We know," Sig said.

Dirk looked up in surprise. "Something sure as hell has gone wacky, Sig," he said worriedly. "I can't figure it. They knew just where I was. They—"

"No," Sig interrupted. "They didn't."

Dirk looked at him questioningly.

"It just—happened," Oskar said. "I heard about it at the yard. There was quite a commotion. A slimy little creature we call the *Raupe* was bragging that *he* started the whole thing. I was told they had found your radio. . . ."

"Did you get the message off?" Sig asked anxiously.

Dirk shook his head wearily. "Hell, no. Didn't even get the damned set warmed up."

Sig frowned. "Now that they have it, *they* can use it. Send false information."

Again Dirk shook his head. "I've got good news for you," he said ironically. "Along with the bad. The set is squashed. *Fini.* Flattened under the wheels of a railroad car. Nobody's going to transmit on it. Not they. Not we!"

Sig stared at him.

"Jesus!" he said. "That's right. How *do* we contact Corny?"

"We don't." Dirk sounded bitter. "We don't know who Otto's contact is in Stuttgart, or we could have tried him. And we sure as hell can't risk trying to buy the parts to build a new set. Not in this burg. Or anywhere else in the Fatherland, for that matter."

"They told me the town is sealed up," Oskar said. "Tight. Even I was questioned when I left the yard. That never happened before."

Dirk nodded slowly. He felt utterly weary. He looked at Sig.

"We're on our own, Siggy baby," he said evenly. "You and me."

Sig frowned. For a moment everyone was silent, each engrossed in his own gloomy thoughts.

"What the hell do we do?" Sig asked finally.

Dirk shrugged. "We lie low for a couple of days. Till the glow wears off the fun and games. Then—we try to get out. Back to our own lines. Back to Corny. And hope we won't be too late. . . ." He stood up. "Right now—I'm going to flake out. I'm beat. But good . . ."

He was lying on his bunk in the stuffy little basement room. He could not sleep. His mind was churning. They'd gotten the information. Vital information that should reach Washington at once. And no earthly way of getting it out . . . The whole fucking mission had caved in around their heads. It wasn't going to be easy to get out—and cross the lines. . . .

He tensed at a small sound at the door. Slowly, cautiously it was pushed open. In the doorway stood Gisela, a tray in her hands.

She looked at him uncertainly.

"I—I did not know if you would be asleep," she said, her voice low. "I did not want to disturb you." She held out the tray. "I made you some hot soup. It will be—comforting."

He smiled at her.

"You bet," he said. "Really hit the spot!"

Gisela looked puzzled. "You would like it, yes?" she asked.

"I'd like it, yes," he said. He sat up.

The girl brought the tray to him. He took the cup of steaming soup. He sipped.

"Terrific," he said. "Thank you, Gisela."

"Bitte," she said softly. "If you please."

He took another sip. The soup was damned good. And hot. It felt great. He looked closely at the girl, standing uncertainly at the bed. Flustered, she looked away. Nervously her fingers played with the ribbon on her dirndl blouse.

"Please," she whispered. "I—wish to say something."

Dirk remained silent. He just looked at her.

"You must know this," Gisela said earnestly. She searched his face. "I did not wish you and your friend harm. I—was afraid."

He started to speak, but she cut him off.

"No, please. You must hear me out." She drew a quick breath. "I knew what Otto and Onkel Oskar were doing. I knew how dangerous it was for them." Her words came tumbling out. "I knew. . . . And then Otto had his—accident." She gave a little sob, unaware of doing so. "I—I loved my brother. He was a good man. And—I love my uncle. I do not wish to see harm come to him."

She took a deep breath. She blinked her eyes to stem the gathering tears. Dirk watched her gravely.

"I did not wish for him to call the police," Gisela went on. "Even though I said it. I knew he would not do so. I said it only because I thought perhaps you might be frightened. And leave. And not make Onkel Oskar do dangerous things. He—he is all I have. I—"

Her voice broke.

"Gisela," Dirk said gently. "It doesn't—"

"No. You must listen to me," the girl implored, her huge eyes beseeching. "You must understand. I *do* want the men to be stopped who can do such horrible things as they did to Wanda. I do!"

The tears brimming in her eyes rolled down her cheeks. She seemed oblivious to them. "She is only seventeen. . . ."

She sobbed.

"And then—today, when Onkel Oskar told us—" She could not go on. Gently he reached out to her and pulled her down on the bed to sit beside him. He searched her lovely face, distraught and moist with tears.

"Gisela," he said softly. "It's all right. I do understand."

And he did. With sudden clarity he understood the agonizing fears she lived with day and night. How painfully she was torn between her fervent need to keep her loved ones safe and her deep desire to help end the misery inflicted on so many others. The impossibility of reconciling the two. He knew her torment and he felt a profound tenderness toward her.

The girl began to sob. She put her face in her hands and cried inconsolably, pouring out the stored-up grief and tension and fear.

Dirk put his hands on her shaking shoulders. Gently he drew her to him. She buried her head on his chest. And wept.

He held her. Silently. Protectively.

And slowly her crying stopped.

He stroked her silken hair. He rested his cheek on it. The fresh, girl scent of her hair caressed him. He felt a surge of compassion and tenderness. He took her head in his hands and lifted her face. Her tear-bright eyes looked searchingly into his. Tenderly he kissed the tears from them, the clear, warm saltiness stinging his lips.

He put his arms around her and pressed her to him.

She melted to him. Her bare arms stole around his neck. Their touch sent his blood racing. She began to weep again. Softly, this time. The weeping of deliverance, of solace, not the racking sobs of anguish and despair.

Slowly they sank back on the bed, holding on to one another.

Every fiber in Dirk's body was aware of the girl's soft nearness and warmth. He was overwhelmed with the desire to protect her, hold her inviolate. And he was tense with desire, his loins ready to burst.

He held her close.

She nestled into the safety of his arms. Slowly her weeping stopped, turned into deep and regular breathing. The last few days were demanding their toll. Gisela felt secure and protected. She let her exhaustion take over.

She slept. . . .

Dirk looked down at the golden head resting on his chest. In sleep the girl's lovely face looked guileless. Young—and vulnerable.

He watched her with regret and with profound gratification that Gisela should be offering him her utmost expression of trust.

He was suddenly enormously happy to be alive. . . .

24

"We can allow ourselves no other conclusion." Colonel Reed's voice was bleak. "We *must* consider them both taken. Or dead."

General McKinley turned to Major Rosenfeld. "What is your opinion, Major?" he asked somberly.

Rosenfeld looked grim.

"We know the French-Moroccan combat patrol came under heavy fire and suffered heavy losses," he said. "The sergeant in charge was severely wounded. His men got him back. At his last sight of our men, they were running toward some woods during the firefight. He does not know if they were hit. They might have been killed. They might not." He took a deep breath. "Their first radio contact was scheduled for Sunday, March the twenty-fifth. Alternate, the twenty-sixth. It is now March the twenty-eighth. London has maintained round-the-clock monitoring of the Gemini frequency. There has been no contact." He paused. "I am forced to agree with Colonel Reed. We must consider the mission aborted. The men—dead. . . ."

McKinley nodded slowly. He looked deeply troubled.

"I assume it is impossible to mount another OSS mission within the narrow time frame available," he said.

Rosenfeld nodded. "I am afraid it is, sir. Gemini was our best shot."

McKinley turned to Reed. "What's the situation at Heidelberg?" he asked. "The town must have been secured by now."

Reed looked troubled. "It has been, sir. Advance elements of the Alsos team are already there," he said. "They entered with the tactical infantry units. They have already sent back information, all of which points to a possible German breakthrough in atomic-bomb research." He looked at the general, who was listening to him gravely. "One of their top scientists in Heidelberg—a Dr. Bothe—had, in fact, been working with a cyclotron at the Kaiser Wilhelm Institute of Physics there. He admitted they were engaged in obtaining radioactive material for a bomb, although he denied that German scientists were close to having such a bomb. No corroboration was possible. All documents relative to the work performed had been burned. In essence, we know no more about what's going on in Hechingen-Haigerloch after capturing the laboratories in Heidelberg than we did before."

"What about the Pash plan?" McKinley asked. "Operation—"

"Effective, sir. Operation Effective."

"Yes. What has Groves decided?"

"The general has reached no final decision as yet."

McKinley frowned. "I don't like it," he said. "But it may be our only course of action."

Rosenfeld looked from McKinley to Reed. He coughed discreetly.

"Sir. I am not familiar with—Operation Effective."

"Sorry, Dave." Colonel Reed gave an embarrassed little laugh.

"Brief him," McKinley said laconically.

"Yes, sir." Reed turned to Rosenfeld. "It is a plan of operation designed to take the Hechingen-Haigerloch area—if necessary. Colonel Pash, who has commanded Alsos from the beginning, will be in charge. It will be an airborne operation. The Thirteenth AB Division will be dropped to secure the area. Alsos scientists will be brought in by plane under heavy air escort. Pash himself will be dropped with a paratroop battalion to seize the actual target . . . as soon as we know *what* it is. A number of C-46's will be used to evacuate the Alsos personnel and any captured German scientists—and whatever equipment and matériel may be deemed important."

"Trouble is," McKinley added. "We don't know what he'll run into. We *could* be landing in a hornets' nest—or dropping a juicy orange in Aladdin's turban!"

Rosenfeld nodded. "I can see that," he said. "Unless we know with absolute certainty that the operation is worth it, the risks might well be too great. . . ."

McKinley sighed. "Any chance at all that your Gemini boys might still come through with some concrete information?"

Rosenfeld shook his head slowly. "I strongly doubt it, sir. We must write them off. . . ."

"That leaves only Pash. . . ."

McKinley fell silent.

The telephone on the desk broke into the heavy silence. McKinley picked up the receiver.

"Yes, Barnes," he said.

He listened, his face drawn.

"Tell them I'm on my way," he said. He replaced the receiver. He looked at Reed. "That was General Groves' office," he said. "It does not look good for Operation Effective. It seems the strike against the Hechingen-Haigerloch Project will be called off." He stood up. "You will excuse me, gentlemen. I am wanted in the office of the Chief of Staff."

He started for the door, hesitated and turned to the two officers watching him solemnly. "An Army Group Task Force may be formed," he said quietly. "A major effort. To seize the Hechingen-Haigerloch area in strength."

Reed looked at him. "Major effort," he said with concern. "That means—time! Sir, it may be too late. When—"

"Last week in April," McKinley interrupted him. "No sooner."

He turned and quickly walked from the room.

Reed looked at Rosenfeld. "Three weeks," he said, his voice flat. "The world was created in only one week. Are we going to see it destroyed in three?"

The steady clackity whirring of Anna Weber's old sewing machine seeped into the dismal little back room—an incongruous accompaniment to Dirk's anger.

Wanda was gone. She had died at last the day after the disaster at the railroad yard. Oskar had buried her in the little garden behind his sister's shop. Her headstone was a row of empty seed packages stuck on twigs and planted in the dark earth. No one would dig up a people's vegetable garden. Had not the Führer himself decreed that they be planted?

Dirk found himself reluctant to breathe deeply. The smell of terror and human decay still lingered in the air.

They were all there. He and Sig. Oskar and Gisela. And Himmelmann. Dirk glared at the scientist angrily.

"Why the hell did you call this meeting?" he asked, antagonism grating in his voice. "You know damn well how dangerous it is for us to run around the streets just now." He glared at the German.

Himmelmann regarded him, a half-smile of disdain on his lips. "Would you rather have had me come to the Storp house?"

"Oh, shit!" Dirk exploded. "That's a goddamn stupid question and you fucking well know it! The Storp place is the only safe house we have. But roaming the streets of this shitty burg, the asshole of the world, isn't exactly healthy either. Not now. And you know that, too! . . . Okay. So you got us here. We'll listen to what you have to say. It had better be good. . . ."

With an air of cool superiority, Himmelmann looked at the angry young American. "If you would listen, young man, instead of indulging in such a masturbatory orgy of words, you might be better equipped to render an opinion," he said calmly.

"Don't give me any static," Dirk snapped. "Just spill it."

Himmelmann shrugged. "Two items," he said, his voice icy. "We have just received a directive from Wehrkreis VII. That is the *Alpenfestung*—the Alpine Fortress. All atomic-research capacities from every laboratory in Germany—except Haigerloch; all stock piles of uranium, heavy water, graphite and all materials essential for the production of an atomic explosive device; all equipment and machinery are immediately and on top-priority basis to be evacuated to the National Redoubt in the Alps."

"Redoubt in the Alps?" Sig was startled. God! They were getting awfully close to home. "What is—the National Redoubt?"

Himmelmann turned to him. "The Alpine Fortress, or National Redoubt, is an area of some twenty thousand square miles of mountain terrain, taking in parts of Bavaria, western Austria and northern Italy. The Führer's personal stronghold, Berchtesgaden, lies within it. It will be the rallying point for all remaining German armed forces, led by the SS. It is here the National

Socialist Third Reich will make its last stand. It is virtually impregnable. . . ."

Dirk and Sig were staring at him. He continued.

"The area has been in preparation for a long time. It contains military supply dumps of every kind. Food, gasoline, ammunition, chemical warfare. There are large caches of poison gas. And rocket missiles. There are concrete bunkers, pillboxes, power stations and heavily fortified lines guarding underground bombproof factories connected by a network of tunnel railways. It is *here* the atomic bomb will be constructed—once the final, vital results of the Haigerloch test are known . . . the proof that makes it possible."

Sig let out his breath. "Holy Jesus!" he whispered.

"You mentioned *two* items," Dirk said. He felt sheepish. Himmelmann had had a damned good reason for contacting them. Even if contrary to their agreement. He realized he had acted boorishly. He was surprised that the tension inside him should have gotten to him that much. But—he could not bring himself to apologize to the scientist. "What's the second?"

Himmelmann turned to him.

"There has been pressure from the *Führerhauptquartier*—the Führer's Headquarters in Berlin. The date for the final test of the Haigerloch reactor has been moved up." He looked gravely from one to the other of the two Americans. "It is no longer April nineteenth. It is now April tenth!"

Dirk was shocked to his marrow. Less than two weeks! There was no earthly way for them to get this vital information to Washington in time, let alone for any action to be taken.

"Will it work?" he asked Himmelmann. His voice was hoarse with anxiety.

"It will," the scientist answered firmly. "There is no doubt. All inhibiting safeguards and theory will be thrown to the winds." The corners of his mouth pulled down in his characteristic cynical smile. "We have been *ordered* to succeed. The pile *will* go critical. It *will* become self-sustaining."

Their eyes were fixed on him. The enormity of his statements beat on their minds.

"And—and after the results are transmitted to that Alpine stronghold, how long . . . ?"

"It is estimated it will take six months to construct the bomb."

"Six months? Can they hold out that long?" Sig felt nauseated. He swallowed, his eyes still on Himmelmann.

"They can," the scientist stated flatly.

"Six months," Dirk said. "Once we know what they're up to, we'll throw everything we've got at them. . . ."

"The *Alpenfestung* can be defended indefinitely. Have no illusions. *No* effort will be spared to buy enough time once the bomb is under construction. No resources will remain untapped. The atomic bomb will be produced for Adolf Hitler!"

The words seemed to reach Dirk from far away. He felt physically beaten. Dammit, they had done their job. They had completed their mission. All they had to do was get the information they had obtained back to Corny. One way or another. And now they found themselves with a new job. A *real* ballbuster. And it was just beginning. . . .

Less than two weeks! That was all they had to stop the Haigerloch Project from being successfully completed. Twelve days. He raged against it. But he knew there was only one thing they could do. It never occurred to him not to try. They were there. They must stay. However impossible it might seem, it was now up to *them* to take action. Destroy the pile. . . .

He looked around at the people standing silent in the dingy little room. He was grimly aware that he was looking at the entire strike force he could muster to stop the deadly project at Haigerloch. A frightened girl. A big, well-meaning yard worker, in over his head. Sig—who still believed the world ought to be a decent place to live. And a renegade Nazi scientist . . .

Himmelmann . . .

He would have to be a key factor in any action to be taken. He'd better remember that.

He turned to Sig.

"Siggy baby," he said. "We start from scratch—against slightly bigger odds this time. That's the rule of the game. Return to GO. Do not collect two hundred bucks!"

Even he felt his foxhole humor fall flat. The hell with it. They still had to go for broke.

PART II

The Week of
2—8 Apr 1945

1

They could not be going more than eight to ten miles an hour, Dirk estimated. He sat at the edge of the open door of the boxcar as it lumbered down the branch track. Sig stood nearby, leaning against the side, idly watching the countryside go by. They had not spoken to one another since boarding the railroad car in the yard along with the half-dozen other foreign workers.

Dirk used the time to take stock. . . .

Four days had passed since Himmelmann had dropped his little bombshell; four days of hiding in the stuffy basement room at the Storp house and racking their brains for an idea as to how to destroy the Haigerloch reactor. They had nothing to work with. No arms. No explosives. No way of communicating. They had gotten nowhere.

Himmelmann had curtly told them that *he* would in no way be able to obtain passes for them to enter the sealed-off security area around the entrance to the reactor cave. The area was ringed with a high barbed-wire fence, heavily guarded. And even if they did manage to penetrate the security area, it would be absolutely impossible for them to get into the caves themselves, let alone close to the reactor.

Everyone, without exception, was thoroughly investigated before being allowed inside. No foreign worker could enter. Himmelmann had pulled his cynical little smile. The pile had once been contaminated, he'd told them. Valuable time had been lost. Obviously, none of the Nazi scientists could take the blame—so it was laid to one of the few foreign laborers working in the caves. Security regulations had at once been sharpened.

Non-Germans, with scarcely any exceptions, were banished from the inner sanctum of the reactor caves. Only a handful of foreigners, a few trusted technicians, still carried the "Red Pass," the ID card with the broad red stripe running diagonally across it.

They had listened to him glumly. They *had* to get close to the damned cave entrance. They had to have some firsthand idea of what they were up against. They had to "case the joint," as Sig had uncharacteristically observed.

It was Oskar who had come up with the solution. Occasionally he had been inside the restricted area. Supply trains arriving at the Hechingen railroad yard sometimes included shipments headed for Haigerloch. The freight cars were shuttled to the area and shunted onto special spurs that dead-ended inside at a series of off-loading platforms. He, Oskar, had at times taken work crews on those cars to do the labor. They entered the area under guard. They unloaded the cars under guard. They left under guard. But no guards could prevent them from using their eyes. . . .

The first opportunity had come today, April 2. With only eight days to go. Four boxcars had to be taken to Haigerloch for unloading. Oskar had taken on the job. He had selected twenty-four men—among them Sig and Dirk, indistinguishable from the other foreign workers. When you want to hide a tree, Oskar had said with a grin, plant a forest. . . .

Dirk watched as the heavily laden boxcars rumbled over the tracks. The countryside as they approached Haigerloch was beautiful and serene. Fields, woods and orchards, their trees in bud, passed in review. He carefully mapped the terrain in his mind as he had been trained to do.

Slowing to a crawl, the train was entering the restricted area, pushed onto a spur by the old locomotive. As it clattered through the barbed-wire barricade, armed SS guards jumped onto each car, scowling indifferently at the silent laborers.

The cars came to a grinding halt. The guards jumped to the ground. A non-com shouted:

"Raus! Raus! Schnell machen!" he commanded. "Out! Out! Make it fast! Get those cars unloaded!"

The workers hurried to obey.

Dirk and Sig found themselves scurrying back and forth, carrying heavy crates between the boxcar and a growing stack on the off-loading platform.

Dirk's arm protested with twinges of pain, but he did not acknowledge them.

As he worked, he listened with his eyes, using them like roaming cameras, committing everything he saw to memory as though recording it on film. . . .

Haigerloch itself, a small Swabian village, romantic and picturesque, was perched astride two precipitous heights above the Eyach River at the edge of the Black Forest. It was a perfect choice for the Project. The narrow, cramped valley was virtually inaccessible to Allied bombers.

Out of the medieval village a sheer cliff reared, towering above the village and the security area immediately below. It was like a gigantic rough wall, almost perpendicular. Dirk estimated it to be between eighty and a hundred feet high. It was topped by a fringe of green shrubbery—and crowned by an original anti-aircraft installation, the most effective protection against enemy air raids: a church. A large whitewashed structure with a cupola-topped bell tower and long, narrow stained-glass windows, their saints and angels solemnly gazing down on the ungodly endeavors below . . .

He spotted it. The single entrance to the cave itself. Around it a boxlike concrete bunker had been built. Massive. Square. A short, chimneylike shaft sticking up in one corner. Air vent? Close to the cliff wall, double doors of heavy steel, set in the cement, stood open, guarded by two armed SS guards.

To the right of the entrance stood a wooden shed, a lean-to built against the cliff wall. Nearby a maze of wires and cables converged on a small house. That would be the communications center. The public-address system. Telephone and radio control rooms. Oskar had mentioned it.

Flanking the cave entrance at some distance from the cliff were two large buildings. The nearer one whitewashed, four stories high, two stories in the steep-peaked roof along with an attic, judging by the windows. That would be the former Gasthof Schwan—the Swan Inn. Conference rooms. Billets for the top scientists on the project. Professor Dieter Reichardt. Security staff. A pile of lumber was stacked in front of it.

Opposite, a half-timbered building set on a massive stone

foundation six to eight feet high, its crooked, unevenly set timbers giving it a patchwork look. In front of it stood several
pieces of construction equipment. A cement-mixer. A brick-
saw. A pile of wheelbarrows . . .

On a siding two spurs removed from where the men were
working, Dirk could see a lone boxcar. It was obviously sealed.
Two SS guards could be seen on the near side. He assumed
there would be two others on the far side. What the hell was in
that car? Hitler's family jewels? Unobtrusively he squinted to
make out the routing chalked on the side of the car. He could
read one word. It seemed to be the place of origin. STADTILM.
It meant nothing to him.

Farther out was the high barbed-wire fencing. He could see
the guardhouses flanking the boom, barricading the entrance,
and the patrolling SS soldiers. Even as he was watching, a staff
car was being cleared through the checkpoint. It drove to the
large white inn and he saw two SS officers dismount and briskly
walk into the building. . . .

They had almost finished the unloading. Dirk and another
worker were heaving a heavy crate up on the stack. Momentarily the man lost his footing, and in an effort to steady himself
without letting go of the crate, he banged his elbow into the
sharp corner of a crate. He swore a lusty oath. He began to rub
his elbow, the left one, as he walked away.

Suddenly one of the SS guards leveled his gun at him.

"You there!" he shouted. "Come here!"

The worker walked over to him.

"Roll up your sleeve. The left arm!" the SS man ordered.

The worker looked puzzled. Since when was an SS guard
even remotely concerned with the injury of a foreign worker?
He began to push up his sleeve.

"Is fine," he said. "Only little—"

"Maul halten!" the guard snapped. "Shut your mouth! Let
me see your elbow!"

The worker complied.

One of the other SS guards, observing, motioned to another
worker.

"You!" he called. "Over here! Roll up your left sleeve!"

Dirk was watching. He felt his legs grow limp. His heart
pounded in his throat. The two workers summoned by the

guards were of the same age. The same build. The same coloring. His!

They knew!

They were spot-checking.

He turned his back to the guards. He did not want to meet their eyes. He began pushing at the crate stack, aligning it. His left arm suddenly burned with pain. He resisted the overpowering urge to rub it. Any second he expected a rough voice to summon him. The skin on his back crawled. . . .

Sig watched the guards in horror, heard their commands. He felt himself go cold. If they challenged Dirk . . .

Frantically his eyes searched for Oskar. There! At the railroad car. He wanted to run to him. But he did not. He walked over.

"Oskar!" he whispered with hoarse urgency. "Get us out of here! *Now!* They are on to Dirk!"

Oskar started. His eyes grew wide. He shot a quick glance toward Dirk at the stack of crates. He pulled a big whistle from his pocket and gave a shrill blast.

"Los-los-los!" he shouted. "Let's go! Quickly! Back to work. We're behind schedule! *Los!"*

As the laborers began to climb onto the railroad cars, the SS guards took up the cry.

"Schnell!" they shouted. "On the cars! Move!"

The men piled on. Dirk ran for the car with Sig. The guards took up their posts—and the cars, empty of freight, slowly began rolling along the branch-line tracks out of the Haigerloch security area.

Dirk felt sick to his stomach. He did not know how. He did not know how much. . . .

But—they knew!

As soon as the SS guards dropped off the train at the barbed-wire perimeter, he rubbed the scar on his elbow. Rubbed and rubbed and rubbed . . .

The air in the conference room at Gasthof Schwan literally crackled with antagonism. Tight-lipped, Professor Dieter Reichardt glared at the two Gestapo officers seated with him at the big table. Normally he considered himself an easy-going man. Slow to anger. He did not relish personal conflict and avoided it whenever he could. But this was too much. *Verflucht!* Did he not have to contend with enough problems without being saddled with the insufferable interference of a high-handed Gestapo colonel? Had he not been as much as *ordered* by the *Führerhauptquartier* to achieve final and complete success? With time cut to the bone—in fact, scraping it raw—and in the process straining to the breaking point the nerves of every one of his colleagues—risky short-cuts and hazardous procedures had already been adopted in order to meet the deadline. Intolerable delays were already occurring. The shipment of vital materials from the *Kernphysik* laboratories at Stadtilm was still sitting on the railroad siding outside, waiting for security to complete the screening of every single man who would be handling the transfer from the boxcar to the caves. Preposterous! And now this—this obnoxious Gestapo upstart wanted to place his *verdammte* watchdogs *inside* the reactor caves! Getting in everyone's way. Inhibiting progress by their very presence. Causing unacceptable delays with their snooping. Outrageous! In no way was he willing to surrender his authority over the Project. When it succeeded, *his* would be the glory. Not to be shared with this—this boor. He would tolerate only a minimum of interference.

He fixed his cold eyes on Harbicht. "I must insist, *Herr Standartenführer,*" he stated deliberately. "It cannot be allowed."

"May I point out to you, *Herr Professor—*" Harbicht's voice was dangerously low—"the Führer has charged the Gestapo with the security at Haigerloch. And *I* command the Gestapo."

"The Führer had also charged *me, Herr Standartenführer,* with developing a process which may well be of cardinal importance to the survival of the Reich!" He looked straight at Harbicht, an icy gleam of anticipated triumph in his eyes. "However, should you personally wish to take the responsibility for possible failure because of unwarranted interference by your men—feel free to place as many of them as you see fit in the reactor chambers." He made a slight bow with his head. "I shall, of course, require a written statement to that effect from you."

Harbicht clamped his jaws shut. He seethed. Abruptly he stood up. He walked to the window and stared out—without seeing. He needed a moment to get control of himself. That insolent, self-important test-tube polisher had bested him. *Him!*

Standartenführer Werner Harbicht. He raged at having left himself open to such humiliation. It was no excuse that he knew the reason why. For the first time in his career, he was not completely sure of himself and his invincibility. He was convinced that two enemy agents were holed up in his area. Enemies—on *German* soil! And he had been unable to apprehend them. In nine full days! Because failure was utterly foreign to him, it unnerved him. He did not know how to cope with it.

He was struck with a sudden thought. Those saboteurs. It seemed impossible that they could have eluded him this long —without local help. Was there a *Widerstandsgruppe*—a resistance group—active in this area?

Like the Kreisaur Circle, built around the traitor Helmuth, Count von Moltke? Daring to call the National Socialist movement a "recipe for disaster"! Von Moltke, of course, had been executed. Only this last January . . .

Or the group of traitors with the code name *Die Weisse Rose* —The White Rose?

That case still made him uncomfortable. It had been a great embarrassment for the Munich Gestapo chief, a good friend and competent officer. . . .

The group members had been students at the Maximilians University in Munich. He still remembered their names: Probst. Graf. Schmorell. And, of course, the Scholls, the leaders, Sophie and Hans. Brother and sister. And their advisor, the Herr Professor Huber. *Germans* all. Disgusting! Their underground propaganda sheet had been filled with lies. About Stalingrad. About Poles being murdered in Warsaw. Hate propaganda. *"Der Tag der Abrechnung ist gekommen!*—the day of reckoning is here!" they had written. *"Die Weisse Rose lässt Euch keine Ruhe*—the White Rose will not leave you in peace!"

Quatsch! Nonsense! Traitorous nonsense. And they had the audacity to paint slogans on official buildings. "NIEDER MIT HITLER!—Down with Hitler!"

The two Scholls had been caught distributing subversive leaflets. But even the Gestapo, despite all the methods of persuasion at their disposal, had not been able to make them betray their comrades. In the end they were, of course, all captured. The White Rose came to a well-deserved end, withering at the end of a rope. . . .

Had the infection spread? Was a seditious *Widerstands-gruppe* active in *his* area?

He was suddenly aware of what he was staring at out the window. A group of laborers unloading supplies from a train. He counted the SS guards. Mentally he nodded. Sufficient. He saw one of them inspect a worker's elbow. Good. They were following his orders to spot-check everyone who might fit the description of one of the enemy saboteurs. He suddenly frowned. It was not enough.

He turned back to Reichardt and Obersturmführer Rauner, who was watching him raptly.

"Very well, *Herr Professor,*" he said, a tone of dismissal in his voice. "For the time being I shall allow you to operate in your own way."

He started for the door. He stopped. Rauner had sprung to his feet.

"Just one thing, *Herr Professor,*" Harbicht said. "For security reasons, I am ordering a program of scatter raids. Throughout the entire area. Random arrests of individuals and groups. Totally unexpected, of course. They will be mounted against foreign workers for the most part, although Germans will not be immune. I regret that it may, of course, interfere with your work schedule to some extent. I will have to hold the prisoners for a while. For—interrogation purposes. But I am confident you will find a way to cope with this necessary inconvenience." He turned from the professor. "It should not interfere with the work in the reactor caves for which you are solely responsible."

He turned on his heel and marched from the room.

2

Sig was deeply disturbed. He hurried down the street toward the Storp house. It seemed to him that the whole mission was falling apart. What he had just seen did not dispel his foreboding.

They had not a prayer of destroying the reactor—and the Gestapo was hot on their trail, with information about them that was uncanny in its accuracy. Dirk's elbow. Obviously they knew exactly what to look for. The near-miss at Haigerloch two days ago proved it. It had to be Eichler. The man hadn't been at the railroad yard for his health. They had agreed on that. It was a relief to figure out how the Gestapo knew—but it did not make Eichler's betrayal less disastrous. It did, however, make it too risky for Dirk to be out more than was absolutely necessary.

But it did not stop him.

They had to have more information, he'd insisted. And more. Information is what makes the war go around, he'd said. And information is what'll give us the key to the job we have to do. Not only information about the immediate Project area at Haigerloch, but the whole damned complex supporting it.

Early that morning, he, Sig, had joined the stream of workers flowing through the streets of Hechingen. He pedaled along astride an old lady's bicycle with high handlebars. He had felt ridiculous, but he had not been alone in his undignified position. People used whatever was available. He'd had no other choice anyway. He couldn't walk, and their own bikes had long since been destroyed in the fiery truck crash. Dirk had lost Otto's bike at the railroad switching yard. The only one they could round up had been the old lady's bike kept in a shed at Anna's place.

He'd cycled all around the area, trying whenever possible to blend in with other riders bent on their own pursuits.

He had been enormously impressed.

The Haigerloch Project was backed up by a gigantic machinery of resources. Seemingly unlimited manpower—housed in huge camps. Factories, tall chimneys, refineries and plants whose functions he could only guess at crammed the region. Motor pools, fields of storage tanks and depots filled with stacks of matériel . . .

How? How in the name of Joseph and Maria could they ever hope to counteract all that?

He felt depressed. The problem seemed insurmountable to him. Damn this whole lousy business anyway. . . .

He rounded the corner into a side street. It was already late in the afternoon, but ahead he could make out the little park and across from it the Storp house. There were a few other pedestrians abroad. He walked quickly. Almost there . . .

Suddenly the nerve-grating screech of tortured tires knifed through the quiet. A Wehrmacht truck came skidding around the corner, sped to the middle of the block and careened to a halt. A dozen SS troops spilled from the back and immediately began to round up every man within reach, shouting and gun-gesturing.

Sig was taken completely by surprise. He found himself staring at a grim-faced soldier moving him toward the truck, a submachine gun pointed at his gut.

Stunned, he obeyed. His legs were leaden. All of a sudden a remark he'd heard back at Milton Hall leaped into his mind. . . .

If your own teammate is taken—kill him! Or he will kill you!
Oh, God—no . . .

He was pushed up against the truck. Around him stood half a dozen white-faced men, staring uncomprehendingly at their captors.

One of the soldiers pointed to a man cowering next to Sig, trembling with fear.

"You!" he barked. "Go! Get away from here! *Los!*"

The man jerked in astonishment. He stared at the soldier.

Slowly, not taking his widespread eyes from the SS man, he began to back away.

"Los!" the soldier barked.

The man ran down the street. Sig looked after him. He had been the only one among them who was elderly, perhaps in his fifties. . . . The rest—

Roughly the remaining captives were herded up onto the truck, covered by the SS soldiers. And as quickly as it had appeared, the truck roared off with its load of prisoners.

As they passed the Storp house, Sig cast a glance of despair toward it.

In the window, where the blackout curtain had been drawn slightly aside, he could see a pale, immobile face staring after him.

Gisela . . .

Oskar almost ran along the darkened street in his hurry to get home. His head was awhirl with the troubling rumors he had heard at the yard. He must warn his friends at once. . . .

As soon as he entered the house, he knew that something was dreadfully wrong.

A chalk-faced Gisela and a grim Dirk were waiting for him. Sig had been arrested.

Quickly they told him what Gisela had seen.

"They—they came for him," she whispered.

Oskar was shaken. "No," he said slowly. "No, they did not. I came to tell you about it. He was caught. By chance. In a terror raid." He looked solemnly at Dirk. "I heard about it. At the yard. Some crews of foreign workers were short. The Gestapo has begun a program of haphazard raids. Anywhere. Anyone. It is rumored that they hope to catch two enemy spies." He looked gravely at Dirk. "You. And Sig. They know about you. They will interrogate everyone they catch in their net. Until they find their men . . ."

He would have been dead, Dirk thought darkly, if he had been caught carrying a gun. As I wanted him to do. Corny was right. Absent-mindedly he rubbed his elbow. Had it been he . . .

He felt the anxiety as a leaden yoke on his shoulders. Sig . . .

"Already the local jail is full," Oskar went on. "They are taking the men they round up to the Gestapo prison in Tübingen. Twenty-five kilometers to the north. It is a very strong prison."

What the hell is the difference? Dirk thought bitterly. We'd have as much of a chance to spring him from the local jail as from the Gestapo stronghold. None at all.

He looked gravely at the two Germans.

"We have a choice to make," he said quietly. "The three of us. Sig will talk. We cannot count on him not to break if they question him." He looked searchingly from one to the other. "The question is—how much time do we have before they come for us?"

Instinctively Gisela moved closer to her uncle. He put his arm around her. Somberly they watched Dirk.

"Our choice is simply this," he said. "Do we clear out now? Hole up somewhere else—until we can get away? Or do we trust Sig to give us enough time to figure a way out of this mess?"

They stared at him.

"If we run," he said soberly, "we write him off. If we stay . . ." He shrugged.

They remained silent. Dirk's shoulders sagged.

"Oh, hell," he said tonelessly, "I can't blame you. I have no right to expect you to cling to a chance as ridiculously small as this one." He looked evenly at them. "Go," he said. "You can make your way to safety. Before—" He took a deep breath. "I will stay. There's got to be a way. Perhaps—Himmelmann can help. I've got to try. . . ."

His mind was in hopeless chaos. There seemed to be no way out. Yet he knew there always was one. If you could only see it. He tried to harness his racing thoughts. If the Gestapo picked up people indiscriminately, they could not possibly conduct full-scale investigations or interrogations. Not of everyone. Not possibly. They would have to let them go after a screening— unless they had reason for real suspicion. Sig was not a professional. Would he panic? Perhaps he *would* be able to convince his captors that he was okay before they got around to investigating him in depth, to checking up on his cover story? He knew before he had finished the thought that it was a forlorn hope. Nothing more. Yet if Sig were to get out, the Gestapo would have to allow him to go free. By their own choice. It was the only way. But—how? *How?* At least—at least he did not have to concern himself with the final alternative. Sig was too valuable to the Nazis to let them squeeze his brain dry. Should he not go free, he would have to die. About that, at least, *he,* Dirk, could do nothing. He did not have that choice to make. Perhaps Sig himself . . .

He turned away from the others. He did not want them to see his despair.

He was aware of Gisela quietly walking toward the kitchen.

"I will make some hot soup," she said softly.

Dirk turned to look after her as she left the room. He glanced at Oskar.

The big man regarded him gravely. He nodded.

"We stay," he said.

3

Here are the three files you requested, sir." Captain Barnes placed the file folders on McKinley's desk.

Without looking up from the report he was studying, the general nodded. "Thank you, Barnes," he mumbled.

"May I remind you, sir. Colonel Reed and Major Rosenfeld will be here in fifteen minutes, as you requested."

"Fine. Have them come in when they arrive."

Barnes looked at the general with a little frown of concern. "Yes, sir," he said. McKinley looked worn out. Small wonder. He worked around the clock almost every day.

As Barnes left, McKinley pulled the three file folders to him. He sighed.

He opened the first file folder.

OPERATION GEMINI.

He sighed again. He wanted to be completely up to date on all three cases before his meeting with the secretary later on. Stimson had a habit of asking pertinent questions and expecting answers.

He riffled through the papers. The dossiers of two young men. Recruiting. Training. Briefing. Cover. Infiltration. Then—nothing. The last entry was from the day before: 031300 Apr 45— No Contact. He bit his lip, feeling a twinge of guilt. Perhaps he should not have okayed a team as unorthodox as Gemini, however urgent the need.

He pushed the file aside.

Operation Gemini was closed.

He looked at the second file. Irritation and frustration rose in him.

REPRESENTATIVE ENGEL, ALBERT J., MICHIGAN.

Of all the problems besieging him, he needed this one the least.

Engel was at it again, despite the earnest intervention of congressional leaders. He still insisted on an investigation of certain "unexplained expenditures." There was no way of placating him anymore. He would have to be shown. They would have to take him to Oak Ridge. But before they did, Stimson wanted to familiarize himself with the progress there. In a way, you couldn't blame Engel, McKinley thought. One billion dollars *was* a hell of a lot of money. . . .

The third file was headed—

OPERATION HARBORAGE.

It was the most important one now—and the one he had to bring up to date before his meeting.

The Yalta Conference in February between Roosevelt, Churchill and Stalin had divided post-war Europe into three zones. Just recently a fourth zone had been added. French. And the Hechingen-Haigerloch area would lie smack in the middle of the French zone. Nevertheless, it was understood at the highest level that it was imperative that Haigerloch be taken as quickly as possible and that any atomic project there fall into American hands. Operation Harborage was the projected MED-Alsos operation against Haigerloch.

Records which had fallen into the hands of Alsos only days before revealed an ominous fact. Degussa, the Frankfurt-based uranium-refining plant, had manufactured ten tons of uranium-oxide briquettes. He knew enough about the project at Oak Ridge to realize the significance of this information. Where were those uranium briquettes? At Haigerloch?

With Gemini aborted and the airborne drop planned by Colonel Pash called off, the final decisions were even now being made for Harborage.

The buzzer on his intercom sounded.

"Yes, Barnes," he said wearily.

"Colonel Reed and Major Rosenfeld are on their way in, sir."

"Thank you."

The door opened and Reed and Rosenfeld entered the office. McKinley motioned for them to sit down. He turned to Rosenfeld. He came straight to the point.

"I asked you here, Major, to find out if there have been any developments regarding Operation Gemini. Any contact at all?"

Rosenfeld looked unhappy. "No, sir," he said. "None. Our last contact with the control officer in London, Captain Everett, was two hours ago. He had heard nothing."

"What is the official OSS conclusion?"

"We must consider the operation a failure, sir. The agents—lost." He looked down. "The monitoring is being discontinued," he added.

McKinley nodded slowly. "Then—with no firsthand information, we are forced to proceed on the assumption that the Haigerloch Project *is* atomic in nature and act accordingly." He turned to Reed. "I have a meeting with the Secretary and the Chief of Staff in two hours. What are the final decisions regarding Operation Harborage?"

Reed cleared his throat. "The task force will be designated T-Force A, sir," he replied. "It will be commanded by Colonel Boris T. Pash under General Devers, Commanding General of the Sixth Army Group. Twenty-first Corps is to provide two mobile infantry battalions and one armored cavalry squadron, as well as other support as may be needed. An Alsos combat unit will be attached to the T-Force with the direct mission of capturing any possible atomic reactor and German research scientists in the area. One infantry company will be assigned to the specific duty of providing security for this scientific unit. General Devers has designated General Harrison to accompany the T-Force as his personal representative. The operation will be a spearhead attack directly on the Hechingen-Haigerloch area."

He pulled a sheaf of papers from his briefcase. "Here are the orders, sir."

McKinley took the papers. He added them to the HARBORAGE file. He would need them at his meeting with Stimson and Marshall.

"I shall recommend that the operation be approved," he said. He looked at Reed. "When is D-Day for mounting it?" he asked.

"Jump-off date is twenty April, sir. It is expected that Haiger-loch will be entered on the twenty-fourth."

"April twenty-fourth," McKinley said. "Three weeks. We should be in no trouble."

4

Five days!

Could he hold out that long?

In five days it would make no difference, one way or another. The final test at Haigerloch would have been successfully concluded—or Dirk would have found a way to wreck it. What he did then, what they made him confess then, could do little harm.

Five days. And nights . . .

Sig stood in the cold, drab office of the Gestapo jail in Tübingen, watching the SS officer behind the desk engrossed in the contents of a voluminous file folder. A nagging headache throbbed in his temples. He had not slept at all during the night. He had been placed in a tiny, glaringly lighted cell that stank of putrefaction and stale urine. No one had said a word to him.

At first he had thought he and the others had been picked up by sheer chance. In a dragnet. His captors had taken his papers —all his belongings—from him. He hoped the Moles back in London were as good as they claimed to be. He knew there had been nothing to connect him with Oskar or the Storp house. But now—as he stood in the dismal office, doubts began to gnaw at him. *Had* it been completely by chance? The Gestapo already knew a great deal about him. And Dirk. Did they know about the safe house? Or—at least that it was located in that particular neighborhood? Was that why the men had been picked up on that particular street? His legs began to tremble. The questions boiled in his mind.

He stared at the SS officer, who was seemingly oblivious to

him. What was in that file the man was examining? What kind of information did he have? How much did he already know? He seemed to have been studying the papers for an eternity.

Five days . . . What horrors did they hold for him?

Obersturmführer Franz Rauner was enjoying himself. He had been in a foul mood when he arrived at the prison in Tübingen early that morning. The short drive from Hechingen had been miserable. It was raining, and a stretch of the road had been all but impassable where an enemy terror-bomber for God knew what reason had dropped a stick. The mud had been hubcap deep.

Yet he was pleased that Harbicht had placed him in charge of the preliminary screening of the subjects rounded up in the Hechingen scatter raids. It was the first real responsibility the Standartenführer had delegated to him since he became his aide. Rauner meant to show his superior what he could do. He had, for instance, some very specific ideas on how to break a man quickly. And economically. He was anxious to try them out.

The trick was—let them do most of the job themselves, before the interrogator took over in earnest. Interrogation by silence. That's how he liked to think of it. It was rather clever, he felt. Give the suspect every chance to let his own imagination conjure up a myriad possible horrors, a myriad reasons why he was lost.

That much he had learned from Harbicht. But he had thought up his own little refinements.

For instance, that thick file he was apparently studying so meticulously. How was the suspect standing in front of him under mounting tension, for a time that must seem eternal to him—how was he to know that the file contained only four unimportant items pertaining directly to him? The only four documents found on his person. His *Ausländer Kennkarte*—his Foreigner Identification Card as a Swiss technician born in Zürich; his work permit and war-service exemption; his *Führerschein*—a valid driver's license issued by the Stuttgart authorities; and a soiled and wrinkled envelope, worn in the folds. The envelope was addressed to Sigmund Brandt, Poste Restante, Postamt Hechingen, Deutschland, and was postmarked Zürich, 18 Jan 1945. It had been opened by the censor and resealed with the standard strip of paper bearing the *Oberkommando der Wehrmacht*—the Army High Command eagle insignia— and the word *Geöffnet*—Opened. It contained a small snapshot —Agfa film, he noted—a middle-aged couple smiling uncertainly in front of some snow-capped mountains, and a rather banal letter from concerned parents trying hard not to show their concern and failing miserably. Rauner put it aside with a small gesture of contempt. He had, of course, no way of knowing that the letter actually had been written by a smashing-looking, twenty-four-year-old London Mole with a forty-inch bust and a pedantic handwriting. . . .

The other papers making up the bulk of the impressive "file" were simply irrelevant circulars and routine orders. Strictly for show. The ashen-faced young man standing before him, watching him with fear-filled eyes, meant nothing to him. Absolutely nothing. Just one of the many fish caught in Harbicht's net. A nobody—with a shiny film of sweat on his pale face. The trick was to make him feel *special*. Singled out . . .

He finally looked up.

"Your name is Sigmund Brandt!" he barked, more an affirmation than a question. It was one of his theories. If you ask your question as a statement, it tends to give the impression that you know a lot more than you do. Someday, he thought fleetingly, he might write a handbook of interrogation.

Sig shied like a nervous horse. "Yes," he said.

Rauner sat up ramrod straight. He glared at Sig.

"Yes, *Herr Offizier!*" Sig said quickly. What was it Dirk had said? Cringe . . .

Rauner referred to the file.

"You are a native Swiss?"

"Yes, *Herr Offizier.*"

"Born in Zürich?"

"Yes, *Herr Offizier.*"

"You are a—scientific technician?"

"Yes, *Herr Offizier.*"

Rauner had run out of knowledge. He bent over the file. He made a show of shuffling a few of the papers. He frowned. He gave a quick glance at Sig. He returned his attention to the file. He pretended to think.

Sig was getting increasingly uneasy. What the hell was in that

damned file? What *did* the man know? How could he be sure
to tell the interrogator just enough, without giving away something the man did not already know? Or holding something
back he *did* know? He could feel the beginning of panic building in him. How could he cope?

"Your work is strictly technical?"

"Yes, *Herr Offizier.*"

"Describe it."

"I—it has to do with electrolytic plating, *Herr Offizier.* I—"

"What else do you do?" Rauner shot the question at him.

Sig started. What else? "Nothing, *Herr Offizier.* That is all."

Rauner smiled a thin, unpleasant smile. "Really?" he said.

Deliberately he returned to the file. He turned over a sheet
of paper and began to make a note on it.

It was going well, he thought, the man was thoroughly cowed.
Give it a few more minutes. He doodled. It was a doodle he did
quite often. It started out being a fish—and invariably turned
into a grotesque phallic symbol. He crossed it out.

Sig was watching the officer. What did he mean—*What else?*
My God! He knew. He knew about the unloading job at Haigerloch! That must be it. He had been caught in the first lie. Would
the officer put two and two together? How could he get out of
the lie? What could he say? He felt cold sweat trickle down his
sides from his armpits. The SS officer looked up and gazed at
him in silence. That damned accusing silence. He returned to
his note. What else did he already know?

Rauner pushed the file aside.

"Very well, Herr Brandt," he said, "suppose we leave that—
for the moment!" He liked the phrase. It hinted darkly at some
vast, secret knowledge in his possession, knowledge that would
be brought to light at a later time. "Suppose you give me a little
more specific information about yourself. Where do you live,
Herr Brandt?"

The thoughts raced in Sig's mind. Did the officer know about
the Storp house? Or at least on what street it was? If so, why had
they not raided the place? Or had they? Were they going to?
Waiting until the rest of them were all there? His mind whirled.
He was incapable of thinking clearly. He only knew he could
not tell the officer where he lived. About the Storp house. Even
if he condemned himself with another lie. He could not take the

chance. What, then? Where? Frantically he cast about in his seething mind. The town. The tour of inspection Dirk had insisted he make. On the lady's bike. To get information. Yes. He'd passed several large camps. Housing foreign workers.

"Arbeitslager Drei," he said. "Work Camp III, *Herr Offizier.* It is a camp for foreign workers."

Rauner nodded impatiently.

"It is the one near the plant with the three tall chimneys, *Herr Offizier.* Between Haigerloch and Hechingen." Thank God he'd used his eyes. Thank God, Dirk had made him do so. . . .

"I am familiar with the camps, Herr Brandt," Rauner said curtly. Enough of that. "Where do you do your work?"

Sig searched his memory. What had he seen? One plant. Large tanks had been in evidence. Plating tanks? What had been the sign on the gate?

"Speziellfabrik A-II," he said. "Special Factory A-II, *Herr Offizier."*

Rauner looked at him. He frowned slightly. He looked incredulous.

"Really?" he observed. He returned to the file. He began to look through it. He had no idea what they did at *Speziellfabrik A-II.* It was not in his province. For all he knew, they made potato dumplings. But it was time for another little pressure pause. Let the suspect's own brain besiege itself with a host of questions to every one *he* asked. Let the doubts ferment. If the fellow did have something to hide—let his own imagination create misgivings as to what *really* was hidden from his interrogator. Let the subject do his own wearing down. . . .

Sig felt utterly lost. He knew with irrefutable certainty that even if his lies were accepted right now, once they checked them out he would be lost. Then—then they would resort to torture to wrest the truth from him. He had no illusions. How long could he resist? Would he scream a full betrayal of his friends when the first fingernail was ripped out? Or would he have the courage to kill himself before being put to the test? It would have to be—soon. . . . If only he could be sure that Dirk and the others had taken off as soon as he was caught. But— damn him!—he knew Dirk would make every effort to complete his self-imposed mission, whatever the odds against him.

. . . He would have to endure. The mere thought of the ordeal that most certainly awaited him was enough to make his stomach knot convulsively and his legs tremble.

Rauner glanced at the man standing before him. He noticed the beads of sweat pearling on his forehead. Good. It was working. Now to tighten the screws a little.

He stood up. Casually he picked up a rubber truncheon lying on his desk. Deliberately he tapped it in the palm of his hand. He was gratified to see his subject's eyes follow every move, flinching imperceptibly with every tap. He felt almost kindly toward the poor bastard. The fellow was reacting exactly as he had hoped. He had a fleeting thought that vaguely disturbed him. The man did not act at all like a trained enemy agent. More like a scared, bewildered peasant. He dismissed it. It would spoil his fun.

He walked over to the prisoner. He circled him in silence.

It was all Sig could do to stand still. Every inch of his flesh tensed in anticipation of the blow he *knew* would fall. Where? His head? His arm? His back? His—testicles? His entire body shrieked to protect itself. The sound of the soft taps as the truncheon hit the officer's fleshy palm was the only sound in the world to him. *Tap—tap—tap—*

Suddenly the tapping stopped. He waited without daring to breathe lest he should miss it. Let him hear the tap. Now. Please, God, please! . . . No sound. He shivered uncontrollably. *Now*—the blow would fall. . . .

But nothing happened.

The officer came around to face him.

"One more thing, Herr Brandt, before we conclude our little talk—for now." He walked to his desk. He pushed a button. "Someone I should like to have take a look at you, Herr Brandt!"

Sig chilled. Someone? Someone who might identify him? Dirk? Oskar? Gisela? Had they picked up one of them. All? What would he do?

He heard the door open behind him. No longer could he control himself. He turned around. He stared.

Two SS guards pushed a man into the room. He was in a wheelchair. He had only one leg—held stiffly out, encased in a heavy cast. On his forehead was an ugly purplish bruise. Sig had never seen the man before in his life.

"Well?" Rauner snapped.

The man in the wheelchair stared at Sig. He nodded his head. "Yes, Herr Obersturmführer," he said. "Yes!"

Rauner waved his hand.

"That is all. Take him away." He turned to look at his subject.

Sig was staring after the cripple. His mind whirled. Yes? Yes —*what?* How could the man identify him? He'd never laid eyes upon him before. Or had he? Or rather—had the man seen *him?* At the Haigerloch railroad spur? At the *Bierstube?* Where? The questions flooded his tormented mind. Questions. Questions without answers . . .

Rauner observed him with hidden amusement. The fellow could not know that his eyewitness, the only man who had had a good look at the foreign agent with the radio at the switching yard, had just indicated that this was *not* the man he'd seen. Had he recognized him, his instructions were to say No!

Again he walked up to his subject, truncheon in hand. Again he began circling him.

"In view of everything, Herr Brandt," he said gravely. "I think it best we have another little—eh—talk. Tomorrow. I strongly advise you to use the time for some serious thought, Herr Brandt." He stopped behind him. It was time for his little clincher. "If by tomorrow you are not prepared to tell me the complete truth, Herr Brandt—"

He suddenly struck Sig's shin a savage blow with his truncheon. Searing pain shot from his leg throughout his entire body. A scream tore from his throat—and hot tears welled in his eyes.

"If not . . ." The words reached Sig through a mantle of pain. "If not—the consequences could become extremely painful for you, I fear."

Rauner returned to his desk. That was it. Step number one. A night of—reflection, and the man would crumble. He felt certain of it. There would be no need for elaborate methods of torture. It was economical. Effective. A minimum of manpower and effort used. He felt pleased with himself. He wondered if Harbicht would write a foreword for his manual. He pressed the button on his desk.

The door opened.

"Take him away," he said.

He sat down at his desk. He removed Sig's identification papers from the thick file and replaced them with a few other items. Dirty, dog-eared identification cards. He was ready for the next one.

For a moment he sat and stared at a paper on top of the file. It was a copy of a *Führerbefehl.* More than two years old. A Führer Order. Never revoked. He read:

All enemies on commando or sabotage missions, even if they are in uniform, armed or unarmed, however captured, are to be slaughtered to the last man. If it should be necessary initially to spare one man or two for interrogation purposes, they are to be shot immediately this is completed.

This last one, he mused. This "Sigmund Brandt." Was *he* the one Standartenführer Harbicht so desperately wanted?

Tomorrow . . .

Tomorrow he would find out.

5

The big clock on the post-office wall showed the time to be just before noon. The place was crowded with people. Gisela had known it would be. It was the hour the foreign mail was available for pick-up. She had selected the time for that very reason.

She walked to the public telephone in the corner. Nervously she looked around. She deposited her coin and waited for the operator.

"Polizei, bitte," she said, a quaver in her tense voice.

Again she waited. She shielded the mouthpiece with a trembling hand.

"Police? . . . I want to report two men," she said in a low voice. "Yes. They are—I don't know—perhaps war profiteers. One is a foreigner. . . . Yes. I know where they are. . . ."

For a brief moment she spoke rapidly into the phone. Police denunciations were not uncommon in Hitler's Germany, but she did not want to be overheard. She hung up and left quickly. No one paid her the slightest attention. She glanced at the wall clock. It was just past noon. . . .

Dirk looked at his watch.

"Noon," he said tightly.

Oskar nodded. He took the old cracked porcelain bowl from the battered washstand and half-filled it with water from the handleless pitcher.

Dirk hauled a piece of white cloth from his rucksack. He tore it in half. He rolled up his right sleeve and held a little knife to his skin. Quickly he made a small cut. He squeezed it to make the blood run.

Oskar watched him.

"Not enough," he said. "It must look to be a bad wound." He grabbed the knife from Dirk and quickly gashed himself deeply on his left forearm. The blood flowed freely.

He dipped one piece of the cloth in the bowl and soaked up the blood, rinsing the rag in the water. It turned bright pink. He bound the other piece of cloth tightly around his arm, stanching the bleeding.

Dirk gave a quick look around the small attic room. The heavy dead-bolt they had installed on the only door to the place was still unbolted, but the door itself was locked. The massive washstand stood close to it. He threw the rucksack into a corner. He glanced at the single window. It was open.

Again he looked at his watch. It was seven minutes past noon. He felt the tension rising. If he had guessed wrong, it might all be over in a few minutes. For all of them. . . . He knew the rivalry that existed between the Wehrmacht—the Regular Army—and the SS. He was counting on the same rivalry existing between the local police and the Gestapo. In fact, he was staking his life on it. His. And Oskar's. And Sig's . . .

Again he glanced at his watch. Nine minutes past. He looked at Oskar. Grim. Waiting . . .

That was always the worst. The waiting . . .

Ten minutes passed. . . .

Suddenly he stiffened. He listened intently. Footsteps could be heard quickly mounting the stairs.

He got up at once. Quickly he moved to the door. Oskar took up position at the heavy washstand.

The footsteps reached the landing outside. He tried to estimate how many. Three? Four?

His thoughts were interrupted by a sudden loud banging on the door.

"Aufmachen! Polizei!—Open! Police!"

At once he rammed the heavy dead-bolt home. The sound was loud and definite. At the same time Oskar shoved the massive washstand in front of the door.

Dirk was already at the window. Across a twelve-foot-wide alley was another building, a warehouse belonging to the Hechingen Textile Factory. From its gable a thick wooden hoisting beam protruded over the alley four stories below, and from the pulley block hung a rope.

The pounding on the door intensified as the men outside tried to break it down.

Dirk was aware of Oskar piling the thick mattress against the washstand and the bolted door.

And he leaped from the window.

He grabbed hold of the rope. The jar made it slip a few inches through his tightly clenched fists, the friction burning them. But he held on. The momentum of the leap carried him toward the open loading hatch in the warehouse gable. He reached for it with his feet. He let himself be carried as far as possible and then he pushed off with his legs as hard as he could. He sailed out over the alley almost to the house on the other side—and swung back toward the warehouse. This time he swung far enough. He grabbed hold of the jamb and pulled himself to safety—in the same instant he heard the submachine-gun fire.

Let the bolt hold, he prayed silently, just a little longer. Let the mattress be thick enough. . . .

Oskar was in the window.

With all his might, Dirk flung the rope toward him.

Let him catch it!

If not—he, too, would have to jump. And *he* had not been trained for it.

Holding on with one hand, Oskar leaned out. He grabbed the rope as it came swinging to him. With his powerful legs he pushed off—soaring out over the alley far below. Dirk reached out and grabbed him, hauling him to safety just as the door to the attic room crashed open.

Quickly the two men raced across the warehouse loft. On the far side a grimy window beckoned. They reached it. It was stuck. Oskar kicked it out. On the brick wall outside was a rusty fire-escape.

They swarmed down.

Below stood two bikes. Oskar's. And Anna's.

They were many blocks away by the time Standartenführer Harbicht's car screeched to a halt at the Textile Factory warehouse. . . .

Harbicht was livid.

The police had screwed up everything royally! They *knew*—dammit!—that the Gestapo was looking for two men, one of them a foreigner. They had strict orders to notify him *at once* if such men were spotted. Instead the blasted idiots rushed in themselves—and *then* notified him! Rushed in with half-assed preparations and no thought to covering a possible escape route. It was no damned excuse that the target room had only one exit and was on the fourth floor. Imbeciles! What the devil were they trying to do? Grab the glory? He clenched his jaws. He'd see *somebody* sweat blood for this!

He looked around the dingy attic room. There was no doubt. It had been occupied by the two enemy saboteurs he was hunting. For some time.

Item. The fresh blood on the rag and in the rinse water in the basin. The man with the recently healed scar on his elbow must have been the one they'd nearly caught in the railroad yard. He must have opened up his wound when he made the leap to the moving train and hit his arm. That would also account for the dropped radio.

Item. A newly installed heavy dead-bolt lock—and the elaborate escape route prepared. Precautions taken not by innocent men—but by trained agents.

Item. A rucksack, empty, left behind. A rucksack like the one carried by the infiltrators at Langenwinkel and at the Lahr roadblock. Empty—except for one tiny object, caught in a fold on the bottom. A small radio tube less than a centimeter long, probably a spare. With the markings: RCA!

He fingered the tube.

The two enemy agents had once again been within his grasp. Once again they had eluded him.

They were both still at large in Hechingen. . . .

He pocketed the tube.

He turned on his heel and left the attic room.

There was much to be done. . . .

Dirk lay on his bed. He felt exhausted. Physically and mentally. His injured arm ached from the exertion. Now came the waiting. . . .

The goddamned waiting . . .

Had the Gestapo bought it?

He looked around the stuffy basement room. It seemed oddly empty—without Sig.

And if they *had* bought it—would it be in time?

Had he succeeded in convincing them that all their scatter-raid captives were worthless to them? Including Sig?

He had agonized over exactly how many "clues" to leave behind. He could not afford to be too obvious. He and Oskar *had* to be the decoys. And from past performance, he had to assume that his adversary was a man clever enough to read much from little—and come up with what had to look like the right answers.

Had he succeeded?

He would have to wait and see.

That stupid, God-awful waiting . . .

There was a small knock at the door.

He started. He was getting really jumpy.

"Come in," he called.

Gisela opened the door. In her hand she held a small bowl and some clean bandages.

"I have taken care of the cut on Onkel Oskar's arm," she said. "He told me you were cut also."

"It's just a scratch," he mumbled.

"I will look at it," Gisela said firmly. "It must be kept clean."

She came over to his bed. She placed the bowl and the bandages on a stool. "Let me see," she said.

Obediently he rolled up his sleeve. The cloth stuck to the clotted blood. He winced as he pulled it loose.

Gisela looked at him, a little frown of concern on her soft face. She sat down on the bed beside him. "It—it does not look so bad," she said, her voice husky. She took his bare arm and placed it in her lap. Gently she began to bathe it, loosening the crusted blood. The water was lukewarm. It felt good. Soothing . . .

He moved his hand in her lap—and suddenly he was intensely conscious of her firm, warm thigh under the thin dress. A flush coursed through him.

The girl stiffened. But she did not move. She stroked his injured arm. Gently. Tenderly.

He let his hand caress her thigh. He had never known his fingertips to be so aware. He was conscious of his heartbeat pulsing in his throat.

The girl lifted her face to him. Tears brimmed in her eyes as they looked into his.

"You—you could have been killed!" she whispered. "Both of you. And I was the one who had to . . . had to . . ."

She buried her face in her hands and wept.

He reached up and drew her down to him. He cradled her in his arms. He felt an overwhelming tenderness. Her warm, soft body moved against his, seeking his strength—and all of a sudden nothing else mattered, nothing else existed.

He stroked her hair. He cupped her face in his hands and kissed the tears from her eyes, her cheeks. Her skin was soft as velvet where his lips touched. The musky fragrance of her mounting excitement fired him.

Her lips met his hungrily, and he drank their sweetness.

She strained against him.

Fumblingly, awkwardly—yet every motion a caress—they freed one another of their unwanted clothing. The cool nakedness of her body burned against his. . . .

And they merged deeply one into the other—oblivious to all else—until that moment when the world compressed to the confines of his bed; when eternity imploded into mere seconds; when all tension crumbled, all disquiet vanished. . . .

6

Sig sat bolt upright. In the distance he could hear heavy hob-nailed boots clanging sharply on the cement floor of the cell-block corridor.

They were coming for him!

He tried to steel himself, but despair washed over him. His heart pounded. His palms were sweaty, his mouth dry. He felt weak.

The fateful footsteps rang in his ears. He prayed they would not stop at his cell. They did. The sound of the iron bolt being thrown back hit his mind like a mailed fist. The door was flung open.

Outside stood two grim SS men. One of them consulted a list. "Brandt, Sigmund," he snapped.

Sig nodded. He did not trust himself to speak.

Curtly the guard motioned to him. "Come!"

Numbly he walked between the two guards. He tried not to think of what lay ahead of him. But it was all there was. Fear was a cold, hard knot in his guts.

The guards marched him into a bleak courtyard. The gray morning was raw and cold. Against a far wall a group of prisoners were lined up. Twenty, thirty men. Guarded by armed SS men. His guards walked him toward the group.

Sig's legs were leaden. He stared with horror at the men in front of the wall. *It—it was not possible. . . .*

One of his guards gruffly motioned him to join the group. He did, moving like a somnambulist.

They waited in silence. A few more prisoners were herded

out into the courtyard and added to the group at the wall.

An SS non-com, a Scharführer, entered the yard. All eyes followed him as he approached the waiting group. He held a list and began to read names from it in an unpleasant, high-pitched voice. The men answered dully. Sig started as his name was called. He heard himself answer as from another world.

The Scharführer put his list away. He surveyed the men.

"You are being released," he shrilled at them. "You will return to your assigned work at once! You will now form a single line and pass by the *Einhaltstelle* over there." He pointed to a couple of non-coms, one with a large box at his feet, the other with a clipboard in his hands. "You will inform the Rottenführer *where* you work. *Verstanden?*—Understood?"

He did not wait for an acknowledgment. *"Los!"* he shouted. *"Schnell! Schnell!"*

Quickly the men began to file by the two non-coms.

Sig was stunned. The tightness of relief in his throat threatened to choke him. He swallowed. Hard. His eyes smarted. He was going free! He did not know how. He did not know why. He did not even want to think about it. They were letting him go!

He found himself in line with only half a dozen others in front of him. Work? Where? He suddenly grew sober. What would he tell them? It would have to be specific. He listened. He tried to hear what the men ahead of him were saying.

". . . Landowski, *Herr Rottenführer.*"

"Arbeitsstelle?"

"Sperrzone Haigerloch, Herr Rottenführer."

The non-com made a note on his clipboard.

"Next!"

Why not? Sperrzone Haigerloch—the restricted security zone around the reactor-cave entrance. At least he'd been there. Knew a little about the place. He'd have to play it by ear. Things were happening too fast for planning.

It was his turn.

"Name?"

"Sigmund Brandt, *Herr Rottenführer.*"

"Place of work?"

"Haigerloch Restricted Zone, *Herr Rottenführer.*"

The non-com made his note. "Next!"

Rummaging through the box in front of him, the other SS man came up with a large envelope. He threw it at Sig.

"Your belongings," he said. He pointed to a field-gray Volkswagen parked nearby. "Go to that car. Wait!"

Sig found himself with two other men. A Pole and a Frenchman. Only these three had given the Haigerloch Restricted Zone as their place of work. They eyed one another in silence.

An SS man came over to the car.

"Get in!" he ordered.

The three men piled in.

A few minutes later Sig was on his way to Haigerloch. . . .

Obersturmführer Rauner sat at his desk staring glumly at the order he had received late the night before. *Verflucht nochmal!* That truly pissed down the drain his chances of getting somewhere. He had been so sure he would be able to come up with a real hot suspect. He had marked two of the scatter-raid subjects for special interrogation this morning. He was all set. An Italian sheet-metal worker, Tittoni or something, and that Swiss technician, Brandt.

But—there it was:

GEHEIME STAATSPOLIZEI   Hechingen, den 5.4.45

AMT IV E-1   15:35 Uhr

SONDERAMT HECHINGEN

GEHEIME KOMMANDOSACHE

Once more he read it, getting more disgusted by the minute:

S E C R E T

Regarding: Scatter-Raid Prisoners.

1. All prisoners, foreign or German, arrested during the current scatter-raid program and *at the time of this order* held at the Hechingen Jail or the Tübingen Gestapo Prison are to be released immediately.

2. All foreign workers shall be ordered to return at once to their assigned duties. Transportation shall be provided where necessary.

3. A list of all names and pertinent data concerning each prisoner released shall be compiled in sufficient copies at once to be forwarded to the following:

    a. Gestapo Headquarters, Amt IV, E-1, Stuttgart
    b. Standartenführer Werner Harbicht, Gestapo Sonderamt, Hechingen
    c. Director, Hechingen Jail
    d. Director, Gestapo Prison, Tübingen
    e. Chief of Police, Hechingen
    f. Chief of Security, Haigerloch

4. This list shall be used by all concerned to avoid arrest duplication in future scatter raids.

> Heil Hitler!
> Harbicht
> Standartenführer

Scheissdreck!—Double shit! Now he would have to wait for another batch of subjects. Do it all over again. Angrily he pushed the release order aside. Lists! The devil take it! Be a hell of a lot quicker and more efficient to stamp some sort of arrest exemption on each man's ID! The brilliant *Herr Standartenführer* had not thought of that, had he? He had a sudden, deflating thought. Perhaps he *had* thought of it. Upon reflection—it was not too good an idea. A stamp—even a hand notation—*could* be forged on any ID card, or a bona-fide card *could* fall into the wrong hands. It *would,* however, be impossible to change the list. Grudgingly he reached for the stack of arrest reports lying on his desk.

The scatter-raid prisoners were already in the process of being released.

He would have to get on with making the damned lists!

Zum Teufel damit!—To the devil with it! . . .

At the checkpoint gate to the Haigerloch Restricted Zone, the SS man dropped off his three charges. He obtained his receipt from the SS non-com on duty, an Unterscharführer, and took off. Sig hung back. Let the two others go first. He might pick up a few pointers.

The sergeant checked their identification papers. First the Frenchman. Then the Pole. He entered their names in a logbook and verified the ID with a record in a large file cabinet.

Sig grew cold. No way could he pass muster.

Neither could he just wander off.

He'd have to come up with something.

His brow wrinkled in thought. What? All at once he brightened. There might be a way—that third way out Dirk was always talking about. . . .

"Your papers," the SS man held out his hand.

Sig gave him his *Kennkarte* and his Work Permit. The man glanced at him. "Where is your zone pass?" he demanded.

"I work in the cave," Sig said. "I am a technician."

The sergeant gave him an ugly look. "Where is your Red Pass, then?"

Sig looked unhappy. "I wish I knew," he said apologetically. "It is a good question. Where is my wallet? I had the pass in it. With my money. And the things you have. That is all they gave me back at the Gestapo jail in Tübingen." He looked innocently at the non-com. "Perhaps the Herr Unterscharführer could ask the Gestapo what happened to the rest?" he suggested. "My wallet. The pass. And my money."

A warning bell went off in the sergeant's mind. Missing pass? Missing money? Gestapo! Not on your life was he going to get involved in that! He was not about to put his fingers on that hot potato! Not he! Dammit—what to do? Of course he could not take the man's word. A foreigner. He cast about for the best possible cover-ass procedure. He went to the file. He searched. There was no record of any Brandt, Sigmund. He frowned. He looked at Sig accusingly.

"I work for Professor Himmelmann," Sig said helpfully. "Professor Gustav Himmelmann. Perhaps you could check with him?"

That was it. Shift the responsibility. But fast. No one could blame *him* if one of the top scientists on the Project vouched for the foreigner. Or—disowned him. He ignored Sig. He went to the telephone. He picked up the receiver.

"Professor Himmelmann," he said. "Security check."

He waited.

Sig watched him tensely. What would Himmelmann do? What *could* he do? Had he miscalculated??

"Professor Himmelmann?" The sergeant spoke with obvious deference. *"Herr Professor,* I have here a foreign worker who claims he works with you. His name is Sigmund Brandt. A Swiss."

In his laboratory, Himmelmann stiffened. One of the Americans! At Haigerloch! Sudden alarm flooded him, but he quickly regained control. Easy. Step by step. Do not rush to conclusions. Investigate . . .

"Yes?" he said coldly. "What about Brandt?"

He listened to the SS non-com explain. His mind raced. The corners of his mouth turned down. They had him. Brandt knew very well he could not refuse to help. Or he would be denounced himself. Brandt was involving him directly. Irrevocably. And he had no choice. No choice whatsoever . . .

"Brandt is one of my technical assistants," he said curtly.

"I—we have no record of him in the file, Herr Professor." The sergeant sounded aggrieved.

"Of course not!" Himmelmann barked. "The man did not show up for work for two days. I had his record pulled pending investigation. I have it here." He thought quickly. He did have a blank record form someplace, left over from the days before the increased security measures went into effect. He could fill it out. Back-date it. It would work.

"He has also—eh—lost his Red Pass, sir."

"Issue him a new pass, Sergeant—what is your name?"

"Brauner," the non-com said. "Friedrich Brauner." He suddenly felt enormously exposed, now his anonymity was shattered. He became uneasy.

Himmelmann went on. "Send him to the cave entrance, Sergeant Brauner. I shall meet him there and sign the pass."

"Sir . . . I—I am not sure." The non-com sounded dubious. It was highly irregular.

"If *you* are unable to handle it, Sergeant Brauner—" Himmelmann made his voice icy—"perhaps I had better take it up with your superior." He paused. He sounded regretful. "I had rather thought it a routine matter. However . . ." Again he paused significantly. "It will, of course, take time. Time we can ill afford to lose." He sighed audibly on the phone. "However, if you think I must—"

"No, *Herr Professor.* Not at all." The sergeant hastened to decline any responsibility. "I shall issue the pass on your authority, *Herr Professor.*"

"Very well," Himmelmann acknowledged. "I shall be waiting." He hung up. His role in the conspiracy to destroy the project at Haigerloch had suddenly increased enormously—and alarmingly. And not at all by his choice. He had the uncomfortable feeling of having his neck in a noose. A noose held by the hands of his colleagues—and his adversaries. . . .

The Unterscharführer unlocked a drawer. He pulled out a pass with a broad red stripe running diagonally across it. He filled it out with Sig's name, stamped it, and entered it on his log. He handed it to Sig.

"Have Professor Himmelmann sign it," he grumbled. "As soon as you see him."

Sig nodded. He took the pass. He stared at it.

The Red Pass. The key to the reactor cave of Haigerloch . . .

He walked into the compound.

He knew the way.

7

The first green sprouts were pushing up in the people's vegetable garden in Anna Weber's back yard. The seeds had been in the ground twelve days now. The carrots seemed to be doing best, followed by the tomatoes and the cucumbers.

Inside, in Anna's shop, the light blazed and the indefatigable sewing machine whirred diligently under Anna's urging.

In the small back room, a council of war was in progress. Wanda's presence was fading and spirits were high. It had started when Sig returned to the Storp house from Haigerloch and triumphantly plunked down his trophy.

His Red Pass.

For the first time they had a real chance of success in their impossible task. The final test at Haigerloch had been scheduled for 1400 hours on April 10. They had sixty-four hours to go.

All five of them were there. All seemed imbued with new hope, except Himmelmann. To his sour cynicism had been added a glum resentment at finding himself much more deeply involved in the action than he had ever intended. And no way to get out. On the stool before them lay a gun. Oskar's Luger. The only weapon they had been able to get their hands on.

Dirk was looking at Oskar. "Five or six sticks," he said. "That's all you can get?"

Oskar nodded. "You must understand. Any serious shortage would touch off an investigation. Dynamite allocation for railroad work is tight." He thought for a while. I can get away with eight sticks. And a few detonator caps. Enough fuse to do the job."

"Not a hell of a lot," said Dirk. He was disappointed. "We'll only be able to do a limited amount of damage."

"There is another possibility," said Oskar.

Dirk looked interested. "Shoot."

"A *Panzerfaust,*" said Oskar. "Or two." He fished out a piece of paper from his pocket. "They were distributing these at the yard yesterday. I could requisition a couple such weapons."

Dirk took the paper. It was a handbill headed "WIE BEDIENE ICH DIE PANZERFAUST?—How Do I Use the *Panzerfaust?*" It had two squares with four drawings in each, one series showing how to prepare the weapon for firing, the other picturing possible positions to be taken by the operator. The instructions were simple and concise. The *Panzerfaust*—literally, Armored Fist—was a simple mass-produced anti-tank weapon; basically a small recoil-less gun firing a powerful, oversized bomb with a charge of three and a half pounds of high explosives. Once fired, the device was discarded. Every man, woman and child from seven to seventy was urged to use the *Panzerfaust* to destroy enemy tanks and trucks. The weapons were easily obtained.

Dirk nodded. "Good enough," he said. "We can use the warheads. Get some."

Oskar nodded.

"And don't forget the tape," Dirk added. "Get a couple of large rolls. Ordinary electrical tape will do."

"No trouble," Oskar said.

"Okay." Dirk looked at Sig. "Once more over lightly," he said. "Give us the layout." He looked at Himmelmann. "Anything you can add, do."

"Two steel doors to the entrance bunker," Sig began. "Two more from the bunker to the cave interior. Directly behind, a large tunnel leading straight back. Immediately inside, off this tunnel right and left, are storage rooms. Drums. Pipes. Metal racks. Crates. Then one or two cross tunnels—" He glanced at Himmelmann.

"One," said the scientist sullenly.

"—one cross tunnel branching off to other areas. At the far end, the main tunnel forms a T. Here there is a checkpoint, constantly manned. No one except key personnel is allowed beyond that point. Not even Red Passes! The main laboratory, the pile itself and the instrumentation control room are located in this deep part of the cave." Sig stopped.

Dirk looked at Himmelmann. "What about it, Professor?" he asked.

"You turn to the right," Himmelmann said tonelessly. "At the T. A small side tunnel on your left leads to the reactor cave and the control room. This tunnel can be sealed off with a heavy steel door set into the rock. Much like an oversized submarine hatch. The main laboratories are opposite, on your right."

"Beyond the steel door?" Dirk asked. "What's the layout?"

"The pile is in the large cave on the left. The instrumentation control room on the right. The pile itself is set in a deep, concrete-lined pit in the cave floor. This pit has an inside diameter of three meters—about ten feet."

"Okay," Dirk said. He looked at the scientist. "Your job will be to see to it that the steel hatch is left open. We'll do the rest." He looked at Sig. "You will handle the communications center," he said. "Make the announcement on the PA system, right?"

"Right."

Himmelmann pulled the corners of his mouth down. "That," he said sourly, "would be extremely foolish."

Dirk looked up sharply.

"Why?"

Himmelmann shrugged. "Simply because you would create suspicion at once," he said. "All communications in the area, including the public-address system, are operated by the *Wehrmacht Nachrichtentruppen*—the Army Signal Corps troops. They use *Nachrichtenhelferinnen*—female Signal Corps personnel. Women! To hear a man's voice over the public-address system would be highly unusual."

"Shit!" Dirk exclaimed in disgust. "Now you tell us!"

Gisela suddenly spoke up. "I can do it," she said. "I can make the announcement."

Dirk frowned. "No," he said.

The girl looked at him. "You cannot say *no*," she said earnestly. "There is no other way. I am quite able to do this thing."

"I don't want to involve you," Dirk said.

She looked at him, eyes big and grave. "You already have," she said quietly. "I am part of—everything. As Otto would have wanted it."

Dirk gazed at the girl for a brief moment. "Okay," he said

reluctantly. "You will go with Sig." He frowned. "Sig can use his pass," he said. He looked at Oskar and Himmelmann. "He may not be able to take even an unauthorized toothpick into the place because of the checkpoint body-search. But at least he'll get in. How the hell do we get Gisela into the area?"

"In uniform," Gisela said. "As a *Wehrmachthelferin.* Anna can make me a uniform. It will be easy."

Dirk looked dubious. "I don't know," he said. "We'll have to work something out." He looked around the room. "That's it, then," he said. "Sig—using his Red Pass—and Gisela take care of the communications center. Gisela makes the announcement. Himmelmann leaves the steel hatch open to the inner sanctum—and Oskar and I'll do as much damage as we can with the dynamite and the *Panzerfaust* warheads." He looked at Himmelmann. "What do you say, Professor? Will it work?"

"Yes. It will work," Himmelmann answered. The corners of his mouth pulled down. "But it most certainly will *not* accomplish your purpose!"

Dirk stared at him.

"What do you mean," he demanded tightly. "We'll wreck the damned pile!"

Himmelmann nodded. "You will damage it. Yes. And in the process you will convince Professor Reichardt and the others that they are indeed on the right track! I know their way of thinking. It would be the only conclusion they could reach to justify the foolish risks you will be taking."

"So what?" Dirk said defiantly. "As long as they are out of the running."

"Ah—but *are* they?" Himmelmann asked pointedly. They all stared at him. "The damage you can cause may be great. But not so great it cannot be repaired. You *are* limited. And I know the capacities at our disposal. The crucial test will be performed. Here—or at the *Alpenfestung,* where facilities even now are being completed. There is sufficient critical material available to duplicate the reactor set-up—and succeed. And if you convince them that they are close to the final solution—they will stop at nothing to reach it! You will have accomplished nothing with your sabotage. Merely a delay of a couple of days at most."

Dirk felt the color drain from his face. Dammit—the Kraut

was right. They would fail—even if they did succeed. . . .

Himmelmann continued. He seemed to take a certain enjoyment in making the situation as bleak, as impossible as he could.

"There is only *one* way you can put a stop to the entire project for a sufficiently long time to make a finite difference," he said. "And that is if you can convince them that they are on the *wrong* track! If they are allowed to perform the test. Without interference. *And it fails . . .*"

Dirk stared at the scientist with bitter resentment. He was being damned unscientific. He was suggesting the impossible.

How the hell was he going to send the Kraut scientists back to the drawing boards?

A depressed silence hung in the stuffy little room.

Sig was concentrating. Something was trying to surface in his mind. Once before he had been confronted with a problem that seemingly had no solution. But it had been there. A "Columbus' egg" solution. Obvious—if you could only think of it. He looked up at Himmelmann.

"Delay," he said slowly. "Several days ago you mentioned a delay that had occurred at the project. When the pile was—contaminated. By a foreign worker."

"Yes," said Himmelmann. "It cannot happen again. Conclusive safeguards make it impossible."

"Why can't it?" Sig asked. "What if we—pushed it along a little?"

They stared at him. Even Himmelmann suddenly looked interested. Intrigued.

"What if *we* contaminated the pile? In such a way it would be almost impossible to discover? Sabotage—without detection of sabotage. What then?"

Himmelmann stared at Sig as if seeing him for the first time. "They would think the pile itself—the geometry of it—was faulty," he said slowly. "It would take many weeks—perhaps months—to discover the real reason and rectify it. The project would have been brought to a standstill!"

Sig moved closer to Himmelmann.

"Let's go over the reactor set-up once again, Professor," he said, oblivious to the others. "Maybe we'll get an idea."

"Of course," Himmelmann said briskly. "I will describe the test briefly." He glanced at Dirk. "I will do it so that your friend may understand also." He smiled his little downward smile. "With my apologies."

He turned to Sig, suddenly all scientist.

"There is a large aluminum cylinder set into the pit in the cave floor, almost filling it," he explained with sudden animation. "The smaller magnesium-alloy reactor vessel has been placed inside this cylinder. The space between the two cylinders is packed and lined with graphite blocks. Ten tons of them."

Sig nodded. "To work as a reflector," he said.

"Precisely." Himmelmann went on. "The pit is then pumped full of water containing an anti-corrosive. Above the reactor vessel is suspended a heavy magnesium-alloy lid, also filled with graphite reflectors. From this lid hang more than a hundred chains of six-centimeter uranium cubes in eights and nines suspended on fine alloy wires. Through a chimney opening in this lid, the neutron source and the heavy water can be introduced."

"The lid is secured to the reactor vessel itself?" Sig asked.

"It is. It is firmly bolted on. . . . During the test the neutron source will be lowered through the lid chimney shaft into the heart of the pile. And the heavy water will slowly be pumped in." He looked gravely at them. "The neutron multiplication levels will be constantly monitored. On the instrumentation panels in the adjoining control room. There is no doubt that the pile will go critical. We will shut down the chain reaction with blocks of cadmium metal if it threatens to get out of control."

Dirk frowned. He looked from one to the other. "You lost me," he said. "What exactly *does* happen?"

"I will explain," Himmelmann said. "The object of the reactor is to achieve intense neutron multiplication. A neutron is one of the components of the nucleus of an atom. Neutrons are required to initiate the fission process. This occurs when a free neutron collides with the nucleus of a heavy element. A few extra neutrons break off and fly away with fantastic speed, and the nucleus splits into two nuclei of lighter elements with the release of—eh—substantial amounts of energy. Creating the potentials for a nuclear explosion. In fission an amount of energy is produced that is a hundred million times greater than in the ordinary burning of an atom. . . . The most fissionable material is uranium. U-235. The nucleus of a U-235 atom contains a hundred and forty-three neutrons. The hanging uranium cubes in the pile emit the necessary extra neutrons. These neutrons must be slowed in order to achieve fission. The heavy water accomplishes this neutron-slowing. Heavy water is a variety of ordinary water. It contains hydrogen atoms of double the usual atomic weight and is therefore about ten percent heavier. It effects the slowing down *without* capturing or absorbing the neutrons, allowing the build-up to continue until the pile becomes self-sustaining. Goes critical." He looked at Dirk with his caustic smile. "Is that clear?"

"Sure," Dirk said. "I couldn't have put it better myself."

"That's where we come in," Sig said enthusiastically. "If we can contaminate the heavy water so that the neutrons *will* be absorbed—the pile will fail!" He was getting fired with the problem. "That is essentially what is done by the cadmium blocks the professor said would be used to check the chain reaction. Of course, we can't use cadmium blocks. They would be detected at once. Besides—they would have to be introduced during the test, which is obviously impossible. . . . "

He suddenly brightened. He turned to Himmelmann. "The heavy water," he asked eagerly. "Where is it stored? Before it is pumped into the pile?"

"In a storage tank," Himmelmann answered at once. "In an adjacent cave. The pipes run through the wall."

"That cave. Is it also behind the sealed steel door?"

"No. It is accessible from the main tunnel. From the left fork."

"Describe it."

"The storage tank itself holds seventy-five hundred liters. Roughly two thousand gallons. It is topped by a heavy access port."

"How secured?"

"Eight bolts."

Sig frowned. "Too much. Go on."

"There is a series of pipes and valves that allow the heavy water to be forced to the pile in the adjoining cave under dry-air pressure."

"The valves?"

"Standard. A gate screwed into the pipe by a stem running

through the body with a turning wheel on top of the bonnet."

"That's it!" Sig exclaimed. "That's how we get the contaminant into the heavy water. Through the valve!" He was getting excited. "How much heavy water is held in the storage tank?"

"A little better than fifteen hundred gallons."

Sig whistled.

"You will need an agent like cadmium that would absorb neutrons," Himmelmann mused.

"Boron," Sig said. "Boron does just that! Boric acid. That's generally available. It's a mild antiseptic. Eyewash. It is an excellent neutron-absorber." Quickly he pulled a pencil and a notebook from his pocket. "We could get boric acid in powder form," he said. "It would readily dissolve in the heavy water. It would be impossible to detect without extensive tests."

He scribbled on the paper. "I figure—twenty-five boron parts per million would screw up the works nicely." He looked at Himmelmann. "Professor?"

"I agree," the scientist nodded.

"One gallon of heavy water weighs 9.16 pounds. Fifteen hundred would weigh—13,740 pounds." He calculated furiously for a moment. "Shit!" he said in disgust. "We'd have to dump in close to a pound and a half of boric-acid powder!"

"That should be no problem," Dirk commented.

"Maybe not," Sig said. "But buying that amount of boric-acid powder sure as hell would raise some eyebrows. Who'd need a bathtub full of eyewash?"

"I get your point," Dirk said dryly.

"Wait! Wait just a minute!" Sig turned to Oskar. "At the yard," he said urgently, "you have machine shops. You do a lot of welding?"

Oskar nodded. "We do."

"What do you use as a flux?"

"Borax," Oskar said. "That is standard. We get it from Italy."

"That's it! Borax contains boron. It's a crystalline powder. Like salt. Or sugar. And it's soluble in water. We'd need about fifty percent more of that than of boric acid. Let's say—two pounds."

"Can we get that much?" Dirk asked.

"Sure. Borax is widely used in welding; it promotes fusion. No one would question a couple of pounds of the stuff." He turned to Oskar. "Can get? Okay?"

Oskar nodded. "Yes. I can get it."

Sig looked at Dirk, his face flushed. "Dirk," he said excitedly. "If we can get to the heavy-water storage room—and have five minutes undisturbed—we can foul up the test, and the damned Krauts won't know what hit them!"

Dirk stared at Sig. He broke into a wide grin. "Siggy baby," he said fervently, "I love you." He grew businesslike.

"Okay," he said crisply. "Here's exactly how we'll do it. Same plan. We've gone over the details already. We'll simply have to make a few changes. Timing is the key to the whole thing, or it will fall down around our ears. Remember exactly what each of you is supposed to do—and when!"

Soberly they watched him. He looked at each one in turn.

"At 0940 hours," he began.

"Come on, Dirk," Sig interrupted. "Give it to us in civilian, please!"

Dirk grinned. "Okay. The operation will start in the morning of April the tenth." He glanced at Sig. "Is that civilian enough for you? . . . That gives us two full days to line up everything we need." He looked at Oskar. "Time enough?"

Oskar nodded. "More than enough."

"Good. . . . At nine forty in the morning," Dirk continued, "Oskar and I will arrive at the railroad yard. I will have Otto's yard pass as before. Just in case. We will proceed to Signal Post Forty-nine, which is in a pretty isolated spot. We will begin the initial step of the operation at exactly nine fifty.

"At nine fifty-five Sig will enter the restricted area at Haiger-loch. He will have no difficulties, using his Red Pass, God bless it! At ten o'clock Gisela will arrive in *Wehrmachthelferin* uniform on Anna's bike. She presents herself at the checkpoint with an eyes-only dispatch for Professor Himmelmann to be delivered personally. Himmelmann will be contacted by the guard." He looked at the scientist. "It is imperative you make yourself available at exactly that time." Himmelmann nodded sourly. "If the guard does not call the professor on his own, Gisela will insist. Himmelmann will confirm that he is expecting the message. His assistant, Sig, will escort Gisela to the cave-entrance bunker to meet the professor. . . .

"At ten ten Sig and Gisela will arrive at the communications center. Sig, you will overpower the guard in the lobby. Gisela —you will have to distract him so Sig can knock him out. Okay? Sig will, of course, not be armed."

Gravely Gisela nodded.

"Okay. Oskar and I should be on our way to Haigerloch by then. And now comes the crucial point. It *must* be exactly on time. . . . At precisely ten twenty Gisela will make her broadcast over the public-address system all through the area and the caves! Got it?"

Gisela nodded soberly.

"Okay. At ten thirty we all meet at the cave-entrance bunker. Gisela, you stay outside. We go in. You know the drill from there on." Again he looked at Himmelmann. "Don't forget, Professor. It is important that you make certain the steel door to the reactor cave area is *sealed and locked!* This is a change. It is vital. We do *not* want to be able to get to the pile itself—or the instrumentation where we could do real damage. But—they must think we tried! They must think we hadn't counted on the locked steel hatch. How *could* we know about it? You then get out and leave the area, establishing your—eh, innocence. Okay?"

Himmelmann nodded. "I understand."

"At ten thirty-four I will set the explosives at the steel door and in the laboratory. Oskar and Sig will make their way to the heavy-water storage room. They will dismantle the valve and dump the borax powder into the pipe. They will reassemble the valve and get out."

He looked at the two men.

"And remember. Leave absolutely no trace that you have been there. That is vital!"

They nodded.

"At ten thirty-nine I light the fuses." He grinned at Sig. "Don't worry, Siggy baby, if you are not through by then—I'll wait a few seconds! Sig and Oskar will then join me and we get the hell out of there! We'll have had twenty-one minutes. We can't stretch it any further. We can expect counter-action at any time after that.

"At ten forty-one the explosions inside the cave go off. Ought to be a real ball-slammer! We need those pyrotechnics. They *must* think that the explosion is the *real* sabotage attempt. They must not even suspect anything else. The steel door probably won't sustain much damage. We may blow a couple of hinges off. . . . But we'll wreck the lab. Making it that much more difficult for them to conduct tests that may reveal the contamination later on. . . . Main thing is—they'll be able to carry out the final test on schedule."

He looked around at them. "If they do go ahead with the test —and I'm betting they will . . . " He grinned broadly.

"Good luck!"

8

The Luger stuck in his belt felt heavy and awkward under his coat as Dirk walked down the dark street. He felt on edge. Seeing demons in every shadow. Hearing the pounce of an ambush with every sudden sound. Ahead of him he could make out the sturdy figure of Oskar hurrying along. Behind him he was aware of Sig.

They were all intently conscious of the risk they were taking. The Gestapo scatter raids at all hours of day or night were still taking place. When the call had come they had quickly decided that the safest way to travel the night streets of Hechingen would be separately. Dirk, who had no chance of bluffing his way through an arrest, would carry the gun. If the worst happened, he would have to try to shoot his way out. With Oskar in front and Sig in the rear, they were hoping to get enough warning in case of a sudden raid for Dirk to find a hiding place. If not—he would have to use the Luger. . . .

It was past ten thirty. Himmelmann's urgent call had come just minutes before. It was imperative that he see them at once, he had whispered on the phone, his voice harsh with anxiety. At the *Zum Güterzug Bierstube*. At once! And he had hung up.

They had debated what to do. They were shaken. Was it a trap? Had Himmelmann caved in? Was he betraying them? Dirk thought not. The man knew where Oskar lived. The Gestapo would have been all over the damned place if Himmelmann had talked. What, then? They had to find out. Himmelmann was crucial to the success of the raid. They had no choice but to heed his summons.

There were few people on the streets. The foreign workers,

wary of the scatter raids, stuck close to their barracks. Even the native citizens were unwilling to be on the streets more than necessary.

The *Bierstube* was only half full. Mostly Germans. The dirty-blond waitress seemed considerably less harassed. The atmosphere of the place was markedly more subdued than when they had been there before.

They spotted Himmelmann sitting alone at a table in a corner. He looked nervous and edgy. Casually they walked to the table and sat down.

Himmelmann did not look at the two Americans. His face had an unhealthy pallor. He talked directly to Oskar, his voice low and tense.

"Listen to me, Herr Weber," he said. "I shall talk to you only. I do not wish to be seen talking to them. They must not address me. Understand? Or I shall leave at once!" He glanced around the room. "I—may be watched!"

Dirk and Sig tensed. What the hell had they walked into? Dirk was sharply aware of the Luger bulging at his waist. It must be apparent to everyone. Instinctively he sucked in his stomach. Sig beckoned to the waitress, and presently each had a stein of beer before him. When they were once again alone, Himmelmann spoke. He looked straight at Oskar—but he was speaking for the ears of Dirk and Sig.

"The Gestapo knows much about you," he said tautly. "The area chief, Standartenführer Werner Harbicht, is determined to catch you. He is your single greatest danger. He will be your nemesis." He paused. Again he looked around nervously.

"You will have to abandon your attempt to sabotage the pile," he said hurriedly. "I will not be able to help you! Tomorrow morning I am being evacuated to the nuclear installations in the *Alpenfestung!* On the Führer's direct orders. I—and *every scientist* not essential to the final test at Haigerloch the day after tomorrow! Already all the other atomic scientists possessing secret knowledge have been ordered to the Alpine Fortress. They—and all their papers, records and documents. From Stadt-ilm. From Celle. From Gottow. Grünau—and Tailfingen. The Gestapo threatens to shoot anyone who refuses! They make certain you obey. . . ." He sounded agitated. He glanced quickly around the tavern.

Dirk and Sig were listening in stunned silence, the foam on

their beer dying unnoticed. They saw their plans crumble in a card-house collapse.

"There is nothing I can do for you anymore," Himmelmann said urgently. "Give up your sabotage plans. Abandon the operation. *You cannot succeed!*"

Sig could contain himself no longer.

"The hell you say," he mumbled. "I still have my pass. I can still get in!"

Savagely Himmelmann turned to him. His eyes blazed in his pale face. Anger made his voice harsh and tight. Anger at finding himself in mortal danger. Anger at having been drawn into a conspiracy he'd sought to avoid. Anger at the ungodly depravity he had been forced to be part of. Harbicht. Reichardt. Wanda . . . Pent-up anger suddenly finding a target.

"If you try to use that pass," he hissed, "you will be arrested at once! And I hope to God you do try! All passes for foreign workers—even *Red* Passes—have been revoked! For the restricted area. And for the caves! There is no possible way for you to carry out your scheme!"

He stood up. Without another word he turned on his heel and walked stiffly from the table, disappearing through the door to the street.

Dirk and Sig stared after the departed Haigerloch scientist.

With him had gone their only hope of success. Of survival.

It was 2307 hours, April 8. Their intricate operation was less than thirty-five hours away.

Already it was abortive. . . .

PART III

The Day of
10 Apr 1945

1

Major General J. Edward McKinley tried to relax. It was a twenty-five-minute ride from the Pentagon to his home in Georgetown. He sat back in the seat of the staff limousine and closed his eyes. Lately he'd developed an almost imperceptible twitch in his left eyelid. It was not noticeable to anyone, but he could feel it.

The car sped along the darkened streets. He opened his eyes. It was no go. He was too keyed up. He'd have to wait until he got home, where he could take a sleeping aid.

He sighed. The burning sensation of an attack of acid indigestion bothered him. That was something else that would have to wait. A Bromo.

He glanced at his watch. He had difficulty seeing it in the dim light. He never had been able to get used to Washington in the brown-out. It was just past midnight.

He belched. It gave him no relief. A new day had already begun. April 10. So far he was not enthusiastic about it.

He'd spent the last few hours in conference with Colonel Reed and some other officers, discussing the latest Alsos situation in Germany.

The Alsos people in Heidelberg had been informed that Patton's Third Army was about to overrun a town called Stadtilm, which might turn out to be a goldmine of information about the Nazi atomic effort. Alsos thought there was even a possibility of an actual pile there. He'd had trouble spotting Stadtilm on the map, but he finally did. Just below Erfurt.

Colonel Pash had broken off his preparations at SHAEF for

Operation Harborage and only two hours before had pulled out for Sixth Army Group Headquarters in Kaiserslautern. He would continue to Heidelberg—and on to Meiningen with a twenty-man task force to wait for Stadtilm to be taken. This meant Pash had to set up the Stadtilm operation on the run. No time for coordinating with field commanders. And the operation might have to be carried out in the middle of the fighting. Not the ideal conditions. It also meant that someone else would have to follow through with the preparations for the ground operations against the Hechingen-Haigerloch targets. It could mean a delay.

McKinley felt uneasy. Undoubtedly Stadtilm was important. Reports had it that one of Germany's leading atomic scientists headed up a laboratory there. But he had a gut feeling about the project at Haigerloch.

Perhaps it was because of the disappearance of the Gemini agents. . . .

2

Signal Station #49 was located in an isolated area on the right-of-way outside the railroad yard proper. It could be reached without having to go through any gate or checkpoint. That was one reason Oskar had chosen it as the place for stashing the high explosives. That—and the fact that the station was serviced only once a month or if an emergency arose.

Dirk and Sig arrived at the shack at 0937 hours. They were early, keyed up by the heady mixture of excitement and apprehension.

Dirk fished a key from his pocket and unlocked the big padlock Oskar had placed on the door to the nearby shack. They stepped in and closed the door behind them.

The place was dimly lit. The windows to the right and left of the door were sooted over. The shack was cluttered with rusty railroad equipment and old tools. In a corner lay a stack of empty sacks. Dirk strode to it and pulled the sacks aside.

It was all there. Two one-pound cans of borax. Nine sticks of dynamite—Oskar was handing them a bonus. Six detonator caps and about twelve feet of standard fuse—more than enough. A large roll of electrical tape—and two *Panzerfausts*. Dirk handled the weapons curiously.

The device consisted of a three-foot-long metal tube about an inch and a half in diameter. It had a simple backsight that could be raised from the tube, and a trigger. The hollow-charge warhead was affixed in the front of the tube. Shaped like two cones joined at their bases, it was about six inches in diameter at its widest point, at the edge of which the foresight pin was mounted. A metal plate screwed onto the warhead itself gave the simple firing instructions.

Dirk carefully dismantled the first *Panzerfaust*. The tail stem of the warhead had four flexible fins wrapped around it so it could fit into the firing tube. He left it intact. Inside the tube was a small charge of gunpowder, which would propel the bomb from the tube when fired. It was not enough to bother with.

He put the two separated warheads aside and picked up the dynamite. He would make three charges. One large one for the steel door, two smaller ones for the laboratory.

He decided to use five sticks for the large charge, two for each of the smaller ones. He placed them together carefully and wrapped tape around to hold them. He handled the stuff with respect. He did not know how old it was: how stable—or how dangerous. He cut a length of fuse and set one end of it in one of the sensitive detonator caps. He had no crimping tool, so he put the cap in his mouth and crimped it onto the fuse with his teeth. He knew a split second of icy fear as he bit down. His mission could end right there.... With deliberate care he made a slit in one of the dynamite sticks, pressed the detonator cap into it and fastened it in place with tape. Finally he wound the fuse around the charge.

While he was preparing the smaller charges, Sig chose the tools he and Oskar would need to dismantle the valve on the heavy-water storage-tank pipe. Oskar had left a selection in the shack.

Dirk glanced at his watch. 0949 hours. It was time.

They went outside to the signal mast. A telephone box was mounted on it. Dirk opened the box. He took a deep breath. He cranked the handle.

"Yard emergency!" he cried, his voice excited. "Quickly!" For a brief moment he waited. Then—"Emergency! This is Weber. At Signal Post Forty-nine. I need an ambulance. At once! There's been an accident!" He listened tensely. "Hurry!" He hung up.

He looked at Sig.

They were committed.

Quickly they returned to the shack and went inside. Oskar had estimated it would take the ambulance twenty minutes to get to the post. It had seemed a long time to Dirk, but Oskar ought to know. Apparently the Germans didn't break their asses over an accident to a foreign worker. . . .

Again he glanced at his watch. 0952 hours.

They had eighteen minutes to wait.

He could relax. He tried.

But he could feel the muscles knotting in the back of his neck. . . .

Oskar nursed the small switching engine along the branch track toward the Haigerloch Sperrzone. He had maintained yard speed for the entire distance. As agreed. He consulted his watch. It was 9:52. Ahead he could see the railroad gate in the barbed-wire fence. It was closed. He was due there in three minutes.

He looked back at the single flatcar behind the engine. Two large, heavy crates were lashed down on it. For the hundredth time he looked them over. Critically. They looked good. They ought to do the trick.

He turned to Gisela standing tensely beside him. He gave her a smile. She returned it tremulously. She looked strangely alien in the field-gray *Wehrmachthelferin* uniform.

"It will go well, my little one," he said encouragingly. "You will see."

Gisela nodded. "I will be fine," she said softly.

Oskar eased the engine to a stop in front of the closed railroad gate. He jumped to the ground, followed by Gisela. He strode to the heavy-wire gate. Two SS guards eyed him suspiciously, their weapons at the ready. Oskar recognized one of them from his previous trips to the area. A fellow named Kurt. Couldn't hurt.

"Open the gate, Kurt," he demanded. "I cannot unload the damned crates out here!"

"We have orders to let nothing through," one of the guards said gruffly.

"What?" Oskar sounded incredulous. "Have they not told you?" He pointed to the crates. "Look!" he said. "It is a special shipment. Look at all the damned signs all over the crates. It is an important shipment. From Stadtilm! Can you not read? *Special Handling*, it says. *Urgent!*"

The guards looked uncertainly at one another.

"Stadtilm?" the guard named Kurt asked tentatively.

"Read it yourself, Kurt," Oskar said. "The damned stenciling is big enough."

It might work, he thought. It *had* to. The *Ami* agent Dirk had been right. Stadtilm *was* important. A magic word. As he had thought it would be from having watched the cars marked STADTILM on the siding during their orientation trip to the Sperrzone. Those cars had been under heavy guard.

"And how the devil will I get the damned things unloaded," Oskar asked querulously, "with these fat-headed new rules forbidding foreign workers in the area?" He looked at the SS guards. "Or are *you* going to do the job?"

"Wait here," the SS guard said sourly.

He walked to the guardhouse. Oskar and Gisela could see him making a call.

Gisela could feel her legs trembling. She tried desperately to stop them. She dreaded that the SS guards would notice. She thought of Dirk. His was the far more dangerous part of the job.

She watched the SS man return from the guardhouse.

"Security has no information about any special shipment," he said, his face grim.

"Dammit!" Oskar exploded. "Is that my fault? Do *I* run your outfit? Very well, I will take the damned crates back to the yard. They can sit there and rot, for all *I* care. *I* have done my duty. *I* am off the hook!" He shrugged elaborately. "Let the *Bonzen* bitch—let the big-shots bitch! It is no skin off *my* ass!" He turned to leave.

"You are ordered to go to the Kommandantur," the SS man said.

"Delays," Oskar grumbled. "Damned delays." He turned to Gisela. "Come with me, *Fräulein Führerin*," he said. *"Die Beamte*—the bureaucrats—are waiting!"

"You go alone, Weber," the SS guard said. "She stays."

"Oh, brilliant!" Oskar exclaimed. "The *Führerin* is from the *Reichsforschungsrät*—the Reich Research Council. From *Kernphysikalische Forschung*—Atomic Research. *She* has all the papers. Waybills. The works. You don't think she will just dump the damned crates and leave without getting an official receipt, do you?"

The SS guards looked at one another.

"Let me see the papers," Kurt demanded.

Gisela pulled a sheaf of papers from inside her tunic. Her heart beat wildly. Please God—let my hand not shake when I hand them to him. . . .

Kurt took the papers. There were a couple of dozen of them. He riffled through them. Gisela hardly dared breathe. Did they look important enough? Were there enough official stamps? And signatures? They had labored hours during the night trying to make the papers as impressive and intricate and difficult to understand as possible. Would their efforts pass inspection?

Kurt frowned over the papers.

"I will need at least six men," Oskar said plaintively. "Those crates must be filled with lead! Who is going to do the unloading, I ask you? Answer me that! Who? The Kommandantur had better come up with some answers!"

The SS guard handed the papers back to Gisela. "Very well," he said. "You go with Herr Weber. To the Kommandantur."

"Listen, Kurt," Oskar said. "You keep a good watch on those crates. Let no one near them until we return. It is most important."

The SS man nodded. "Make it fast."

He and the other guard rolled back the heavy gate far enough to let Oskar and Gisela through.

Oskar felt enormously gratified. It had worked! Try to push in a load of hay, the *Ami* agent had said, and it will be much easier for them to let a couple of straws go through!

Briskly he and Gisela walked into the area toward the Kommandantur in the Swan Inn. . . .

The ambulance was two minutes early. It skidded to a halt on the service road outside the signal-post shack. Two attendants dismounted.

Sig came running from the shack.

"This way!" he called. "He's in there. Bring a stretcher. He is badly hurt!"

Quickly the two men opened the back of the ambulance and hauled out a stretcher. They hurried to the shack and entered.

They stopped short.

They stared at the Luger held steadily in Dirk's hand.

Sig stood in the doorway behind them. One of the attendants turned to him, eyes wide in his ashen face.

"What is the—"

"Quiet!" Dirk snapped. "We are not here to make conversation. Do exactly as you are told and do it fast—and you will be all right!"

Open-mouthed, the two ambulance attendants stared at him.

"Take your clothes off," he ordered. "Your pants. Your shirts. Your jackets. And hurry it up!" he barked.

The men started. They dropped the stretcher. Quickly they stripped.

"Okay, Sig," Dirk said. "Tie them up!"

Sig moved at once. Using the heavy electrical tape, he lashed the two men's hands together in the back and wound great loops of tape tightly around their ankles, immobilizing them. Finally he placed strips of tape across their mouths, sealing their lips.

Quickly he and Dirk began to exchange their own clothing for the uniforms of the ambulance attendants.

Dirk looked at his watch. 1008 hours.

In another couple of minutes they would be on their way to Haigerloch. . . .

There was only one man on duty in the downstairs reception hall of the farm building serving as the Sperrzone communications center. He looked up pleasantly as Oskar and Gisela entered.

"Can I be of help?" he queried.

"Yes, please," Gisela said. She gave the man a big smile. "I have here this announcement to be read over the public-address system," she said, touching her chest. "I show you."

She walked to the end of the desk. She began to unbutton her uniform tunic. She gave the man a coquettish smile as she slowly loosened the buttons one by one. The man was watching her with evident interest. He was not aware that Oskar had walked quietly around the desk from the other end.

Neither was he aware of the powerful blow to the side of his neck which instantly obliterated his enjoyment.

At once Oskar slung the unconscious body over his shoulder. "Quickly!" he urged. "Upstairs! Before anyone comes."

They hurried up the steps.

They paused before a door marked:

LAUTSPRECHERSYSTEM
KONTROLLE
ZUTRITT FÜR UNBEFÜGTE VERBOTEN

PUBLIC-ADDRESS SYSTEM
CONTROL ROOM
ENTRANCE FOR UNAUTHORIZED PERSONNEL FORBIDDEN

Oskar nodded.

Without knocking, Gisela entered.

A young *Wehrmachthelferin* was sitting at a desk, making entries in a logbook. She looked up in surprise. When she saw Gisela in her non-com uniform, she jumped to her feet and came to attention.

"Name?" Gisela asked.

"Siebert, Maria," the girl answered, her young voice clipped and precise.

"Maria," Gisela said quietly. "If you will make not the slightest sound, you will not be harmed." As she spoke, Oskar appeared in the door with his unconscious burden. He eased the man to the floor and closed the door.

The *Wehrmachthelferin* stared at the two intruders, eyes bulging, color gone from slightly parted lips. She stood rooted to the spot, uttering not a sound.

"Excellent," Gisela said. "I—we should not have liked to hurt you." She walked up to the girl. "Turn around," she said. "Put your hands behind your back." Without a word, the girl obeyed.

Oskar, who had been busy taping the unconscious man's hands and feet, handed Gisela the roll of tape. "Use plenty of it," he said.

Gisela did. "Sit down," she told the girl.

She taped her legs together and fastened them to one leg of the chair. She tore off a few strips of tape. "I am sorry," she said softly. She pressed the strips firmly over the frightened girl's mouth. "You will be all right," Gisela said. "Do not worry. Whatever happens . . . "

Oskar was at the instrument panel.

"One minute," he said. "It will be exactly ten twenty in one minute."

Gisela joined him. Now that the time had come, she felt calm and confident.

"It is much like the set-up at the yard," Oskar observed. "You flip those two switches. One for the area. One for the caves. You speak into this microphone." He turned to a row of buttons. "I will activate the alarms when you are finished. The horns. The sirens. Is it clear?"

Gisela nodded solemnly. "It is clear."

Gisela's mind churned. Would they believe her? All the people out there? Dirk had said they would. They already knew much about him and his friend. The enemy. It was a handicap they could not get around, he had said. So they would make it work *for* them! They would take advantage of the knowledge the Gestapo already had. Someone was bound to learn of their presence in the area, Dirk had pointed out. This way, they would let *everyone* know. *Their* way! They knew the saboteurs were real. They would believe. She could still hear his words. "Pour it on, Gisela. Create as much chaos and panic as you can!"

"Now, Gisela!" Oskar said tensely.

She flipped the two switches. She gripped the microphone stand with both her hands. Her knuckles showed white.

"Achtung!" she cried. She was startled at the desperation in her voice. "Attention! Attention! Red Alert! Red Alert! Emergency!" Her voice was shrill with alarm. "Evacuate! Evacuate! All personnel, evacuate the area immediately! Enemy saboteurs have penetrated the caves! Explosion imminent! Repeat—*Explosion imminent!* Evacuate! Evacuate! . . . "

Oskar stabbed at several buttons.

At once a cacophony of Klaxon horns and sirens screamed their wailing warnings, echoing urgency and danger throughout the area. And underlying the din, the sudden, growing, many-voiced roar of terror and panic . . .

Oskar took Gisela by the arm.

"Come," he said. "We must hurry. There is little time." They ran from the room.

Bursting from the main entrance of the communications center, they instantly found themselves swept into a savage crush of milling people pressing toward the area exit. Pushing, shoving, tearing, frantic to get away from the caves. *Explosion imminent!* Past rumors of a super-explosive power being born in the depths of the caves fed their panic. Oskar grabbed Gisela's arm as she was being carried away in the boiling stream. The blaring horns and piercing sirens fanned the alarm of the crowd. *Evacuate! Evacuate!* Gisela stared in horror at the tumultuous scene. It was her doing! It was bedlam. . . .

Oskar bucked and butted as he shouldered his way through the horde pouring away from the cave entrance toward the exit gate. His hand was firmly locked around Gisela's wrist as he plowed ahead.

They had only a few minutes to reach the bunker at the entrance to the cave. . . .

Dirk slammed on the brakes. The ambulance screeched along the street, narrowly missing the people scrambling to get out of the way. The Klaxon horn shrieked its constant warning —*bah-boo! . . . bah-boo! . . . bah-boo! . . .* The streets were alive with people running away from the area near the caves. He pushed on more slowly, literally nudging people out of the way. Ahead was the checkpoint entrance to the restricted area—the Sperrzone.

A riotous, chaotic crowd of men and women was flooding through the gate. The air was filled with shouts and screams, sirens and horns.

Slowly the ambulance plowed forward, horn wailing. . . .

They were at the gate.

Several SS guards were feverishly trying to control the terrified mob. The crush was so dense that Dirk was forced to stop. A couple of SS men began to fight their way toward him. He leaned out of the cab.

"Get those goddamned people out of the way," he screamed at them. "We've *got* to get through! Do something, dammit!"

One of the guards shouted something at him.

He could not make it out.

"For Christ's sake, *get us through!*" he screamed.

The SS men began to clear a path before the ambulance. Cursing and threatening, they forced the fleeing workers to give way. Inch by inch Dirk prodded the vehicle into the gateway bottleneck. Suddenly the bells in the church tower high atop the cliff began to peal, clanging out their warning.

They were through.

The crowd of people thinned. The furor and turmoil lessened as more and more of the workers fled. The violent uproar began to die down.

They were at the bunker.

Dirk looked around anxiously.

There!

Oskar and Gisela were making their way toward the ambulance.

Gisela gave Dirk a long look. Her eyes shone. Tears streaked her dirt-grimed cheeks, and she had a small cut on her forehead. She looked triumphant.

And beautiful.

Dirk leaped from the cab.

With Sig, he tore open the back doors to the ambulance—and quickly hauled out a stretcher. A couple of blankets lay folded on top. At once they ran for the bunker entrance, followed by Oskar and Gisela.

The two SS men guarding the bunker entrance were still at their posts, frantically herding the last few people from the caves. They eyed the ambulance crew apprehensively as they came running for the entrance.

Urgently Dirk shouted over his shoulder to Sig and Oskar. "Hurry! We may still get him out in time!"

They were at the bunker. Dirk glanced at the SS guards. "Keep the doors open till we get back out!" he called. "Pray God we make it!"

The SS men exchanged a troubled look. They stood aside.

The four ran into the caves.

The corridor inside was empty. The workers and technicians getting ready for the test had fled.

Dirk was startled by the depressing dampness. They ran toward the cross corridor in the back. Every second counted.

They reached the guard post. It was abandoned.

They turned right toward the heavy steel door that would seal off the reactor cave itself.

It gaped wide open!

Dirk and Sig put the stretcher down. They ran to the door. For an instant Dirk was tempted. Could they destroy the pile? For good? He rejected it. Himmelmann was right. It was a chance they could not afford to take. Stick with the original plan. . . .

Quickly they examined the steel hatch. It was a couple of inches thick, swung on a series of massive hinges. There were two heavy locks set into it about two feet apart. Sig worked them. They would lock automatically if the doors were slammed. At once they pushed it shut. Hard. The locks sprang home with a single metallic click.

Dirk ran to the stretcher. He tore the blankets aside. Beneath them lay the dynamite charges. The cans of borax. The *Panzer-faust* warheads. The tools.

"Get going!" Dirk said. "You've got five minutes!"

At once Sig and Oskar grabbed the borax cans, a blanket and the tools. They raced down the corridor toward the heavy-water storage room.

Dirk picked up the five-stick charge. "Gisela," he said hurriedly. "Take the two small charges. Place them in the lab. Just inside the door. One on each side. Where they can be easily reached." He was already running for the steel door.

Gisela snapped up the two charges and ran for the door to the laboratory. . . .

Sig stopped just inside the storage cave. In a glance he absorbed the layout. The huge heavy-water storage tank stood about three feet off the cave floor on a sturdy wood-and-steel platform. A maze of pipes with a variety of diameters ran along the walls and to the tank itself. Some were studded with meters and gauges and valves. Sig was certain he could identify some of the equipment. The access-port cover on top of the tank was firmly bolted in place, as he had known it would be. A pipe from what seemed to be a liquid-air or nitrogen cold trap led to the top of the tank above them, controlled by a valve set close to the tank wall. A second pipe also entered the top portion of the storage tank. A dry-air source? It, too, had a valve on it. At the bottom of the tank a heavy pipe ran toward a small opening in the wall, where it disappeared. There was a valve at the tank itself, and another a couple of feet from the wall. The pipe slanted downward. It was the pipe through which the heavy water would flow to the reactor in the floor pit in the adjoining cave.

He made his decision. He pointed to the valve on the pipe between the storage tank and the cold trap.

"We'll use that one. Up there," he said. "We can dismantle it without screwing things up. The pipe slants into the tank, and the borax powder will roll directly down into the heavy water. It'll have plenty of time to dissolve before the test."

He looked around. He spied a tall A-ladder on rollers. He ran for it.

Oskar was already spreading the blanket on the floor under the valve above. Any borax spillage would have to be caught. They must leave no trace.

Sig positioned the ladder and at once they climbed up. The valve was easy to reach.

Quickly Oskar began to dismantle it. He loosened the bonnet screws and lifted out the stem and gate. Below was an opening in the pipe about two inches in diameter.

Sig had opened the cans of borax crystals. He suddenly swore.

"Shit! How the hell do we pour the damned stuff into the hole in the pipe down through the valve housing? Some of it is bound to be caught in the body. We'll never clean it out completely!"

"They may not discover it," Oskar said.

"They will. Once they run into trouble, they'll check everything. Dammit—we should have brought a funnel!"

"A funnel?" Oskar frowned.

"We've got to have something to pour the borax through. Make it out of paper. A thin sheet of metal." He swore angrily. "Dammit! There goes the time!" He started down the ladder. "I'll take a look around. There's got to be something. . . . "

"Wait!" Oskar said eagerly. "This will work."

Balancing himself precariously on the ladder, he took off his right shoe. He peeled off his sock. With his knife he sliced off the foot and dropped it to the blanket below. He held up the tubelike sock.

"Here," he said, a wide grin on his face. "We can pour the borax through this!"

Sig grabbed the sock from him. He stuffed it through the valve body into the hole in the pipe. With the screwdriver, he spread out the fabric so that an opening was formed. He held the top open.

"Pour it in!" he said.

Dirk worked rapidly. Quietly. He wanted to place the charge at the door where it would do the most damage. It had to look good.

Suddenly a gruff voice shattered the silence.

"What are you doing there?"

Dirk whirled at the voice.

At the checkpoint desk stood an SS man. One of the guards from the bunker entrance. He glared suspiciously, his Schmeisser machine pistol trained unwaveringly at Dirk's gut.

Dirk felt his heart stop. Then pound in his ears.

It could not end like this!

Instinctively his hand twitched toward the Luger in his belt. He checked himself at once. He could not risk a shot.

He did not stand up. He turned back to the charge at the heavy door.

"Am I glad you showed up!" he exclaimed fervently, without looking back at the SS man. "I found it! The explosive! I think I can defuse it. Quickly! Give me a hand!"

He did not breathe. He listened with every cell of his body. The guard was walking toward him. Closer. His hobnailed boots heavy on the rock floor of the corridor. Closer. Bending down to look . . .

Now!

Dirk exploded from his crouched position. His hunched shoulders slammed into the Schmeisser. It flew from the guard's hands to clatter along the rock. In the same motion he grabbed the man's uniform at the waist, threw himself backward to the floor and sent the guard flying over his head to crash against the rock wall of the tunnel.

Dirk was on his feet at once. In an instant he was at the side of the fallen guard lying crumpled at the wall.

He stopped. His breath came in agonized gulps. His hands fell to his side.

It was over.

The man's head lay at an odd angle to his body. The force of the crash had broken his neck.

Gisela stood in the door to the lab. White-faced, she stared at the dead SS guard.

It had taken less than twenty seconds. Twenty seconds between life and death. . . .

The charges were all set. The two *Panzerfaust* warheads had been placed with the dynamite. One at the door. One in the lab. Ready to blow.

Dirk felt a sudden stab of pain in his arm and chest, a sudden chill numbing his mind. He had a flash vision of a rubble-strewn office in Holland—and Jan. . . .

He shook himself mentally.

When *this* explosion went off, he'd be far away.

He glanced at his watch. Almost 1040 hours.

Sig and Oskar were running late. . . .

Frowning, he turned to Gisela. "Get on the stretcher," he said. "Pull the blanket over you."

Anxiously he glanced toward the storage room. 1040 hours. They were on the ragged edge. He still had to light the fuses. . . .

There! Sig and Oskar came running from the cave.

He did not wait for them. He dashed for the lab. He had it figured to the second. Charges one, two and three. With progressively shorter fuses. They should all go at once. . . .

Finished. All three fuses were sputtering. He ran to the others. Sig was already at the stretcher. He was staring at the dead SS guard, eyes wide. He threw a quick glance at Dirk, but said nothing. Oskar was packing the tools around Gisela, spreading the extra blanket over her.

Dirk took hold of the stretcher.

They raced for the exit. . . .

Only a few people, running around dazed and confused, remained outside the bunker.

They ran for the ambulance.

Any second now . . .

They shoved the stretcher with Gisela on it up into the open ambulance. Sig jumped in with her.

Dirk ran for the driver's seat.

Suddenly a hollow, booming explosion rent the air. The mountain shook. Almost at once the steel doors to the cave entrance flew open, spewing out a dense cloud of dust and smoke. One of them was wrenched from its hinges. Tumbling end over end, it slammed into the wooden shack nearby. The ventilation chimney on the bunker roof burst from its base and shot high up into the air. Rocks and boulders broke loose from the cliff wall and crashed to the ground below. Stones and gravel rattled down in a rain of rubble.

Clouds of black smoke billowed from the cave entrance as the workers outside, shouting with terror, ran from the bunker opening. . . .

Dirk was in the ambulance cab. He had already started the engine. Oskar slammed the back doors shut and raced around the ambulance to enter the cab on the other side.

Suddenly he stopped dead.

From the direction of the communications-center building, two SS guards came running.

The guards from the railroad gate!

One of them pointed to Oskar.

"Da ist er!" he shouted. "There he is!"

They were only a few feet away.

Oskar gave a quick glance at the ambulance already slowly moving away. He clamped down on his teeth so hard that the muscles in his jaws corded. Then, with a quick wrench, he started to race away from the vehicle, closely pursued by the two SS men.

In the rearview mirror Dirk saw the brief chase.

"No!" he cried involuntarily. "No! No!" He pounded his fist on the steering wheel in impotent frustration. His eyes burned. His throat tightened. "No, dammit! No . . . "

Oskar was caught. Surrounded by jostling, screaming men, arms pinned by the SS guards. He did not glance in the direction of the moving ambulance.

And Dirk did not stop. There was nothing they could do. He knew with absolute certainty that Oskar was a dead man. Only —it would take a long time for him to die. An eternity of torture. Before the final heartbeat. A dreadful thought stabbed him. *Would Oskar talk?* Had their efforts been in vain after all? Angrily he pushed it from his mind. He speeded up, hit the Klaxon horn savagely. The milling crowd had almost disappeared.

He raced through the checkpoint gate and careened past a staff car, which narrowly gave way before it sped through the gate into the devastated Haigerloch Sperrzone. . . .

In the back seat sat an SS officer. Ramrod straight . . .

3

Standartenführer Harbicht barely managed to suppress his fury. He had no desire to display in front of Rauner and Professor Reichardt his rage at having failed to protect the Project. The enemy agents had actually bested him. The thought burned bitter in his mind.

There was only one minor consolation. It was, of course, important, but it did little to salve his badly damaged ego.

The saboteurs had failed!

He had spent better than an hour inspecting the damage the explosives had done to the cave installation. As soon as it had become apparent that no further danger existed, he had ordered the technicians and scientists rounded up and returned to the cave. Reichardt had been one of the first to show up. Pale and frightened, he had joined Harbicht in examining the blast damage.

The vital question was: Could the crucial test ordered by Berlin still be carried out on schedule?

Harbicht was all too vividly aware of the importance of the question. The dire ramifications of it—should the answer be *no!* If the test had to be called off because of *his* failure to provide security. Impatiently he pushed it from his mind, refusing to dwell on it.

The laboratory was totally destroyed. Reichardt had declared it to be of little consequence at this stage of developments. Anything that needed to be done could be carried out in alternate facilities.

The vital reactor cave and control center were virtually undamaged. That was the essential fact. Harbicht experienced a touch of gratification. Obviously the enemy saboteurs had not known about the massive steel hatch that sealed off the heart of the installation. It gave him a sort of perverse pleasure to contemplate the dismay and frustration they must have felt when they discovered the locked door! The blast they had set off had sprung it, but it had been impossible to open it. His own men had been forced to use torches to cut the remaining hinges so as to gain entrance to the caves beyond.

The cave that held the heavy-water storage tank, apart from being shaken up, had sustained no damage. It was far enough removed from the source of the explosion. But technicians were nevertheless checking everything, every gauge, every valve for signs of cracks or warps, any sign that tightening and adjusting were necessary.

Some minor damage *had* occurred both in the reactor cave and in the control center. From the very force of the explosion. The key word was *minor.* Reichardt had assured him the necessary repairs and clean-up could be accomplished in two or three hours. The critical test would go on as scheduled—with only an hour's delay.

Harbicht was aware of a vague uneasiness in the back of his mind. Something he had overlooked? He had carefully examined everything. Gone over every possibility. Was there some point he did not see? He did not try to force it. He knew from experience that if something was worrying at him, it would surface faster if left alone.

He had briefly questioned a few individuals who had been in contact with the saboteurs. Two SS guards, a young *Wehrmachthelferin* and a man who had been too groggy to be coherent. And he had painstakingly pieced together the ploy the saboteurs had used in order to gain access to the caves. He felt a grudging respect for their ingenuity and audacity.

He also felt a stinging anger at the realization that he himself had passed within arm's length of the saboteurs as he arrived at the Haigerloch Sperrzone. They had escaped cleanly. All but one . . .

A German . . . A traitor! He had been right. The enemy agents had indeed been helped by a local *Widerstandsgruppe.* He felt the rage rise in him. The man was being held at the local security office at the Swan Inn.

It was time to have a little talk with him. . . .

Harbicht openly studied the man standing before him, his arms held firmly by two SS guards.

A large man. Well built. Strong. Obviously a man used to working with his hands. Not the brain behind the operation. He had a bruise over one eye and his clothing was torn.

The man met his gaze steadily. He looked determined. Stoic. Harbicht sighed inwardly. So many of these unimaginative clods were that way. He would not be easy to break. Certainly not in a hurry. And time was the only commodity he, Harbicht, did not have. The man simply *had* to talk. *Now.*

He turned to Rauner.

"Who is this man?" he asked.

Rauner stepped in front of Oskar.

"Name?" he barked.

Oskar did not answer.

Rauner got a dangerous look on his face. His eyes narrowed. "I asked you your name," he said.

Oskar remained silent. He thought back to what the *Ami* agent had said. When they had been talking about—interrogation. Keep your mouth shut, he had said. Do not even give them the time of day, he had said. Say nothing. As soon as you open your mouth, it is damned difficult to close it again! He said nothing.

Rauner eyed him maliciously. He'd be damned if that peasant would make him look incompetent in front of Harbicht. With measured steps, he walked behind Oskar. Suddenly he grabbed one of his arms and twisted it to his back.

"One last time," he snarled. *"What is your name?"*

Oskar did not answer.

All at once Rauner pulled his twisted arm upward with as much force as he could muster. There was an audible snap as Oskar's shoulder left its socket.

Harbicht was watching him intently. A low, hoarse groan escaped the man's throat, but it was quickly cut off. Pain flooded his eyes and the muscles in his strong jaws knotted. He did not turn. He stared straight ahead, eyes hooded. Interesting. Not bad for a curtain-raiser . . .

Rauner let go of the arm. It fell, hanging useless at Oskar's side.

"Now, now, Obersturmführer," Harbicht said, his voice mildly reproachful. "The man is quite right. We do not have to ask him his name. We have his papers, do we not?" He turned to the desk behind him. "Ah. Yes. Here they are." He studied them briefly. "Weber," he said. "Oskar Weber. Foreman at the railroad yard at Hechingen." He looked at Rauner. "You see, Obersturmführer, we already have that information." He turned back to Oskar. "You must forgive the Obersturmführer, Herr Weber. He is impetuous." He shook his head regretfully. "I am afraid you have been hurt needlessly. This time." He looked at Rauner. "Have this man taken to the infirmary," he instructed him. "Have them take care of that arm of his. I will talk to him there."

The infirmary was antiseptically white and clean. There was the usual pungent odor of disinfectants. Glass cases with glass shelves and glass doors held trays of gleaming instruments and rows of bottles and jars. Two stony-faced female attendants in white smocks were on duty. A variety of medical equipment and machinery stood neatly against one wall. The only thing out of place was a massive wooden chair with a high back and long, broad arm-rests standing in the middle of the room.

Oskar stood, stripped to the waist, held by the SS guards as Harbicht entered.

"Ah!" he said. "They are taking care of you. Good. That shoulder of yours must be set." He nodded quickly to the attendants.

The two women walked over to Oskar. They looked at him dispassionately. One of them took hold of his shoulders, the other grabbed his limply dangling arm. With a quick, powerful pull, she jerked the arm forward and upward.

Oskar winced. For a second he screwed his eyes tightly shut. Then he looked at Harbicht.

Harbicht nodded. "You stand pain well, Herr Weber," he observed quietly. There was a trace of admiration—and regret—in his voice. "Perhaps we should find out just how well. . . . "

Again he nodded, his head moving with a quick, jerky motion. "Strip him!" he said.

The attendants at once obeyed.

Harbicht was watching closely. It was always a moment of humiliation. He did not want to miss it. He was interested in seeing how this man Weber would handle it. He could make use of that knowledge.

Oskar stood stock still. Like a mannequin. Letting the attendants manhandle him. Interesting. The man had enough sense to know when resistance was useless—and enough obstinacy not to cooperate.

They pulled off his shoes. On one foot the man was wearing a black sock. On the other—nothing. . . .

Harbicht started. The man wore only one sock. Why?

A fleeting thought invaded his mind. There was another annoying puzzle still unsolved. A pair of abandoned boots. The boots left behind by the missing Decker. It still gnawed at him. And now this. A missing sock. Why? With the unerring instinct of a good investigator, he knew that the two ridiculous incidents were nevertheless significant. It greatly irritated him to know also that he had little chance of ever learning why. He resented being defeated by a pair of boots and a sock. . . .

Oskar stood naked. Roughly the women attendants pushed him down in the large chair. Quickly—with the expertness born of practice—they fastened a leather strap from the back of the chair around his chest. They clamped both his wrists to the long arm-rests with two more straps, his hands lying flat on the ends of the boards. And they trussed his feet to the sturdy legs of the chair. He sat naked. Utterly helpless. Utterly vulnerable . . .

Harbicht contemplated him. . . .

A railroad worker. It would be he who had engineered the ambulance feint—although he surely had not thought of it. It would be he who had rigged the crates filled with bricks that he brought to Haigerloch. It was he who had been the brawn at the communications-center takeover. Had he also planned it? Harbicht dismissed the idea. It *had* to be the work of the two *verfluchte* enemy agents. . . .

He felt uneasy. The nagging feeling just below the level of consciousness still disturbed him. Something was not right about the sabotage mission. What was it?

Even though the saboteurs had not been able to reach the pile itself—had they really done the best they could? Granted the limitations of the explosives they could bring in: had they? Thank God someone had had the presence of mind to slam the security hatch. He smiled a cold inward smile. He had already talked to half a dozen men who claimed to have done it! . . .

His mind was working rapidly, trying to analyze the situation before he began to question the traitor-saboteur. He had to produce results at once. . . . The sabotage attempt had been, at best, inefficient. Not in keeping with the brilliantly conceived and executed penetration operation. Still—what *could* they have done once inside? Once they discovered the locked steel door? If they had used all their explosives at the door, they might have blown it open. But then they would have had no explosives left to destroy the pile itself. . . . From Reichardt he had learned the importance of the heavy water. If the enemy agents had blown up the storage tank, a far greater delay would have resulted. If, indeed, it would have been possible to replace the heavy water at Haigerloch at all—within the time frame available and at the present stage of the war. Could the saboteurs have known about the alternate installation at the *Alpenfestung?* Not possible . . .

Then *why* did they not destroy the heavy-water supply? Why? They might not have known the storage cave was accessible to them, of course. Possible—but not likely. They obviously knew where the reactor cave was located. But, then again, they had not known about the steel security hatch. Or were they not aware of the importance of the heavy water? Did they not know it was kept separate from the pile? He doubted it. That, too, would be out of keeping with their obvious familiarity with the Project. . . .

He frowned. He was indulging in seesaw reasoning. It would produce no concrete results. The answers would *have* to come from the man strapped in the chair before him.

He felt irritated. Something was escaping him. Somehow he still did not see the complete picture. Angrily he cleared his mind and fixed his cold eyes on Oskar.

"Now, Herr Weber," he said evenly. "I have a great many questions to ask you. Questions that *do* require answers." He looked steadily at him. "I should like to know, for instance, who else belongs to your group—your *Widerstandsgruppe* in Hechingen. Where are they? And who on the inside at Haigerloch helped you?" He smiled unpleasantly. "And—why are you wearing only one sock? Many more . . ." He paused. He sighed. "However, in the interest of expediency I shall limit myself to two questions, Herr Weber. Two questions to which I admit I must have immediate answers."

Again he paused. "One: Where are the two enemy saboteurs with whom you worked? Two: What was the *real* purpose of the sabotage raid?"

A blinding realization gripped Oskar. He did not betray it by a flicker of an eyelash. But he felt himself go cold. The officer suspected! But he would not *know*—unless he, Oskar, talked. Oh, God! Would he have the strength to keep silent? . . . Dimly he was aware that Harbicht was talking.

"You are, of course, quite correct in your surmise that you will be—ah—tortured, Herr Weber. But perhaps you have no clear comprehension of what that actually means. Let me assure you, ultimately you will talk. My purpose, admittedly, is to convince you of the futility of keeping silent. To persuade you to talk *now*. I am confident I will succeed."

He snapped his fingers at one of the attendants. The woman went to a glass case and took out a tray of surgical instruments. She brought it to Harbicht.

"Normally I am not this—eh—frank with my subjects, Herr Weber, but in this case time is important, and I have hopes you are a man who can see reason. To help you, I shall perform a small demonstration."

He picked up a scalpel. It was razor sharp, with a wicked curved point.

"Pain, Herr Weber," Harbicht continued, "is alive! It leaps. It twists. It soars. No place is inaccessible to it. It has no limits. . . ."

He touched the scalpel gently to Oskar's chest. The cold steel seemed to sear his skin.

"The human body has many points that are especially sensitive to pain," Harbicht went on, like a lecturer in a classroom. He placed the tip of the scalpel on the base of the nail on the middle finger of Oskar's right hand as it lay in the leather vise. "Here, for example. A particularly sensitive spot."

He pressed the scalpel down through the nail. Oskar stiffened convulsively. Liquid fire shot from the tip of his finger through his arm. He groaned through tightly clenched teeth, and he strained his arm against his manacle, trying to free it, unmindful of the leather strap that was tearing the skin on his wrist.

Harbicht removed the scalpel. He dropped it into a metal bowl with a sharp clatter.

"You see, Herr Weber," he said pleasantly. "Pain can be quite excruciating, can it not?"

He looked closely at Oskar.

"Yes. Of course," he commented matter-of-factly. "And still —there are other factors, Herr Weber. More terrifying . . ."

He nodded curtly to the other white-clad attendant. She at once went to a small table and opened a drawer.

"You see, Herr Weber," Harbicht explained. "Knowing *where* the pain will strike, as you did just now, *how* it will be inflicted, gives a strong man an edge. An advantage, if you will. He can anticipate it. He can steel himself to endure it. As you did. Yes . . ."

He smiled. A terrible smile which never reached his eyes. He motioned to the attendant at the table. The woman came over.

"However, Herr Weber, we can take that edge away! I think you will be amazed at the difference it makes. When you no longer know *where* the pain will strike. Or *how*. Or—*when.*"

He reached. The attendant handed him a small black object. He held it up for Oskar to see.

"A blindfold, Herr Weber," he said. "Simply—a blindfold." He shrugged. It was a strangely chilling gesture. "We could, of course, blind you. But that seems so—permanent. It might remove a certain, shall we say, incentive to talk. No. A blindfold is quite as effective."

He threw it at the attendant. The woman at once placed it across Oskar's eyes.

Blackness . . .

Fear enveloped him at once.

He felt himself straining to hear. There was utter silence. What were they doing? His naked flesh crawled. What would they do to him? He waited. The pain would strike . . . *now!* . . . He shivered . . .

Nothing . . .

Harbicht spoke.

"Finally, Herr Weber," he said, "there are the fears in our

own minds. The special fears we all possess. They are the most powerful. That special place on our own body where we fear pain the most. That secret, intimate place we must hold inviolate at all costs . . ."

He paused.

"Where is yours, Herr Weber?" he asked almost seductively.

Oskar fought against the leather straps binding him, already slippery with his blood. They gave not a fraction of an inch. . . .

Where?

When?

His mind screamed.

Suddenly he felt a light, cold touch on the nipple of his breast. A short cry burst from his lips.

"Here, Herr Weber?" Harbicht whispered.

A cut slicing into the skin of his abdomen made him twitch with sudden shock.

"Here?"

Oskar was trembling. He knew it. He could not stop. He waited. . . .

Oh, God . . .

He listened.

He could hear nothing—except his own tortured breathing.

Suddenly he felt a sharp hard tap on his testicles. He screamed. He could do nothing else. Waves of agony washed over him, spreading to every nerve end in his body. He was suddenly aware of his testicles utterly unprotected beneath him. He struggled against the leather straps. He sobbed.

"Ah, Herr Weber!" Harbicht exclaimed with pleasure. "The secret spot! Not so different from other men, are you, Herr Weber?"

His voice suddenly grew brusque. "Where are the enemy agents, Weber?" He shot out the question. "What was your *real* purpose?"

Oskar's mind whirled in a turmoil of anguish. With all his being he wanted to end the pain. He would talk. No! Gisela. The others. Anna . . . He could not sacrifice them. If he talked, he would perpetuate creatures like this Gestapo beast. *He—would —not—talk!* . . . He heard himself sobbing. He stopped at once. He heard a low, rumbling sound. Something was being rolled across the linoleum floor. Something big. What was it? . . .

It stopped. He listened, struggled to understand. . . . Clanks. Scrapes. Snaps . . . What were they going to do? . . .

A sudden, sharp pain shot through him as if with a life of its own. Something had been clamped with a tight, sharp bite into one of his nipples. . . . He jerked violently as an iron grip clutched one of his testicles. . . .

Alligator clamps . . .

And he knew!

He sobbed. His mind shrieked.

He tried to steel himself.

The fiery shock went through him. A million white-hot needles stabbed into every nerve. The pain raged through his loins. It was the only reality in the whole world. There was only one thing to do. Stop it! Stop it any way possible. At any cost . . .

As suddenly as it had been turned on, the current was switched off.

Talk! Tell them anything!

At the edge of his mind, through the cotton-wool silence in the room, he was aware of someone talking harshly to him. The Gestapo colonel? He could not focus.

But one clear thought reached him in his sea of pain.

Talk now—and everything he had lived for, everything he had endured, would be in vain. . . . In an instant he would obliterate himself. And all the others . . .

He—would—not. . . .

Yet he knew with absolute certainty he could not bear the torture any longer. His will would be shredded in an instant. There was only one way to end it.

Death.

But how? How? His aching arms were held tightly by the leather straps. His legs. The skin was torn and bleeding where he had strained against his bonds in his spasms of raw agony. He had been wholly unaware of it. Unaware? . . .

The massive pain had overridden all other hurts. There, perhaps, was the hope. The way he could rob the Gestapo colonel of his triumph . . .

Suddenly the blindfold was torn from his eyes. He found himself staring into the face of his enemy. His tortured eyes, peering from their sockets as if in the rictus of near-death, sought and met the cold, derisive eyes of his tormentor.

Oskar smiled. It was a hellish grimace.

He could do it.

There *was* a way.

"Ready, Herr Weber?" Harbicht mocked. He nodded imperceptibly.

Again the searing current burned through his tortured body. *Now . . .!*

He bit down. With all the power he could muster he bit down.

He felt his teeth meet and grind together, severing his tongue. And there was no pain. Only the terrible fire billowing from his loins . . .

He felt the hot blood spurt and well in his mouth. He felt it pour down his throat . . . all without pain . . .

He breathed. Deeply. Exultantly. In triumph. The moist, velvety warmth rushing into his lungs brought him deliverance. . . .

Harbicht held up his hand.

"Enough," he said. "He is unconscious."

He snapped his fingers. "Revive him!"

Suddenly he stared at his victim, bent over him. How could the man look—serene?

Alarm assailed him. A trickle of blood was seeping from the corner of Weber's mouth. Harbicht grabbed his chin. He pressed the jaws apart. A cascade of blood welled out and gushed across his fingers, drenching the man's naked chest.

And a crimson lump.

It plopped to the floor. . . .

"*Verflucht!*" Harbicht cursed. He slapped a vicious blow across Oskar's lifeless cheek. "The bastard drowned himself! In his own stinking blood!" He stared at the body.

The words of Aeschylus, learned long ago and long forgotten, came to his mind to mock him. *Pain lays not its touch upon a corpse. . . .*

Abruptly he turned away.

"Get rid of him. He is of no further use to me."

He strode to a washbasin and turned the faucet on. He held his hands under the streaming water and rubbed. Rubbed and rubbed . . .

His only lead had been destroyed. But he felt coldly determined. He would find the enemy saboteurs. *By God, he would!*

He forced himself to think calmly. The enemy agents and their German accomplices would still be in Hechingen. They would have to be. He had given the alarm as soon as he had learned of the ambulance. It had not left the area. He would find it. Even if he had to turn over Hechingen brick by brick . . .

And—when he did . . .

The shrill clanging of a bell interrupted him. It was the telephone. One of the SS guards answered it. He held the receiver out for Harbicht.

"Herr Standartenführer," he said.

The Gestapo colonel took it.

"Harbicht!" he snapped. He listened. Stonily. Without a word he replaced the receiver. Slowly he turned to gaze wide-eyed at the dead man slumped in the massive chair.

It had been Professor Reichardt on the phone. The final, crucial test of the Haigerloch pile had been completed.

It had failed!

4

Dirk was getting increasingly uneasy.

There was well over half a tank of gasoline left in the tank of the ambulance. It was more than enough to take them where they had to go. No problem.

It was the time that worried him. It was moving too fast.

He glanced at his watch. It was nearly 1900 hours. They had been hiding in the ramshackle barn close to eight hours now. Too long? Or not long enough? There was a fine edge between letting enough time go by for the immediate scramble of pursuit to die down—and staying in the barn so long that discovery became imminent. Or—Oskar talked . . . It was Oskar who had suggested the abandoned barn near the village of Bodelshausen on a side road about four kilometers north of the main Hechingen-Haigerloch road. They had picked the barn as a place to hole up in case something went wrong and they became separated or were unable to return to the house. With Oskar's capture they had headed straight for the barn. Once they left it, it would be the final, irrevocable step in writing Oskar off. He knew it. Gisela knew it. They had to give Oskar every possible chance to get away. Get out of it and join them. But time was getting to be critical. . . .

He looked toward the girl.

She stood silent, rigid, quietly looking out through the large crack in the side of the barn. Looking down the little road that snaked peacefully through the wooded hills. She had stood there for hours. . . .

Sig glanced at Dirk. He knew the anguish his friend was feeling.

By now the Haigerloch test had been run. He'd pretty near give his right arm to know what had happened. But all he knew was that they were in greater danger than ever before. A danger that grew with every passing moment . . .

Dirk had made the right decision. When he'd seen Oskar detained by the SS guards and had spotted the Gestapo staff car racing into the Sperrzone, he'd known it would be only a matter of minutes before a general alarm was sounded. Not time enough for them to get out of the area without being spotted. And with Oskar caught, they could not risk returning to the house. Holing up in the barn had seemed the only thing to do. But by now eight hours had gone by. If they were to go on to Stuttgart and lose themselves in the big city as they had planned to do if it became impossible to stay in Hechingen, they had better get started. There seemed little chance now that Oskar could talk himself out of his dilemma. If he could have done so, it would have happened long ago. . . . Forget about escaping. They had him. And he *did* know of the emergency rallying place at the barn. He *could* be made to talk. In eight hours. Sig tried not to think about it. But all his senses were acutely alert for the first signs of approaching trouble.

He bit his lip. The mission which right now should have been completed successfully might turn out to be no more than an exercise in futility—if the Gestapo forced the truth out of Oskar. What should have been a time of triumph had become a time of uncertainty and grief.

He looked at Dirk. He felt he had to say something. The brooding silence was getting on his nerves. Any moment he expected to hear the laboring noises of approaching vehicles.

"It worked," he said, attempting enthusiasm. "Your crazy ambulance trick. It sure worked! It was a hell of an idea!"

Dirk did not look at him.

"Yeah," he said, his voice lackluster. "It worked. Hell, that gimmick was used a long time ago. Only the Greeks didn't use an ambulance. They used a wooden horse."

Sig felt a momentary irritation. Shit! He knew the Trojan Horse story as well as Dirk. He was only trying to pull them out of the doldrums. He didn't need a lecture in history, for crissake! He calmed down.

Dirk walked over to Gisela. He put his arm around her waist and drew her to him. She leaned her head against him.

"He won't come, Gisela," he said softly.

She looked up at him, dry-eyed. "I know," she whispered.

"We'll have to leave. Soon," he said. "It won't be safe here much longer. Oskar knows of this place." He cursed himself the instant he said it. Quickly he glanced at the girl.

For a moment she closed her eyes. She gave a small sob.

"You will have to come with us," he said. "You can't return home."

She nodded bleakly. "What about Tante Anna?" she asked.

"She'll be okay," Dirk assured her. He hoped he sounded convincing. "There's no way they can connect her to the raid. We made sure every scrap of uniform material was removed from her shop."

"She is Oskar's sister," Gisela said tonelessly.

Sig joined them.

"We'd better take off," he said.

Dirk nodded. He turned to the girl.

"Gisela," he said earnestly. "You do understand?"

She nodded heavily.

"Look. You know this area?"

"Yes."

"How do we get to Stuttgart?"

"This road." She glanced out the crack in the barn side. "It runs into the main Tübingen-Stuttgart highway. Just outside Hechingen. It is only two or three kilometers."

Dirk frowned. "Is there a way to get to the Stuttgart road without getting too close to Hechingen?" he asked. "A back road? That joins it?"

"Yes," she said. "Over Rottenburg. It does not link up with the main road until around Tübingen." She frowned. "It is a little longer that way. Maybe ten, twelve kilometers."

"That's okay." Dirk looked searchingly at the girl. "Will you show us?"

She nodded.

"I will show you."

Dirk drove the ambulance as fast as he dared along the narrow, winding mountain road toward the village of Rottenburg. Every foot traveled, every second spent out in the open, increased his edginess. Dusk was beginning to mantle the countryside. Soon he would be forced to turn on his lights or be reduced to a snail's pace.

He felt dangerously exposed. Like a tin duck moving across the target line in a shooting gallery.

They had sixty kilometers to cover before they hit the city of Stuttgart. . . .

Gefreiter Meissner stared incredulously through his binoculars. When he and Keller had been ordered out on their bicycles to patrol an area of the hills north of Hechingen in search of a *verschissene* ambulance, the last thing in the world he'd expected was actually to find it!

"Donnerwetter!" he exclaimed. "By thunder! There it is." He pointed.

Far below on a winding road a gray ambulance, the red cross prominent on its side, was careening into the mountains.

He whipped his map from his pocket. With a stubby, dirty-nailed finger he searched and traced.

"That would be the road to Rottenburg," he said excitedly. "And Tübingen."

He glanced at his partner.

"Josef-Maria!" he exclaimed. "Close your mouth before a bat flies in! And get on the *verdammte* radio!"

He had learned nothing.

Hours of questioning, threatening, investigating had produced not a single lead. And Reichardt had not the slightest idea of why the reactor had failed! There was obviously something radically wrong with either the geometry of the pile—or the theory itself.

Harbicht clenched his teeth.

The saboteurs had vanished. And the ambulance. Had they had time to lay a false trail? If they had, he was totally unaware of it. He had *no* trail to follow. False or otherwise. Frustration was bitter in his throat.

He paced his office. He was not satisfied with the evaluation of the reactor failure made by Reichardt and his staff. Not at all. The nagging suspicion that there was an aspect of the case totally unperceived refused to leave him. Capturing the enemy saboteurs was imperative. When he did, he would find the answers. He was convinced of it. But he would have to wait until he had something concrete before he went to Reichardt—or over his head, preferably. Had the saboteurs had inside help? Inside information? If so, from whom? That might be another source of information to shed light on what really had happened. As it was, he was left with a single lead.

A dead man.

There was a knock on the door and Obersturmführer Rauner hurriedly entered. He had a notebook in his hand. Harbicht turned to him.

"What did you find?" he asked at once.

"We searched the house of the man Weber," Rauner said soberly. "Very thoroughly. He lived there with his niece. A girl named Gisela Storp. She cannot be found. She—"

"The girl with the saboteurs," Harbicht interrupted impatiently. "Go on!"

"Yes. Undoubtedly. There was evidence of other people having lived in the house." He paused. He frowned. "But—we found no positive leads."

"What else?" Harbicht snapped.

Rauner consulted his notebook. "Weber's supervisor at the railroad yard, a Yardmaster Schindler, gives the man the highest recommendations—"

"Fool!" Harbicht spat.

"He was known to frequent a *Bierstube* called *Zum Güterzug*. He was seen there in the company of others."

"Who?"

"We had an informer checking the place," Rauner said. Again he referred to his notebook. "Weber was seen there with his nephew, one Otto Storp, a railroad worker who died in a recent yard accident. With two men unknown to our informer, and also at the same table—" He looked up at Harbicht. "—although it is uncertain if they were together or merely sharing the table as is the custom of the place—with a professor—"

"Name?"

"Himmelmann. Professor Gustav Himmelmann. Apparently the professor stopped in occasionally."

Himmelmann! Harbicht remembered the man. From his briefing by that Berlin general at Haigerloch. He felt the familiar jolt of excitement which discovery always brought. With the certainty of the experienced investigator, he knew he had run across a vital piece of information. *Himmelmann.* The inside link? He looked piercingly at his subordinate.

"I want a full report," he ordered. "Weber's friends. Family. Co-workers. And Himmelmann. Everything. Understood?"

"Jawohl, Herr Standartenführer!"

"And I want it *now!*"

Rauner tapped his notebook. "I have it all here, *Herr Standartenführer.* I shall write it up at once." He clicked his heels.

He turned to leave.

The shrill ring of the telephone stopped him. He put the notebook on the desk. He picked up the receiver.

"Gestapo!" he said crisply.

He listened. His eyes stretched wide. He turned to Harbicht. *"Herr Standartenführer!"* he said excitedly. "The ambulance! It has been spotted!"

"Where?"

"On the road to Rottenburg—and Tübingen!"

Harbicht was already half out the door.

Rauner dropped the receiver. He started for the door. He stopped. Quickly he turned, scooped up his notebook and put it in his tunic pocket.

He ran after Harbicht. . . .

Rottenburg had been left behind. They were entering Tübingen.

Dirk pushed the button activating the Klaxon horn. It was a risk. But if the alarm was out in Tübingen, they would be stopped whether their damned horn was going or not. This way they'd get through town faster. . . .

It was getting dark. Dirk turned the hooded headlights on.

He sped through the streets toward the *Stadtmitte,* the center of town. He was gripping the steering wheel so tightly his knuckles showed white. His arm hurt.

Traffic was a little heavier—but it obediently gave way. He was nearing an intersection. A policeman was directing traffic. He cleared the way for them—and they raced through.

A few moments later they were on the open road speeding toward Stuttgart.

Thirty kilometers to go. . . .

Harbicht sat next to the driver, rigid with impatience. In back were Rauner and two SS men. All were armed. Tübingen was ahead. They had taken the direct route. There was a chance—a slim chance—they could cut off the ambulance before it reached town from the Rottenburg road. He urged the white-faced driver to greater speed.

They entered town. The driver leaned on the horn, scattering other vehicles, bicyclists and pedestrians. Ahead was an inter-section. A policeman was directing traffic.

"Stop here!" Harbicht called.

The driver skidded to a halt next to the startled policeman. Harbicht impatiently beckoned the man over.

The policeman gave him a stiff-armed salute.

"Heil Hitler!"

"Have you seen an ambulance?" Harbicht shot at him.

"Ambulance?" The man scratched his ear.

"Yes! Ambulance, you idiot!" Harbicht thundered.

"Ah, yes!" The man brightened. "The ambulance. It came through here. Going very fast." He drew himself up. "I gave it the right of way!"

"Why the devil didn't you stop it?"

"Stop it?" The policeman looked thunderstruck. "But—it was an emergency. It was quite clear. I had no reason to—to stop it."

Harbicht knew the man was right. "Imbecile!" he snapped. "Which way did it go?"

"On the Stuttgart Strasse," the policeman answered fretfully. "Stuttgart."

"How long ago?"

"Five, ten minutes."

Harbicht's thoughts raced. It made sense. The saboteurs knew they could not remain in Hechingen. Stay hidden from him. But Stuttgart. A large city. A city of half a million. They could lose themselves in the crowds. Once they did—with half the city in ruins, government offices, records and registrations destroyed, thousands of refugees living in the rubble and con-stantly shifting about, the two enemy saboteurs would be al-most impossible to find. It would be like tracing a snowflake in a blizzard. . . .

But find them he *must*. He was certain they could provide him with the answers to all his questions—and suspicions. They —and they alone.

He had thirty kilometers in which to catch up with them. He turned to the driver.

"Stuttgart!" he ordered sharply. *"Fast!"*

The sign briefly caught in the sweeping headlights of the ambulance read:

ECHTERDINGEN
Kreis Stuttgart

"It is only a few more kilometers after Echterdingen," Gisela said.

Klaxon blaring, they barreled through town. . . .

They were racing through the darkness of a small grove of trees. The long, horizontal beams from their headlights sliced the tree trunks in two—miraculously restoring them as they roared past.

They emerged at the crest of a long hill gently sloping down before them. Abruptly Dirk slowed the careening ambulance— and stared ahead.

In the far distance lay the city of Stuttgart. Above it flared the searing crimson and orange hues of leaping flames, turning the horizon blood red. Countless large fires were blazing through-out the city. The city of Stuttgart was a primary bombing target. Home station of the 10th Panzer Division. Heavily destroyed in massive raids by the RAF Bomber Command and the US 8th and 15th Air Forces. Periodic raids currently being mounted to keep the Daimler-Benz tank, truck and aircraft-engine facto-ries from rebuilding and to prevent the main railroad station in the heart of the city, a vital, strategically located railroad hub connecting the Rhine Valley with the Danube, from being re-paired and able to function. . . . Corny's briefing had been detailed.

They were seeing the results of another air raid.

Directly below, the road crossed a railroad line. The bombers had destroyed the tracks for some distance in either direction. The road itself was heavily damaged also and pockmarked with bomb craters at the crossing. A cluster of houses just beyond the tracks had been hit. A few of them were still burning.

Dirk sent the ambulance speeding down toward the demolished tracks.

Near the crossing the road became almost impassable. Dirk had to slow to a crawl. Carefully he threaded the ambulance between the craters, twisted rail sections and splintered wooden ties. . . .

They were through. The road ahead was relatively clear. The fires from the burning buildings made day out of darkness. Dirk accelerated. The ambulance careened down the road toward the cluster of fire-bombed houses.

Suddenly a figure dashed out onto the road. A woman. Caught in the harsh headlight beams, she waved her arms frantically. Dirk was forced to come to a skidding stop. The woman ran to the vehicle.

Her clothing was torn and singed. Her face was dark with soot and ashes, streaked with tears and dirt-caked blood from a cut above one eye.

"Gott sei dank!" she cried, her voice at the edge of hysteria. "Oh, God be thanked you are here!" She clutched the open window of the ambulance door with both her hands. They were gashed and black with soot, the fingernails torn and bleeding. "Come! Quickly! We cannot get her out!"

"Get who out?" Dirk asked.

"Lisl! Our girl. She is trapped. My husband cannot— Oh, God! Hurry! Please hurry! The fire—" Her sobs choked off her words.

Dirk cast a quick glance at Sig and Gisela. The girl at once put her hand on his arm. She looked at him, eyes big and imploring. "Please," she whispered.

He jumped from the cab. Sig followed.

The woman was already running for the house, which was engulfed in flames. They raced after her.

On one side of the house was a small ground-level window to a basement. Timbers and masonry shattered by the bomb explosion blocked the window—one heavy, smoldering beam was wedged tightly across it. Pressed toward a tiny opening in the jam of rubble was the face of a little girl. Eight? Ten? Tear-stained, singed, eyes wide with horror and fear. She was screaming. Smoke billowed around her from the window, washed red by the flames behind her.

A big man was savagely hacking and slashing like a man possessed at the beam blocking the window, wielding a hefty tool, a broad-bladed, flat-tipped dagger. He chopped with the honed edge of the thick blade; he sawed with the sharp, saw-toothed edge. Automatically Dirk identified the tool. He had seen it once before. At Milton Hall. A souvenir. It was a Red Cross dagger. Carried by German rescue workers. Desperately the man was trying to cut through the massive beam. It was an impossible task.

The instant he saw Dirk and Sig come running up, he threw the tool aside.

"Here!" he shouted. "Lift here!" He ran to one end of the heavy timber. The masonry debris had been cleared away. It was possible to get a grip on the beam. "I cannot move it alone. The three of us . . ."

He bent down and grabbed hold of the thick log. At once Dirk and Sig followed suit. Straining, they lifted. Dirk could feel the skin on his palms scraped raw as his hands slipped on the rough surface of the scorched beam. His injured arm sent jolts of pain through him. His chest burned. But he struggled to move the timber until he trembled with the effort. . . .

Slowly the beam shifted. Bricks and masonry rubble began to trickle down around it. And suddenly it was free. With their last burst of strength, they heaved it away from the building.

The woman was already at the window. She reached down and pulled the screaming child through the small opening. She ran from the flame-engulfed house. . . .

Gisela was with the woman and her daughter. The child was not seriously injured. But she was frantic with terror. Her mother held her in her arms, rocking her gently.

The man came up to Dirk. He grabbed his hand. He pumped it up and down. "May God thank you!" he said, emotion making his voice hoarse. "I do!" He threw a haunted look toward the house. "We were taking shelter in the cellar when the bomb hit." His words came tumbling out. He felt the need to talk away the terror. "The stairs were blocked. The window was the only way out." He shivered. "Lisl was the first one through—and then—then she ran back to get her doll before we could stop her. It is a fine doll. In the uniform of the BDM. Like her sister. And then—the beam and everything fell down, trapping her inside. And we—we—" His eyes went from Dirk to Sig. "Thank God you came along!"

Sig looked toward the blazing building. Flames were shooting from the basement window. It had been close. He shuddered, and looked away. He glanced up the road toward the railroad crossing. And froze.

Bearing down on the tracks from the hill on the far side was a car. A German staff car. Roaring, wide open, for the railroad right-of-way!

He grabbed Dirk by the arm. Urgently he pointed.

The staff car reached the tracks. It skidded to a stop, slewing sideways down the road in a cloud of dust. Then it started up again and began threading its way through the craters.

They had seen the car before. Racing into the Haigerloch Sperrzone!

Dirk grabbed Gisela. "Get in the ambulance," he shouted. "Quickly!"

The big man stood in Dirk's way.

"You must take Lisl to the hospital," he demanded.

"We can't. She'll be all right." Dirk turned to follow Sig and Gisela, who were running for the ambulance.

"The big man stepped in his way. He seized his arm. "You must!" he growled. "She is hurt. The ambulance—"

Dirk tried to break loose. The man's grip tightened desperately on his arm. "Take her," he screamed. "Or—"

Without warning Dirk shot a knee into his groin. With a choked gasp, the man doubled over. At once Dirk struck him a stiff-handed blow across the neck. He crashed to the ground.

Suddenly—over the roar of the flames—Dirk heard the sharp, staccato barks of submachine-gun fire. Instantly small geysers of dirt spewed from the ground close by. At once he pushed the woman down to the ground.

"Stay down," he yelled at her.

He shot a glance toward the staff car at the crossing. Two soldiers had jumped out and were firing at him. The car was slowly worming its way through the crater-pitted area.

Dodging and weaving, he sprinted for the ambulance. The woman lying dazed on the ground next to her unconscious husband, clutching her child to her, stared after him in shock.

He was at the vehicle. Sig and Gisela were already in the cab.

He leaped in. At once he started up. The ambulance jerked forward even as a burst from the submachine guns shattered the windows in the rear door. He gathered speed. He tore down the road—wide open. He glanced in his rearview mirror.

The staff car had made its way across the tracks. The two soldiers jumped back into the moving vehicle.

It shot after the ambulance in close pursuit. . . .

5

The powerful headlight beams of the ambulance rushed ahead of them into the gloom, searching out a path through the ruins. Stuttgart was a mere shell of a city, a sea of rubble.

Dirk stuck to the main thoroughfare. He dared not attempt to lose his pursuers by darting through the smaller side streets. He might easily end up in a cul-de-sac. At least the main street had been cleared. Blackened hulks of gutted buildings lined it, their empty, soot-ringed windows like dead eye sockets, as the ambulance roared past below. Mounds of shattered bricks and crushed concrete piled up against the house walls looked like coarse, miniature alluvial fans.

As they neared the Altstadt—the old part of town at the city center, surrounding the main railroad station—the devastation grew worse. They still had not been able to shake their pursuers.

Sig sat tensely in the cab. Instinctively he pressed his feet down into the floor. Flash impressions of the ravaged city hammered on his mind. . . .

Skeletons of buildings crazily askew, threatening to topple at their very passing . . .

The single defiantly standing wall in a heap of debris, its white-painted propaganda slogan a mockery: "AM ENDE STEHT DER SIEG!—*At the End Stands Victory!*"

A church, its gutted interior starkly laid open, the large crucifix at the altar standing alone amid the rubble, the cross and the left arm of Christ sheared away, leaving the scarred right arm raised in a macabre Nazi salute . . .

Dirk was forced to slow his headlong rush. The street was fast becoming impassable. They were racing into the target area of the last attack. . . .

Fires were raging, flames shooting from buildings showered with incendiaries, acrid smoke billowing from the intense magnesium incandescence. Rescue workers, firemen and civilians were desperately fighting to quell the holocaust. Trucks and fire engines blocked the rubble-strewn street.

Dirk sent the ambulance flying into the havoc. He hit the Klaxon horn. Its wail was hardly audible in the din. He glanced in the rearview mirror.

The staff car was catching up.

He skidded around a fire engine. A bomb had blasted the sidewalk open. Water from a broken main was gushing out into the street to form a shallow, muddy stream. Dirk hit the slippery muck at full speed. The ambulance slid and began to spin. He fought the wheel. The vehicle slammed against the paint-blistered hulk of a burned-out truck lying overturned in the gutter. Metal crunched and screeched against metal. The ambulance caromed off, out of control. Dirk struggled to straighten it as it plunged forward directly toward a gaping, still smoking bomb crater. He stomped on the brake. He tore at the wheel, swinging it about. The ambulance slewed. Grating and grinding in protest, it reared over on two wheels before crashing down to fling itself around a pile of rubble and careen down the street.

They were bearing down on a large apartment building blazing with incendiary fires. Several injured people were lying on the sidewalk. A man wearing the green armband of the Hilfspolizei, the auxiliary police, ran into the street, frantically trying to flag them down. Veering crazily, they shot by him. Outraged, he shook his fist after them, barely managing to scramble out of the way of the staff car roaring after. . . .

The ambulance barreled wildly into a park area. Huge mounds of debris. Broken tree trunks, their splintered tips pointing accusingly into the night sky, their crushed and withered crowns lying scattered on the rubble-covered ground . . .

Ahead, bathed by the fire from several blazing houses, loomed two large buildings, one squat and stark, the other ornate and baroque. With a strangely unattached part of his mind,

Sig recognized them. The Altes Schloss and the Neues Schloss —The Old and the New Castle. The middle of the broad avenue between them had been cleared, and it snaked between piles of broken masonry. They raced past. From the decorated façade of the New Castle, rows of mutilated stone figures kept a ghastly vigil. Armless, legless, headless they stood, grotesquely guarding windows gaping on gutted emptiness within.

The Old Castle squatted in a nest of rubble. Goethe had once panned the building, Sig remembered irrelevantly. "Hardly fit even to be a stage set," he'd written. It was now. It would make a splendid medieval ruin. . . .

Dirk braked violently. The street ahead was completely blocked. A building hit by a bomb had collapsed across the roadway. Along the ground, gasoline from a wrecked fire truck flowed in a river of flame.

Quickly he made a sharp right turn, tires squealing, and careened into a narrow path that had been cleared through piles of rubble.

With piercing suddenness, a siren began to wail. And another. Until the smoky, dirty haze shrouding the city was filled with urgent alarm. A distant crisscross of blue-bright searchlights stabbed into the red-tinged night sky, reaching for the deep-throated drone rumbling steadily high above.

The bombers were returning!

Gisela was chilled by anxiety. She knew where Dirk was headed. Straight for *Theaterplatz*—Theater Square. Immediately bordering the Central Railroad Station, always the target of the bombers! Should she warn him? But where would he go? She turned to him. . . .

Suddenly the earth erupted in front of them. Chunks of masonry ripped through the air. Huge slabs of concrete shot high before smashing down into their path. A hurricane of dust and grit swirled around them. Noise slammed into their minds. The ambulance was lifted into the air. It crashed back with a bone-breaking jar and shuddered to a stop against the mass of rubble.

They were out of the disabled vehicle in seconds. Dirk looked around.

The bombers were raining new death and destruction on the already mortally wounded town. Ground-shaking explosions drowned out the constant noises of roaring fires, crashing buildings, the ululating wails and whines of sirens and horns. . . .

Far to the right, the sky was bright with flame. That would be the Daimler-Benz factories, Dirk thought. On the Neckar River . . .

They were at the edge of a huge field of rubble hillocks. Ahead the whole ragged skyline seemed ablaze. The Central Railroad Station was being showered with high explosives and incendiaries. A large and still solid building loomed close by. Two massive structures at each end of a long gallery. Dirk whirled on Gisela.

"What's in there?" he shouted.

"Das Stadttheater!" she shouted back. "The State Theater!" Her eyes grew round with alarm. Dirk followed her frightened gaze.

The staff car was tearing into the square.

Quickly he grabbed Gisela's arm.

All three sprinted for the theater.

The main entrance was blocked by rubble. They ran around the corner. The explosions of the bombs blasting the railroad junction tore asunder the air around them; the falling incendiaries were like giant, fiery hailstones. A side door came into view. It had been cleared of rubble. Dirk rushed up to it and pushed. It gave way. They ran into the building.

Scrambling around a cracked wall that was leaning precariously, they found themselves at the edge of a huge,.empty stage.

The theatre had been badly hit in an earlier air raid. Beyond the bare proscenium arch the auditorium was gutted. The entire roof had collapsed and the floor had caved in, plunging seats and flooring into a basement two stories deep. The walls, shorn of their décor, were raw and scorched, exposing chipped and pitted bricks. At the far wall was a jumble of blackened timbers. Ringing the space halfway up the walls, steel rods that had been sheared off when the balcony had been torn from their grip still grasped chunks of concrete as if loath to let go completely. Moments before, incendiary bombs had hurtled through the gaping roof into the yawning auditorium pit, and the rubble and debris in the basement far below were blazing fiercely.

The stage itself was bare. Cracks and gashes had been gouged out of the wooden floorboards by falling masonry, especially in the large center trap area. From the steel-pipe gridiron high above in the fly loft hung a jumble of set pieces, flats, lighting equipment and catwalks. Smoke curled over the lip of the proscenium from the blazing auditorium on the other side.

Dirk ran out onto the stage. Sig and Gisela followed. They raced across to the far side. Along the wall a massive, long pinrail was mounted. The tangle of ropes and heavy counterweights needed to hoist scenery and equipment up into the fly loft ran from the rail to the gridiron above. On the stage side, next to the proscenium, torn and twisted wiring hung from a mangled switchboard. A door between the pinrail and the board stood a couple of inches ajar. Dirk ran to it at once. He pushed against it. Hard. It did not budge.

He looked around quickly. Another door farther upstage, at the far end of the pinrail, was completely obstructed by rubble and broken scenery cleared off the stage at some time past. In the rear of the stage was a small opening in the bare brick wall where a breach had been blown by a bomb exploding outside.

He started for it.

And stopped dead in his tracks.

Several men came running from behind the leaning wall, across the big, empty stage.

Two SS officers and two SS men. All armed. Dirk had the Luger in his hand. Halfway across the stage the Germans spotted him and the others. They came abruptly to a halt at the brief command of the senior officer. An SS Standartenführer.

The two SS men immediately trained their unwavering Schmeisser machine pistols on the three fugitives standing dumbly at the pinrail; the officers held their Lugers ready.

Dirk threw a quick glance toward the break in the rear wall. It was the only way out. The only avenue of escape.

They had no chance whatsoever of reaching it.

Backs to the pinrail, they stared at the SS men.

The senior officer took a single step toward them. He stopped. He stared at his trapped quarry. The look of triumph blazing in his eyes rivaled the brightest flame of the hell raging below.

Dirk stood motionless. For a brief eternity the two men stood stock still, staring at one another.

The SS colonel would be Werner Harbicht, Dirk thought. The officer Himmelmann had warned them against. Their nemesis, he'd said. He'd called the shots. . . .

Harbicht had not missed Dirk's glance toward the ragged break in the wall. Without taking his eyes from his cornered prey, he barked a short command. One of the SS men ran to the break and took up position, still covering the three captives with his Schmeisser. Rauner and the other SS man closed up on either side of Harbicht.

Dirk's mind was in turmoil. But one fact stood out with glacial clarity. They were alive! Harbicht and his men had not gunned them down. As they could have done. . . . He fought to bring order to his whirling thoughts. To reason clearly. *Why?* He, too, was armed. Why would the SS officer take the chance of being killed? There was only one answer. He wanted them alive. *Needed* them alive. Why? Information. With lightning lucidity he knew.

Oskar!

The big man had *not* talked. If he had, Harbicht would have shot them down the moment they were trapped. He *had* to take them alive. Make them talk. . . .

He shivered.

There *was* a way to cheat Harbicht. One single, certain way.

The Luger suddenly felt heavy in his hand. All it would take would be three rounds. One for Sig. One for Gisela. One for himself. Had that been Oskar's way out? . . . His hand twisted on the gun. He'd have to act fast—before the Schmeissers could disable him and leave him or either of the others alive. . . .

All at once he felt completely calm. He had made his decision. He would carry it out as fast as he could. Gisela first. She must not suspect for an instant. Then Sig. He would understand. They would be the victors after all. . . .

He felt himself tensing.

He did not look at his friends. He dared not meet their eyes. He cast one last glance around him. A final gaze at the place that would be the last his eyes would ever see. . . .

The gutted theater auditorium. The raging fire below. The scarred and ravaged structure itself. Ruins . . .

His eyes swept the dismal vastness of the stage, once the setting for the brightest make-believe. Now marred and dead, tiny curls of smoke rising from the cracks and rifts in the flooring. And above—high above—the flourishes of play-making, the colorful set pieces once bathed in brilliant stage lights.

His eyes suddenly focused. There—high above—suspended from the gridiron by a single, heavy rope—hung a large section of a hanging catwalk, several floodlights still clamped to its iron railing. . . .

His heart pounded. He needed time. Just a little time, please God . . .

The seconds raced by.

He was suddenly aware of movement out on the stage. Harbicht was motioning his men to fan out. At once Dirk called to him, at the top of his voice.

"Colonel Harbicht!"

The Germans froze. Harbicht stared at Dirk.

"You *are* Colonel Harbicht?" Dirk shouted.

Harbicht nodded curtly. He contemplated the enemy saboteur. American? Certainly not British. No *Engländer* ever lost his accent that thoroughly. He was vastly intrigued. The terrorists were cut off. They were his. He could afford a little cat-and-mouse game. He could afford to let himself be amused. And he did need them alive. He would listen to what the man had to say. For a while. Whatever it was, it could be put to use. Later . . .

Without turning, Dirk spoke urgently to Sig, standing behind him with Gisela. "Don't look up now," he said. "Wait. There is a heavy section of a catwalk hanging above. Trace the rope that is holding it. Find the pin it's fastened to. Got it?"

He heard Sig's constricted voice from behind him. "Yes."

"Tell me as soon as you've found it."

Harbicht was calling to him.

"I am Standartenführer Harbicht!" he responded.

"Can we make a deal, Colonel?" Dirk cried. "Let the others go, and I'll tell you anything you want to know!"

Harbicht smiled coldly. "I fear that is not possible," he called. "You—or one of you—will tell me anyway!"

"How about the girl?" Dirk shouted. "She can be of no use to you."

Harbicht gloated. Interesting. His tolerance had paid off. Useful. An attachment between the girl and the obvious terrorist leader. *Very* useful . . . The girl. Harbicht was suddenly filled with cold hate. The girl. A German. *Ein Verräter!*—a traitor! Without her help, and the help of other contemptible scum like her, the saboteurs could not have succeeded. Could not have shown him up the way they had. The girl . . . She least of all would be let go.

Dirk heard Sig hiss from behind him.

"Got it!"

"Work the rope loose," he growled. "Hurry! Gisela! Stand in front of him. Cover him!"

He heard her voice, husky with tension. "Yes, Dirk."

Harbicht was smiling again. A derisive grimace.

"Throw your gun away," he cried. "Come over here. Slowly. With your hands on your heads. All three of you." His voice was mocking them. "Then we will talk *deal!*"

Dirk's thoughts were racing. Time. A few minutes. Seconds, perhaps. He had to stall. How? Oh, God, how? . . .

Sig was working feverishly. The first few turns came off easily. He was down to the last belaying loop. It was caught and wedged so tightly by the enormous weight of the catwalk that he could not budge it. Desperately he ripped and clawed at the jammed rope, splitting his fingernails. He made no headway. . . .

Dirk riveted his eyes upon the Gestapo colonel. The man was the only thing in the world that existed for him. He stood like a menacing SS Mephisto clad in his black Nazi uniform, feet firmly planted on the stage floor, oblivious to the spirals of smoke rising around him. He seemed to have stood there in the middle of the empty stage for hours. . . .

Stall!

"Colonel Harbicht!" he yelled. "Perhaps you are right. Perhaps you *can* get us to talk. But—it will take time. *Do you have that time?*"

He strained to make out what was happening behind him. It was impossible. . . . What was Sig doing, dammit? What was holding him up. He fought down the urge to turn around. *Hurry . . .* !

"If you will let the others go," he continued, "I will talk *now!* Answer any questions you may have!"

Harbicht made a small gesture of dismissal with his hand. Somehow it was a gesture infinitely sinister. "Only *one* question is of interest to me," he cried. "Answer *that* for me. *Now!* And I may be inclined to discuss letting the girl go free!"

"What is it?" Dirk yelled.

"Tell me *why the reactor test at Haigerloch failed.*"

Dirk's heart skipped a beat. *The test was a bust!* And the Germans did not know why! They'd pulled it off. God dammit, *they'd pulled it off!* . . . More than ever it was imperative that they not talk. The thought was sobering. He took a firm grip on his Luger. He shot a desperate thought at his partner. *Sig!* . . .

"I don't know what you are talking about, Colonel," he shouted. "You should know that already. We blew it up!"

Harbicht glared at him. He did not comment. It was enough. The charade was over. He would give the order to fire. Only one of the terrorists was armed. The leader. They would shatter his knees. He smiled a chilling smile at the thought. The man would still be able to use his tongue. . . .

Sig was sweating. His hands were bloody. The rope would not come loose. . . . One last thing he could try. But the SS would surely see him do it. He would have to try to move the belaying pin itself. Jiggle it in its socket. The rope might slip off. Just might . . . But he would have to use all his strength. He placed both his hands on the head of the pin. With all his might he pulled. He pushed. He jerked and jerked. . . .

Harbicht saw the sudden movement. He froze. In that single instant he knew with blinding certainty that something was irretrievably wrong. He raised his hand. . . .

There was a sharp whoosh. The rope flew from the belaying pin. It whipped up into the air.

Out over the stage the heavy catwalk hurtled toward the stage floor from the gridiron above, the rope screeching through the pulleys.

For a split second the SS soldier guarding the break in the wall glanced up. In that same instant Dirk fell to one knee and emptied his gun at him. The man toppled over—dead before he could even register the cause of his alarm.

The catwalk crashed to the stage. The fire-weakened floorboards over the center trap gave way in a thundering cascade of charred and splintered wood. The catwalk, the flooring and the SS men plummeted down into the inferno raging in the storage rooms below the stage.

All but Harbicht.

At the last possible moment he grabbed hold of a protruding plank. Desperately he fought to hold on. To pull himself up. To crawl to safety.

Dirk and Sig and Gisela stood petrified with shock, their eyes fixed on the sight. . . .

A gaping hole had opened up in the middle of the stage. A hole into hell itself. Below, fire and smoke boiled and belched in unbridled fury. Sprawled across the blazing papier-maché rocks from some Wagnerian opera, tangles of burning tree limbs, carts, benches, stools, picture frames—a jumble of a thousand theatrical props—two figures were being consumed by the flames. Costume mannequins? Or Rauner and the SS man . . .

Harbicht was hanging over the seething pit like a pig over a roasting fire. His uniform was beginning to smoke.

Dirk took a step toward him. The singeing heat drove him back.

Harbicht's eyes met his. The hate in them seared Dirk's own, or was it the scorching heat from the pit below?

The skin on Harbicht's hands and face was blistering. His hair blazed.

He screamed. The hellish sound knifed across stage as he slipped from the charred plank and plunged into the blazing pit below. . . .

Dirk turned to the others.

For a brief moment they stood together. Silent. In infinite closeness . . .

Then Dirk took Gisela's arm. They ran along the pinrail to the break in the rear wall.

Outside, the sirens were sounding the All Clear.

PART IV

The Hour of
0500 — 0600
16 Jul 1945

1

"Five-minute warning!" the PA speaker boomed. "Five-minute warning!"

Dirk could feel the tension mount all around him. He glanced at Sig standing next to him, staring out over the Alamogordo desert into the far distance. He wondered what his friend was thinking. Was he seeing in his mind's eye the Fat Man atop his hundred-foot steel tower ten miles away, ready for the final test? Code name: Trinity . . .

Or was he back at Haigerloch—and what might have been? . . .

For a moment, as he gazed into the raw morning twilight, his own thoughts went back. . . .

They had returned to Hechingen two days after the raid on Haigerloch. They had nowhere to stay in Stuttgart, and with Colonel Harbicht dead, it had seemed reasonably safe. But they did not go near the Storp house. They kept a watch on Anna's place for a long time before approaching it cautiously.

Anna had been overjoyed to see them. Even the ever busy sewing machine was momentarily forgotten. Somehow the absence of its clackity whirring made the seamstress shop seem a different place.

No one had bothered her. No one had even talked to her—except some man named Schindler, who said he was the yard-master at the railroad yard, complaining that Oskar had not shown up for work and did she know where he was?

She had gone to the house and had found no one there. She had assumed they were all together.

When they told her that Oskar had been caught and was

dead, she sat down at her sewing machine. Quietly she had run her fingers over the motionless flywheel and the still needle arm. Then she had looked up, her old, world-weary eyes dry.

"He was a good man, Oskar," she said. "A good brother . . ." And she had bent over her machine and sent the flywheel spinning.

For ten days they had stayed with her, out of sight. And then, on April 23, a US combat task force had barreled into town hell-bent for the reactor caves at Haigerloch. It had been an incredulous captain of Combat Engineers whom Dirk and Sig had bade a cordial welcome!

Dirk had made certain that Anna and Gisela were placed under the full protection of the Americans. . . .

He suddenly felt a longing pressure in his chest. As soon as the world stopped its insane ride on the roller-coaster of war, he'd get off. Hechingen would be his first stop. . . .

He glanced around him.

It was still quite dark at 0525 hours. It was cloudy and a drizzle dampened everything and everybody. Only a few stars were visible in the sky. It was a miserable morning, but no one seemed to notice.

Base Camp was located ten miles from the bomb tower, the nearest point at which anyone was permitted out in the open. Between the camp and the tower—five miles away—was the Control Dugout. Only people whose duties made it absolutely necessary were allowed there. Most other observers were at a point twenty miles from the epicenter of the explosion.

He fingered the little piece of smoked glass he had been given with a strict warning not to watch the blast without using it. Ten miles? Typical brass exaggeration, he thought. An implosion-type atomic-fission bomb, they'd called it. What the hell kind of an explosion—atomic or not—could create a light strong enough to hurt your eyes at a distance of ten miles?

Oh, well. He'd use it. Everyone had a piece. Even General Groves, who stood only a few feet away, and another general with him. Rosenfeld called him McKinley.

"One-minute warning!" the PA system blared. "One-minute warning. Assume blast positions!"

He started to lie down. . . . Lie face down on the ground, he had been instructed, feet toward the blast. Close your eyes and cover them with your hands as the countdown approaches zero. After the flash you may sit up or stand up. Use the smoked glass as you watch the explosion. Be prepared for the shock wave which will follow in approximately fifty seconds.

All around him the observers were lying down, faces to the ground. General Groves. General McKinley. Rosenfeld. He glanced at Sig lying next to him. He winked.

"Okay, Siggy baby," he said. "To coin a phrase—*this is it!*"

"Thirty-second warning!" Even the tinny voice over the PA speaker sounded tense. "Thirty-second warning!"

The silence along the ridge grew more intense. Dirk was aware of his heartbeat speeding up. He gripped the piece of smoked glass tightly in his hand. Easy. He loosened his grip. No need to break the damned thing.

"Ten seconds!" The taut voice on the PA rang out over the campsite. "Nine—eight—seven—"

Dirk stopped breathing.

"—three—two—one—NOW!"

At the instant of the final shout, a flash swept the entire countryside with a light brighter than a dozen midday suns. Even though Dirk's hands were clasped tightly across his eyes, the tremendous light burned through. He was shocked to the core. Ten miles! It was just not possible. . . .

Dazed, he got to his feet. He placed the glass before his eyes.

On the horizon an immense ball of fire was still expanding, orange and red, purple and blue flame swirling, soaring thousands of feet into the air. The earth had opened up. The sky split asunder. . . .

A monstrous dark cloud was growing rapidly, billowing upward, reaching for infinity itself. It dwarfed the world.

A shock wave of unimaginable pressure slammed into him. Instantly a sharp blast tore the desert silence, followed by a thunderous Doomsday roar. . . .

For the briefest instant his eyes were blinded in a bombed-out factory building in Holland. . . . He was hugging the ground of a vineyard on the bank of the Rhine. . . . Hearing the blast from a dank cave at Haigerloch . . . Staring down into a fiery pit in a gutted theater . . .

He turned to look at Sig standing next to him. He saw his own terrified awe mirrored on the face of his friend.

Together they had seen the flash, heard the thunder, felt the shock wave, and watched the towering mushroom cloud that would change the world. . . .

The author acknowledges with appreciation the valuable assistance given him in researching this book by Mr. Siegfried G. Bart, wartime president of Bart Manufacturing Company, a prime contractor for the Manhattan Project; Colonel James C. Stowers, chief of the Manhattan Project, New York; Mr. William F. Heine, Atomic Energy Information Service; and Dr. Edwin L. Rodgers, Sherman Oaks Hospital, California.

The terms "atomic research," "atomic bomb" and "atomic physics" have been used in *The Haigerloch Project* rather than the current "nuclear research" and "nuclear physics" because they were the terms in general use during the time the story takes place.

Bibliography

The following books and publications in English are among those which, together with the author's own experiences, investigations and documentation, as well as foreign publications, have furnished authentication and facts for *The Haigerloch Project*.

Asprey, Robert B. *War in the Shadows*. New York: Doubleday & Company.

Bar-Zohar, Michel. *The Hunt for German Scientists*. New York: Hawthorn Books.

Bauer, Eddy. *Encyclopedia of World War II*. New York: Marshall Cavendish Corporation.

Boldt, Gerhardt. *Hitler: The Last Ten Days*. New York: Coward, McCann & Geoghegan.

Cave Brown, Anthony. *Bodyguard of Lies*. New York: Harper & Row.

Delarue, Jacques. *The Gestapo*. New York: William Morrow & Co.

Dollinger, Hans. *The Decline and Fall of Nazi Germany and Imperial Japan*. New York: Crown Publishers.

Dyer, George. *XII Corps: Spearhead of Patton's Third Army*. Baton Rouge, La.: XII Corps History Association.

Eisenhower, Dwight D. *Crusade in Europe*. New York: Doubleday & Company.

Feger and Liehl. *Picturesque Black Forest*. Jan Thorbecke.

Fermi, Laura. *The Story of Atomic Energy*. New York: Random House.

Fest, Joachim C. *Hitler*. New York: Harcourt Brace Jovanovich.

Gaines, Helen Fouché. *Elementary Cryptanalysis*. New York: American Photographic Publishing Co.

Gallagher, Thomas. *Assault in Norway: Sabotaging the Nazi Nuclear Bomb*. New York: Harcourt Brace Jovanovich.

Glasstone, Samuel. *Effects of Nuclear Weapons.* U.S. Atomic Energy Commission.

Goudsmit, Samuel. *Alsos.* Henry Schuman.

Groueff, Stephane. *The Manhattan Project.* Boston: Little, Brown and Company.

Groves, Leslie R. *Now It Can Be Told.* New York: Harper & Row.

Heisenberg, Werner. *Physics and Beyond.* New York: Harper & Row.

Hymoff, Edward. *The OSS in World War II.* New York: Ballantine Books.

Irving, David. *The German Atomic Bomb.* New York: Simon & Schuster.

Jungk, Robert. *The Big Machine.* New York: Charles Scribner's Sons.

Kahn, David. *The Codebreakers.* New York: Macmillan.

Kaufman, Louis, Barbara Fitzgerald and Tom Sewell: *Moe Berg: Athlete, Scholar, Spy.* Boston: Little, Brown and Company.

King & Batchelor. *Infantry at War, 1939-1945.* New York: Marshall Cavendish Corporation.

Lattre de Tassigny, Jean de. *The History of the French First Army.* London: Allen & Unwin.

Lysing, Henry. *Secret Writing.* New York: Dover Publications.

Manvell, Roger. *SS and Gestapo.* New York: Ballantine Books.

Manvell, Roger, and Heinrich Fraenkel. *Himmler.* New York: G. P. Putnam's Sons.

Masterman, J. C. *The Double-Cross System in the War of 1939 to 1945.* New Haven, Conn.: Yale University Press.

Michel, Henri. *The Second World War.* New York: Praeger Publishers.

Michel, Henri. *The Shadow War.* New York: Harper & Row.

Morgan, William J. *The O.S.S. and I.* New York: W. W. Norton & Company.

Mosley, Leonard. *The Reich Marshal.* New York: Doubleday & Company.

Pash, Colonel Boris T. *The Alsos Mission.* New York: Award Books.

Pia, Jack. *SS Regalia.* New York: Ballantine Books.

Pratt, Fletcher. *Secret and Urgent.* New York: The Bobbs-Merrill Co.

Schlabrendorff, Fabian von. *The Secret War Against Hitler.* New York: Pitman Publishing Corporation.

Schwarzwalder, John. *We Caught Spies.* New York: Duell, Sloan & Pearce.

Seydewitz, Max. *Civil Life in Wartime Germany.* New York: Viking Press.

Smith, R. Harris. *OSS.* Berkeley: University of California Press.

Smyth, Henry D. *Atomic Energy for Military Purposes.* Princeton, N.J.: Princeton University Press.

Sunderman, James F., ed. *World War II in the Air: Europe.* Franklin
    Watts.
Von Roon, Ger. *German Resistance to Hitler.* New York: Van Nostrand
    Reinhold Company.
Winterbotham, F. W. *The Ultra Secret.* New York: Harper & Row.

Sunderman, James F., ed. *World War II in the Air: Europe.* Franklin Watts.

Von Roon, Ger. *German Resistance to Hitler.* New York: Van Nostrand Reinhold Company.

Winterbotham, F. W. *The Ultra Secret.* New York: Harper & Row.